The Thorn Bearer

Penned in Time—Book One

Pepper Basham

Vinspire Publishing

www.vinspirepublishing.com

ISBN: 978-0-9903042-7-2

PUBLISHED BY VINSPIRE PUBLISHING, LLC

Dedication

To my parents, Jay and Ginger Williams,
Who taught me the beauty of forgiveness and always
dreamed big dreams for me

Pepper Basham

Prologue

April 1914

Death hovered in the shadows of the room, a shapeless presence as familiar to Ashleigh Dougall as the scent of morphine. Two years of nursing in the mountains of western North Carolina taught her to accept the invisible company as a passage of life. Sometimes it came as a thief to steal a final breath, other times it appeared as an angel of mercy to end a prolonged illness or a satisfied life, and then, there were moments when it entered as an arm of justice. Precisely what her father deserved.

She cringed at the dark turn of her thoughts and wiped a weary hand across her brow. Her father's ashen complexion and sunken cheeks proved a striking indicator of the pain his illness wrought, but it couldn't compare to the agony he'd inflicted. Years of a secret tyranny as malignant as any cancer. She pushed away from his deathbed, but her stand jolted to a stop by a grip on her wrist.

A frigid fear rushed through her at her father's touch, weakening her and forcing her back into the chair. Every muscle fiber tensed to the defense, but nothing prepared her for the desperate plea in his dark eyes.

"Forgive me." His staggered breath eked out the words. "Forgive me."

Ashleigh tried to pull free, the otherworldliness in his voice tugging at the fabric of her hate, but his fingers pinched tight, riveting her in place. He'd trapped her all over again.

"I ruined you…ruined you to any man." He drew in

another ragged strain of air. "Took liberties with you…"

Ashleigh succeeded in pulling free and placed the chair as a barrier between them.

"Forgive me."

She grappled for breath. His gaze pleaded for something she could never give – a freedom he didn't deserve. The raw nakedness of his declaration shivered through her, exposing his monstrous sin after years of silence. The hideous ache of her lost childhood nearly crippled her back to her chair, but she fisted the back of the chair and stood to her full height. She would never forgive him.

He'd thrived within the walls of a lie, moving their family from their estate home in England when the debt grew too large and the rumors stung too close to truth. Nestled on the outskirts of Asheville they'd resumed his sickness within Grandmama's house until Ashleigh had grown strong enough to stop him.

Bile rose into her throat and she jerked back from those haunting eyes.

"Ashleigh." He moaned, snagging her gaze back to his before he lost consciousness.

A creak of boards at the door shook her attention away from the deathbed and to the empty hallway. Had someone overheard her father's confession? No. She raced to the doorway, only glancing back to note the weak rise and fall of her father's chest as he lay in his frail final hours.

Afternoon sunlight from the open balcony door provided the only presence in the hall. She kneaded her fingers into her head and breathed out a sigh of relief. Her secret needed to die here, with her father. No one else could ever know. It would ruin them all.

The sunlight beckoned her away from the deathbed and into the warmth and fresh air. A honeysuckle breeze cooled the tear-stains on her cheeks. She wiped her cheeks, wishing the stains on her soul cleared as easily. *God, help me.*

She massaged her neck and eased out to bask in the full glow of afternoon, but a movement from the garden along with her sister's desperate voice stilled her steps.

"Father is dying. Ashleigh is as good as gone." Catherine's voice hitched with a sob as she gripped Sam Miller's arms. The wind had loosed enough of her hair from her loaf bun to send several locks framing her face. The stark contrast of ebony hair and piercing blue eyes were noticeable even from Ashleigh's place on the balcony. Paired with her sister's height and exposed, slender neckline, she was the perfect model of a Gibson Girl. Catherine had always been the pretty one.

Sam, their neighbor and friend, had fallen for her the day she'd arrived from across the Atlantic.

"It isn't right." Her words pierced into the afternoon birdsong. "The eldest should marry first, and yet Ashleigh is engaged."

Ashleigh bit back the sarcasm tickling her lips. *Now Catherine claims the status of eldest?* In every other way, responsibility, sacrifice, management, and control, Ashleigh had been forced to act as eldest as Catherine requited any such expectation, but when the title suited her, she wielded it as a skillful sword.

Ashleigh looked to the tiny stone on her finger, a choice made out of friendship and necessity more than love – a way to ease her mother's financial burden at Father's passing. Michael Craven's polite affections were safe and logical. A good decision. And yet she couldn't move her gaze from Sam. The way his fingertips tenderly brushed a tear from Catherine's cheek sent residual warmth across Ashleigh's face. Her chest squeezed tight with a sudden longing.

Catherine buried her head into his shoulder. His broad, strong shoulder. Ashleigh raised a palm to her cheek, remembering the feel of his jacket when he'd comforted her in the past. The little sister. The tag-along. He'd made her laugh – to forget all the heaviness she carried. There had been safety in those arms, in the authenticity of his friendship.

Her heart trembled a rhythm.

Those aqua eyes paired with his boyish smile—

It was a good thing he belonged to Catherine.

"Catherine, I can't give you the life you deserve yet." The gentle hum of Sam's Appalachian accent curbed smooth like the strums of a bass. "You're used to servants and teas and fancy store-bought clothes. In a year, maybe I can give you those things, but I don't even have a ring yet—"

"I don't need a ring." She pulled him closer. "Your love is all I need."

Ashleigh held her breath, Sam's hesitation a sign of his uncertainty. Catherine's inconsistency had wounded him once. Would he still wish to marry her?

With a large sigh from those sturdy shoulders, he cupped her face with his palms and the sweetness of it wrenched a gasp out of Ashleigh.

"Then, Catherine, will you marry me?"

Sam's thumb lingered on her sister's cheek, his tenderness a sweet pang in Ashleigh's chest and a poignant reminder. Love required a full heart, a whole woman. A cost she could never afford.

Chapter One

May 1, 1915

There is a distinct difference between marrying a man you do not love, and falling in love with a man you cannot marry. As Ashleigh Dougall locked eyes with Sam Miller across Manhattan's crowded dock, the sting of that truth stripped all doubt. Pinpricks of fresh awareness rifled through her like the sharp May wind off the wharf of the Atlantic, bringing to life a shocking realization.

Heaven help her. She was in love with her sister's fiancé.

Even through the space of noisy travelers and hurried porters, Sam's grin tripped her heartbeat and introduced a myriad of emotions she'd reserved for three-volume novels and daydreams. Ash-brown curls twisted in an unruly manner from under his brown Fedora and shadowed his best feature – his eyes.

In love with her sister's fiancé? A man who'd become her dearest friend? Nonsense.

But her mental reprimand did nothing as her pulse skittered into rhythm with *Alexander's Ragtime* from the pier. She waited for her mind to catch up with her errant heart, to blame the high emotions of departure, but each thought confirmed the growing attraction. He'd provided escort for the long journey from North Carolina and only *now* her emotions swelled from girlish fancy to—

No. The idea was utter madness and complete betrayal, a family trait of which she would not fall prey. Whether she blamed youthful blindness or disappointed hopes, the truth remained: Sam was ever faithful – and forever Catherine's.

Or the woman he thought her sister was.

Ashleigh drew her day suit jacket taut. Rumors had made their way across the Atlantic in Mother's letters and Fanny's quick missives. The faithful maid gave more insight into Catherine's notorious flirting and dogged pursuit of Edensbury's elite, flaunting a wealth her family didn't possess. After a year abroad to help her mother grieve, nothing had changed.

A child's scream pierced through her mental fog. Ashleigh turned in time to see a little girl tumble forward and land in a crumpled mess of lace and cloth on the dock floor, arm pinned beneath her.

A woman with the same blush of auburn hair, rushed to the child's side. "Alice, are you all right?"

Without another thought to the maddening confusion of her heart, nursing instincts quickened Ashleigh's steps to the pair on the dock. The older woman pulled the child into her lap.

"My wrist hurts, Mama." The girl's cries were muffled against her mother's chest.

Ashleigh dropped her valise and reticule and lowered herself to the dock beside the pair. Their faded, but pressed clothes, suggested poor – but hardworking. Like so many she'd served over the past two years in the rural North Carolinian Mountains.

She met the mother's frantic gaze with the cool calm of her specialty. "My name is Ashleigh Dougall. I am a trained nurse. Might I be of assistance?"

Alice whimpered. "I can't move it, Mama."

"My girl, Alice, has hurt her wrist." The mother's voice pitched higher, a sudden awareness raising her volume and drawing attention from the passersby. "If it's broke what are we going to do? I used my last dollar to pay for our tickets. How am I going to—?"

"Let's see what we have here, first. What do you say? I've watched magical recoveries with little girls and wounded wrists before." Alice peeked her teary gaze from her mother's shoulder. "I shouldn't wonder if this might not be the perfect setting for another bit of magic." Ashleigh smoothed her words into softer tones and the spell worked.

The mother's breathing slowed. Alice sniffled and squinted at Ashleigh, her eyes a beautiful umber hue.

"Hello, darling, I'm very sorry for your spill. I would like to help you. I'm a nurse and know a bit about things like bruised wrists and skinned knees. May I look at your arm, Alice?"

The little girl tightened her hold on her doll, proving the wound was more a sprain than a break. Painful, but not as serious and certainly a less expensive fix.

Sam emerged in Ashleigh's periphery a short distance across the dock, his whistle at full volume. She caught his gaze in a solid hold of unspoken messages. He paused. Ten years of friendship worked its wonders. He surveyed the situation and increased his pace toward them, resuming his tune along with the band.

She turned to the little girl and lowered her voice to increase the suspense. "My friend Sam has a secret. Do you like secrets?"

Alice's whimpers died altogether. A smile tickled at the corners of Ashleigh's lips in response to the interest glittering in Alice's golden eyes.

Sam removed the newspaper from beneath his arm and knelt at Ashleigh's side, bringing with him his usual scent of soap and lemon. Heat swirled up her neck and planted firmly on her cheeks, no doubt darker than her mauve day suit.

She acknowledged him with a nod, but kept her

attention fastened on Alice's movements, in part to monitor her injury and in part to gain time to cool the sudden warmth around her chest at his nearness. "Have you ever had a LifeSaver? I wouldn't wonder if one or two might be the medicine you need to feel better. What do you think, Sam?"

Alice's sharpened gaze fastened on Sam.

"Well…" His rich bass voice melted into conversation. "You have to be pretty special to get a piece of *my* candy." He pulled a colorful roll of paper from his pocket and slowly opened the wrapper.

Alice didn't miss one twist of Sam's fingers.

"So, Alice, I need you to reach those fingers out for that candy, and if you use both hands, Sam will put a LifeSaver in each."

"Two?" Her lips wobbled into an 'o' shape.

"Two." Ashleigh looked to the mother. "If she can clasp this candy, then it will confirm my suspicions of a sprain rather than a break."

The mother gave a feeble nod.

In an easy sweep of his hand, Sam popped a piece from the wrapper with his thumb, tossed it up in the air and caught it in his mouth. He sighed and closed his eyes with a look of utter satisfaction. "Mmm, that's some good candy."

A smile unfurled on Ashleigh's lips. *Such a boy.*

The temptation proved too much for Alice's resolve. With the slowest of motions she unclenched her left fist, dropped her doll on her lap, and brought her left hand to join her outstretched right one.

As Sam placed a LifeSaver in her left palm, she fisted it without a hint of discomfort, eyeing the candy as if it was manna from Heaven. For a poor little girl with a well-worn gown, it just might have been.

Alice raised the red piece into her mouth, her eyes brightening with a hidden smile.

"The red ones are my favorite, but Sam likes yellow best." Ashleigh made a face and Alice's grin unhinged a little more.

"Bright and cheery, Miss Alice," Sam added with a wink. "I'm a big fan of lemons."

Ashleigh bit back a comment about one sour thing deserving another, but her expression must have hinted her thoughts.

"And I'm never sour, Miss Ashleigh," he added with a raised brow. "I'm as sweet as country boys come."

She rolled her eyes, but her smile expanded despite her best attempts. A connection had always existed between the two of them -- an easy acceptance. From the first day her family moved into the grand Victorian beside his smaller cottage in Asheville, North Carolina, she'd found the strained relationships of her family bearable with Sam and his father nearby. Harsh family secrets stung less with the kindness of her surrogate big brother. Her chin tilted with resolve. She would not forfeit their friendship to a girlish romantic notion, even if her wayward sister taunted a threadbare hold on his heart.

She tugged at the floral scarf about her neck until it loosed. "Alice, I'm going to wrap your wrist with my scarf until you can see the physician aboard. It will hurt less, if it moves less."

Alice's umber eyes widened. "A silk scarf? For me?"

The wonder on the little girl's face fed the dream in Ashleigh's heart– an orphanage for little lost souls – of war, or worse. Every child deserved an opportunity for love and a family. Michael's desertion propelled her into the choice all the more. Heaven knew what her former fiancé had done with his ticket. Wherever he was, he'd most likely sold it weeks ago to pay off a foolish debt. The expensive trip had only proved another one of his grand schemes unraveled into disaster – except this time he gambled her future.

With a few quick and gentle movements, the scarf twisted around Alice's wrist in a makeshift bandage of gold, blue, and rose. "My gift to you for being such an excellent patient. Now, let's get you aboard so the physician can properly see to your arm." Ashleigh reached for her reticule and started to stand. Sam was at her side to assist her. The perfect gentleman.

Catherine doesn't deserve him.

Sam leaned close to her ear. "Nice work, Nurse Dougall. No wonder your patients love you."

The intimacy of his whisper sent tingles rushing across her neck, renewing the whole battle of fight or flight within her. She offered him the briefest of smiles and turned back to the mother and daughter. "Have a safe journey."

With a wink in Ashleigh's direction, Sam placed another LifeSaver in Alice's unharmed hand. Yellow.

"And a happy one."

The mother and daughter offered their thanks again and then rushed off to the third class gangway, leaving her alone with Sam. *Alone with Sam.* That had never been a problem before.

But now?

He stood at her side, his usual grin hitched at the corner. Her heart gave a responsive flutter. *Problem?* The sweet hum under her skin confirmed much more than a problem. It awakened a frightening flare of emotion she could barely contain, and being out of control terrified her. All she needed was to get aboard without saying something to alter her friendship with him forever and possibly brand her as frivolous as her sister. Surely after two years nurses' training and a childhood diet of pretension, she could douse her feelings long enough to board the ship?

But Sam knew her. His tender way of etching out the truth held a surgeon's precision.

A cheer from the crowd pulled Ashleigh's attention to the emotionless steel of *The Lusitania*. Dwarfing the crowded pier, the ocean liner provided a solid diversion of elegance and ingenuity. It was a massive display. The Cunard Company's Scottish princess. A stronghold of black paint and billowing smoke framed by the four towering funnels and five passenger decks readied to whisk her back to England and away from her failed wedding plans.

Running from her disappointment with Michael to the world of pretention with her sister? A lesser of two evils? At least Catherine's behavior was predictable and didn't leave her holding a one-way ticket-turned-escape-plan.

She studied the great display of white and red flags, fluttering in the strong ocean gusts. People of all shapes and sizes, from every social class, painted a blur of smiles, bidding their farewells from the cascade of decks high above, but one face came into focus among the masses.

Ashleigh's breath stumbled on a gasp. The ship's funnels blurred. The crowd's noise droned to a murmur.

Michael?

Her reticule slid from her hand, dropping to the pier, fingers too numb to snatch it in time. *Impossible.* He'd disappeared eight months before their wedding without explanation only to show up now? Here?

Her knees weakened. She'd given him her friendship and a promise of her future, and in return? He'd left her holding a 'good-bye note' and a heart filled with as many questions as the debtors knocking on her door to locate him. No. Her eyes must be playing tricks on her, her troubled thoughts creating ghosts.

She bent to retrieve the small bag, muscles moving as if in slow motion, but Sam reached it first. Concern in his eyes softened the tension in her face.

"Are you all right?"

"Yes, thank you." She took her reticule from him and nodded toward the ocean liner.

"This fell from your bracelet." Sam handed her the intricate locket her Grandmama had given her as a parting gift. A charm with a portrait of the two of them together. "You don't need to lose any more. It looks like there is only one more left on your bracelet."

Ashleigh took it with a small smile. She'd removed all the charms from her father, except the one given to her his last Christmas. The piano. Somehow, since it had been presented from the entire family, it didn't hold the same corruption as the other charms. Those gifts came with a meaningless apology for the corruption he continued to bestow on her. Perhaps Grandmama's elegant charm fastened on the old bracelet would prove the past didn't have to direct her forever. "Thank you."

"And the ticket man had this for you."

She took the small envelope from him, her name scrawled in elegant hand on the front. A quick look confirmed her suspicions. "It's from Grandmama's distant acquaintance, Mrs. Ragan. My room adjoins hers and she's providing escort for me, but I believe it's more a formality than anything else. I don't suspect we'll engage in much conversation since she cares little for the society in which she is traveling."

"Ah! She sounds delightful." He nodded, his gaze searching hers, almost as if he could see her heart. "Are you sure you're all right, Ash?"

His nickname drew a larger smile from her. "Just overwhelmed by this *Palace of the Seas,* I suppose."

The ship loomed overhead, calling her attention back to the railing where she'd seen Michael's image, but he was as absent as he'd been on their wedding day. She was finished with him. A new life with new dreams waited just across the ocean and Michael wasn't a part of it.

Sam sighed and a hint of mischief tipped the corners of his lips. He assessed the ship, hands tucked in his pockets. "You Brits sure like to show off, don't you?"

Her caution ebbed in light of his easy banter, their friendship an acceptable substitute for romantic fancies. *Oh, how she would miss him.* "Poor Sam, you're not going to allow a ship to wound your fragile American pride now, are you?"

Sam winced and slapped his palm against his chest, feigning a wound. "Whew, nice shot. I think my quick wit is rubbing off on you." He leaned close and winked. "Your mother might disapprove."

Ashleigh adjusted her gloves to keep her gaze from his, but warmth swirled in her stomach, nonetheless. "She has a tendency to disapprove of me quite often. And *you* never help."

He took off his hat and ruffled his curls. "You mean she still hasn't forgiven me for teaching you how to swim? That's an important skill to lea—"

"Swimming mildly irritated her and bicycling, well, she didn't care for that too much either. But climbing trees? Frog gigging? She may never forgive you for those."

Sam's brows inched higher with each accusation.

She razed him with a look. "Not suitable for a lady, you know."

"A lady? You were ten–"

"Twelve."

"Twelve?" One brow tipped skyward and he scratched his chin. "Well, you were still just a kid, not a lady."

A grin eased onto her face. "Mother had high hopes that I would be some day."

Sam hesitated, as if considering the thought, and then tilted his head to examine her. "A lady?" His expression softened, a tender caress. "I don't think frog gigging affected that outcome."

For one split-second she bathed in the fresh spill of sweetness his affectionate gaze produced. *But it could never be.* His love resembled an elder brother's or perhaps a dear friend, but nothing more. She shifted under his gaze.

"Well, Scott was too young and I could never convince Catherine to try new things."

"Ah, I see the way of it." Ashleigh shook her head and stepped back, Catherine's name a presence between them as never before. "Corrupt the young, impressionable Dougall sister. Of course, it didn't help that I thought you hung the moon and stars."

"You've always been a smart girl. At least you have your priorities straight." A twinkle deepened his eyes. Had they always been so blue?

"Smart girl, indeed? Where was Catherine when I was ankle deep in a sinking boat trying to pick off some poor frogs? Not within half a mile, I'd say."

"You know, Catherine always disappeared when I mentioned slimy critters or dirt. It usually ended up just you and me." His gaze grew intense. "And we've been through a lot together, haven't we?"

She couldn't manage his seriousness. Her feelings edged much too close to the surface already. "The fact I engaged in questionable outdoor activities is the core of our friendship? Why does it suddenly feel less glamorous than I imagined?"

"Maybe not so glamorous, but certainly genuine." His smile faded. "I can't imagine Millington without you."

At the vulnerable look in his eyes, something cautious and hard inside her chest melted. She settled into the feeling like coming home. *Sam.* How long had his face replaced Michael's in her dreams? A sharp sting eclipsed the touch of sweetness, his tenderness suddenly too painful, pleading for her complete confidence.

She wanted to trust him completely, anchor her faith in the kindness of another man, place her hope in the possibilities of something more, but she couldn't. Memories suffocated hope, reminding her of who she was...and who betrays. Men. Men like Michael. Or her father.

A protective cloak of pretension as ingrained through her family as the dominant gene for dark hair cooled her heated cheeks, numbing her feelings. "Millington is my true home."

"And people always come back home, right, Ash?"

She cleared her throat. "There's plenty to be done in Edensbury, so I shan't know how long Mother expects me to remain. She was determined to place an ocean between her and Grandmama once father was no longer around to play referee. Although I'm certain the thought of living in Grandmama's manor house gives little consolation." She shrugged. "And with my nurse's salary, I hope to make my own contributions to the war effort."

"The orphanage you've talked about?"

"You *were* listening?"

He quirked a brow. "Now why would you think I don't listen?"

Michael never did. The thought humbled her. The past eight months since his absence proved better clarity than the previous two years. Michael had never loved her as much as he loved himself. She'd agreed to marry him on a whim of grief after her father's death, a means to ease her

19

mother's financial burden and she'd hoped their love might grow in time.

Hope had never served her well.

"An orphanage seems an insignificant thing for a man, I suppose."

"I'm not Michael." The tension in his voice drew her eyes to his.

His gaze roamed her face, as if memorizing it. She stepped close and placed her hand on his arm, his muscle tensing beneath it. Her words nearly stuck in her throat. "I know you're not."

He tilted his head, watching her. "Do you realize we've eaten dinner together five nights a week for the past three months?"

"What?"

"And lunch every Sunday?"

Some of the best memories of her life – a friendship forged deeper over the past year. "Yes, I know."

"There's going to be this giant hole in my life when you leave." He shook his head. "First Catherine and now you?"

I'm not Catherine. She searched his gaze and forced a strained whisper. "We can write letters."

His expression darkened. "They're not the same."

She stood in silence, willing the safe numbness to stay wrapped around her heart. No, they weren't. No tender glances or shared secrets at the table. No easy banter or welcome laughter. Letters could never be the same, but neither would their relationship. Her pulse shuddered into an erratic staccato and she distanced herself with a step. "I must go."

His forehead crinkled in thought. "Do you have everything?"

Have everything? No, she was missing a husband, a

honeymoon negligee, and a piece of her heart to the wrong man. Blessed escape was the only answer. "Yes, thank you, dear Sam." She took a deep breath. "But I suppose I must be off."

He nodded, but didn't move. "S'pose so."

"My bags?"

"I had a porter take them after I picked up the tickets."

"Then–" Ashleigh replayed his word in her mind. Her gaze snapped to his. "Tickets?"

Sam nudged her forward. "There's the line for boarding?"

"Tickets? Sam?"

He led her to the gangway, his jaw working. A certain sign of trouble. "I already told you, Ash. I couldn't just let you leave."

She caught his arm. "Sam?"

"I haven't seen Catherine in a year and our engagement happened so fast. Maybe I rushed things." He took his hat off and ran a hand through his hair, squinting from pale midday sun. "Her letters - they've been fewer and farther between. Things have changed. I need to see her."

Ashleigh's throat tightened. "What do you mean?"

His stare brooked no argument. All heat fled her body.

"I'm going with you to England."

Chapter Two

Ashleigh's eyes grew wide as his words sunk in and then she sent him a look that took the chill right out of the May morning. Maple brown, with the faintest flame of oak-gold around her pupils – Sam felt every flicker, hot enough to steam the *Lusitania*.

Not the reaction he'd expected.

"You're going to England?"

He opened his mouth, but Ashleigh interrupted - her cheeks almost as pink as her hat. "You'll travel across the entire Atlantic to secure your relationship with a woman who doesn't –" Ashleigh jerked one glove from her hand and squeezed it, her tone controlled. "For Catherine?"

Her hesitation hit him in the chest. Exactly. A woman who hadn't written in over four months. He was no Sherlock, but the clues sent a clear message. He had to know why.

"Of course I would. I can't keep living in uncertainty. If things are over between us, I need to end it face-to-face." Sam shrugged. "Plus there's the simple fact you shouldn't sail across the Atlantic alone."

"Grandmama provided a suitable chaperone with Mrs. Ragan." Her body stiffened and she looked toward the ship. "Despite what you might think or believe, I am no longer the twelve-year-old knee-deep in muck. If the past year hasn't confirmed it, perhaps the past eight months have."

Actually, the thought had flitted through his mind a few times since they left North Carolina, and the little-girl pout on her lips right now wasn't helping her argument, but through her father's death and Michael's betrayal she'd proven the 'little girl' lay far behind. She was a strong and honest woman.

Something inside him twisted as tightly as a double-overhand knot. Michael should have been with Ashleigh on their wedding cruise. On *this* ship. He stifled a growl. *Michael was an idiot.* He'd thought it a dozen times, but said it? He'd feel better if he could tell Michael in person. Maybe with a fist or two.

His desertion changed a lot of things, most of all her. The shadows under her eyes, the dimmed emotions, the need to leave for England. *No one leaves home without a good excuse.*

Just like no fiancé stops writing letters without an excuse. Usually a bad one.

"Well, if your Grandma was so sure of Mrs. Ragan, she wouldn't have encouraged me to come—"

"Grandmama forced you into this?"

He bit back his smile at the thought of Victoria Dougall's gift of persuasion. Of course, it didn't take much for him to agree to her urging. Take care of Ashleigh and sort out his relationship with Catherine all in one trip? Sounded like a win-win and long overdue.

"Ash, your grandma is the picture of gentility and temperance, but we both know she has the persuasive abilities of a cattle prod."

His words hit their mark. The fire in her eyes dimmed.

"Besides, someone needs to watch over you." He took Ashleigh's arm and ushered her closer. "Ash-honey, I can't just leave you after what Michael did."

Softness flickered over her countenance. Tears formed in those coffee-colored eyes, drawing him closer. Her eyes had always been his downfall - round, dark, pleading. When she was little, he'd caved into giving her a treat or taking her along on an adventure. Unguarded, they glowed with a million emotions.

"Mrs. Ragan doesn't know you. I do." His thumb pulsed a squeeze. "And I have no intention of letting you sail alone."

She slipped her arm free from his hold and the familiar transformation began with each step she made up the gangway. That infuriating emotionless glaze cloaked her expression. If he didn't hate it so much it might have been a fascinating study, but she walled herself in with it: Protected herself from something, but he'd never figured out what. He'd rather she burst into tears or slap her hand against his jaw than distance herself with that confounded look.

A porcelain doll, dark mass of hair pinned neatly beneath her rose hat to show off her slender neckline, lips firmed into a grim line of determination, and he knew-- because of the past, and Michael's betrayal--their relationship was changing.

An ache swelled in the place where his heart thumped a slow rhythm. He couldn't lose Ashleigh like he'd lost Catherine. He needed to keep her safe. Close. Protected.

"You needn't feel obligated, Sam." She blocked his entrance up the gangway. "Go home. I'll be fine."

"Obligated?" He tipped up the rim of his hat to get a better view of her face. She finally turned her attention toward him. She wouldn't stay behind that confounded mask. Not if he could help it. "I've never taken our friendship lightly, even when frog gigging. Friends look out for each other." He offered an exaggerated sigh and pushed past her. "And I don't think Mrs. Ragan has the constitution for it."

Life shimmered into her expression with the hint of a smile to relax her features. She snatched the newspaper he had under his arm, and hit him against the shoulder. "I do not need an overprotective nursemaid along."

Sam followed her to the far railing facing the sea. "Then it's a good thing your charming and handsome neighbor came instead, isn't it?"

She turned and lifted a much-too-innocent brow. "Really?" Her gaze slid down him and back up to his face, as if questioning his declaration. "And who might that be?"

"Flattery will get you nowhere." He grinned. "I'm still going."

"You're stubborn to a fault."

"Kind of like someone else I know." He grabbed the paper from her hand and nudged her shoulder with it.

She opened her mouth to speak, but he shook his head.

"No more arguing. I'm going. You're stuck with me, whether you like it or not." He turned his back and strolled toward one of the deck chairs without another glance in her direction. After all the hurt she'd been through, the last thing she needed was to be alone.

If she'd been his sister, Michael wouldn't have been able to hide from Sam's wrath. How could Michael have done this? His reputation as a playboy only bore skin deep. A lifetime of friendship and memories confirmed it. He'd been certain Michael had changed his ways and committed to Ashleigh. How could he have been so wrong?

He reclined back in the chair and flipped open the paper, peering over the top to gauge Ashleigh's reaction. She looked lost among a sea of farewells. Instead of following suit with the other travelers and waving toward the pier, she faced the channel that led to open sea. What was she thinking? Devising a plan to get him kicked off the ship?

Her hat dipped to one side, obscuring part of her forehead as faint sunlight haloed her face. From her willowy frame to her dark curls, she reminded him of her sister.

His Catherine.

He wasn't so sure anymore. Ten months ago the thought would have never crossed his mind. Seven months ago the tone of her letters changed. Four months ago she wrote to question their engagement, asking to end it – and she never responded to his last three letters requesting a reason for her concern.

He fisted the paper. He'd find his answer now for better or worse.

A large advertisement in the center of the newspaper grabbed his attention.

NOTICE!

Travelers intending to embark on the Atlantic voyage are reminded that a state of war exists between Germany and her allies and Great Britain and her allies; that the zone of war includes the waters adjacent to the British Isles; that, in accordance with formal notice given by the Imperial German Government, vessels flying the flag of Great Britain or any of her allies are liable to destruction in those waters and Travelers sailing in the war zone of Great Britain or her allies do so at their own risk. The Emperial German Embassy.

His blood cooled, caution chilling his skin. Germany sent a warning? He slammed the pages together and stood from his chair, looking to the gray horizon. The calm sea didn't match the storm brewing in his chest. Why would Germany send America a warning? The horizon gave no answer, but his senses jumped to full alert. Scaremongering tactics? Spineless threats meant to discourage trade with Great Britain? Surely nothing more.

A shrill whistle pierced the air.

The ship came alive under his feet, vibrating into motion away from the pier. A new explosion of shouts erupted from the people at the ship's railing followed by a cloud of flags and handkerchiefs raining down to the pier. He stepped forward to meet Ashleigh, readied to protect her from any threat beneath the seamless sea. *Calm down. No need to worry. Germany would never torpedo a passenger ship.*

"I suppose you'll not be reasonable and leave?" Ashleigh's dark brow shifted, gaze almost pleading.

"Nope, I've never been very reasonable, you know."

Her smile bloomed, and the very sweetness of it drew him closer– as sweet as her violet scent. "Forgive me for speaking harshly to you, Sam." Ashleigh looked down at her hand against his arm, her teeth skimming over her bottom lip. "I want you to be safe, and there's no need for you to risk your life on a ship sailing toward war-torn—"

He blocked her words with his finger against her lips, the heat of her breath warming his skin and traveling up his arm to hook in his throat. A loose tendril of her hair brushed against his hand and he twisted it around his finger, ending with a firm tug. Her entire body swayed forward, face inches from his, and his voice got stuck somewhere between his dry mouth and heavy tongue. "I care about you too, little girl."

Little girl. Right. What was he doing? This was Ashleigh, practically his sister, and much too young. For him. He straightened and steadied his breath, untwining the dark ribbon of hair from his finger and stepping back. "You don't want anything to happen to *me*? Well, we're in the same boat."

She laughed. "Precisely the problem."

The ship jerked as it backed into the bay. Ashleigh stumbled forward into his arms, hat knocked back from her hair and the full scent of violet an onslaught to his senses. She certainly didn't feel like a little girl either. Heat seeped from his body. Where had that thought come from? He steadied her, but quickly moved back a step.

Ashleigh adjusted her hat and gave him a stiff pat on the shoulder. "Perhaps you are nice to have about."

"Just keep that in mind the next time you start complaining about me. What would you do without me?"

Her hand fisted at her chest and the unnamed emotion flickered across her face again. "I have no idea, my dear Sam." She looked back to the horizon and half shrugged a shoulder, the pixie expression in full bloom on her face. "Get a bit of peace and quiet, no doubt."

She sent him a wrinkle-nosed grin over her shoulder before she returned to her quiet watch from the railing. The wind tossed her dress, pressing silky material against her frame, and sending his thoughts skittering in a very different direction than he'd ever planned for Ashleigh.

He cleared his throat and looked away.

He needed to see Catherine and sort out their relationship for certain. After all, it had been a year since he'd seen her. His gaze met Ashleigh's. *And a lot can happen in a year.*

Chapter Three

A cool sea breeze whistled across the Boat Promenade Deck along with the laughter of children playing Deck Quoits or spinning tops. Three days aboard the ship had only reminded Ashleigh of the first-class lifestyle her family used to know. Posh surroundings of golden trim and delicate wooden carvings led the way across floors of lush carpet and marble. Stewards waited on the whims of the rich and famous – who overlooked small oddities or atrocities, as long as the social status wasn't affected.

It was a dazzling display of a world as pretentious as her father's faith, but sadly fitting for the part she played now. She'd attempted to convince Michael to purchase a second class private room to save money, but with his usual flare for the extravagant, he booked the best her grandmamma could afford, thrusting Ashleigh back into pretension at its peak. Even the relationship with Sam stung with unspoken truths. Oh how she craved simplicity and authenticity!

She'd prayed for two days about Sam – begged for guidance and peace. Pleaded for God to remove this undeniable attraction. Maybe it took such a shocking realization to force her to her knees. It had been too long.

Sometime before the day waked with dawn, she'd released her fear to God and made a resolution: Friendship first and foremost. Her mind clung to the thought, her heart lagged behind a little, but whether her sister deserved it or not the uncertainty of being jilted should never fall to anyone – even Catherine.

"A penny for your thoughts?"

She slowed her pace to a stop and looked up, Sam's

Fedora low over his eyes. He looked like he belonged in one of those new moving pictures.

"Oh, I have an entire purse full of thoughts, but most of them revolve around a single coin." She hoped for a grin, but knew she failed.

"Michael?"

"I suppose it's the fact we were to travel together on this ship, but I can't stop wondering – why did he leave?"

"None of this was your fault, Ashleigh." Sam's voice bit into the words and his jaw tightened. "Michael was the fool and coward. I'm sorry he broke your heart."

Her gaze dropped from his. She'd been disappointed and hurt over Michael's desertion, but heartbroken? "People do many foolish things for want of love, I think."

As Sam wrapped his hand around hers, she knew her heart was far from broken. Its rhythm beat too quickly. Why had she been so naive to believe her friendship with Michael could be a substitute for real love? Sam's nearness, his compassion, marked a stark and painful contrast. She'd been so blind.

"I'm sorry, Ash. I know you two weren't deeply in love, but you *were* friends – and this isn't the mark of a friend." He released her hand with a sigh and rammed it back into his beige slacks pockets. "Some things are unforgiveable, and betrayal is near the top of the list."

The wind ruffled the curls across his forehead and her fingers twitched a surprising longing to touch one. She fisted her hands at her sides. "I was blind in so many ways."

"What do you mean?"

Confession? Would the truth truly set her free? "Many times people make decisions without weighing the full cost." She took a deep breath and focused on the gray horizon. "One chooses to see a person as one wants, instead of as he or she truly is." As he did with Catherine. As she'd done with Michael. An ache for understanding pooled in her stomach.

"You couldn't have known Michael would do this, Ash. It shocked us all."

"You're right, I didn't see clearly until later. But as time has proven to heal many of the wounds Michael left behind, it has also clarified other feelings. Time is a powerful friend or adversary."

He drew in a sharp breath through clenched teeth and removed his hat, moving it from one hand to the other as they walked. "Time has certainly been an adversary for me."

His sober expression stilled her reply and she searched his face for clarification.

"Catherine asked to end our engagement." He ran a hand over his jaw, his eyes care-worn. "In her letter over four months ago. She doesn't think we want the same things anymore. Says she's changed."

Words and thoughts of a hundred possibilities crashed into the thousands of emotions pounding in her chest. Sam and Catherine were no longer engaged? Sam was...free? Her throat tightened around a fissure of hope.

"Why didn't you tell me before now?" She forced the words out on a whisper.

"I'm not sure." He shook his head and squinted, as if the words hurt. "I think speaking it out loud made it real, more painful."

"Words have a way of adding spines to our fears."

"More like spikes." His palm pressed his chest as though the confession pierced him. "I thought absence was supposed to make the heart grow fonder."

The hurt on his face eclipsed her attraction with impressive power. He didn't need another woman throwing herself at him when his heart was so full of her sister. How selfish could she be? "Oh, Sam, perhaps your presence will remind Catherine of your love for her. She's never handled distance well." Ashleigh squeezed his arm and he covered her hand with his. "She's always been a horrible correspondent." Ashleigh offered a smile and squelched hope yet again. "When she sees you, it will all be set to rights. How could she deny such a faithful heart as yours? No woman could."

His gaze zeroed in on hers, nearly nailing her to the deck planks. "Maybe that's the problem. I'm not a game-player and women seem to like those sorts of men."

"Heavens, Sam, not all women." She turned from the intensity of his gaze and resumed their walk, her arm still tucked within his.

"I don't know." He absently caressed her hand, the touch sweet and tender, an extension of their friendship. "That's why I've never liked this idea of you leaving. What if—"

Comprehension dawned and she brought them to a standstill in the middle of the deck. "Our friendship is quite capable of handling time and distance. You must know that."

He tilted his head and examined her face, his expression unreadable. His thumb smoothed across her knuckles. "Yes, Ash. I *do* know it."

An almost imperceptible shift in his touch tripped a tingle of awareness up her arm. She slipped her hand from his and looked ahead, her stomach twisted as if pinched by tweezers.

Movement, small and white, caught in her periphery and wavered like a flag. A boy, no more than three, attempted to climb an empty deck chair propped against the railing. His white, cape-like coat flurried behind him as he pushed one pudgy knee after another onto the chair seat. A matching cap topped the golden curls twisting around his round face. No one along the shaded deck seemed aware of him or his dangerous plan.

Ashleigh picked up her pace. "Look, Sam."

She caught the boy's gaze just as he came to a stand on the chair, chubby hands wrapping around the railing, and chin tucked over the top. The familiar tilt of his smile and playful glint in his green eyes flickered a warning to Ashleigh's memory. *How did she know him?*

"Hello, Duck. Are you searching for the water?"

He turned back to the railing and heightened on tiptoe, scratching the chair across the deck until his feet almost slid off.

Ashleigh drew him up in her arms as the chair toppled. "You are an adventurous one, aren't you?"

"Where are his parents?" Sam swept the deck another glance, but the long promenade gave no hint of an answer. A handful of people braved the chill in the open air with a few wrapped in blankets on the deck chairs, and none seemed concerned about the welfare of a toddler.

The boy pointed toward the horizon. "Me tee water."

Ashleigh's smile bloomed in response to his sweet voice. "Yes, you do. Aren't you a clever boy?"

"This big boat." His green eyes grew as wide as saucers and tugged at her heart all the more.

"Yes, this is a big boat and you're quite small to be wandering about on your own." Ashleigh bounced him against her hip and smiled at Sam. "He's such a darling. Reminds me of you on one of your good days."

Sam bent to eye level with the boy. "Don't let Miss Ashleigh fool ya, buddy, she's not all sugar and spice either." Sam shot her a wink.

"There's the pot calling the kettle black."

His grin arched and the gentleness in it swelled her

heart three sizes. Large enough to toss propriety to the wind and wrap him in her arms, if a certain little boy hadn't taken up residence in them already. *Thank God for small favors.*

"What's your name, little fella?" Sam tickled the boy's chin.

"Free," he answered, holding up two fingers.

Sam scratched his head and peeked up at her with wrinkled brow. "He's clever like me too, I see."

Their gazes caught just above the little boy's cap. She couldn't look away and Sam's expression faded from gentleness to curiosity. Heat crept up her neck and she blinked out of his stare.

"Stephen?" A woman emerged from the main companionway, her gaze frantically searching the length of the deck until landing on the boy in Ashleigh's arms. "Stephen." She tossed a glance back through the companionway, sprigs of brown hair flying about from a gust of wind. "Stephen's here. On this side."

She stomped toward them, her button-boots clapping a thunderstorm of noise, her pale eyes aflame. "There you are, you little devil. I can't turn my back on you for one second." Her deep southern accent softened the harshness of her words in a sickeningly sweet contradiction. "You're gonna be the death of me."

Ashleigh instinctively drew the little boy closer. "I found him atop a deck chair, *alone*."

The woman registered her slight by aiming the full fire of her gaze. "Hand him to me."

"Annette? You found him?"

A man emerged from the companionway in a slight jog, brown jacket flapping behind him like broken wings.

She knew that voice.

Ashleigh's breath clung to the roof of her mouth, not even strong enough for a whimper. *No.* The shadow of the black fedora could not hide the familiarity of his face.

Michael Craven.

She couldn't move, couldn't think. Her gaze trapped in his, trying to make sense of the obvious mistake. How was Michael here? He'd disappeared. Gone from her life forever.

"Daddy!" The child's squeal split through her mental fog and drove the confusion deeper.

Ashleigh looked into the little boy's face and back to Michael, who stood frozen in place halfway across the deck.

The brunette snatched the boy from Ashleigh's numb arms, sending her mind into motion. Slow motion. One by one, as rocks dropping into a pond, each truth pierced into her heart, rippling shock out to her arms and legs. Clarity, nauseating clarity, weakened her.

Michael's disappearance. The secrecy. The little boy's familiarity. It all pieced together and forced an unbelievable and heart-wrenching picture. She gripped the railing for support. Eight months peeled away to unearth insecurity and hurt afresh. He'd lied to her, deceived her, and abandoned her.

"Ashleigh?" Michael's voice broke like a nervous youth's.

And now he was using the ticket purchased for their wedding cruise to travel across the Atlantic with another woman? Her hand tightened around the railing. Energy exploded through her limbs with added adrenaline and pushed her to her full height.

She gritted her teeth. "Michael, if this is your idea of a surprise to our wedding cruise..." She sent a glare to the woman holding Stephen. "...I think you over packed."

Without warning and out of her periphery, Sam darted forward with enough fire in his step to ensure one thing:

Michael Craven might not make it off the *Lusitania* alive.

Sam wasn't sure how he made it across the deck so quickly, or exactly when he fisted Michael's shirt with enough strength to lift him from the deck boards. All he knew for certain was what Michael Craven deserved. A little dent in those pretty-boy features to humble him a notch or two. He reared his fist back to make its mark against Michael's nose only to see a flutter of white in his periphery.

The little boy, green eyes wide, stared at him in wonder, or silent reprimand. No child should see his father bested and bruised, inside or out. Some of the fight in his veins fled. He shoved Michael away and stood between him and Ashleigh.

"Goin' soft, pal?" Michael's lips cocked into a grin. "I'm sure you've been waiting to give me a good saucer or two, haven't ya?"

"Get the kid out of here and I'll tell you what I really feel about you – without a single word."

Michael shook out the wrinkles Sam's fist had formed on his shirt, his smile fading. "I can't say I don't deserve it."

The declaration stole Sam's words. Did he regret hurting Ashleigh or was this another act of charm to diffuse responsibility? Oh, the past months built a stack of Michael's sins to justify a solid pounding, with hurting Ashleigh at the top of the pile.

"Didn't take you long to move in on my fiancé, did it, Sam? I knew it would happen sooner or later." Michael straightened his tie and cleared his throat, his voice more confident than the look in his eyes.

Sam started back to place a fist in Michael's stomach, but Ashleigh held a vise-grip on his arm.

"Stop this, now," the brunette screamed, causing the little boy in her arms to whimper. "How can you do this to a man who is practically your brother, Sam Miller?"

The woman knew him? Sam really looked at her, taking in the round hazel eyes, pale freckles across her nose, and honey curls. "Annette Dixon?"

He switched his attention to the little boy at her waist. Those eyes? The face? *Almost four years ago – when he'd found Michael in the back room of a pub.* Air clenched in his lungs. He pulled his friend up by the jacket, bringing him to face-level. "Michael, what have you done?"

Michael shoved Sam away. "Something I'm willing to fix." His gaze shifted from Sam to settle on Ashleigh. The fire in Michael's eyes dimmed. "We need to talk."

Ashleigh hitched a breath and Sam slid his palm down her arm to let her know he wasn't going anywhere. Her gaze flitted to his, the pleading look bringing him closer, as a guard.

He turned back to Michael. "I think it's a little late for talking, don't you?"

"It's late for a lot of things, but seeing you, Ash." He ran a hand through his hair and took a step forward. Ashleigh tensed. Sam moved closer. Friend or not, he'd beat Michael to saw dust if he placed one hand on Ashleigh.

"We were friends once. I'm not a monster. I want you to understand."

Sam forced a humorless laugh. "Not a monster. Just a coward."

Michael's eyes narrowed to slits. "Coward? The only cowardly thing I've done is not tell Ashleigh about Stephen."

Sam gestured toward Annette with a toss of his head. "You didn't forget someone, did you? You're wheeling away with your son and—"

"His wife." She announced, pale eyes challenging him. "On o*ur* wedding cruise."

Michael squeezed his eyes closed and released a long stream of air through his nose.

"W...Wife?" Sam stuttered. A blow to the face would have been less painful. He couldn't grasp the situation fast enough. "Your wife?"

The word felt strange on his lips, sour, wrong. Not only had he fathered her child, but married Annette and then took her on the wedding cruise meant for Ashleigh? It was unconscionable. Had desperation really forced him to such a low? Back in Millington when his schemes merely upset a business owner or riled a jealous suitor, he'd excuse them as a part of Michael's makeup. Sam's father had taken time and love to draw Michael away from his harsh grandparents and into the fold of his family, but trouble pursued him like the Baskerville hound. Evidently the stains of his past couldn't be changed. He was lost – and there was no hope for reform.

"Ashleigh, give me ten minutes to explain. Annette has family in Ireland, and it was one less ticket to buy."

"You're married?" Ashleigh pushed passed Sam, her voice hard and stance unswerving. "And on *our* wedding trip?" Without warning her hand made contact with Michael's cheek. He covered his cheek and stumbled back.

Annette lunged forward, nearly dropping her son. "How dare you."

Ashleigh turned with raised hand. "Don't embarrass your son by trying, *Mrs*. Craven. I think you've already neglected him enough for one day, don't you?"

Sam pulled his dropped bottom lip up into a slight grin. Well, at least one of them got a bruiser in – and Ashleigh deserved to release a whole lot more than Sam. Her anger proved fairly potent, judging from the red handprint emerging on Michael's cheek. Underneath all her compassion and wit burned a fighter.

She stepped back, her shoulder rubbing his, and that's when he noticed her trembling hands. Even fighters reach their limits. He placed a palm to her back and she leaned against him with the slightest touch.

Michael's jaw tightened, a dangerous flame flickering in his eyes. He'd always been better at running away than facing the consequences, but then he would come back, repentant like a child, winning everyone over with his charm. There wasn't enough charm on the entire ship to help him now. His deeds caught him.

Ashleigh turned to Sam, lips twisted into an impressive snarl. "I retract my earlier comment. I was not blind. I was stupid." She faced Michael again, jaw set and eyes in slits. "I should be grateful to you, Michael. You kept me from making a grave mistake in marrying you and realizing much too late who you really are."

Maybe he shouldn't be too concerned about her taking care of herself. Though he wasn't relinquishing any of his big brother influence any time soon. His protective impulse flared a brighter warning at Michael's approach.

"I had every intention of marrying you. Of being the husband you wanted. But this all happened so quickly —"

"Quickly?" Ashleigh laughed, and the harshness in it even surprised Sam. "From the looks of your little boy, this has been going on for some time."

"I didn't know about Stephen." Michael ran a hand through his hair, their discussion beginning to draw a crowd. "Can't we find a place to talk, privately?"

"We have nothing to discuss." Ashleigh stepped further away and adjusted her hat. "You have proven to be a cad, and a coward besides. How can you even admit to caring about me from what you've done?"

Sam added. "And you were like family to Dad and me, Michael. Why didn't you come to us with the news? We would have—"

"Confess to you?" Michael jabbed the air with his finger. "Provide another problem for your father? All I've ever done is cause problems for him – and I could never have been as good as you. Once you're offended, then you cut people off." He shook his head and rubbed at his red cheek. "I couldn't stomach the thought of your self-righteous condescension. When would my next problem be the last time you could stand me? I've had to make enough sacrifices over the past eight months." His gaze went to Ashleigh. "I wasn't interested in lowering myself even more."

"To hear yourself talk, you'd think you're the only one who's suffered here." Sam glanced over at the little boy, large green eyes round and curious. He lowered his voice, a battle of emotions hammering together in his chest. Sam sighed. "Dad and I have always been there for you. We've been family." His gaze traveled to Annette's and back. "You didn't have to run away."

"I'm not running, Sam. I'm fixing my mistakes."

"By making other ones?" The muscles in Sam's shoulders unwound.

"Michael." Annette seized his arm, her eyes flashed. "I've heard enough and will not be-"

"You've gotten what you wanted, Annette." Michael stopped her with a look and she withered back. "Allow me a chance to explain." He looked at Ashleigh. "I will not be thought of as a coward, whatever else you might think of me."

"Too late."

"Listen to me." Michael's voice lowered, almost to a

whisper, but the flame in his eyes brightened. Sam pulled Ashleigh away from the glare, but he couldn't protect her from Michael's words. "I'm not the only one who's kept secrets. I heard your father's deathbed confession."

A visible change swept over Ashleigh's countenance. Her dark eyes widened and her face paled. She clenched a fist to her chest and sagged against Sam's side for a moment. He gripped her waist to keep her from slacking to the deck. What had Michael said? *Her father's deathbed confession?* "Ash?"

When she looked up at him tears clustered in her eyes – tears and...fear? He didn't know to what Michael referred, and at the moment, he didn't care. He needed to get Ashleigh away from Michael as quickly as possible. "That's enough. Let's go."

"No." Ashleigh stopped him, her words wobbled and then hardened with a steeling lift of her chin. "I'll see him."

"Ashleigh, you don't have to do—"

"It's all right, Sam." Her gaze softened and held his.

For one second she lowered the guard around her heart. Tears, usually rare and controlled, slid silently down her cheeks. She didn't brush them away or try to hide them as she usually did. She only stared, her hand holding his in a vice grip. The last remnants of the little girl he used to know disappeared. Something deep and meaningful passed between them – something beyond words.

Pain squeezed his chest and then released, leaving a hollow feeling behind. She was one of the strongest people he knew, but how much more could she carry before breaking? And how could he let her talk to Michael, only to be hurt again?

"I have to do this." She leaned close, never breaking eye contact. "But promise me one thing." The plea in her eyes held him in place. "Whatever happens, promise me

41

you'll always be my friend."

"Ash, I don't—"

"Please, Sam."

He placed his hand over the one she rested on his arm. "I promise. You will always have my friendship."

She smiled, a sad, lonely smile, and took a deep breath. With a final squeeze she released his hand and turned to face Michael. "You have ten minutes and then I want to be rid of you."

Michael flinched at her words, but kept his gaze steady. "That's all I need."

"If you do anything else to hurt her..." Sam stepped closer, using his two-inch height advantage to add weight to his words. "So help me, Michael..."

Michael stared at the deck, his cheek tightened like an overly extended rubber band.

"And only if Ashleigh is sure—" Sam checked with her again, hoping she'd say no. Was he releasing a lamb to the wolf?

Her gaze steeled and emotions dropped away. The porcelain doll appeared. "I'm certain."

His soul shook. Darkness hinged on Michael's threat. Would this meeting or his secret change her forever? How could Sam keep from losing the people he loved the most? He sent a final look to Ashleigh as she disappeared around the curve of the ship. He wouldn't be too far behind, but he'd give her the benefit of his doubt and he'd keep his promise to her. No matter what.

Chapter Four

Michael offered his arm, but Ashleigh ignored it and walked two steps ahead of him toward the bow of the ship. A wild mixture of fear and anger burned through her. All this time, she'd found solace in the knowledge that only her long-time maid, Fanny, knew of her father's sick betrayal, but now...

Whatever Michael had to say, she'd face it, alone and free of eavesdroppers or friends who would never look at her the same way again.

She braced herself for the lone battle.

The horizon bloomed soft and blue with the misty blush of afternoon. An artist's masterpiece. No, not alone. *Dear God, help me.*

Her boots clipped harsh clatter against the deck and they walked in silence. Oh, if she'd been a man she'd left much more than a handprint on his cheek. Michael never cared for her. Not like a groom for his bride. Yet another betrayal to add to the list of deceitful men in her life!

She cast one last glance to Sam before his face disappeared behind a white wall of the ship. Except Sam, or his father. Would Sam have been able to face this discussion with her and still loved her when he knew the truth?

"I shouldn't have announced about your father, Ashleigh. You just wouldn't listen any other way and I had to get you to listen."

"Obviously self-control has never been one of your virtues." Ashleigh stepped between the rows of lifeboats for privacy and then turned on him, voice low. "What do you want?"

"What do you mean?"

Did he think she was a complete idiot? She clenched a fist at her side and wondered if she should make a matching mark on his other cheek. "For your silence. Is it money, because you know as well as I do, the only person with any money in my family is Grandmama, and if you go to her with this news I will—"

"No, no." He held up his hands to stay her onslaught. "I'm not as bad as that. I'd never wish to wound your grandmother." He took a deep breath and shoved his hands into his pockets. "No one should have to hear such news."

Hear it? Her other fist curled around her reticule. *Imagine living it.* She hoped the fire in her eyes wilted him. He took another step toward her without one hint of a burn.

"I didn't know about Stephen before I proposed. I promise." Michael groaned and searched her gaze, a glimmer of his charm trying to shine through in his softened expression. She wouldn't be fooled. "I received Annette's letter the day before I left. The week after we made our travel plans."

She moved away from him, back against one of the whitewashed lifeboats, hands ready to battle her way out if necessary. "Why didn't you tell me? If nothing else, our friendship demanded your honesty."

"Honesty?" He raised a brow, his gaze darkened for a moment and then cleared. "I didn't want to hurt you, I didn't—"

"Hurt me?" A joyless laugh erupted from her lips. "And leaving without explanation would wound me less?" She rubbed her forehead with a gloved hand, the continued pulse in her head transforming into a headache to match the pain in her heart. "Oh, Michael, if I mattered to you at all, you should have told me the truth."

Michael examined his shoes, with little less than a

grimace. How could her heart have been satisfied with this? With him? Memories and moments filtered through her thoughts, spilling onto a clear canvas in her mind. Their engagement had been built on the hope love would follow their friendship – a way to relieve her mother of the financial burdens of two unmarried daughters, but apparently Michael had never even loved her as a friend – not if this was his treatment of her heart.

"So what is it you *do* want from me? How can we end this to ensure you keep my horrid secret and I never have to see you again?"

His shoulders slumped forward; an attempt at feigning regret? How could she believe his reactions? His promises now? "I hate we're ending things this way, like enemies. I never thought I'd see you again."

"With tidings such as these, I should think not. I'm sure you'd prefer to disappear into complete obscurity to save your pride, but unfortunately that choice hasn't been given to either of us. So why bring up my father's confession? Why talk about it now? I would expect a coward like yourself to run from confrontation."

"That's just it, I'm not a coward." His gaze narrowed and he ran his hand through his hair, upsetting his dusty blond curls into chaos. "Do you know how hard it is to live up to your reputation? When you agreed to marry me, I thought I could finally bring some good into my life — that maybe your reputation could remove some of the marks in mine, but you were so perfectly controlled and...good."

She rolled her eyes, her face a continual flush of heat. "I'm glad the knowledge of my father's sin has rectified your high opinion of me, but my past was not of my own making. I hadn't gambled away my family's money, or lost my cares in a bottle now and again." She waved her hand in the direction of where they'd just come. "Or sired a son outside of marriage."

She tightened her lips to keep more accusations in check. She'd already said enough. Too much, if Michael's heated response was any measure.

He stepped forward and lassoed his fingers around her wrist in a burning grip. "You see, that's the point. You've always pretended to be this perfect person, when underneath..." His gaze trailed down her and she cringed. "You want to throw my past in my face? Well, now two can play at that game." His words snaked out on a whisper. He tugged her close, his nose inches from hers. Ashleigh pulled against his hold, but his grip tightened, digging into her arm like ropes, like the hold of her father.

She froze. A chill trickled down her neck and thudded against her heart. She couldn't breathe. Fear strangled her with a million memories. She couldn't force one ounce of pent up air from her throat. Her lips formed the word, "No", but her voice didn't add any volume to it. She was trapped all over again.

Michael groaned and released her arm with a forceful push. She nearly collapsed to the deck before catching herself against the cool wood of the lifeboat.

"You're making me out to be a monster and I'm not. I've made some big mistakes, but I wanted to do right by you. I just couldn't."

Her soul trembled with the rush of pain those memories revived. Time's blessed distance cushioned the full potency of her father's poisonous choices, but with Michael's profession, she was back to cowering in the corner of her room...waiting.

How had he overheard her father's confession? Reality hit. Wait, he'd known since her father's death? *But that had been almost a year.*

"Wh...why did you stay with me all those months

when you knew?"

He looked at her then, her greatest fear ignited. The reflection of her past mirrored in his gaze. Shame flushed her skin with trembling heat and knifed into the marrow of her soul. His look, his disgust, confirmed all the doubts she'd ever felt. *She would never marry now.*

He rubbed his chin and walked to the railing. "I couldn't even put it into words at first, let alone confront you." He shook his head and sighed, his voice softer, almost regretful. "Whether you believe it or not, Ashleigh. I did…I do care about you, but I needed you to trust me with your past secret, so I could trust you with mine about Annette. You never let me in. You just kept teaching Sunday School and nursing sick people as if nothing was wrong."

"One doesn't usually discuss such things at dinner parties and church functions, Michael."

"And then the more I thought about it..." He lowered his gaze to the deck. His Adam's apple blobbed from a swallow. "How could I be with you after knowing...?"

His gaze slid down her body, adding pulse to the shame flaming through her. Her father's betrayal burned through the fog of ten years and brought each hideous memory into perfect focus. Every lurid detail, every whisper in the dark collided like a paint-stain upon her soul. Her father had caught her again. Perhaps not in a closet in the library or the corner of her bedroom, but here, in broad daylight, his evil slithered up from the grave and stole more of her life. Not only her past, but her future too. She was drowning. *Oh God, where are you?*

Bile swelled into her throat, mingling with tears, but she wouldn't give in. *No.* Her father didn't deserve it. She'd learned to fight eight years ago when she left a scar on her father's cheek and earned her freedom from him. She would not back down to Michael's threat. If she was drowning, she'd bring him with her. "And you blame me for this atrocity? Look at me!"

His head came up, eyes wide.

"Do you honestly think I had some hand in this wicked crime?"

He stepped back and cleared his throat, blotches of red deepening her handprint on his cheek. "You could have told someone. Anyone."

"Who would have believed me, Michael? My father – an elder in the church and respected gentleman in Asheville?" She wanted to scream, grab him and shake some sense into his empty head. "I was a child. I didn't even know what was happening."

He distanced himself by a few more steps, his face deepened to carmine. *Yes, move away from the soiled woman.* A surgeon's scalpel to her chest couldn't have hurt worse than his obvious disgust. She couldn't ignore the past anymore.

"If you listen carefully you will hear yourself and be ashamed. He was my *father*." A sob strangled her voice into a whisper. She hated tears. "How dare you blame me?"

He straightened, even leaned forward to offer a hand to her trembling arm. "That reason is enough to call off our marriage, but I didn't. Don't you see? I did the right thing. I was going to go through with it."

"You are such a martyr." She jerked away from his hold and licked the sarcasm from her lips.

"But there was something else which made my decision to leave even easier."

She shrugged, exasperated. "Learning of my tainted past and the presence of your son wasn't enough to break off our engagement? Please, astonish me."

"Don't pretend ending things broke your heart." He

stepped closer, any semblance of gentleness fleeing his expression. "I didn't see it at first, but when I looked back on the past few months before I left, the signs were everywhere. You're in love with Sam."

She held his gaze, her pulse throbbing a gallop in her throat, but she refused to acknowledge his claim. How could he possibly know? She hadn't known it until she was boarding the ship.

"Playing the part of a coward is one thing, using this shallow accusation to become a *victim* is quite another. Unlike you, I've never had a hidden attachment to someone else." *Until now.* She thrust her chin forward. "Is this who you truly are? This weak man who hides his own guilt behind children and women? I'm glad I discovered it now before I spent the rest of my life—"

"I know I'm right. At first I didn't want to believe it, but then little things kept happening. A look here, a laugh there. Doubts started creeping in." He skewered her with a look. "A man can tell when a woman is in love with someone else."

"This is preposterous. I never expected you to stoop so low as to use –

"And then the letter came about Stephen and I thought, why should I fess up to my flaws? Have my dirt shown to the world?" He stepped closer, his face flushed. "It was the perfect storm of situations to make my decision clear."

The look in his eyes sliced through her breath. Haunting. "Oh, you've made many things clear today." She didn't budge, but faced him with as much fury as he shot at her. Her voice constricted to a whisper. "I should thank you for rescuing me from a marriage built on sympathy and pride, but if you think by demeaning me you will save yourself, you are wrong. Those who step on the hearts and lives of others to gain acceptance rarely leave without bloodstains on their souls."

The last ounce of her strength shuddered. One more man trying to overpower her, except this one used pride instead of strength. Exhaustion swept over her body, taking anger's power with her. She wiped her gloved hand across her cheeks and leveled Michael with a final stare. "You may have your judgments. You may find comfort in comparing our pasts, but know this Michael -- you have triumphed over no one today."

She turned and walked from him. If her Promenade dress hadn't constrained her, she would have run. Run from Michael, the past, and the truth that no man would ever want a soiled dove like her.

Sam hurried across the deck, each turn of the ship ending in disappointment. Where was she? He'd given them half an hour to finish whatever conversation they needed, but that was enough. His second turn of the ship gave no new information.

Michael's allusion to Jonathan Dougall's death-bed confession held a mysterious warning. Ashleigh's quick response proved even stranger. What did Michael know? He racked his brain for memories to reveal the answer without a hint. The simple fact Mr. Dougall never nurtured a friendship with Sam's father, despite his father's attempts, was enough to leave a bad taste in Sam's mouth. As Sam grew into adulthood, he finally was able to label his dislike for their neighbor. He never seemed genuine. Reclusive and sometimes moody in the privacy of his home, but a gregarious and somewhat winsome speaker when in public, Sam had watched with growing caution at the man's duplicity.

He knew what it looked like. His mother had been the queen of it.

Sam came to a stop in front of the Verandah Café nestled near the bow of the ship. Only a few people enjoyed the breezy atmosphere of wicker seats and columns twined by faux vines. Ashleigh had made a little routine of going there to sit after her morning walk on the deck, but none of the hats resembled hers.

He leaned against the wall and looked to the horizon. *God, where is she?* He couldn't shake the need to find her. Something was wrong, and now she was missing? Maybe she knocked Michael clean off the ship. Sam's grin almost edged up at his wayward thought, but quickly stilled. No, that would have been too easy on Michael. A long life with Annette Dixon's demanding nature would prove much more just.

"I heard from Evans, myself."

The raised voice near him caught Sam's attention. Two men, white jackets identifying them as waiters, stood nearby, cigarettes in hand. Sam pushed himself away from the wall to keep up his search and shy away from ship's gossip.

"I overheard Dr. Garry talk to Johnson about munitions on board."

The words brought Sam to a stop. *Munitions? On a passenger ship?* He closed his eyes in frustration. He hated war.

"Said there are boxes of it in the hold."

The shorter man of the two tapped his cigarette and blew out a long line of smoke. "Don't waste your breath worryin' about munitions, Jimmy. I heard we have the promise of the British navy as escort on the way back. Once we reach the war zone, I'd like to see the Jimmies go after a fleet of our own."

"I don't like it." The taller man called Jimmy shook his black head. "Let the captain gamble with his own life,

51

but not mine."

The men looked Sam's way then, but Sam had heard enough. First a warning from Germany and now this? The entire situation chiseled at his peace. Top it off with the mess with Michael and it threatened to bore right into his soul.

He started back toward the stern, glancing into the Music Room as he passed. No one among the stained glass and plush red cushions resembled her. He marched through the passageway leading to the grand staircase and took the elegant steps almost two at a time, inciting a few disapproving looks from a few elderly ladies he passed.

When he reached her stateroom, the sound from inside wrenched his heart. Sobbing. In ten years of friendship, he'd never heard Ashleigh sob. She always been the one her family turned to for strength, ever controlled and thoughtful. Even when her father died, she'd barely shed tears in public, reserving a few for the solitude of her grandmother's lounge, but nothing like the mournful cry on the other side of the door.

The next time Sam saw Michael Craven, he'd pummel him to dust.

Hope never served her well. Proof walked somewhere in first-class with a new wife and a beautiful son.

Ashleigh collapsed on her bed in a heap of tears. "I hate him. I hate him."

She rammed her fist against the bed. Strength escaped with her tears until she dropped to her knees. *Tainted. Unloved.* Unloved? In one last act of betrayal, her father's hands reached up from the grave and strangled her future.

She'd almost succumbed to the beautiful lie she'd told herself for years; the dream she could live beyond her scars, build a family on this shaky foundation she kept underneath her hope, but she could never have a future with any man.

Blinking through tears, she noticed her Bible nestled in the folds of her pillows. *Where were you, God? Where are you now?* She pushed to a stand, pulling the book with her, her fingers wrapping like a claw around the binding. *It was all a lie.* Her life. Her future. Even her faith.

With one fluid movement, she threw the heavy book across the room. It thudded to the ground, and loose papers came unbound and fluttered like a fallen bird to the rug. Deafening silence followed. Her eyes burned at the irony. She was still alone and God remained as silent as he had all those terrifying nights as a child.

"You don't care about me." Her words caught in a broken whisper. "All those promises? All of that love? It was never meant for me."

A sob racked through her. "All things work together for my good?" She laughed, harsh in the stillness. "You've lied too." She squeezed her eyes closed. Her voice lost vibrato. "I'm ruined."

Sinking back onto the bed, she pulled the pillow against her chest and muffled her sobs against it. "Where were you when I needed your protection the most?" She listened into the silence, frantic for anything, one ounce of solace to touch the raw ache. A*s absent as you are now?*

She'd learned God sends rain on the good and the evil. From a child her Grandmama had not only taught about the Christians' response to suffering, but had lived it. But Grandmama never knew this true monster of suffering, did she? God forbid anyone experience this hideous parasite of shame. Not even God wanted to listen to her.

You are not your own.

She fisted the pillow as the words whispered through her spirit. "No, I'm a puppet on a string and my father controlled it all." She looked up to the ceiling, tears cooling her cheeks. "You say you love me? Is this love?"

Her gaze trailed the dim room and rested on her Bible, still clumped in a pile on the floor. The letter her grandmother had given her before her trip jutted from the crinkled folds of her Bible. Like the warmth of her comfort, the familiar handwriting winked from among the heap on the floor. The letter meant to encourage her as she left the wounds of Michael's disappearance behind for the challenges of England, but could it still provide comfort? Even now, when the truth stung through her system like lidocaine?

She crossed the room on weakened legs and knelt to retrieve the Bible. As a course of habit, she smoothed back the leather binding and drew the book to her chest, begging for comfort to pass from its pages. The letter's pages rained to the floor like tear drops, but she gathered them up. If only Grandmama were here in truth; to hold her and whisper that all would be well.

But it would be an empty promise. All would never be well again.

She sat on the edge of the bed and pressed the pages against her lap. The paper on top of the stack gripped her attention.

Sorrow and despair, whether justified or not, are anchors pulling you down below your lifeline until you drown in it – pushing out what hope has to offer you.

Her grandmother's words fit with such perfection a tingle trembled up Ashleigh's spine and snagged her thoughts for more.

When you grieve – pray
When you dream – pray
When you're confused – pray
When you're joyous – pray

But do not stay alone with your prayer. Hold it before you like a beacon and step back into your life, wherever you are, no matter how dark. Place hands and feet to your prayers by focusing on others instead of your pain or disappointments. Life holds infinitely more meaning when it is wrapped within a love for others.

Ashleigh crumbled up the letter, tears traveling down her face with new fervor. Pray? She didn't want to pray. The few words she had for God right now weren't appropriate in the least.

Pray.

Her grandmother's voice whispered through her spirit and nudged at a faint glimmer of hope. *False hope.* Nothing could expunge her past. She squeezed her eyes closed and her grandmother's face emerged, gray-blue eyes penetrating into Ashleigh's shattered thoughts.

Pray and do the next thing.

Pray and do the next thing?

She didn't want to pray.

Pray and do the next thing.

What is the next thing? Breathe? Step one foot in front of the other?

The paper pricked her hand as needling as her conscience. She tossed it to the bed, singed by the command. How could she pray? Those words were nothing more than lifeless ink on a page, but somehow they pierced into her callous spirit like a scalpel. Her vision blurred and breath surged into her lungs through sobs until she finally wiped a dampened sleeve across her face.

"I'll do what you want, Grandmama, but not for God. For you."

She picked up the paper and began to unfold it. *Step back into your life?* What life? She didn't have anything. Certainly no future worth mentioning.

A life wrapped within a love for others?

The orphanage. Her spine straightened. She could find a makeshift family in poor, parentless children. Sam's desire to be with Catherine? She firmed her chin.

Very well, she would do the next thing. Find joy where she could – in the lives of others. She would search for her own contentment in the happiness she could help others find.

Sam's smile came to mind, taunting a paper-thin hope. She squelched it. After all, no man deserved half a woman for a wife. She knew society's expectations, and there was no home for someone like her. She would live this life alone. By her own strength. Without God's help.

Chapter Five

Michael struck again, and this time he hit a home run directly into Ashleigh's heart.

Whatever he'd said or done left an almost visible mark on her behavior. Strangers might only see a content lady going through the activities aboard ship, but *Sam* knew – and she wouldn't talk about it. Every time he'd tried to get her talking over the past two days, she changed the subject or begged for silence.

She hovered beneath a shadowed smile, but something deep and dangerous had shifted in her. A secret emerged. He hated secrets. They usually upturned lives, just like Michael's, but what had happened? Did Michael have something to hold over her? Some hidden stain on Ashleigh's character? One gaze into those honest eyes reminded him that she was not a deceiver ... but something haunted her.

"Add eight more points to my score, Sam." Ashleigh pointed her shuffleboard cue at him and raised a brow. "You're not even trying."

He placed his disc on the ground and readied his cue. He hit his disc across to score ten points, his gaze focusing in on hers. "I want to help you."

Ashleigh's smile froze and then wilted into a pitiful frown. "This is a private burden I must bear alone, Sam." Her reply rasped with emotion to soften his annoyance a little.

"Alone?" Evidently she shared it with Michael. He curbed the surprising edge to his thoughts and shifted a step closer to her. "You don't have to carry this burden alone."

A crinkled dipped across her forehead. She bit her

bottom lip and turned her attention back to the game, hitting another disc. She added eight points to her score, but the mischief in her grin didn't reach her eyes. "Perhaps you could renew your tennis matches with Catherine once we arrive in England. It's good exercise, an opportunity to rekindle your relationship, and...Catherine always loves winning."

More talk about Catherine? It seemed every time he probed for an answer about her conversation with Michael, she'd resort to bringing Catherine into the conversation. She seemed determined to distance herself from him, but why? Sam missed his next shot and frowned. Losing at shuffleboard. Losing his fiancée. Losing his best friend?

Ashleigh slid the disc back across the scoring triangle and gained ten more points with a smile to show for it. It was worth every ounce of pride he swallowed. Was this what his relationship with Catherine used to look like? This easy friendship and tender affection? A few faded memories floated forward, but "tender" wouldn't be a word he'd use to describe them. He remembered their kisses. Heat skimmed his collar at the thought. But the camaraderie? The simple pleasure of being in each other's company? He'd never known anything else. She'd been the first woman to stir his heart and it became his interpretation of normal, but could it be different? *Should* it be? Like this?

Ashleigh's grin turned playful, and much more genuine. "You always lose when you're distracted."

Fine, he'd play along, for her sake. Maybe in time she'd share her burden with him. "And this from experience?"

She tapped her cue onto the ground, the tension in her shoulders easing. "Years of well-placed distraction. Didn't you ever wonder why I always ordered tea and cakes just as we sat down to start a game of chess or backgammon?"

"You used by appetite as a distraction?" He laughed and the affection for her pinned into a deeper place in his chest. "Nice choice. I do love to eat."

"Know your opponent. Isn't that the strategy?"

He narrowed his eyes with his grin. "And all this time I thought you were the sweet and innocent sister."

Ashleigh's eyes grew wide and all color fled her cheeks. What had he said?

His fist tightened around his cue and he moved forward. "Ash, I was only teasing."

She excused his words with a shake of her head, avoiding his gaze. "I'm fine. I'm sorry. Please, I'm fine."

Perhaps a distraction might work for her too. *Oh, if he ever saw Michael again...* He offered his arm. "Speaking of food, it's time for the second seating at lunch. And I'm hungry."

Her gloved hand slid in place, but her smile remained stiff and fake.

"So how long do you plan to stay in England? A year?" He swallowed the tightening in his throat. "Or more?"

The question worked its magic and her gaze found his. "Oh, a year at the very least. There's no knowing how long it will take to establish the orphanage."

Sam sighed into step. "I can't imagine walking to the house next door and not seeing you. And there's the fact that Dad loves you like a daughter."

An authentic glow lit her eyes. "Your father is a wonderful man -- and since you've made such a valiant choice of escorting me across the Atlantic, you're forced to do with my company a bit longer. Scott will be thrilled to see you. You're like the mischievous older brother he's always wanted."

Sam laughed and led Ashleigh to their table, sending the room an appreciative look with his craftsman's eye.

The rose painted dome of the Dining Saloon, framed by golden arches, rose above them filtering sunlight through scenes of stained glass. Their table hugged the railing of the central well, where they could look down at the lower level of the Saloon. Sam never grew tired of cataloguing each feature in his memory. Ideas for future furniture spurned from the carvings among white plaster and carved mahogany. It was a masterpiece of fine workmanship, and something Sam was certain he wouldn't have seen in third class.

Tinkling glass and tings of silver mingled with the murmur of people around them. *First class travel.* He shifted in his swiveling dining chair. What could a furniture maker's son know about traveling with film stars and playwrights?

His spine straightened like the back of a chair, along with every muscle in his body. He was not meant for a life like this on a regular basis. It was exhausting. Would Catherine expect it?

"Will there be a lot of house parties in England?" Sam tried not to wince.

"Catherine has always maintained an active social life, Sam, even in Millington."

Sam's nod came slow. "Dinners at the café and local dances sound a lot different than house parties." He rubbed his jaw. "I'm not much of a socialite, you know."

Ashleigh moved her hand to touch his in her usual comforting manner, but then she stopped. Her fingers curled back toward her and she finally drew them into her lap.

Odd. He'd gotten used to her natural displays of affection. Why the sudden change? Was this about Michael too?

"Dear Sam, you are a gentleman where it counts the

most."

"You'll have to show me the ropes on Thursday evening at the Talent Show." He raised a challenging brow. "Give me some hints on how to be polished and civilized."

She caught her laugh. "A challenge, I see. Well I'm no expert at them, either."

"That's right, I think you ended up hiding away in the library during Catherine's dances."

She narrowed her eyes, but couldn't stop her smile. "Halfway through the night I usually ended up with company, if I recall."

"Ah yes, it's where I beat you in chess."

Her brow tilted. "Where I taught you how to beat me in chess."

"But the truth still remains, that I beat you."

"You're incorrigible."

Sam relaxed in his chair, warmed by the playful glint in Ashleigh's gaze. A true sister couldn't have been any better. She fit so well into his heart. It was like she'd always belonged there. His thoughts flinched on the word 'sister' and his chest tightened with an unnamed feeling, deep and low. As he responded to Ashleigh's familiar smile, it swelled just beyond recognition. She was beautiful.

His thoughts rammed to a stop. Why hadn't he noticed until now? He pulled at his collar and looked down at his plate without seeing it. Of course, she was beautiful. He'd always thought she was a pretty girl. He glanced back across the table. Nope, neither of those words fit the woman sitting across from him. He wasn't sure how to handle the tightening around his heart. Whether it was from Catherine's long absence, her refusal of him, or the braided pain he shared with Ashleigh, his relationship with her suddenly shifted into unknown planes. And wherever it was going…his heart didn't seem to mind the detour one bit.

Two more days of travel and they would arrive in Liverpool -- a notion which gave Ashleigh both relief and pain. The constant pull of her affections with Sam's presence warred with the truth of her past, but she craved his closeness. His friendship. As they sat for dinner, their conversation flowing with the freedom she wouldn't experience with her sister present. Hope wavered out of reach. Perhaps having him as a brother-in-law would be better than nothing at all.

If she kept repeating the thought like a mantra, it might make it all the way to her broken heart.

"Is your fish okay?" Sam whispered.

The concern in his sunrise blue eyes pulled her from her worries like a drowning man from the sea. Three more days and a train ride – then she could disappear into Catherine's shadow and tend her wounds, free to distance her heart from an impossible romance.

"Yes, exquisite. Yours?"

He winked and her mantra disappeared in the drumming of her heartbeat. He used his fork to point to his plate. "I'll have to admit first class is worth the food, but nothing can beat the company."

A flutter danced through her chest and knocked off the residual chill. *What had Catherine ever done to deserve him?* Nothing. Barely written him, and the letters she *had* written were paltry in comparison to his lovely messages. And now?

The air thickened, like breathing the steam above a boiling kettle. She jerked her gaze from his to break the spell, the cool sea breeze from the open porthole a welcome balm for her cheeks. Catherine's interests waxed and waned with her moods, an obvious juxtaposition to Sam's consistency.

Her history left a trail of broken hearts. Ashleigh's gaze flickered back to Sam's. But if Catherine *did* prove to be as fickle as her past, would Sam allow Ashleigh to help him heal through his heartbreak? Could he ever look at her the way she'd seen him look at her sister? Not with her secret.

"No matter how many times we dine in this three level Saloon, I still feel like a fish out of water." Sam laughed and shook his head. "I can't get those clichés out of my head."

Ashleigh followed Sam's gaze to the rose painted dome two-levels above them. Sunlight filtered through its frosted glass and haloed the gold and white decorations centering each table.

"Well, with a head like yours…"

"Sarcasm again, Miss Dougall? What have I created?" He crossed his arms in front of his chest and donned his most fatherly expression. His mock frown eased into a smile. "I kind of like it."

"Miss Dougall?" A steward, trimmed navy suit in perfect form, lowered a silver tray to the table. "Pardon me, but you received a telegram."

Ashleigh released her held breath and retrieved the envelope from the tray. Controlling her natural impulses to touch him proved harder than expected, but it was necessary. She couldn't continue to feed the impossible hope of a future with Sam. Not now. Add to it the underlying tension of their safety aboard the *Lusitania* and her emotions teetered too close to the edge. And then there were whispers of munitions aboard?

"Thank you." She focused on the paper in hand and read it aloud, thankful her voice worked at all. "Contact me when arrive. Safe trip. Jess."

"Jessica Ross? Your friend from nursing school?" Sam added another serving of ham to his fork. "Is she still fighting for the rights of women around the world?"

Ashleigh tweaked a brow at his sarcasm. "She's certainly fighting, but more for the lives of British soldiers at present. Give her opportunity, though, and she'll throw herself in front of carriages and motor cars again in no time."

"She's at the Front?"

"She took advantage of her father's connections as the war started." Ashleigh smoothed her hand across the telegraph paper. "I think her primary goal now is to recruit more nurses. Evidently, there is dire need."

Sam's gaze shot up from his plate. "You're not considering it, are you?"

Oh dear, she'd opened a kettle of fish. Best to play ignorant. "Considering what?"

"Ashleigh." He lowered his cutlery until his hands pressed against the table, his lips set. Warning in his tone. Obviously, he was not fooled. "You're not going into that war."

Ashleigh took her time answering, slicing at her potatoes to avoid his gaze. Michael's face surfaced in her thoughts, followed by her father's – both forcing her to conform to their demands. Her jaw tightened. Sam would not be the next one.

"Well, I'm certainly not going anywhere until I've fulfilled my commitment to Dr. Ross for—"

"Ashleigh." He breathed her name on a growl.

She steadied her expression before lifting her face to him, annoyance rising to a boil within her.

"You don't belong at the front lines. It's hard enough for men to see the—"

"Must I continually repeat myself?" She kept her voice

controlled, even consolatory, though stomping *his* foot would have been more gratifying. "I am quite capable of making my own—"

"It's not only about the danger, Ashleigh. It's about the pain of watching people suffer or seeing a human stoop to the lowest level of morality. You've never had to deal with things like..."

"Haven't I?" The whisper took on more volume than she'd planned and heat bolted from her stomach to her face. *If he only knew.* "Lest you forget, I have worked as a nurse for two years and as far as the ill effects of man's decadence, I am keenly aware—"

"I know what happened with Michael hurt you, but when it comes to the depravity of human nature in war?" He tossed his napkin on the table and sat back. "You and every other woman—"

"And traveling toward war-torn waters isn't meant for women either? What will you do about that one, Sam? Turn the entire ship about?"

"You don't understand. War is the province of men, not—"

"That is enough." Each bone in her body trembled to move, attack, something. How dare he presume she was as weak-willed and pampered as her sister? "Don't you think every mourning widow or fatherless child is as much a part of this war as the soldiers?" She drew in a deep breath. "We will not agree on this point. Let us divert our conversation to something safer, shall we?"

"Yes, let's talk about safety." His fingers chopped the table, causing tiny waves in the water glasses. "I love your kind heart. It's one of the most beautiful things about you, but your compassion always gets you into trouble. Going to the front lines is as safe as jumping off this ship. You can't save everyone, A—"

"I would rather take risks on something as noble as compassion then allow fear to stifle my life and anyone else's I might influence. If this war lasts two years, maybe three, my brother could enlist. If America joins, then you?" She pushed herself away from the table and tried to keep her voice down. "God forbid that one of you should be injured and there isn't a nurse willing to risk her hat pin to help you."

"Calm down, Ashleigh. You know that's not what—"

"And what did you mean?" She crossed her arms and waited. Should she dare hope he might impress her with a logical reason? She would never be more than a child to him, and she was full up of men pushing her about like a pawn on a chessboard.

Sam leaned forward, elbows propped against the table, fingers threaded through each other and that infernal big brother expression pasted on his face. "You're not even twenty-three, Ashleigh. There are some things women aren't supposed to—"

"Excuse me." She stood and tossed her serviette onto the table. "I've suddenly lost my appetite." She lifted her hand as Sam followed her to a stand. "No, please stay. Eat. Fill your mouth with something besides words you'll regret."

She fled from the Saloon, but even in the throes of annoyance a swell of pride surged higher. She'd spoken her mind to Sam – not backed down like a child. Her feet slowed. And she wasn't afraid of his wrath or retribution. He would never really try to force his will on her. Not Sam. There was a sweet freedom in the thought.

She barely made it to her stateroom before Sam caught up to her. In one quick motion, he tugged her into his arms. His warmth spread through her, shocking her anger and body completely still.

"I'm sorry, little girl." His breath fanned the top of her head where his chin rested. "I just want you to be safe."

She closed her eyes and soaked in the moment. Perfect. His embrace filled empty spaces in her heart no one else had ever touched. And *this* was what she could never have. Tears squeezed beneath her eyelids. His lemon scent made sour so sweet.

No! She hardened her thoughts against them and stepped out of the haven of his arms, but he wouldn't let her escape. His hands cupped her shoulders, his face close and oh so tender.

"I don't like the idea of you putting your life in danger." His expression softened to a smile. "But you're right, there's no one else on this Earth who'd take better care of the wounded than you."

The tension seeped from her body and loosened her hold on her tears.

Sam's thumb moved to sweep one from her cheek and a glimmer of something alive and beautiful passed between them. It registered in his eyes. Attraction? From him? It couldn't be.

She fluttered back from his touch, stung by the painful irony. "I forgive your mule-headedness, *this* time."

He blinked from his trance, brow crinkled in confusion. "Yes, um..." He tilted his head and examined her face again. "Well, with my track record I'm sure there will be more opportunities for your forgiveness."

It was only a flicker of attraction. Nothing more. Easily doused with time, and...Catherine. "I'm certain it will take all of your stubbornness to match my sister's, as you well know."

The intensity of his stare continued. He gestured with his chin toward the hall. "Come back to the Dining Saloon and eat." His brows gave a playful wiggle. Her stomach squeezed tight. "I promise to play nice."

"Thank you, but I think I should like to retire for a while."

"I'm sorry, Ash." He stepped forward, palm trailing down her arm and leaving a tingle. "You know I mean well, even when I'm bossy."

The gentleness in his eyes deepened the wound. She waved him away. "Go on. Finish your meal. I'll see you in the morning."

He paused, watching her a little longer. His smile inched broad. "Fine. I'll let you get away with hiding for now, but I'd better see you then."

Ashleigh slid into her stateroom and sighed onto the bed, fresh tears marking warm trails down her cheeks. How could she keep pretending with Sam Miller in her life? Her natural regard for him made conversation easy, but nothing prepared her heart for his touch. How could she continue the charade? How could she cool the lightning attraction blazing through her? She picked up her grandmother's letter again, seeking the closest tangible piece of her possible. Could she provide hope? Insight? Strength to make it to Edensbury?

Dearest granddaughter,

Many people face heartbreak throughout their lives. Some fall under the weight of their sorrow, some harden like stone, and others blossom from it, as lovely as a winter rosebush in bloom. Trials are a part of life, and pain with those trials. It grieves me to see you face so many within your young life. How you choose to heal from these wounds will determine what will become of the woman inside of you.

We are not promised an easy journey. A world filled with broken people will only produce broken hearts in one way or another, but God lives inside of you – the mender of broken things. He has guided you throughout your life, and he holds you even now.

God lived inside of her? Then where was He? Hadn't He seen what was happening?

You may not feel his presence, but deep in the most hidden places of your heart, He is with you. The still small voice of love and comfort. You are His and He has a specific plan for your life.

Evidently the plan didn't involve a husband and children. What man would want her? Ashleigh glanced in the mirror. Her pale face and hollowed eyes bore little resemblance to a child of God. If she could look inside her heart, she'd see even less of a reflection. She didn't even want to talk to Him. What possible plan could God want with her filthy heart or stained life?

God has given you the unique talent to hear and heal people. Few are called to such an intimate selflessness, but God chose you for it. Take the gifts you have, the life within your breast, and use it to bring hope to others. When you hurt, do not hold it close to your heart, clenching it so tightly you cannot see anything but your own pain – reach out. In helping others, you will find healing for your own heart.

A prayer almost formed on her lips, but she snapped her mouth closed. She didn't need Him – and He didn't love her. In only a few more days, she could disappear back into a life of nursing and hope her grandmother's words rang true.

Chapter Six

Sam stood at the entrance of the Saloon Lounge and pulled at his uncomfortable cravat. Why did sacrifice have to come wrapped in a tuxedo? He leaned against the wall and watched the entourage of glitz and glamour pour past him into the immaculate room.

The sweet scent of wine mingled with the trill of laughter and drew his attention inside the Lounge. Sam's craftsman's eye took in the Georgian style architecture surrounding jade green carpet. Dark mahogany framed the softly lit room, encasing the walls from entryway to the green marble fireplaces at each end, which must have stood 12 to 14 feet. It was beyond anything he'd ever seen, a masterpiece of woodwork and color, topped with a vaulted skylight of stained glass depicting the months of the year. Unbelievable.

His father wouldn't be able to view the rich colors from Sam's photographs, but at least he could appreciate the workmanship shown in the black-and-whites.

Millionaires and film stars? Musicians and businessmen?

His photography and his father's furniture business had given him a secure and comfortable life, but nothing in his little mountain home came close to this. It was a spectacle of wealth. A vision of the perfect life?

Sam shook his head. Not for him. Not at the core. No amount of money could buy away the tension simmering from one end of the room to the other. The *Lusitania* would enter the war zone in the morning, and Sam wondered if the whispers aboard were true. Submarine warnings? Slower speeds?

During Sam's morning walk, crewmen were uncovering lifeboats and swinging them out to the readied position. A simple precaution? He hoped so.

The cravat around his neck nearly choked him and he pulled to loosen it. Either he was letting the ship gossips get to him, or something was wrong – and tension didn't only stem from the war. He'd resorted to near begging to get Ashleigh to attend the famed Seaman's Charity Concert on their last night aboard. She'd tried hiding away for the two days since their argument.

Had she felt the spark between them too? Like lightning. It nudged a curiosity only time with her could answer. And he wanted an answer.

He stepped aside to allow an older couple into the Lounge and glanced back toward the stairway in time to catch Ashleigh in his line of vision. But this was no Ashleigh he'd ever seen. Her dark hair, typically twisted into a knot at the back of her head, piled in elegant ringlets. Some spilled over and framed her face, matching her eyes. The simple dresses she usually wore were replaced by a gown of black lace covering cloth the color of dawning blue. The material moved with the curves of her body as she descended the grand staircase.

Sam stood in shocked stillness. Heat swelled in his throat with each move she made toward him. His body responded to her as a man would to a beautiful woman, drawing his attention down the length of her body again. As their gazes met, warmth flooded his chest to match the heat pulsing through his arms and legs. He swallowed the gathering tension in his throat and forced his feet into motion until he stood in front of her.

"You look beautiful."

Her cheeks blushed darker. "I thought I would make wise use of my trousseau, but it's much too glamorous for me." She glanced down at her dress. "It's more suited for Catherine, I'm afraid."

"I only wish I'd brought my camera tonight so I could capture you." He couldn't help but stare and try to place this woman before him with the little girl he'd always known. Maybe he was the captured one. If he could get his brain out of whatever fog her presence cast on him, then he'd be fine. Maybe. And just maybe, he kind of liked her spell.

Her eyes had never been as fascinating as they were tonight. And her lips? His pulse hammered beneath his Adam's apple. He was clearly losing his mind.

An impish grin molded onto those glossy lips. It'd been cute a few days or months ago, but now it was attractive. He gave his cravat another tug.

"You're enjoying this too much, little girl."

"I promise not to get used to it." Her smile lost its glow. "We're both pretending tonight, aren't we?" She swept him an appraising look. "You're in a tuxedo, and clearly as dapper as any gentleman here."

"But tonight, I'm a furniture maker's son puffed up as a millionaire." He offered his arm.

"And I'm a bankrupt Lord and Lady's daughter who is playacting as an heiress."

She bit her lip and hesitated before slipping her arm through his. Did she feel the difference between them too? The newness? The caution and fragility? Like catching the first rays of sunlight over the mountains through his camera lens. Too long, and the shot is lost. He placed his hand over hers on his arm, determined not to lose the memory.

"Well, let's put on our best act and see how we fare among the elite. What do you say?"

In response, she lifted her head a bit higher and donned a very regal profile.

Laughter came from within the Lounge, mingling with the tinkling of silver and the scent of cigars. A men's ensemble sang at the front of the room. Sam's shoes sank into the lush carpet as he navigated around the tightly placed chairs to a half-empty table. The upper crust at the table welcomed Sam and Ashleigh with nods and a few handshakes.

He leaned close to Ashleigh's ear to quip about how misplaced he felt, but her violet scent distracted his senses and drew him closer. She looked up, expectantly – her face so close to his, the caramel swirls in her eyes danced in the candlelight.

He chuckled through his embarrassment and allowed his gaze to travel to her lips a little too long. He cleared his throat. "I was going to make a joke about being a fish out of water, but…um…I got distracted."

Her gaze flickered unfocused for an instant and then her eyes grew wide and she snapped her attention to the stage. Sam sat back in his chair, attraction doused by her obvious discomfort. What was he doing? A few days ago she thought he was engaged to her sister and now he was flirting with Ashleigh? No wonder she turned away. That type of apparent inconsistency had his mother's name written all over it.

His emotions cooled. He was *nothing* like her.

Ashleigh leaned close, keeping her face forward. "I doubt I can perform the part of an heiress as well as you play the part of a charming millionaire. I almost thought you *were* flirting with me."

He forced a grin and played along with her mistake. In fact, he needed to believe it too.

"I imagined myself to be one of those extravagant Vanderbilts from back home." He took a hold of his lapel, relaxed in his chair, and lifted his nose high. "Be sure to return to Millington soon, Miss Dougall. I would greatly enjoy your company at my small estate at Biltmore for one of my house parties. Nothing much. Only a few hundred people—"

"Shh." Ashleigh laughed and covered his mouth with her hand. "One of the Vanderbilts *is* at the next table. Besides, you were a better actor when you were flirting."

Because I wasn't acting.

She pulled her hand from his mouth and folded it in her lap.

"One of the Vanderbilts is on this ship?"

He followed Ashleigh's gaze to where a man held the nearby table captive. His suit, dark hair, and especially his eloquent gestures spoke of refinement – but there was genuine kindness in his ready smile. If Sam had to imitate a rich man, maybe this one wouldn't be so bad.

Ashleigh's voice remained low. "I believe he's a first cousin to Mr. George Vanderbilt of Asheville. Gwyn or Alfred. Something like that."

Sam looked down at her. The gentleness returned, deep and sweet, and brought with it a question. What would it be like to fall in love with his beautiful friend? He'd been enamored with Catherine ever since they were children. Never Ashleigh, but was it such an odd thought? The six year age difference mattered when they were children, but now? The realization produced an unsettling result, with an even more shocking reaction. Uncertainty. He curbed the urge to brush his fingers down her cheek.

"So, Miss Dougall, how would a young aristocrat, like Vanderbilt let's say, impress a lovely heiress such as yourself?"

His gaze held hers, and even with the dim lighting her cheeks blushed rose. Maybe she wasn't immune to what was happening between them.

She looked over his head and the impish glow returned. "He could accept one of those delicious desserts from the waiter."

"Ah, saved from my expert acting by another distraction."

She wrinkled her nose with her grin. "I'm an enormous fan of perfect timing."

He thanked the waiter and turned back to her. "And I'm an enormous fan of dessert." He pointed his fork at her, which was probably against some kind of social rule. "Even though all the food aboard has been excellent, none of it can compare to Grace's cooking. I told Father we should steal her from your grandma so she could feed two poor, unfortunate bachelors."

"Unfortunate indeed?" She tsked and took up her fork. "Steal Grandmama's cook, not to mention best friend?" Her sweet smile held him captive again. Would her lips taste as sweet as this trifle? "Hardly heroic just to feed your unending appetite?"

"We need her. Do you remember what happened the last time I tried to cook?"

Ashleigh's nose curled like the little girl he was still trying to envision– but no, he failed.

"I still can't understand how one turns blueberry muffins into something the consistency of chalk."

Sam raised his loaded fork to his grin and winked. "Talent."

Her gaze softened and held, longer this time. But not long enough. *Attraction.* He was attracted to Ashleigh Dougall, and…the feeling settled into place like the perfect fit.

Ashleigh stiffened and looked back to the stage, her fist pressed to the base of her neck. The rapid flow of her breathing confirmed she felt it too. And it terrified her.

How had he gotten into such a mess? Two sisters? One didn't want him anymore. He caught Ashleigh's profile from his periphery. But what of the other? And how had his heart turned in such a direction?

Ashleigh had been with him since Catherine left. Had she replaced Catherine in his heart? No, certainly not. He couldn't just toss away ten years of friendship and two years of courting to…to…

He focused on the Scot on the stage, telling jokes. This world was a crazy place, and Sam's heart bore witness to it. Silence built the tension between them as a pianist performed classics, followed by an amazing Welsh choir. After a burst of applause, a sudden hush fell over the room as a man in uniform, expression serious, approached the concert area, cap in hand.

"Is that the captain?" Ashleigh asked.

"I believe so. Captain Turner. From what some of the passengers said, it's customary for the captain to give a farewell speech on the last night of the voyage."

"Good evening, ladies and gentlemen." The captain began in a gravely tone, his square face held a firm countenance. The very reflection of seaman. "I have no talent to share with you tonight."

The crowd's laughter eased the tension a bit as he continued.

"I hope you have enjoyed the journey thus far." He shifted his white cap to the other hand his brow hinged in wrinkles. "We've received word that German U-boats have been reported off the coast of Ireland, particularly Fastnet."

Murmurs broke out through the crowd, but the captain stayed his hand against their questions. "There's no need for concern. Readying the lifeboats, as many of you witnessed this morning, is a simple precaution under such times as these. And we've doubled our lookouts as an added safeguard. You can feel confident that upon entering the War Zone in the morning, we shall be securely in the care of the Royal Navy."

A man's voice called from the back of the room. "Are we still to keep from lighting our cigars on deck?"

"Yes, sir. Again, this is merely a precaution. We shall keep the ship darkened until we are out of danger. No doubt many of you felt the ship slow earlier this evening. We hope to clear Fastnet protected by the cover of darkness. In the morning, a cruiser should arrive to escort us into Liverpool."

A few more questions filtered through the guests and then the captain excused himself from the room. His reassurance of protection doused anxiety like a dry cloth on a wild flame. Few people, rich or poor, would sleep tonight.

Sam escorted Ashleigh from the lush Lounge to the chilled air off the Boat Deck. A light fog cloaked the ship in misted darkness, and beyond the railing hung a black void of ocean. The lights and chatter from within posed a contrast to this quiet, dark world.

They walked in silence, Ashleigh's arm tucked tight in the crook of his elbow and her body warmed his side. Another overwhelming sense of her rightness had him tugging her arm a little closer.

"Do you make anything of the captain's words?"

He shrugged away his concern and rubbed a hand over the one she had nestled on his arm. "The *Lusitania* carries passengers, not soldiers. Not even Germany would want the bloodstain of innocent people on their hands, no matter how big a bully they are."

Her raised brow challenged his declaration.

"Besides, we're on one of the fastest ships on the

Atlantic. No U-boat can outrun her." Perhaps if he repeated what he kept telling himself it would help take away the nervous edge.

A frown crinkled her brow. "Unfortunately, speed and wisdom do not always dine at the same table. At least there have been some life boat drills I've noticed during my morning walks."

From what Sam had seen, it didn't boost his confidence in the sailors' abilities to rescue people from a sinking ship. He guided them to the railing where fog whispered through the darkness. The breeze brought the full impact of Ashleigh's violet scent back to him and he closed his eyes to drink it in. His body warmed and his thoughts followed less chaste imaginations than usual.

Perhaps distraction *was* a good option.

"This Dr. Ross you're going to work with – is he any relation to your friend, Jessica?"

"Yes, her older brother. David Ross. It seems they have a family tradition of medical professionals. Their grandfather is the doctor with whom I worked in rural Warm Springs. Their father, a surgeon, recently joined a medical team near the Front. And then, of course, there is David."

That was the first time he'd noticed her using Dr. Ross' first name. A nerve twitched in his jaw.

"David and I share a common goal -- providing support for the orphans and widows of the war." She pushed away a loose strand of her hair, but the wind wisped it back across her cheek.

She gazed out over the water. The silence brought the lost look back to her face. He'd caught glimpses of it since Michael's disappearance when she thought no one was watching, but it had become more frequent since Monday. Whatever Michael had said or done, it had stolen something from her.

"What can I do to help you heal? Ever since Michael…"

"Please, Sam, let's not discuss Michael." She pulled her arm from his and pinched the collar of her cape close around her neck. "The only way to fix it is to place it in the past."

"Ash." He coaxed her to meet his gaze. "I don't know if I agree with that. I've tried to keep my past in the past, but it's still right here." He placed his hand over his chest and shook his head, the ache below his palm swelling into a pain. "Just below the surface, and as painful as the day Mother left. I'm beginning to wonder if there comes a time when we need to face our wounds for what they are."

She remained silent, but her fingers twisted the edge of her gloves, wrinkling the material at the hem. Her eyes lifted to his, as dark as the night around them. He moved a breath closer, close enough to touch the stray curl resting against her cheek. An invisible tie surged between them.

She raised her hand, as if to touch his cheek, but stopped and stepped back. The wind chilled the space between them like unspoken words. He craved a touch from her, something to answer the unspoken question bouncing between them in the darkness.

"Perhaps we should go inside." She took a few steps toward the companionway, then half turned to him. "Sometimes the past is the safest place for pain. Time helps dull our senses to it."

"But I'm beginning to wonder if it's like one of those tumors you've talked about in nursing. If you leave it inside of a person instead of remove it, then it can eat away at the person, right?"

Her brows drew close, gaze studying the deck. "Some are so large, and so deep, that they are inoperable."

"What does the patient do then?"

She lifted her face, china doll impassive. "They die." She blinked and moved further away from him, shadows falling over her face. Her cryptic words clung to the fog-soaked air.

He wouldn't leave the moment in darkness, not matter what she wanted. "Or God sends a miracle?"

Her lips tipped into a sad smile. "Miracles?" She sighed, a slight hint of longing in her voice. "Some things can't be fixed. And many times, God never sends a miracle. Good night, Sam."

The nip in the air penetrated Sam's jacket and settled around his heart. Something much bigger than Michael's deception hid behind Ashleigh's words, more menacing than the unseen enemy lurking through those dark waters – and it was eating away at her soul. She tugged against the bond between them, but he'd do everything in his power to keep his hold. And maybe even … create a miracle?

Ashleigh stifled a yawn. The ship's foghorn just after dawn had roused her from a restless sleep and the gentle lull of the ship's afternoon movements weren't helping her muddled mind. Perhaps within the next half hour she'd retire to her cabin for a short nap before her promised chess match with Sam. The last thing she needed with his competitive streak was syrupy thoughts.

She'd kept their conversations as safe and superficial as possible all morning. After the tremulous close to last night's events and the draw Sam's 'pretend' flirting had on her will, serious topics stayed clearly out of the question. She *wanted* to be genuine and honest with him. Everything about the easiness of their friendship urged her to be authentic, which was the very reason why she had to keep a close rein on her behavior. Her faith in Sam made her weak. His friendship softened her defenses in ways nothing else ever had. She trusted him – a dangerous commodity when the truth would alienate him forever. Better he care for the person he thought she was than discover her secret and despise her.

He was a difficult man to keep at arms' length, though. She knew every curl of his hair, every expression of his face, every golden flake in his eyes. He seemed to work through her defenses with the ease of a master surgeon – and there was nowhere to escape him apart from jumping ship.

She glanced at the choppy sea and pondered the thought for half a second. She wasn't that desperate yet. If he ran his fingers across her cheek or focused on her lips again, she might be. Heaven help her, she'd almost puddled to the floor at his touch.

Sam stood a few feet away, hovering over his Brownie box camera with the care of a mother with her newborn. His hobby had grown into a little business back in Millington, even finding some of his photographs of Appalachia in a few magazines, but Ashleigh had never become adept with the tiny device.

He'd removed his cap to more easily work his camera and the sea breeze ruffled the curls at the base of his neck, teasing her fingertips with a tingle. Would they curl around her fingers or smell like lemons? Her breath turned shallow.

What if last night hadn't been pretend? If the playful banter and easy trust melded into a remarkable romance? Would he be able to look beyond her stains to see her for who she truly was? Love her beyond them?

He glanced up at her over the rim of his camera and topped his grin off with a wink. Her smile bloomed with a breathtaking flutter in her stomach. If only…

A woman of substantial girth and even more impressive hat passed between them, blocking her from his charm long enough for her face to cool. It was one of those hats of older fashion; almost the size of a carriage wheel with enough flowers and feathers to ensure the woman held near-royal social status...or wished to. Having been removed from higher society for the past few years, the hat surprised even Ashleigh. When the woman moved out of the way, Sam's wide-eyed gaze still followed her slow gait across the deck, parasol making a rhythmic click against the wood.

Their gazes locked, they shared a pinched-lip smile that burst open in shared laughter.

"So *that* is what I'm going to see in this high society of England?" he whispered, steadying his camera with a hand and leaning closer to her. He tilted his head to catch another glimpse of the woman. "Why would she need a parasol? She's thoroughly protected from the rain underneath that umbrella of a hat."

Ashleigh caught her snicker in her gloved hand, glad for the light-hearted distraction. "Balance, my dear Sam. With a hat of such...magnitude, the poor woman could barely stand upright without some assistance, don't you think?"

"Really?"

"When those hats were in top fashion a few years ago, Mother insisted on the largest one in the shop. Don't you remember? It had at least three ribbons, a bird's nest, and..."

"The ostrich feathers."

"That's the one." She tapped his shoulder to add to her words. "One gust of wind and she would've blown over if not for her faithful parasol keeping her stable." Ashleigh shook her head and pressed a palm to her stomach. "What women suffer for fashion? I was thankful for simple nursing uniforms to keep me from the tedious use of decorative hats and pinching corsets."

"And you're even more beautiful without them." His gaze roamed over her, a caress, and his hand rose as if to touch her hair. "I've always preferred your hair uncovered."

He blinked, as if he hadn't intended to voice his thoughts. Warmth fused to her cheeks.

He looked back to the horizon, cleared his throat and gestured toward the green-gray mounds of land in the distance. "I'm glad the fog cleared so we could get a view of the Irish coast."

She swallowed down a heated breath and followed Sam's gaze to the horizon. The last remnants of morning fog clung to the green coast on the horizon. A mixture of relief and fear washed over her. *Land.* With the warnings of torpedoes, nothing looked more reassuring, but with landfall came a closer step to Catherine -- Ashleigh's next conflict.

"Are you all right?" Sam's voice broke through her thoughts.

"Why didn't you bring your plate camera? Didn't you say it made clearer photos?"

"It's with my luggage." He shook his head and placed his palm over his heart. "Besides, it's my pride and joy and much too nice a camera to toss around on the deck of a ship."

His boyish grin tugged her closer. Oh, the power that man had over her emotions! Her stomach twisted at the thought. Another man with power over her? No, it wasn't the same. It was new and gentle. Safe? Her rapid pulse begged to differ.

She stepped toward the railing and looked out toward

gray-green mounds against the horizon. Sunlight sparkled across the waves, a bridge of gold across the water. It was easy to see God in the vastness of the sea and the strength of those waves. She closed her eyes to the sun's warmth and breathed in the salty air. Her thoughts almost formed into a prayer. But God didn't care. Not for her, or He would have stopped her father years ago.

"Ash, come take a look at this view."

She pushed away her thoughts and walked to Sam's side. Carefully she leaned close to the small leather-bound box on its precarious tripod perch. His giddy delight in teaching her how it worked dampened a little of her nervousness at his closeness. She reached to steady the little box at the same time as Sam and their fingers brushed against each other. A tingle shot from her hand to her heart. She attempted to pull her hand away, but he captured her fingers and placed them on the side of the camera, firming his palm over them.

"Hold it like this." His voice breathed past her ear, nearly weakening her knees to the deck boards.

He stood behind her now. His arms hemmed her in on either side, breath warming her cheek. She swallowed, or tried to, but her dry mouth wouldn't cooperate. *Ignore these ridiculous feelings, Ashleigh.* The only problem was they weren't ridiculous. They were wonderful.

She took a deep breath and looked back through the lens, trying to ignore the safety in the haven of his arms. It was remarkable how one could frame a piece of the world. The monstrous ocean wasn't as frightening in such small doses. In fact, the angle at which the sun glazed the water held a magical, almost hypnotic quality. So vast and mysterious, and yet as beautiful as starlight's reflection in a pond.

"It's beautiful. It truly frames the world."

"One of the many reasons I'm obsessed with it, I think." Sam's voice rumbled low, vibrating from her earlobe down her neck. He guided the camera to a different scene, nearer the coast. She ignored the influence of his closeness on the chaos in her stomach. "Can you see the coast now?"

"Oh, yes, it's lovely." She pulled back and smiled up at him, but hadn't calculated the distance.

His face hovered above hers, eyes so intense she thought he might read her rebel thoughts. His brow tilted upward, slightly, as if he was searching for an answer to an unvoiced question.

She didn't have an answer. She *couldn't* have an answer. But she did look down at his mouth as if he'd spoken it. Two inches and their lips might touch. *Oh, Heaven help me!*

As if drugged, she drew her attention from his and back to the camera. The sea rumbled out to meet the distant shore with waves as confused as the emotions crashing in her heart. She couldn't wait to get off of this boat. There would be plenty of opportunities to flee Sam's presence in Edensbury. She knew all the hiding places.

As a child, hiding had been a survival skill honed to near perfection.

She blinked the framed scene back into view. A strange stream of bubbles broke into her line of vision making a surprisingly straight path through the waves. A fish? Whale? Whatever it was, it moved fast.

"Sam, look here. There's some strange fish coming toward the ship."

He offered a doubtful smirk as he took the camera. "A fish coming toward the ship?" He peered through the lens. "I don't know of any fi—" His body stiffened. "No."

A chill of awareness trembled down her spine. "What,

Sam? It can't be—"

"Torpedo on the starboard side!"

The shout rang down from a place above her followed immediately by another from somewhere else on the boat. Sam's gaze locked with Ashleigh's and everything slowed. Sounds muffled except for the thrumming of her heartbeat in her ears. Sam pushed his camera aside and took her into his arms as an explosion sent them staggering like ragdolls toward the railing. *No, dear Lord. We've been hit.*

Chapter Seven

Sam steadied her against his chest as the vibration rocked to a stop. "Are you okay?"

"Yes." She pulled back and released her grip on his jacket. Her hat crooked to one side so she pulled it off altogether. "You?"

"Fine." He sent another glance down her body and then scanned the crowd, his hands keeping a firm hold on her shoulders.

Some people righted themselves and went into immediate hysteria, running to the railing or snatching up their children. Others resumed their promenade without more than a nod. Was she dreaming?

"We've been hit?"

Sam offered a lopsided grin. "Don't worry. It will take more than one torpedo to sink a ship this large. Besides, we're so close to land—"

A second explosion, larger than the first, cut off Sam's words. The impact ripped them apart and slammed Ashleigh to the deck, face first. She bit back a cry as her wrist twisted beneath her, but quickly rolled onto her back. The world shuddered into a mass of chaos covered with a charcoal cloud. Flames burst into the pale blue sky and rained hot debris against her cheek. She covered her face and sat up, dusting the ash from her skirt and taking in the swarm of frantic people. Her stomach clenched. *Could the ship survive two explosions?*

"Ashleigh."

Sam called through a myriad of cries and shouts. He reached toward her, pressed between a crowd of people. Had the shock of the explosion knocked him so far down the deck? She pushed herself up on hands and knees, but almost lost her balance again. Was she dizzy? She pressed a palm to her head.

Sam was by her side, steadying her with his hands on her arms. "Are you hurt?"

"No, I don't think so, but I may be dizzy—" She saw it then, the deck clearly slanting toward the sea. A steep downhill tilt. Her worse fears ignited. "Good heavens, Sam, the ship."

Sam gave her a gentle shake and drew her gaze back to his. "Let's get to the port side." He reached for her hand. "And don't let go."

A mass exodus erupted from the companionway, spilling toward them in a wave of panic. Sam pushed ahead, keeping a vice grip on her hand, and wedging them nearer to the companionway.

"Do you think we'll make it to shore?"

"I don't know." He glanced back from where they'd walked and his jaw tightened. He fastened a sober gaze on her. "We're going down fast."

She followed his stare. The deck's angle already brought waves into view at the bow. Officers in white suits worked to guide the multitudes into some order while attempting to move toward the lifeboats, but streams of people blocked their path.

Sam pushed ahead. Seconds stretched to minutes, but he never let go of her hand, taking the brunt of the stampede. The increasing tilt of the deck added to their slow progress, as gravity tugged them toward the starboard side.

With a final pull Sam drew her with him into the temporary haven of the companionway. Ashleigh leaned against the wall a moment and closed her eyes, trying to quiet her fears with a deep breath. *One step in front of the other.*

"Go through to the port side, away from the sea. There might be a chance at lowering those lifeboats in time." He squeezed her shoulders and stepped back. "I'm going to my room for life vests."

His words jarred her attention wide awake. Below? Even now waves lapped into view at the bow, and only a few minutes had passed since the explosion. There wasn't time. She gripped his sleeve. "I'm going with you."

"Not this time."

Her hold tightened with her resolve. "You will not risk your life for me. It's too dangerous."

Sam raised a brow and stepped back, breaking her hold on him. "I need you to listen." His voice almost pleaded; his gaze followed suit. "I need to make sure you're safe."

The ship groaned underneath, confirming the concern on Sam's face. A shudder ran through its massive form, nearly shaking them to the ground again. The diamond reflection from the shaking chandelier overhead sparkled over Sam's face with rainbows. Ashleigh glanced up in time to see it break from its place in the ceiling and dangle, readied for a free-fall toward Sam.

"Sam!" She grabbed up her skirts and dived forward. The chandelier snapped. She tackled him to the ground as the glass fixture pelted them with glass, missing them by inches.

Ashleigh didn't move. His rapid breaths matched hers as she lay atop him, the scent of lemon forcing a fresh wave of tears. *Too close.* She fisted his shirt and buried her face into his shoulder, ignoring the impropriety of their position or the accusing voices from her past. None of it mattered right now, as they waited for the next breath – if there would even be a next breath. Mere inches and he'd have become a part of devastation of bodies certain to crowd the bottom of the sea.

He wrapped his arms around her, warm, safe, and as close to Heaven as she'd ever known on Earth. "You saved my life, little girl," he whispered into her hair, and punctuated his words with a kiss to her head.

She rested in his embrace for a moment, crowding out the doubts and fear with the overwhelming awareness of him. His arms tightened, strong, yet gentle. *Oh yes, she loved him*--and for what time they had left, she'd clasp those feelings just as Sam held her now.

She lifted her face from his shoulder and lost her gaze in his. Tenderness swelled along with more tears. Ashleigh sniffled and pushed up from his chest, her lips quivered into a smile. "I think you owe me a favor for my good deed."

Sam sat up and leaned forward to wipe a tear from her cheek, his smile crooked and soft. The sweetness of his red-rimmed gaze probed deep, touching a hollowed out part of her heart with a glimmer of hope. "Hmm, you going to hold this over me for the rest of our lives?"

As short as those might be.

"Live." She patted the wrinkled spot where her hands had fisted his shirt. "Live through this thing with me."

His hand cradled her cheek and for the briefest second, he looked as if he might kiss her. Her gaze rested on his lips, wondering what it might feel like to kiss her friend. Her smile grew with the thought. Kissing friends? The notion warmed her to her toes.

Another massive shake of the ship broke the spell and sent her back into motion. What on earth was she doing? Clearly tragedy had her going mad. She readied herself to stand, but Sam took hold of her elbows and brought them up together.

"I'm going for the life vest." He held up his hand to stop her protest. "Go to the port side and look for a lifeboat.

I'll find you."

He pulled back but she caught his arm, forcing her tight voice to work above a whisper. "My stateroom is closer. Here." She took the key from her pocket and planted her boots against the slant of the ship. Too fast. How could this giant ship sink so quickly?

Sam's palm closed around her hand, his gaze lingering on hers, unspoken messages passing between them. She didn't want to let go of him. What if he never came back?

"Sam…"

He seemed to read her thoughts. "I'll find you."

With one last squeeze of her hand, he took the key and disappeared toward the stairway, down below in the bowels of the dying ship. Her body itched to run after him. To be with him if the worst happened. She could die wrapped in his arms.

An elderly woman stumbled in front of her and fell to her knees in a heap of tears. "We're going to die."

Ashleigh sent another look in the direction of the stairway and drew in a deep breath for strength. *Oh God, if you hear me at all. Please bring Sam back to me. Please keep him safe.*

She tucked her fear deep inside and allowed the cool-calm of indifference to separate her logic and emotions. Get to the port side of the ship and find a lifeboat.

Ashleigh leaned down to the woman and placed a hand to her bent shoulder. "Come now, you'll be trampled if you keep to the floor."

"We're sinking. The ship is sinking," the woman muttered. A hint of watery brown eyes peeked up from beneath weathered hands.

"Yes, it is." Ashleigh patted the lady's arm and offered a tight smile. "But there's no time for hysterics. The only thing to be done is to find a safe way off the ship, isn't it?"

The woman stared up at Ashleigh, no doubt searching for courage Ashleigh didn't feel. But she knew how to fake it. How to give something she didn't possess. And…it usually worked.

The woman dried her eyes with her dainty handkerchief. "Yes, of course."

"Very good. Now step this way and hold to my arm."

Ashleigh pulled the woman with her to the port side, but the view revealed its own difficulties. Whereas the lifeboats should have dangled over the open sea, the angle of the ship shifted them inward toward the deck. A few boats near the stern rested against the deck and were already filled with people, but how were they going to lift a boat full of people over the side of the ship? Was that even possible?

Ashleigh walked out of the companionway, the elderly woman still fastened to her side, and scanned the stern for Sam. He couldn't have gotten below and back in time. She started for the nearest lifeboat.

A sudden chorus of screams pierced the scramble of noise around her. Ashleigh looked in time to see a crowded lifeboat sliding down the deck toward her, an avalanche of human bodies and white wood. With the selectivity of a freight train, it closed in on its victims and ran them over, busting against some of the other boats as it crashed down the incline.

Ashleigh lurched toward the wall, away from the crushing boat and tried to bring the poor woman with her, but she let go of Ashleigh's arm just as the ship barreled down on them. With the sudden release of the woman's weight, Ashleigh's back slammed against the ship's inner wall, knocking breath from her lungs. She slid down the wall, trapped in place as the horrific scene unfolded before her. Thousands of pounds of boat and people crushed the woman and dragged her body along to the bow where it settled with a deadened thud in a heap of wreckage.

Ashleigh held her stomach as she stood, grappling for the next breath. She'd seen some frightening things in her career thus far, but nothing prepared her for the mass destruction of this tragedy. Tens? Hundreds? Dead already. She locked her knees to keep them from shaking and pulled her gaze from the pile of debris slowly covering with sea water. She struggled to a stand, releasing her breath a quiet sob.

Oh dear God, where are you? Please help me.

"Ashleigh."

Sam came up beside her, but his voice melded in with a new chorus of screams from above. Wood screeched and pounded louder, closer. A crescendo of screams chorused in terrifying reality as another passenger-laden lifeboat careened out of control. Sam's eyse grew wide. Ashleigh turned her face into Sam's shoulder. *Not again.*

"Oh dear God." Sam's words quivered through his body to her. She knew what he witnessed, and the sudden silence of screams alerted her to the same fate as the first boat. He pressed a life vest into her hands. "Put this on."

She blinked up to him and took the cumbersome item, untwisting the ropes of the white flotation device. He helped it over her head, zipped the straps of the vest into a tight bow, and tried to lighten the moment with a grin. "Aren't you glad I taught you how to swim now?"

She rolled her eyes at his banter. "I certainly hope I don't have to practice it."

Sam's gaze sobered. "Me too, Ash."

He grabbed her hand and pulled her up the steep incline through the mass of people, sandwiched between an open sea and the unyielding wall of the *Lusitania.* She could barely keep her balance. The deck tilted to her left as she climbed higher up the ship, toward the dangling lifeboat nearby. Ashleigh glanced behind her down the long sweep of the deck. The front of the ship dipped into the ocean now and wept waves over the wreckage of humans and white wood, pulling more of the ship downward. Fear as palpable as the cool spring breeze pinched at her breath.

Children with wide-eyed stares, mothers screaming, and men trying to keep busy, busy and unthinking, because the next few moments dangled as precariously as the lifeboats over the open sea. They were sinking fast. No more than ten minutes had passed, if that, and already the water seeped over the edges of the ship. How many would never make it to the lifeboats? Or even out of the bowels of this great dying ship? *Oh God, please keep us safe. Keep Sam safe.*

"Take this one, Ash." Sam pushed her forward into the crowd, his gaze fixed ahead on the white boat. An officer, voice commanding calm and order, allowed women and children through.

She turned at Sam's command. "Where is *your* life vest?"

Her hand went to the knot of her own vest and she began to untie it, but Sam covered her hand. "No, Ash." He squeezed her hand. "I'll find one, but first we have to get you out of here."

Tears, hot and unwelcome, surfaced at the edge of her vision. If she lost him? "You must promise me, Sam."

He pushed a tendril of her hair back and his fingers dropped to touch the tip of her chin. "I promise I'll try. Now, hurry ahead. They're loading."

She held his gaze, a sudden need to memorize his face, savor his voice. "Sam, I...You..." Her voice floundered, heavy with emotion and uncertainty.

He placed a finger to her lips and crooked a grin. "Not necessary, Ash." He stepped closer, one hand gentled against her shoulders. "We've gotten beyond words in this friendship, don't you think?"

She nodded, unable to voice anything even if she wanted. She blinked back another onslaught of tears and forced a smile. Women and children first, like three years ago on the *Titanic* when hundreds had died. Hundreds, thousands.

Sam knew he'd never see the inside of a lifeboat.

"You need to go, Ashleigh. Now."

A convulsion of clarity riveted her to the spot. Her heart ripped at the seams. She loved him. Without a hue of doubt, she knew she'd never love anyone else, and even if her past kept her from sharing her future with him, she had this moment. This second and maybe never again. She touched a palm to his cheek and leaned in, trailing his smile with her thumb. "Sam, I—"

"One more seat."

The voice, the warning, killed the moment. She pressed her eyes closed.

"Go." Sam's voice came out in a rasp as he took her arm. "Here," he called. "Here is one."

She lost Sam's touch within the crowd of hands moving her forward. They guided her up the steps and into the lifeboat, blocking her view of him. Women and children pressed together on the benched seats, welcoming her forward. She looked back onboard to catch another glimpse of him, but only strangers' faces stared back – men. All men. Staying behind to die.

Sobs and whispers passed through them and the boat began its slow and uneven decent. Two officers aboard took the boat's paddles and pressed them against the side of the *Lusitania*, pushing the boat free from scraping the ship as it scaled down the side toward the water.

"Sit still, Stephen."

Stephen? Ashleigh came face to face with Michael's wife, her navy hat still in perfect place on her golden head. She wrestled with her fidgeting son, who struggled for freedom from his mother's hold…and he didn't have a life vest.

The boat teetered back from another push against the side of the ship and a few women screamed in response. Some people from a lower boat deck even tried to climb aboard, angling the boat in a precarious dip toward the sea. The boy's mother screamed and loosed her hold on him to grab for the bench seat and Stephen fell forward into Ashleigh's arms. She scoured Mrs. Craven with a look, and then wrapped an arm around the boy as she began unlacing her life vest.

"It's all right, luv. Just a bit bumpy, isn't it?" She tapped his nose to keep his attention on her instead of the women screaming at the back of the rocking boat. "Would you help me unlace this bit here?"

She put a loose string in his hand to keep him busy as she continued to remove her vest.

Ashleigh pulled the life vest around the lad. It was too large, but with some quick, inventive tying, she strapped him into it.

"What are you doin'?" Michael's wife asked, wide-eyed, hands gripping the seat.

Ashleigh barely grazed the woman with a glance. "He needs a life vest."

"I planned on holding him. I keep a tight hold on the men in my life."

Ashleigh fixed her with a stare, much too aware of the implication in the woman's words. Of all the things to do as they teeter in a lifeboat of a sinking ship? Insult her? A wicked smile itched to reply. Maybe Michael did deserve her. She was going to cause a whole lot more trouble for him than a fiancée with a tainted history.

She bit back a retort and tightened the straps around Stephen with a sharp zip. The boat inched lower, until the ship's onlookers were barely visible above the railing. *Where was Sam?* She searched the faces, desperate to locate him before she lost sight behind the massive wall of the ship.

Her gaze landed on Michael's face. Tears marked trails down his cheeks as he watched. Her fingers fisted the life vest straps around Stephen until her fingernails dug into her palm. He leaned forward, the look in those sea mist green eyes penetrating through her hurt like a cry for help.

Thank you. He mouthed the words and she released the breath she'd been holding. *Michael.* She'd wanted him to hurt. Wanted him to feel pain like she'd felt, know the sting of loss…

But not like this. Never this.

What if we always received the first wish of our hearts? She shuddered at the cruelty of her own reaction and blinked at the burning in her eyes. With the next shift of the boat, it dipped below the railing's view and out of sight of the onlookers. *Please, Lord, keep Sam alive.* The boat scraped against the side of the ship and Michael's wife pulled at the boy's arm.

"Give him to me."

Ashleigh released the boy and at the same time, a loud crunch shook the lowering boat. The little boy tumbled from his mother's arms back against Ashleigh's chest and then…they were airborne – falling toward the sea. A chorus of screams rose around her as people rained to the ocean. She wrapped her arms around the boy and closed her eyes, as the cool waters of the Atlantic swallowed her down into darkness.

Sam nearly crawled over the edge of the ship when Ashleigh took off her life vest and wrapped it around Michael's son. Ridiculous woman! She couldn't swim well enough to give her life vest to someone else, but even in the middle of his frustration with her, a rush of pride settled around his heart. There she went again – risking her life for someone else. He smiled. Like she'd done for him.

He gripped the railing and whispered a prayer for her safety, watching until her dark head disappeared with the curve of the ship. His face still hummed from the warmth of her touch. His mind still reeled from the look in her eyes which almost urged a kiss. He warmed to the thought. He could give his heart to someone like her. *Blazes, he could give his heart to her!*

The ship creaked beneath him as he clung to the railing for one last look. The forty degree angle of the deck made it harder to stand, but he'd hold on until time ran out. She glanced up to the railing, searching for him, and he tried to move into her line of vision – reassure her and see those beautiful dark eyes on him again, but the lifeboat lowered out of view.

Heat pressed behind his eyes. At least *she* would survive to touch other people's lives like she'd touched his. Her friendship had been one of the best things that had ever happened to him. How it had evolved from a tag-along to this vital existence, he couldn't remember, but he was pretty sure it started the day Catherine sailed away.

A loud crunch of metal pulled his attention to the railing, followed by screams from below – from where Ashleigh's lifeboat had disappeared. An officer at the lifeboat chain stared over the edge, motionless, eyes wide and face pale.

Heat fled Sam's body. He pushed through the crowd to hear the commotion.

"What happened?" an officer demanded over the crowd.

The young sailor blinked up to the officer. "I...I lost control, sir."

Lost control? Of what?

The young man blinked. "The chain, sir, it broke..."

The life boat?

Sam pressed against the railing, leaning as far as he could to see, but his attempts proved futile. Where was Ashleigh?

Another officer pushed forward, his face pinched in concern. "She can't suspend from mid-air for long without–" Another crunch sounded, followed by more screams. The other chain broke, releasing the full weight of the boat to the ocean below.

A lifeless thud silenced the screams.

No!

Ashleigh!

The officer took off his hat and ran a hand through dark hair. His gaze steeled forward. "To the next boat. There's nothing more we can do for boat 12."

Whatever just happened to Ashleigh's lifeboat was not good, and from the deadening silence of screams? He had to find her. From all he could piece together, Ashleigh's boat came unhinged from one side and dumped all its passengers into the sea. And the thud when the remaining davit broke? Sam's stomach dropped. It had to be from the lifeboat falling on top of the passengers it had spilled into the sea.

He half ran, half slid down the port side deck of the ship toward the bow. The strict tilt of the vessel pushed him starboard and his back slammed against the ship's white wall of metal, stealing his air. He leaned forward to catch his breath and took in the heart-wrenching portside scene. An avalanche of people, deck furniture, and shattered lifeboats slid like lifeless pucks on a shuffleboard toward the sea. Smoke-filled air blew around him, carrying screams and a boy's cap. People climbed over each other to gain the highest spot on the boat, away from the waiting water. And Ashleigh was somewhere among wreckage and the savage ocean.

Against the tug of the slanted deck, he crawled to the railing and hung on, sliding toward the bow until sea water lapped over his shoes. Keeping his balance with a hand on the railing, he tossed off his shoes and jacket, took a deep breath, and dove into the cold Atlantic.

Sam broke the surface to as much chaos in the water as aboard ship. Wreckage and bodies littered the sea, blocking his search. Most of the dead wore life preservers, and the tragedy was no respecter of age. A baby basket drifted by, overturned and a woman floated facedown, golden curls waving behind her with a trail of deck chairs and overturned furniture.

Was Ashleigh among these unfortunate souls, where not even their life preservers saved them? Wait, Ashleigh gave her life vest to Michael's son.

Oh no! Sam swam harder, looking from emotionless faces to the panic-stricken. Wails of infants and moans of women hemmed in on all sides. The great ship's stern loomed above him now, almost parallel to the ocean, and casting a giant shadow over part of the wreckage below. The liner tipped away from him, ready to collapse into the sea.

"Ashleigh!"

His voice barely made a ripple in the waves of agony around him, but he had to try. "Ashleigh!"

With a groan above all others and a dying heave, the great *Lusitania* rolled over into the ocean, its massive funnel's sinking last. Water poured into them, creating a whirlpool of bodies and debris and tugging Sam into it. He fought against the vortex, against the suction of the merciless sea.

It held like death.

He couldn't keep fighting. His muscles protested, his lungs screamed for relief. He filled them with air as the current sucked him beneath the waves. Down passed swirling debris and darkness, pulling him into one of the massive funnels and a watery grave. Ashleigh's face entered his mind. *Dear God, save her.* Then all went black.

Chapter Eight

Ashleigh swayed down the ramp as she exited the fishing boat. After four hours on an overturned lifeboat, clinging to little Stephen and the next breath, and then another few hours on the fishing rig with other ragged survivors, her body rebelled. Her legs trembled, weak from long-term exposure to the freezing Atlantic, and her mind wafted between grief and numbness.

After the boat spilled them into the icy sea, Ashleigh swam away from the dangling lifeboat before it spiraled like a bullet toward the water. She squeezed her eyes closed, the deafening thud and sharp silence of screams still clear in her ears. It was a miracle they'd survived.

A miracle? Sam's words came to mind. *Sometimes God sends a miracle...*

A voice softly nudged her spirit. *I am with you.*

Are You? Then why didn't You stop the torpedo? Or Michael's deception? Or Father? Or Sam's...?

She tightened a tattered wool blanket around her and Stephen, but it couldn't ward off the internal chill. Stephen's head nestled in the crook of her neck, his blond curls matted from dirt and water. He whimpered and she squeezed him closer.

Lord, don't let him remember this day.

Her thoughts rammed to a stop. She'd prayed? She groaned against it. The prayer came without effort. Naturally. If only it really mattered.

Queenstown's dock welcomed the motley crew of survivors into the lantern lit dusk, a beacon of safety for the living and resting place for the dead. People crowded the pier, half looking for loved ones, half offering assistance, but not one familiar face greeted her.

Her body protested the walk down the gangway but she shuffled to the dock and caught her breath. A gruesome procession lined the far end. Tens, if not hundreds, of bodies lay in rows on the ground, waiting for identification. Ashleigh moved mindlessly with the crowd toward the corpses. Wails of loss, sobs, and incoherent mumbles spun a tale of tragedy all around her. She released a slow breath, bracing herself for whatever might come next in this story. Her mind wouldn't consider Sam among those bodies. She tucked Stephen closer. Or Michael?

No, not even Michael, as misguided and harsh as he had been.

An endless sea of lifeless faces were strewn on the dock, with more being added as each recovery boat arrived. Tears she'd kept controlled during the arduous ride aboard the fishing rig rushed to the surface as she passed the small bodies of a baby and little girl.

The price of war?

She paused before Stephen's mother's body, but held Stephen's face close to her chest so he couldn't see. Perhaps he wouldn't recognize this shadow of her in the faint evening light. How had she died? When the lifeboat fell? Or like others who'd fought to stay alive while they waited in the water, exposed to the baking sun and chilly sea?

The trail continued – and she followed, catching a breath as she paused before each male victim, but there was no sign of Sam or Michael. Her knees almost buckled when she saw a small body with a familiar scarf tied about her neck. *No.*

Just when she thought she'd cried all her tears, warm and silent fresh ones trailed across her cool cheeks. *Alice.*

Ashleigh looked away and turned her attention to

town.

Though a few of the bodies were unrecognizable, none of them fit Sam's or Michael's build or clothing. Should she feel relief yet? Would she find them alive, maimed, out of their minds? Or would they disappear with numerous other nameless faces into the grave of the sea?

She followed the lantern lights beyond the dock into town. Half the people were partially dressed, some wrapped in blankets, others weeping. Worst still were those with vacant expressions – where pain pushed them beyond their minds' capacities.

Quaint buildings framed the cobblestone street as it rose up a hillside. At the peak of the hill, pale spires crowned the roof of an enormous cathedral. Its white tip shone in stark contrast to the black night.

I am here.

The voice came again, but Ashleigh ignored the whisper. She forced her mind into action. She needed food and a room for her and Stephen. A small pouch between her breasts contained enough to purchase both, but where?

Stephen whimpered again.

"Hungwi."

Hungry? Of course he was hungry. The biscuits aboard the fishing skiff had long since been forgotten.

"No worries, luv. I'll see to you." Her raw voice scratched out the words and she forced another step. Her wet skirt slowed her pace and the cobblestones pinched into her stocking feet. At least they were off the water.

Warm lights from a shop window welcomed her forward. There were others from the wreck already inside, their wool blankets and disheveled appearances giving them away. She reached up to run a quivering hand through her tangled hair and caught her wearied reflection in the window glass. Half of her hair matted against her head, thick and flat. Dried blood?

The shop lights drew Stephen from his frightened posture and he lifted a curious gaze green gaze to the room. His father's eyes.

"Oh, darlin', you've come just in time." A woman, hair aflame with orange and red, drew Ashleigh into her arms. "I've but one room left and it goes to you and the sweet lad here."

"How kind of you." Ashleigh's smile pierced into her sun-scorched face. "Would you have a bit of food as well? I can pay."

"Pay?" The woman's grey eyes softened. "I think you've paid enough today. Sweet saints above, this tragedy's struck at the heart of our town. Many of the townsfolk heard the explosion from the beach, and watched the ship go down. It's a miracle any of you are standin' here."

Ashleigh fought for composure, and the woman shook her head. *Another miracle?* "Thank you for your kindness."

"Ah, but the good Lord would ask nothing else, would he? Who knows if the lot of you is angels in disguise?" The woman teased a grin from Stephen with a tickle to his chin. "My name's Elsa Roop, and this is my father's bakery, but we have three bedrooms for hire upstairs." She guided Ashleigh to a table. "Sit here with Mrs. Dunby and have some biscuits while I fetch more tea."

Ashleigh stopped the woman with a touch. "Do you know if there are more boats to come in tonight?"

"I can't say, miss. There've been all sorts comin' to the wharf for hours." Her expression took on a knowing look. "Looking for someone?"

"Two young American men."

The woman's brow creased. "I shall put a word out and

see what I can find."

"Thank you." Ashleigh eased into the chair and broke a biscuit in half for Stephen. His navy suit twisted with wrinkles. The simple act of kindness encouraged more tears. She couldn't seem to stop them and she hated crying.

The tragedy. The loss. Neither words nor thoughts could wrap around it.

She'd wanted Michael to suffer, but not like this. And Sam? She'd rather him know the truth and reject her than lose him at the bottom of the sea. *Dear God, please save him. Save them both.*

It was almost eleven o'clock when Ashleigh finally placed Stephen in bed, clean pajamas snug on his little body. Mrs. Roop worked another miracle in sending for fresh clothes. Her own new shirtwaist and skirt sagged a little from being too large, but they were dry. She tucked the blankets around Stephen; his deep and even breaths whispered of a restful sleep and peaceful memories. The sweetness of his golden curls framing his cherub face caught her breath. *Dear, motherless boy.* Her sigh quivered. Was he an orphan now? Her fingers glided over his soft cheek. What were they going to do?

She stood and slipped from the room, leaving the door ajar to hear him from below.

Ashleigh followed Elsa's humming to the kitchen.

"You're not asleep?" Elsa stared at Ashleigh, then understanding filled her eyes. "Ah, your heart is restless for your sweetheart, is it? Go on." She waved a spoon toward the door. "I'll see to the lad while you're gone." She stepped over and touched Ashleigh's arm. "Me brother just got back from the wharf and it's none too easy to look upon, he says."

Ashleigh straightened her shoulders, readied for the battle. "No." Visions of their arrival a few hours earlier flashed through her mind in heart wrenching detail. "But I must try to find him." She cleared her throat. "Them."

Elsa nodded. "Of course you must. Take the lantern by the door and my coat to keep you from the evenin' chill." Elsa gestured forward. "And no worries about the wee babe. You've enough on your mind."

Ashleigh nodded, unwilling to tempt her voice again, and stepped from the house.

The scene on the street mirrored the one from hours before. Men and women roamed about, many with vacant expressions and soiled clothes, so caught up in the visions of the past day they had difficulty seeing the present. She knew. Screams and silence still echoed in her ears and she wasn't certain which one was worse.

She followed the trail of lanterns to the crowded wharves, where men continued to unload their boats. The eerie pale glow of the gas torches added haunting solemnity to their task. Her throat tightened. Most of the people being brought from the boats came in horizontal form, not walking…or breathing.

She approached a man in uniform. "Hello, sir. I'm looking for…" The word caught in her throat. "The morgue, if you please."

He gave her a keen examination and his gaze softened. "Which one, Miss?"

Which one? She steadied her breathing, eyes burning. "How many are there?"

"Four, as far as I know."

Ashleigh looked away to gain her composure, her fist pressed against her chest. "I see."

"And two hospitals." His voice perked up a little, more hopeful than her heart. "One private. Have you checked those yet?"

She pushed her fear down deep. No, she would not

imagine the worst first. Her gaze, and a touch of hope, steadied on him. "Might you point me in the direction of the nearest one?"

She took his instructions and made her way through the night to the first place. Moans greeted her in the doorway, followed by the sickeningly sweet scent of morphine combined with whisky. People lined the walls, half on cots, half spread across the floor in a patchwork array of wounded, dead, or dying. She assessed the patients nearby, mentally cataloging those who might see the light of another day, and those whose wounds suggested a nearer end to their sufferings. Of course, appearances were never an assurance.

A woman, arm limp at her side, moaned to the nun who attended the scratches on her face. A man lay still and pale, scarlet seeping through the bandage about his head. On and on the rows grew, no respecter of class, race, or age.

Ashleigh walked among them, nursing instincts rising to cover her pain. The cool numbness of logic stole away the chaos of feeling. Each room opened into another, filled with rows upon rows of strangers.

The second hospital yielded the same results. No one had seen a light-haired man fitting Sam or Michael's description. Gone? A sharp sting sliced through her deadened senses. *Not Sam, Lord? Please, not Sam. I'll give You every part of my life, but spare him. Please.*

She grabbed the doorframe for support, as the ache in her heart swelled through her chest, stealing her breath. He couldn't be gone. Tears came, blurring her vision. How would she make it through the morgues? All four of them? Searching for the one face she ached to see alive.

"Ashleigh?"

She wiped a palm across her face and turned away

from the room. Now she was hearing things.

"Ashleigh."

She stopped at the sound of her name. Was God calling her again? She looked around. A nun walked by, sending her a cursory glance, but nothing else. Was she still hearing Sam's voice, even beyond the grave?

"Ashleigh," the voice repeated, raspy, weak, but wonderfully familiar.

Ashleigh pushed away from the doorway and searched the faces nearby, frantic to find the owner of the voice.

Across the small crowded room, a cerulean blue gaze came into focus, blurring out every other sound or sight around it. Was it Sam? The face, head...the entire upper body was covered in some sort of gray ash. His hair lay matted against his head in a heap of black soot. The black lips spread into a white smile and those piercing blue eyes cut out all uncertainty. *Sam.* She stumbled forward with a sob. *Alive.*

She fairly ran across the room and collapsed to her knees at his bedside. "Sam. You're alive." She took his lifeless hand into hers and kissed it, tears dropping from her cheeks to wash against his gray skin. "I thought..."

The possibility muted her words. She couldn't speak it. She pressed her lips back against his hand, afraid to let go. *Thank the Lord.* The prayer slipped out unbidden, but what else was she to do when her heart beat so full with gratitude? Her tears left trails on his hand. She swept her fingers over them to reveal some sort of gray powder.

"Coal dust," Sam rasped. "Funnel."

It took a few seconds for his words to register. Her lips came unhinged. "You were pulled down into a funnel?"

He nodded and offered a weak smile. "Spit out."

She touched his face, her thumb wiping back one of his tears to show skin underneath. "Oh, thank heavens."

He raised a brow. "Miracle?"

She couldn't help but smile. "It would seem so, wouldn't it? Are you going to force me to admit you were right about something?"

"Always right." His gaze caressed her face. "You okay?"

Ashleigh brushed back a strand of his soot-covered hair. "After the boat collapsed, I was pulled atop an overturned lifeboat." She laughed and squeezed his hand again. "You're alive." She took a handkerchief from her pocket and began to wipe at his face, her pulse slowing. "The ship sank so fast. The loss..."

His weak smile softened. "You're safe." He whispered the words as if that was enough for him. "Michael?"

"I don't know." She lowered her eyes to the tattered blanket draped over his lap, her thoughts darkening. "I haven't checked everywhere yet, however."

He sighed his regret.

"I have his son, Stephen."

His eyes widened. "How?"

"I caught him in my arms as we fell. His mother didn't—"

Sam gave the slightest squeeze to her hand and the bond between them forged deeper. "Can you walk?"

He gave his head a slight shake and pushed himself up to a taller sitting position. "Not without help. Weak."

Side effects of hypothermia. Hopefully it would be temporary weakness and no permanent nerve damage. She stiffened her shoulders to keep a cringe away. Four hours or more in those cold waters didn't promise full recovery. Muscles pulled taut against his soiled shirt. Sam was young and healthy. Her throat went dry. Two facts she wasn't likely to forget.

"If I support you, do you think you could walk?"

He lifted a brow and a corner of his mouth in challenge.

"If I didn't know you better, my dear Sam, I would suspect you of doubting my abilities."

His smile spread to a full white grin, a striking contrast to his gray-hued face.

"Let me check with your nurse and see if I can take you with me."

His hand tightened around hers, stopping her from leaving. She turned back to him, twin trails of tears making paths down his coal-covered cheeks.

"You're safe."

His words whispered with the same relief pumping in her heart, but safe? Until her emotions cooled to indifference, she was anything but safe in Sam's presence.

Chapter Nine

Sam thought we would never have full feeling in his arms and legs again…until Ashleigh informed him they were sharing a room. Pinpricks of heat spiked up his legs jolting his heart to life. Not that there was any fear of impropriety. His arms drooped as limp as a string and his fingers barely moved at all.

But his thoughts worked perfectly fine. Too well, in fact, probably making up for his general numbness from the chin down at present.

Lamplight from the street lanterns haloed Ashleigh's pale face as they made their way along the cobblestone path. Lying weak and useless in the hospital for hours gave him time to pray and worry, fearing the worst. He relived their trip over in his mind, a whole ream of new feelings waking. Ashleigh? When he recognized her as she walked from patient to patient in the hospital, energy surged through his weakened body like heat to a furnace. She was alive. Though her dark hair hung in tangled webs about her shoulders, and her face and lips were discolored from exposure, there was no other sight more beautiful than Ashleigh Dougall in her shapeless, oversized gown and dark hair falling loose around her shoulders.

"Oh, praise be, you found your man." A middle-aged woman, red hair barely contained in a bun, bustled forward.

Sam shot Ashleigh a look for clarification, but she only nodded.

"Ms. Roop, this is Sam." Ashleigh's gaze didn't meet his. "Sam, this is our gracious hostess, Ms. Elsa Roop."

Elsa laughed. "Well, now that sounds a bit more high and mighty than what I am." She examined Sam closely, grey eyes atwinkle. "But what's this, laddie? You look like you jumped into a barrel of pitch."

"Coal dust." Sam forced his voice above a whisper.

Elsa's eyebrows shot northward. "Well, no doubt there's a story to be told in that, but from the looks of you both, it needs to wait for a good night's rest." Elsa reached to the counter and handed Ashleigh a small loaf of bread. "Take this for your man and I'll bring up some tea."

"And Elsa, could I trouble you for some warm water? I'll need to help clean Sam up a bit."

Sam's body stiffened.

Elsa's brows shot high again and her gaze swept him from shoeless feet to his forehead. "You'll have your job cut out for you, and that's a fact." She snapped a towel on her thigh. "I'll bring up some good hot water for you."

"Thank you." Ashleigh shot a sassy grin to him. "He's certainly a mess, isn't he?"

Her gaze softened with uncovered admiration. He never remembered feeling love like this from Catherine. Was it time's hand or something much more basic which drove his doubt about Catherine deeper?

"So, Sam, do you think you can make it up a flight of stairs?"

He stared ahead at the narrow, wooden stairs and willed strength into his legs. He wasn't too sure he could make it, but he wouldn't admit it to Ashleigh, not after all she'd endured. He nodded.

With slow and labored movements, they mounted the steps. "We need to get you cleaned up and in bed. The more rest, the better. I went out and bought an extra pair of thick socks, in the hopes I'd find you."

"Socks?"

The concern etched in her brow softened into a small smile as they paused on the stair landing. "To save those big feet of yours from the ill effects of the Atlantic."

Tenderness swelled up in him, warm and alive. His sweet friend. Now bound to him by another tragedy. "More flattery." His raw voice barely worked, throat contracting with a combination of exposure and emotion.

Ashleigh helped him up the next short flight and then offered him a triumphant grin. "Whatever it takes to make it up the stairs, my dear Sam." She drew in a deep breath, as if to prepare herself, and stopped in front of a door. "Here we are."

The small room offered little as far as decoration or space. Only a large bed, wooden posts carved with homespun charm, a wash stand of similar style, and a spindled chair with a pillowed seat. Ashleigh led him to the chair. He collapsed, exhausted, his body screaming for rest.

Ashleigh rubbed the back of her neck and smiled, her eyes tired. "Stay with me for a few minutes yet, Sam." She lifted one of Sam's hands and began to rub his fingers. "I need to tend to you before you nod off to sleep."

Sam pulled his eyes away from her hands and met her gaze. "You need sleep?"

Her brows bent. "I thought about going out to see if I can find Michael."

Sam shook his head and tried to sit up straighter to reinforce his objection. "No. You rest too."

"Calm down, Mr. Miller." Her voice soothed with the same effectiveness as her warm hands on his skin. She massaged his hands to life and moved to his wrists.

"Maybe a few hours of sleep would help." She touched her forehead a moment and then moved her hands up his arm, friction building under his cool skin. "Morning will bring more clarity, I'm sure."

More clarity of loss and devastation. He'd only caught a glimpse of the row of bodies lined up along the dock to know the sunlight wouldn't make the massive loss prettier or less heart wrenching. The same ache he'd felt since being pulled from the sea crashed against the confusing warmth in her touch. His last words to Michael, harsh and angry, still hung in the air, in memory. *His* memory. Was it worth it? No. Regret aged him, weakened him, but Ashleigh's hands on his shoulders jerked his foggy brain to full alert.

"What are you doing?"

"Waking up your skin." It was working. Her hands wrapped around his upper arm. He flexed against her touch, or because of her touch, and residual warmth poured through him. "Hypothermia can cause temporary or permanent damage to the nerves under your skin. We must assist the circulation to work properly again."

She moved to his other hand and began the same ritual, her gaze fixed on her task. He wanted to study her, sort out these new emotions pumping from her touch to his heart, but his eyelids drifted to a close. Her methodical movements drew him deeper into sleep. The pinpricks of discomfort in his fingers subsided. She wrapped something warm around his hands and placed them in his lap. He sighed into a comfortable sleep...until something touched his feet.

"What?" Only his weakness kept him from jumping clear out of the chair.

The glint in Ashleigh's eyes turned impish. "Ticklish is a good sign." Her brow raised in mock warning. "No nonsense now; you're my patient."

"Not my fault. You."

"I'll have no excuses, Mr. Miller. We must save these big feet of yours." She pinched his big toe. "Even unsightly things such as these."

He tried to squirm away, his jaw tightened to hold in a

115

laugh or scream. "Leave feet alone."

She grabbed at his foot, her bottom lip clamped between her teeth in a grin. She was enjoying his torture a little too much. So was he. It brought a welcome distraction from the dark thoughts at the edge of his consciousness.

"Your arms and legs, especially fingers and toes, are most susceptible to nerve damage because they are the farthest from your heart and least likely to have appropriate blood." Her hands covered his foot and began rubbing hard. Warmth spiked up his leg.

"Stop. Please." He cringed, laughed, and almost cried altogether.

Ashleigh released an exaggerated sigh. "One more foot, Sam. Be a big boy about it, will you?"

He would have frowned at her, if he'd been able.

A slight knock at the door gave him some relief. Elsa swept in with a steaming pot in hand and a few cloths draped over her shoulder. Her gaze fastened on Sam. "Well now, your eyes have a bit more life to them. Can't tell if your face has color underneath all the soot, but the eyes are a good sign."

"He's showing good signs all around," Ashleigh answered, folding her hands in front of her like the dutiful nurse. "Good feeling in both his hands..." She bit back her grin and looked at him. "And his feet."

"Torture," Sam muttered to Elsa, hoping for an ally.

Elsa sat the pot down on the floor and wagged her finger at him. "Consider who is the one sittin' in the cozy chair and who's the one washing dirty feet." She raised a brow as she pulled the door closed on her way out. "Torture indeed."

"Miss Elsa is one smart woman."

Sam nailed Ashleigh with a look and then sighed out the last of his fight. His body couldn't take much more, and

Elsa was right, he wasn't the only exhausted one in the room. How long had Ashleigh searched for him in the cold night? How many lifeless faces had she passed by before finding him? After she'd taken care of a little boy who wasn't hers and found lodging for them? All with the same visions and dark thoughts as himself.

Perhaps all this time his focus had been on the wrong Dougall daughter and it took Catherine's broken engagement to bring him to his senses. Why had he never seen Ashleigh, not really seen her, until now?

"I know you're tired." Ashleigh draped a blanket over his legs and a cloth over her shoulder. "But you need to have a good wash." She gestured toward the bed. "Imagine if Stephen wakes up in the night to find a man covered in coal dust beside him. He'll think every childhood nightmare has come to life."

Sam cast her a playful glare before looking to the bed. Light filtered over the boy's face. The physical similarities between Michael and Stephen swelled an ache through Sam's chest. Sam's hand gripped for the arm of the chair, but it was a weak hold, his fingers barely responsive. In the dim stillness, he still heard the moans and cries of those in the water around him. Over and over the sounds sloshed about with wreckage and corpses, until they faded into a throbbing sore.

His eyes closed against the pain, but he couldn't stop a raspy sob from shaking his body. Another followed, quivering through each weakened muscle. He didn't even have the strength to lift his arm to wipe away the tears. So much pain. So much regret.

Silent sobs shook him. Wave upon wave of memories, sights, sounds, the weight of massive loss -- the last whimpers of life drowning out around him as he floated among wreckage and bodies until everything became a murmur of confusion and the frozen pain in his limbs started to numb out his life.

A soft touch to his arms brought his gaze up. Ashleigh knelt by him, tears and sweet compassion in her eyes. "We will get through this." She squeezed his arm, holding his gaze, so strong and certain. "We *must* get through this."

He ached to wipe the single tear from her cheek, to cradle her face in his palm again, but his arm barely made it to her shoulder. "Yes." His words slowed with emotion. "But time to mourn."

"Yes," she whispered and cleared her throat. "There should always be a time to mourn, shouldn't there?"

She dipped the cloth into the pail and stood behind him. With a gentle back-tilt of his head, she poured warm water through his hair, and then massaged the soap into his scalp. Tingles shot down his neck as her fingernails skimmed his ears. He groaned at the touch and the pressure, his body relaxing back into the chair. Her fingers paused. He held his breath and kept his eyes closed, waiting. From a regular nurse, the action would have encouraged nothing but mindlessness, but from Ashleigh? The intimacy of the act comforted him to his core, yet awakened an ache...for her. She brushed his damp hair back from his forehead and continued moving the cloth over his face, occasional skin-to-skin touches elevating the temperature beneath the cloth much more than the tepid water.

Her gentle stroke moved over his cheeks, face so close that the firelight flickered aflame in the dark of her eyes. She stayed focused on her work, casting glances to him as she went through her task. His breath caught when the cloth moved down his neck.

Her hand stilled, acknowledging his reaction, but she didn't look at him. The rapid rise and fall of her chest clued him in to the fact she might not be as immune to his reaction as she portrayed. When one of her hands steadied against his shoulder, he mustered up the strength to take hold of her wrist and tug her closer. That's when he saw the tears, glimmering with the firelight in her caramel eyes.

"Ashleigh?"

"I'm sorry, Sam." She shook her head, spilling more tears.

Strength infused his muscles and he slid his arm around her shoulders, pulling her against him. Fear held her emotions in check and her body on-guard. Fear from those deep wounds she couldn't share. Her breath shivered against his neck with a touch of her soft lips.

His heart broke for her, for them. "It's okay to mourn, Ash," he whispered into her hair. "You're safe with me."

His words broke some invisible barrier in her. With a shudder, she buried her face into his shoulder, her sobs encouraging his own. Having this strong, independent woman grow vulnerable in his arms brought out his deepest protective impulse, and somehow, in the pale flicker of firelight, he knew he loved her. He rubbed his clumsy hand over her head, resting in the rightness of her fit with him. Her warm tears seeped through his shirt right over his heart. Nothing but the crackle of the fire and a few quiet sobs broke the silence. They comforted each other as only the closest friends could do – without words.

He smiled through his tears and rested his cheek against her head. He'd take his time. Earn her trust that his heart was no longer her sister's, but one thing was certain, he'd never known anything as dear and precious as this.

Ashleigh sat back and wiped her cheek with the back of her hand, smearing some of the coal dust from his shirt onto her forehead. Her smile formed, timid and beautiful. "You need your rest, Sam."

He cupped her cheek. "Tell me?" He swallowed to wet

his parched throat. His thoughts drifted back to the night of the Talent Show. Had that only been yesterday? "About your wounds?"

Her gaze flew to his, and for one moment he thought she might give in to his plea, but then as quickly, her protective, porcelain expression cloaked her emotions. She slipped back from him and his hand fell to hers, wrapping around her wrist.

"Ashleigh?"

"I'll send a wire to your father in the morning so he will know you are safe. I should send Mother a wire, as well. Catherine will worry for your safety."

"You can trust me."

She dropped her cloth into the basin and stared at the floor, her shoulders slackened forward. "Oh Sam, I do trust you," she whispered and dropped her cloth into the basin. "But, I..." She sighed.

"I'm sorry." His thumb slid across the soft skin of her wrist. "I shouldn't push you." They'd been through enough today, especially her. "We both need rest."

"Right."

He looked at the one bed in the room and attempted to sort out how on earth he could share a bed with her. "Maybe I'll sleep here?" He patted the arm of the chair.

She narrowed her eyes. "No. It may be...against propriety, but...well...I think God will understand, don't you?" She shrugged. "After all, if we sleep to either side of Stephen, then we wouldn't... it might not be as..."

"Good plan." He tried to stand and nearly lost his balance.

She slid her arm around him, their bodies tight against each other.

"I'm...I'm sorry." Sam muttered against his embarrassment. Some hero.

Ashleigh looked up at him, her lips tilted on one side. "More proof of your stubbornness. Quit talking and get to bed." She snapped her mouth closed. "Um…some rest. Get some rest."

Even in the dim light he could see the deepening shade in her cheeks. She nodded toward the bed. "The owners have clean clothes for you to wear." She scanned down his body. "Can you…um…manage on your own?"

A sudden rush of heat set his face on fire. "Yes." There was no way on this planet he'd make it through her undressing him. "If I sit?"

She sighed beneath his weight, as relieved as he – though somehow her relief didn't make him feel as good.

"The clothes are here." She led him to the bed and helped him to a sitting position. "I'll…leave the room so you can—"

"Yes." He fisted her wrist before she could move away.

She blinked and looked up at him, questions in her dark eyes.

"I love you, Ash." The words slipped out with ease.

Her chapped bottom lip unhinged.

"You know…" He grinned up into her lovely face, growing lovelier by the second. "You're my dearest friend."

She closed those lips into a sad smile and slipped from his hold. "Then I advise you to get changed so this dearest friend of yours can enjoy some rest as well." The door squeaked open and she stepped into the shadows of it. "And I love you too, Sam. Always will."

Chapter Ten

The obvious disrepair of the rock walls and utter neglect of the road didn't prepare Ashleigh for the poor condition of her Grandmama's family manor house, Roth Hall. One gray stone wall of the west wing, which faced the hills and cold north wind, lay like a jigsaw puzzle against the other, opening the interior to the elements, the faded green walls of the former ballroom barely visible through a motor car-sized hole. A massive branch from one of the ancient oak trees protruded into an upstairs window. Wasn't that Scott's old bedroom…and the wing in which she was going to secure the orphanage?

Another disappointment. Were any of her dreams ever to come true? Certainly none very easily.

Gray afternoon fog swirled before the motor car, adding gravity to the scene. Ominous and sad. Much like her memories of this home. So much had happened in the eight years since she last stepped foot across the columned threshold. So much had changed, but more things had been buried deep inside her – creeping into everyday life on occasion. Like now.

Her early memories, those of wealth and parties, where Grandmama's reputation painted a bright banner over their home, faded into the desolation of her father's poor financial choices. Not even her mother's American money had been enough to slake their thirst for the appearance of a wealthy life. No doubt where Catherine developed the need.

Debts rose and tensions rose higher, until their family was forced from their father's estate in Suffolk to make their home under Grandmama's roof in the quiet and rural town of Ednesbury. An act which stole her mother's joy and sense of self-importance.

And her father's soul.

When Grandmama moved the family to America and leased the Hall, Ashleigh hoped the move would change her parents, but her mother resented returning to the states as a pauper...and her father only sunk deeper into his debauchery.

The memories where her nightmares began took palpable presence. Footpaths he'd traveled, a tree he'd watch her climb, the steps from the side garden to the house – all visible reminders of him, like scars.

"Are you all right?"

She offered a smile, she hoped. "It's been a long time." She buried her face down into Stephen's curls, his head nestled on her shoulder. "Over eight years."

Sam's eyes lit with the wonder of a child as he peered out the window. "I can't believe this is your home. It's enormous. How did you cope with moving to the house in Millington?"

"Size has very little to do with a true home, don't you think?"

"It makes it a lot more impressive. When you spoke about your family home, I pictured red-bricked colonial at best or maybe a little rock cottage by a stream – not this." He gestured forward, wide-eyed. "Were the Dougalls an extremely wealthy family?"

"This isn't the Dougall's ancestral home. It's the Spencers'. Grandmama's."

His raised brow begged for further explanation. "After Grandmama's younger brother died in the Boer War, Great-grandfather broke with tradition and entailed his property to his only daughter, instead of a male cousin."

"And that is bad?"

Ashleigh grinned, another notch of pride growing for her grandmama's family. "Scandalous." She leaned her head back against the pillowed seat. "Estates are rarely entailed to women, but Great-grandfather saw the good of passing it on to Grandmama. She had married well and had always shone a sharp business mind. Leasing the house for those eight years probably saved it."

Sam's hesitation cautioned Ashleigh to Sam's following questions. "So what happened to your father's money? He came to live in America with your grandmother. Something must have happened."

Ashleigh sat up straight and turned to face him as the autocar slowed in front of the house entryway came into view. "I'm surprised you haven't heard this story through the local gossips of Millington."

"I'm not much of a gossipmonger." His lips twisted up into a grin and the air suddenly warmed around them. "But I'd heard something about his losing money."

"Father married an American heiress to increase his funds."

Sam laughed. "Your mother is an heiress?"

"*Was* an heiress," Ashleigh corrected.

"I'm sorry, I just didn't realize…"

"No need to apologize. Mother's fortune was depleted before we moved to North Carolina. Father did not inherit Grandmama's sensibilities for management nor self-discipline. Mother knew no other life than one of extravagance. Combine those habits with poor investments and the costs of running an estate, and the end results is..."

"Living off of your grandmother."

Ashleigh frowned and nodded, the wheels of the car crunching gravel as it came to a stop. "I'm determined to make it up to her if I can. She doesn't expect it, but I want to. She's sold parcels of land to gather enough money to run the estate at half-staff."

"I never knew your grandma was so wealthy. She lives simply."

Another reason to aim to be like her. "She's never been one to flaunt wealth. I suppose she lives on what she needs, which isn't a great lot. She sends a monthly allowance to Mother, of course, but only keeps three servants. Most of her money goes to the estate, but if she could see it now..." Ashleigh sighed at the scene out the window. What had her mother done with the money? "The tenants pay a small fee, but the biggest loss was selling the southern part of the estate to the Cavanaugh's."

Lord Cavanaugh was a sweet man, but his wife ruled with the arrogance of a queen and the generosity of a miser. "All the Cavanaughs needed was more control. They already owned Edensbury."

"Somebody owns a *town*?"

Ashleigh grinned at Sam's surprise and nodded toward the butler coming toward their stopped motor-car. "You are in for a great learning experience, Sam. By the end of your visit, we may even have you speaking in proper English."

The glint in his eyes belied the scowl on his lips. Those same lips she'd been tempted to touch as she washed his face and hair in Queenstown. Her fingers twitched at the tactile memory of his soft hair between them.

But all was different now. Roth Hall forced a wedge between them with her sister's name on it. No doubt Catherine's presence would draw him back into their romance. It always worked that way. Dreaming of Sam Miller's heart ended here.

Sam took her wrist and ran a thumb over her bracelet. "Did you lose another charm in the sinking?"

Only the locket remained on the chain, and the photograph within it faded from exposure to the water.

How to answer truthfully? "I suppose so. It isn't so glamorous anymore, is it? But Grandmama's lovely locket made it worth the entire bracelet."

"I'm sorry, Ash."

She patted his hand and then wrapped her arms around Stephen. "Nothing that can't be replaced, my dear Sam. Now, let's see what sort of stir our arrival might cause, shall we?"

The motor-car door opened and Sam stepped out first, examining the stone walls with another admirable gaze, then he turned to take Stephen. The little boy reached for him without hesitation. Two more days in Queenstown as Sam recovered and a day ride to Edensbury had already secured a bond between the two.

If her childhood butler was shocked by Sam's or Stephen's arrival, his placid expression never conveyed it. Jackson closed the motor-car door behind her and offered a slight bow, his slicked-back hair much more gray than she remembered.

"Miss Ashleigh, I wasn't aware of your arrival time or I would have sent a car and greeted you properly." He cleared his throat as if embarrassed. "I apologize, but I was unable to gather the staff —"

Ashleigh took the older man into her arms and his stance thawed a little. "It is good to see you, Jackson." His words registered then and she stepped back. "You knew I was arriving today, didn't you? I sent a telegram."

Jackson's expression gave nothing away. "We had been watching for you since Monday afternoon, Miss. I've had no other communication of a change in your schedule."

She caught the warning in Jackson's gaze and the old caution of years ago winkled its way to knot in her throat. The dance of secrets waltzed in full turn in this house.

Ashleigh motioned toward Sam. "Jackson, I'm certain

you remember Sam Miller from your days serving us in Millington?"

Sam offered a free hand. "Nice to see you again, Jackson."

"A pleasure, Mr. Miller, as always." Jackson turned to Sam. "Might I inquire after your father's health, sir?"

"He's well, Jackson, thank you. And you?"

"I'm glad to see you safely arrived." He glanced behind them at the car. "Your bags? Should I send a man to the station for them?"

Ashleigh's stomach dropped. Did the telegram even reach Roth Hall? "We have no baggage, Jackson." She took a deep breath and touched his arm. "We were aboard the *Lusitania*."

It was the largest display of emotions she'd seen on the butler's face since she'd fallen headfirst from her mare when she was ten years old. His hand went to his chest and he lurched forward to draw her back into his arms. "Miss Ashleigh, I had no idea."

She smiled into his shoulder and patted his back with another hug. Grandfather Dougall had hired him years ago, and he'd proven more constant than an English rain. "How could you?" Her mother had received her letter with her travel plans. Surely she'd passed it on to the staff? "Obviously the telegram didn't come through." A breath of doubt kept her caution alive.

"You both must be exhausted. Come inside."

Ashleigh heard the exact moment Sam entered the house from his hum of appreciation. Despite the outer wear and tear of time on the exterior, the Great Hall maintained an impressive air of generations of refinement. Georgian designs carved into the oak panels in the walls and stair rails framed a two-story room with arched ceiling molded to Grecian proportions. An open terrace from the second floor allowed curious onlookers to stare down on guests entering the house, or perhaps a daughter spying for her father's arrival.

Ashleigh shuddered. Father was dead. She need not fear him anymore. Jackson called to a housemaid, who quickly assisted them and won Stephen over with a biscuit and the promise of a bubble bath.

"Well, Sam, I believe you've completed your duty to Grandmama on seeing me safely to Edensbury."

He scratched his head, eyes squinted. "The last part didn't work out so well, I'm afraid. I hadn't planned on a torpedo."

The errant curls at his ears distracted her. She folded her hands in front of her to keep from touching him. Already the familiarity of running her fingers through his hair and over his face itched for repetition. Were those feelings a byproduct of her past as well? An unwholesome desire? She swallowed through her tightening throat and met his gaze. "You made certain I boarded the lifeboat, didn't you?"

"Yes, but—"

"Had it not been for your urging me to board the boat, there is a good chance Stephen would have suffered the same fate as his mother."

Sam winced.

"Then I think you've certainly completed your duty, my dear Sam."

He gave her a measured look then took a step closer. "It was more than duty, Ash. Much more."

His expression sent messages his words didn't, but she couldn't respond to them. Every piece of her heart cried out to reach for it, but how could she? She'd never marry him without him knowing the truth of her past – and the knowledge would alienate him, or at the very least create an emotional rift. No, he could do much better than her. Or Catherine.

"I treasure our friendship."

"And what if…" He paused and shifted his stance. "What if there's more to our friendship. I mean…" He rubbed the back of his neck and looked past her, studying some distant image.

"I don't—" Ashleigh squeezed the words through her breaking heart. "You and Catherine—"

"Ash." Instead of retreating, he closed the gap between them, his gaze roaming her face with a sweet longing. "I came here to clarify my relationship with Catherine. Not necessarily to continue it." He took her hand. "It's honorable to end things in person. If nothing else, our past and friendship deserve it."

"End things?" The words eked out on a whisper. Her muscles tensed with the sudden knowledge that Sam might be free. What would she do if he was actually free?

"Ashleigh?" A voice swelled from the other side of the great hall. "Is it you?"

Moriah Dougall emerged from the shadows of the hall; her pale blue house dress billowed around her and brought out the strands of silver reflected in her mother's soft brown hair. The red-rimmed eyes gave fair warning to her mother's current emotional state and the strong scent of wine hinted to her amount of consumption. Ashleigh drew in a deep breath for strength and whispered the shortest of prayers. Maybe God was still listening. After all, Sam was alive.

"Hello, Mother."

"It has taken you long enough, hasn't it?"

Her mother's harshness rained upon Ashleigh's exhaustion. She fisted her hand at her side to maintain composure and inwardly groaned at the flush of tears in her eyes. Would she never harden to her mother's selfishness?

"I sent word by telegram, but I don't believe it arrived."

"One can never trust the wire. Not with a war going on." Her mother waved her hand in the air and then sent a full-length look over Ashleigh from toe to forehead. "Have you lost all sense of propriety while living in the Appalachian wilderness? You look positively wretched."

Ashleigh lifted a hand to her hair and tried to smooth back a few unkempt strands. Her lack of care for her appearance had long been a thorn in her mother's side, but with Ashleigh's toiletries at the bottom of the sea, she hadn't considered them.

"Mrs. Dougall, it's good to see you again." Sam stepped forward and offered his hand. "You're looking well."

"Sam?" Her mother's hand went to her chest and a smile flushed her face. "Oh my, what a surprise! Sam Miller?"

"Yes, ma'am." He kept his hand out until her mother took it, but his other palm pressed into Ashleigh's back, adding comfort in the aftermath of her mother's careless words. She almost leaned into him to absorb his strength.

"Ashleigh sent no notice you'd be coming as well?" Her mother pierced her with accusation.

"Because Ashleigh didn't know until we boarded the ship." The slightest edge tinged Sam's words. "It was a surprise from Grandma Dougall. She didn't want Ashleigh traveling alone, and I was a willing victim. A houseful of lovely ladies? How could I go wrong?"

Her mother offered a brief smile at the compliment, but a frown quickly replaced it. "Jackson should be here to get your bags."

"He has already taken our items up to the rooms,

Mother." Ashleigh sighed and decided to change the conversation to safer ground. "How are you feeling?"

"How do you suppose I'm feeling?" Her mother rubbed her forehead and produced an impressive pout, before turning and walking toward the drawing room. "I've been worried sick about your safety with no news to your welfare. You were supposed to be here three days ago. Three days of worry."

"You can imagine it was difficult to get away after the sinking."

"The sinking?" Mother stopped right outside the drawing room door, her face a wreath of exasperation. "What are you talking about?"

"In my letter I told you of my travel plans aboard the *Lusitania.*"

Her mother's expression showed no recognition of the name at all. All the weariness of the past few days alighted on Ashleigh's shoulders like a heavy cloak. Home, sweet home?

Sam cupped her elbow. She smiled up at him, grateful he understood all the nuances and ridiculousness of her mother.

"I don't recall what your ship's name was, dear, only that you would sail on one." She shook her head. "Come, let's sit in a more comfortable place. My feet are sore."

Sam leaned near her as the followed. "I knew your mother was…um…"

"Self-absorbed? Demanding? An emotional pretzel?"

His grin hitched to one side. Her heart twisted up like a pretzel in response. "To name a few."

She rolled her eyes to add some levity to her mother's behavior. "I'm sorry to say it, Sam, but I don't even think a yellow LifeSaver will help."

"That's pretty serious."

Ashleigh's smile faded as they opened the door to the Drawing Room. She faced him before entering, taking this one second to warn him. "You are in a house of actors now. Guard your heart, Sam."

"Are you going to stand in the doorway until winter?" Mother's voice called from the Drawing Room. Ashleigh entered and moved to sit in a chair across from her mother, Sam nearby.

"I've called for tea," Mrs. Dougall announced as they entered the room. "Now, I'd like to know what is going on."

With as little detail of the events as possible, Ashleigh told her mother the tale of their journey, carefully leaving out Michael's conversation with her and the sleeping arrangements in Queenstown.

To her mother's credit, she actually paled as the story continued, and by the end had tears on her cheeks. "Oh, how horrid!" Her hand flew to her chest and her eyes bugged. "And Sam was pulled into a funnel?"

Ashleigh looked to Sam, a swell of gratitude at the fact he sat, alive, beside her. "Yes, Mother. And I'm extremely grateful he is still with us."

His stare lingered, soft and sweet, stirring to life the same emotions awakened aboard the *Lusitania*. "You have to love those miracles."

Chapter Eleven

The sound of a male voice drew Catherine Dougall's feet to a stop within the shadows of the drawing room door. Who was her unexpected visitor? She closed her eyes, trying to place the familiar tones. American. Southern.

Her breath caught. *Sam.*

She slid further into the shadows to gather herself. Sam? Here? Her thoughts shot into a flurry of possibilities. Oh, this would prove most unpleasant, especially since breaking their engagement through a letter. She bit her bottom lip. He deserved more than a letter. She knew it, but breaking his heart in person was a situation she had no desire to experience.

Another peek around the doorway brought doubts with it. Though disheveled, Sam's good looks had only matured over their year-long separation. His boyish smile sent a delightful thrill of warmth over her skin, pricking sweet memories of lingering kisses and sincere affection. Dogwood summers and spring dances with the scent of cherry blossoms. Gentle touches and tender words. She leaned back against the wall, pressing her palm to her chest. Oh how she'd missed his sincere attention--unglossed by society's rules and her family's broken reputation.

She frowned. If only he were rich, or titled at the very least. Poor people were trampled on or forgotten, their homes stripped from them, and their families' reputations tattered into gossip and cynicism. The sting of her family's return to Edensbury burned a deeper need to save her name, her family's name. When they'd left in shame and near poverty eight years before, the townspeople had not forgotten. They'd snubbed her mother, but Catherine's attempts to repair their wounded reputation were slowly working.

The past year she'd learned how to use her assets well – staging dances and refining her flirting to impress earls and dukes … and their sons. She'd spent opportunities hosting simple teas with those influential women in the community who would come, slowly building a small selection of supporters, Elaine Cavanaugh – Drew's mother, being one of them. Mother had made it perfectly clear that the only way to keep from losing their home and what little respect their name still held was to marry rich. Couldn't she be the daughter to redeem her family?

She lifted her finger to her lips, a plot stirring to light. Perhaps Samuel Miller was exactly the spark Drew Cavanaugh needed to set his tardy marriage proposal into motion. Their little intimacies and his continued liberties promised a wedding ring soon, and even his notoriously hostile grandmother seemed accommodating. All he needed was the proper incentive. Her grin tipped again.

Sam's laughter spilled from the next room. She quelled a sliver of guilt gnawing at the edge of her stomach and peeked around the corner. His gaze fastened on Ashleigh with such intensity, it paused Catherine's approach. Guilt darkened inside her chest. Attraction? For Ashleigh?

The golden charm bracelet at Ashleigh's wrist mocked Catherine, stabbing the anger deeper into a childhood wound. Father had given the expensive Italian bracelet to Ashleigh for no apparent reason than to flaunt his love for his favorite daughter. Some of the intricately designed intaglios seemed to be missing from the golden chain, but there was a new charm added – shaped like a locket. Ashleigh had never learned how to take care of expensive things. How could she have lost so many of the charms? It fueled Catherine's animosity.

The hurt crashed alive from its one-year sabbatical and nursed the ache of insecurity – a poignant reminder of how unloved and insufficient she'd been. Until now.

No, she'd not be reduced to second in his death as she'd been in his life. She would marry well, and first, if it was the last thing she did. Prove to them how they'd underestimated her.

"Sam, darling, what a pleasant surprise."

All heads turned, an aspect she always enjoyed experiencing, but her attention remained on Sam. His response encouraged her. Wide blue eyes, sharp intake of breath, palm to his chest. A perfect welcome. But the genuineness of his unadulterated sincerity surprised her into a stumble. He was quick to her assistance, scooping her into his arms before she slipped to the rug in an embarrassing heap. What on earth just happened? Stumbling?

"Catherine." Her name emerged on a rasp.

An awareness of something real and sweet trembled to life in her chest. What had she forfeited for the right connections? The taste of wealth? She shoved the thought aside and used her blunder to her advantage.

"Sweeping me off my feet, I see?" Her attention trailed slowly up to his eyes, halting only a split second on his lips for good measure. "To what do I owe this pleasant surprise?"

He tilted his head and examined her with as much focus as she had him. She squirmed beneath the intensity of perusal, hoping her downcast expression communicated shyness, instead of discomfort. What was wrong with her?

"Well, I should make Fanny aware of our addition to supper." Mother stood, her gaze disapproving of Catherine's obvious flirting. Well, her mother branded practically every conversation with the subtle mantra; the right connections marked the difference between power and poverty, so falling into Sam's arms probably didn't elevate expectations.

Catherine sighed. And a furniture maker's son didn't hold connections to restore the Dougall reputation, but he might be the perfect means to that end – especially if it meant besting her 'perfect' sister in the process.

Catherine turned to Ashleigh. "I see traveling doesn't agree with you, does it, dear?"

Ashleigh didn't even flinch. "As you know, I've never been one for flaunting fashion."

"No, certainly not." Catherine laughed. "With your shapeless nursing frocks and such, you were more akin to the Bloomer Girls than anything else."

Ashleigh raised a brow in answer and slowly stood, less troubled by Catherine's slight than Catherine wished. "I think that's my cue to freshen up and make myself more presentable."

Sam released his hold on Catherine and stepped to take Ashleigh's hand. "Ash-honey, there's no one who has faced the last week with as much beauty and strength as you."

A look passed between them, barely a second, but it spoke volumes. Catherine's pulse jumped to the defense. He cared for her in a very different way than when she'd left a year ago. Then it had been simple brotherly fondness, but now...? Why did she suddenly regret the loss of his sincere affections?

"I think your eyes are still clogged with sea water." Ashleigh's grin tipped before glancing back at Catherine. The lighthearted glow died an immediate death. "Excuse me."

Catherine would not lose the affections of another man

to her little sister. She turned her full charm on Sam. "Well, what have you to say about showing up without notice?"

He pulled his attention from the doorway and shoved his hands into his pockets, gaze examining her face again in his unnerving way. "I thought you wouldn't be happy to see me, since your last letter brought an end—"

She placed a finger to his lips. "Oh, you poor dear, did you take my indecisiveness to heart? Surely you know me better than that." She trailed her finger from his lips to palm his cheek. "All true engagements are broken at least once to ensure their sincerity, you know."

"Is that so?" He raised a brow and a hint of the sweet glow in his eyes dimmed. "I've been pretty sincere from the start."

"Yes, of course," she whispered, hoping the doleful look on her face translated her regret. "A year is a long time, and I've never been separated from you like this. How was I to know the response of my heart?"

His silence pricked at her conscience ... and her fear.

"You're right. It has been a long time." He lowered his voice. "We need to talk."

"Of course," she repeated, and wrapped her arm around his, drawing him close and allowing her fingers to make subtle circles across the inside of his arm. Her year in England had taught her one thing: she had the power to get what she wanted from men. Maybe she'd lost the opportunity with her father where Ashleigh was concerned, but not with Sam. She could win him back, if she wanted.

"Tell me of your journey. Was the dining as fine as I've heard?"

He hesitated. The look in his eyes paused her. What was it? Disappointment? Fatigue?

The contents of Ashleigh's telegram came to mind. The *Lusitania*. "*You* were on the ship that sank?"

He nodded, slowly, and Catherine launched herself into his arms, determined to help him forget her oversight. "Oh, Sam, I'm so glad you're safe."

His arms settled around her and nudged a gentle peace she'd never been able to duplicate in her other conquests. There was something safe in his embrace. True. Her heart opened to the feeling like greeting a long lost friend. Had she missed it? *Yes.* Could she keep it? She squeezed her eyes closed. No, it offered only temporary solace as she awaited Drew's decision. She smiled against his shoulder. But why waste beautiful admiration, though.

"Did you receive the telegram?" Sam's voice rumbled in his chest at her ear.

She stilled at the question. A coin given to the proper person here and there secured all mail was delivered to her instead of her mother, controlling what news passed to their weak-willed mother. But Sam? Grief and compassion edged into her heart, tools as unfamiliar to her as cooking pots and electric toasters. He brought them out in her. Always had. "I'm so sorry for the loss and pain you must have experienced."

A sigh pulled from his shoulders, confirming the depth of his sadness. He stepped back from her to rest his hands on her arms. "I wouldn't be here if it weren't for God's grace and your sister."

Catherine controlled a bristle. Bested by Ashleigh again? Definitely not. "And how is your father? I suppose the dear man must be worried sick for you? Have you given him the news of your safety?"

His expression turned as tender as any she'd remembered. A woman could lose her purpose in such a look. Her heart warmed in a new way, urging another turn of affection – slow and effortful, like the workings of a rusted clock. She was frightfully out of practice with sincerity.

"Ashleigh sent him a telegram to let him know we were safe. I wish I could have the same report for Michael." He lowered his head, his voice thick with emotion. Her heart broke, a little, enough to buoy concern. "We searched for him, for his body, among the shoreline and the morgues, but never found anything."

"Michael was aboard the *Lusitania*? But I thought..." Her words trailed off as her mind whirred with questions.

"It's a long story." He lowered onto the settee, as if he couldn't bear the weight any longer. "Meant for another day."

She joined him on the velvet settee and covered his hand with her own. "I am truly sorry for your loss." A surprising rush of tears threatened her voice, unbidden and strange. "And I hope your time here will help you heal."

"So do I."

She braided their fingers together and offered him her most disarming smile. "I'm particularly gifted in helping you forget your heartaches, as I recall. Especially in Grandmama's hallways and on long summer picnics."

Sam's brow wrinkled. He placed his other hand over their clasped ones and stared down at them. "Catherine, we've both changed." His blue gaze came up, clear and kind. Too kind. As if she'd lost the fire of his affection. Fear skittered up her spine lodging like desperation in her throat. *She needed him.*

"No, Sam." Oh heavens, did she really have to resort to more tears? "Please don't give up on me. Please say you still care about me."

"I'll always care about you, Catherine." A shadow fell over his features, curbing the sweet glow of love she realized she'd missed. He was so *good*, one of the few faithful men left who didn't have to be coddled into commitment. And it *almost* satisfied.

His eyes filled with apology and perhaps a touch of regret? She didn't like the look of finality on his face. "You were right. We're not the same people we were a year ago and…and I'm not the one for you."

"What?" She shot to her feet, palm pressed to her chest. "You came across the ocean and survived a sinking ship to tell me this?"

"Catherine."

He stood and reached for her hand but she jerked back, forcing more tears into view. "I can't believe this, Sam Miller. After all we've been through, you had to bring my horrible decision face-to-face?"

"Did you think I could let it end through a letter? We started this relationship face-to-face, I needed to resolve it the right way. In person. Our friendship deserved that much."

"And this is how you treat your friend, is it?" She sighed and massaged her fingers into her head. Disappointment at her failed plan etched a painful gnaw in her stomach, but something deeper made her feel sick.

"Come on, Catherine, you know as well as I, it ended months ago for you. It took longer for me, but clarity of time has helped." His earnest gaze searched hers, probing almost to the core of who she was. "We're meant to be good friends, but only friends. I'm sorry."

"You're sorry?" She stepped further away, unfamiliar shame flickering a flame beneath her cheeks. No one needed to see beneath her skin. She righted herself, smoothing her palm across her shirtwaist. No, she couldn't reflect her disappointment. It would make her weak, and successful women could not appear weak. She'd learned as much from Drew's grandmother. Power surged from Lady Cavanaugh, an addictive sort of wealth and power

Catherine craved. A marriage with Drew would elevate her entire family, 'save' them from the squandering humility they'd endured since Father's practical bankruptcy. Yes, she'd be the best sister then.

"I care too much about you to let a letter be our final conversation, my friend."

Pain twisted in her chest at his declaration. What had she forfeited in Sam's love? A tiny piece of her heart ached for the simplicity of what Sam once offered her, but it would never satisfy. Not when she had so much to prove and so much to lose. She meant it. He'd shown her nothing but love's faithfulness and generosity, and she'd treated him deplorably. The awareness pierced her with inward reflection which panged for a second along with a gaping emptiness. True tears slipped freely down her cheeks, shocking her with their presence.

No, she couldn't give in to weakness. She pushed the emotions aside and accepted her fate and choice. With a deep breath, she stepped close to him and placed her hand to his cheek. "I should have taken better care of your heart."

"I don't belong in your world, Catherine. I know now, I never really did."

The look of compassion in Sam's eyes chipped away at her anger. It had always been that way. He, the moral compass to her wayward heart. "You're right, I suppose." She swept the grand room a glance and looked back at him. "You've never been fond of society." A smile formed, slow and genuine. "And you would hate all the pomp and expectations, wouldn't you?"

"Friends, then?" He offered his hand, his sad smile renewing a tug-of-war with her heartstrings.

She hesitated, the weight of this finality adding sting. She placed her hand in his and quirked a brow, readied for the salvation of distraction. "And upon the quick forgiveness of friendship I must beg my pardon, for I am off to London in the morning."

"You are?"

"I've a house party which should last at the very least a fortnight." She fluttered her eyelashes ever so slightly, but the thought of running away from Sam's unsettling presence and the ache of his rejection couldn't have come at a better moment.

He tempered his unnerving intensity with a slight grin. "Be careful in that world of glitz and glamour, Catherine Dougall. Lots of things that sparkle leave burn marks behind. Not every man has your best interest at heart and certainly not every one of them is a gentleman."

Her smile faltered for a second as his warning sent a shudder through her confidence. She would be careful, but she would not settle for failure – no matter the cost.

"Sam?"

A man's voice came from the boy Sam once knew. Scott Dougall stepped through the large doorway, but the only resemblance the young man kept was a shock of dark hair and his dark blue eyes. *Same as Catherine's.* Sam's gaze made a quick inventory of the woman of which he'd ended a relationship. A small light of fear lit her expression at his warning. Once she'd attempted to cover with her glib response.

Sam walked toward Scott with outstretched hand, creating more distance from the root of the heat in his face. "Scott Dougall, I hardly recognize you."

"Jackson told me you were here." Scott took Sam's hand, grin growing with each step. "Finally, some decent conversation."

"You're almost as tall as I am. What have they been feeding you over here?"

Scott's mouth set in a grimace. "Nothing as good as Millington. English food can't compare, especially at the boarding school."

Boarding school must have been a big change for Scott when he moved from Millington's close-knit schoolhouse. "Then you'll have to come back with me." Sam steadied a palm to the boy's shoulder, leaning close to add camaraderie. "Think we can convince your mother?"

"I see you have plans to make," Catherine interrupted, standing. "I must attend to my packing. Do forgive me." She sidled up to Sam and slid her hand up his arm, her warmth and touch twisting his thoughts. When had she learned to offer caresses like those so freely. Heat pulsed into his neck. She was playing a dangerous game.

"Oh, Sam, don't be vexed with me." She warmed his cheek with a kiss and then sauntered to the doorway as if across a stage for the world to view.

What had Ashleigh said about a houseful of actors? "I've never been good at holding a grudge against you, Catherine."

"Ah, the perfect man." She sighed and tossed a last look over her shoulder. "Perhaps, when I return, we can become reacquainted? I might not mind a country life shared with a gentleman."

She disappeared out the door and he released his breath.

"I wouldn't set my cap at her if I was you, Sam."

Sam shifted his attention to Scott and cocked his own smile. "Is that so?"

Scott nodded and hitched a thumb over his shoulder in the direction Catherine disappeared. "That one is trouble. If you're going to fall for one of my sisters, it ought to be Ashleigh." Scott shrugged. "But as Catherine says, what do I know about women? I'm nothing but a boy."

Sam shook his head. "I think every male on earth gets lost in that murky quandary, Scott."

"Which is all the more reason to take you up on your offer." Scott patted Sam on the back. "I like this idea of going back to Grandmama's. What do you say we talk about it over some of Ellie's fabulous pastries?" Scott lowered his voice. "It's the only thing she cooks that's worth eating anyway."

Ashleigh caught Catherine's reflection in her dressing table mirror as she entered the room. From their meeting downstairs, Ashleigh knew nothing had changed between them. The same contempt of unknown origin burned in the sarcasm in Catherine's words and the sneer on her perfectly manicured lips. Like now. "To what do I owe this pleasure?"

Ashleigh ignored her contempt. "Sam has only arrived and you are leaving? He survived a sinking ship and untold hardships to see you. Don't you realize how much he wishes to resolve things with you?"

A question flickered in Catherine's eyes. "Resolve?"

Ashleigh faltered. Had he resolved things with her or resumed them? With Catherine's flare for getting what she wanted, it seemed quite possibly he could have fallen right back into her hold on his heart. "Can't you postpone your trip? If nothing else to show him you value his efforts and friendship."

"Sister dear, I have a previous engagement. Some of us still have engagements, of course." Her slender eyebrow pointed like the dagger in her words. She returned to powdering her nose. "Besides, I've been practically fettered to this old house for the past year while you've gotten a college degree and scared away a fiancé. It's time for some freedom."

Ashleigh's lips pinched closed. Perhaps coming home had been the wrong idea. From her first encounter with her sister in the drawing room until now, each haughty look and slighting phrase proved why an ocean apart was the best sibling situation for the two of them.

And Catherine sat there in a new gown which had to have cost much more than her mother could afford. She sent a glance over the gowns littering her sister's four-poster bed, each one exquisite, modern, and...new? Where was she getting all this money?

Ashleigh fingered the edge of a blue brocade sleeve. "I know very well the weight of being a caretaker, but Sam has—"

"You are such a saint, aren't you?" Her words dropped into a whisper Ashleigh barely heard. "Everyone's favorite."

Sam's favorite? The question knifed a fresh pain to her chest. Was she, or had Catherine already begun to renew their affections. Ashleigh released a breath through clenched teeth and refused to enter into the same argument and bout of jealousy. She turned to her sister's bed. The gowns draped across it were made up of garden colors, a couple with questionable neckline drops. There was even one of the newest hobble-skirt styles in pale blue. "I've noticed you haven't taken much of the English accent since you've been here. I thought perhaps you might have, with all your social connections."

Catherine smoothed back her dark hair with her palm. "It isn't useful. I haven't the patience for things which aren't useful to me."

"And Sam?" Ashleigh's tone hardened. "Is he *useful?*"

The same questioning look entered Catherine's eyes. "Sam? Sam is vital, I assure you."

Ashleigh dropped to the bed with a sigh, keeping her

thoughts from following Catherine's words into possibilities. "I understand his arrival was unexpected. And I understand you want some freedom from Mother, but—"

"No, you don't understand." Catherine turned on her, ice blue eyes in slits. "*I* am the eldest, but you're the one they all want. You're the one they've always wanted. Sweet Ashleigh." Her lips curled. "Do you realize how many times I've heard, 'If only Ashleigh were here?'" She took a deep breath and turned back to her mirror, brush clenched so tightly her knuckles turned white, but her words came in barely controlled smoothness. "It's no matter. I have my plans."

Her face paled to match her knuckles. Anger. Anger Ashleigh had never completely understood, but experienced the wrath in bounds. Years of insults and undermining. If the orphanage failed, Ashleigh would return to the states without one glance back to this house or her sister.

Did her sister even know how to value Sam's heart? Ashleigh didn't put one ounce of confidence in her. Catherine brushed through her long, midnight hair and ignored her presence.

"Perhaps it would be better if you left him alone, Catherine." Ashleigh turned to the window, the wear of the day evident by the pale orange light off the horizon. "He deserves someone who will know her own heart regarding his."

The sunset's colors drew her thoughts to the *Lusitania* as she'd watched the fading day from the top of an overturned lifeboat, Stephen clutched to her. Her eyes flickered closed and Sam's face came into full view. The way their eyes met when he woke the morning after the accident, staring at her from across the bed, Stephen between them. Warmth rushed over her in waves, bringing an inward glow with it. If only…

"I see."

Catherine's voice dashed the memory with a chill. Ashleigh opened her eyes and met her sister's, the faintest smile lifting her glossy lips.

"You're in love with him."

Ashleigh controlled her expression into disinterest, but her pulse stuttered forward. "I've always loved Sam, as has Scott. In fact, everyone who meets Sam eventually loves him. This isn't news."

Catherine stood, giving Ashleigh a full-length measured look. "No, you really love him." She stepped closer and slid her voice to a whisper. "But he's not yours."

There was no use denying it. "No, he's not."

Catherine's grin curved with sarcasm. "Do you plan to win his heart while I'm gone? Use all of your…" She swept Ashleigh another glance. "Charm?"

Ashleigh's emotions fell cold. "I have no intention of playing games with Sam's heart. Evidently, that is more your sport than mine. He deserves *sincere* affections." She squeezed the words out through clenched teeth and broken heart. "And he wanted that from you."

"That's right, sister. Me." Catherine scoffed and pulled the brush through her hair again. "And though you doubt it, my affections for him are sincere. You're too young to realize there are different forms of love, but I can assure you, I will make up for my absence once I return – and he will be mine."

Ashleigh held Catherine's gaze. "He isn't stupid, nor will he remain blind to your liaisons forever." Catherine's eyes narrowed, but Ashleigh didn't back down. "So, *if* you do love him, then I would tread carefully."

"Or you'll steal him from me?" She released a light, humorless laugh. "Is that your threat?"

"No, Catherine. If Sam stops loving you, it will never be from my doing. His friendship means too much to me." Ashleigh walked to the door and placed a trembling hand on the knob. Her anger quaked beneath the surface. "You'll only have yourself to blame."

Chapter Twelve

Ashleigh peeked into her room, keeping her feet hushed by the rug in case Stephen still slept. His giggle answered her question and loosed some of the anger knotted in her stomach after her talk with Catherine. She'd never been able to understand Catherine's hostility toward her, but for years Catherine's competition grew more ruthless. Their early childhood held nothing beyond ordinary sisterly discord, but from Catherine's thirteenth or fourteenth year something changed. A drastic shift curbed their relationship and finally grew into an insurmountable chasm Ashleigh had no intention of trying to cross.

She'd attempted too many times, only to be wounded by Catherine's words or actions. Ashleigh was finished trying to make her sister care.

"Well now, look who finally showed up?"

The sight of Fanny McCloud's familiar smile, with all of its genuine love intact, brought welcome peace with it. The woman, fifteen years Ashleigh's senior, sat on the floor with a set of blocks Ashleigh recognized as ones she and her siblings used to enjoy.

The small white coif at the back of Fanny's head unsuccessfully held in her wealth of auburn hair. Her smile welcomed in the comfort of someone who knew all her family's secrets – no pretension or anxiety in a slip of the tongue.

Stephen snuggled up on her lap without an ounce of the past few days' tragedies shadowing his countenance, an added bounce to his clean curls. He was so young, perhaps he could find healing from his tragedy in the love of a new family.

"Oh, Fanny, are you a sight for these wearied eyes."

Fanny's face softened into a look of understanding. She patted the floor beside of her. "Jackson told me what he knew, but not nearly enough." Her gray gaze grew sharp, defied by the curl of her Irish tones. "And this wee lad favors Mr. Michael Craven too much to be a coincidence. I suspect you have quite a yarn to spin."

Ashleigh dropped to the floor, her skirt billowing about her enough to invite Stephen into its pillow-shape. She buried her face into his honey scented curls, eyes stinging. "It's more like a nightmare. All of it. Even the good parts are twisted and—" She looked up through watery vision. "You will never know how grateful I am to have one person in this world with whom I need not pretend."

Between a mixture of tears and distracting Stephen, Ashleigh relived the events of the past week, from boarding the magnificent ocean liner to the horrible aftermath at Queenstown. She carefully kept her feelings for Sam tucked away from the other details.

"Oh darlin'." Fanny's words whispered out on a sigh. "There aren't words for it."

"No." Ashleigh shook her head and placed the blocks into another tower for Stephen to knock down, his little hands clapping at his success.

"I don't sense the same anger toward Michael I read in your letters."

Ashleigh paused and studied the floor, doing an internal assessment. Michael deserved her anger, but the look in his eyes as she'd descended in the lifeboat with Stephen in her arms scraped at her resentment. In that moment, the sorrow and gratitude reminded her of the man she had once called a friend. Selfish, yes – but with the right motivation to curb his selfishness, he had contagious energy, rock-solid determination, and a strong desire to right his wrongs. He always worked so hard to make up for his mistakes. His sorrow was genuine.

Maybe in those last seconds, when their eyes met, he died knowing she wasn't his enemy. Perhaps he died free from the hold of his past. He'd hurt her and she ached from the sting of his betrayal, but...she didn't hate him.

"He was wrong." Ashleigh lowered her face into Stephen's hair. "But having Stephen here somehow softens my anger toward him. Desperate people make poor choices in many cases. I wonder if his own experience of being an orphan made him determine his son would have a father – even if it meant leaving me."

"Poor child. To have to face all this hardship alone."

Ashleigh rested her cheek against Stephen's head, a smile teasing to unfold. "I wasn't alone, Fanny. Sam was with me."

"I see."

Ashleigh opened her eyes and looked over at her dear friend.

Fanny's lips pursed before she turned to place the blocks in the bin, methodically, silence increasing the sudden tension in Ashleigh's stomach.

"You see?"

"Your feelings for Sam."

Ashleigh ran a hand through Stephen's curls, considering her reply. A few creases at the corners of Fanny's eyes hinted of the years gone by, but she'd not lost one wit of quickness in her observational skills.

"Sam has always been dear to me, Fanny." Ashleigh didn't have to lift her head to feel the woman's keen stare. Her lifelong familiarity with their family attuned her perception all the more to the workings of the Dougalls, better than a clock. She met her gaze. "I have nothing to offer him except my friendship. He came here for Catherine, not me, and I'm–" She released a slow breath, contemplating her words. "Better suited to a single life of service."

Fanny's silence stung of disagreement, but Ashleigh forged ahead. "Sam and I have spoken a little about Stephen's future, and have agreed it is best he stay here. He can be our first orphan."

Ashleigh cupped a golden curl, lighter than his father's. "Unless Sam discovers any remaining family for him back in Asheville, of course. I only need speak to Lord Cavanaugh about the use of one of our old buildings near the village. Since they purchased the property a few years ago, I don't believe it's been occupied and its vicinity near town and the hospital would be excellent."

Fanny's auburn brows perked. "Aye, Lord Cavanaugh would have been delighted to share his property with you. Especially with your grandmother's connections here. But the fine man passed away six months ago and his wife has taken over running the estate."

Ashleigh stomach cinched tight. "Lady Cavanaugh?" She stifled a groan, visions of the sallow-faced tyrant from her childhood coming to mind. The one clear memory she had was of the woman thundering through the shops in town, head high, voice pinched to set anyone's nerve on edge. "Well, I shall have to try and speak with her. Until the north wing of the house can be prepared, we must have a place to work. You know as well as I, Mother would never let orphans stay in the main part of the house."

"Aye, but time and circumstance have a way of changing our 'nevers'." Her knowing look pierced with implications.

"And some nevers are for the best. I have nothing to offer Sam, or any man, except my friendship and my skills as a nurse. I'm soiled goods."

"Codswallop," Fanny said, standing and brushing at her skirts. "I see you're feeding yourself the same rotten food you were before we moved back to England last year."

"What's that supposed to mean?"

Her fiery gaze burned with rebuke. "You know exactly what I mean. I love you like my own daughter, but I'll not have you believing the lies from the shadows. God's created you as something else altogether, but you're not listenin' to his voice." She tugged a squirming Stephen out of Ashleigh's arms. "And if you ask me?"

Which Ashleigh most certainly did not.

"You're giving in without a fight. You were a victim once. You're not a victim anymore – unless you choose to be." Her gaze narrowed. "And you're much smarter and stronger than that."

Fanny's footfall disappeared out the door and Ashleigh squeezed her hands together in her lap. Stronger? She lifted her chin. Yes, she was strong. Strong enough to let Sam go and experience a life with a woman who could give him her whole self. If not Catherine, someone else – someone besides her.

Chapter Thirteen

The quiet hush of the small hospital stirred Ashleigh's calm, along with a sense of loneliness. A suppressed cough to her right or a stifled moan to her left alerted her of the suffering, but the sterile walls and tranquil atmosphere curbed the watchful grief at every corner of the building. It was a nice facility, holding about thirty wounded in this first room. The familiarity and consistency offered a subtle balm to the ache of relinquishing Sam to her sister.

Catherine would be home soon, and the knowledge punctured a small bubble of hope she'd nursed in secret. No matter how much Sam's gaze spoke to her heart, Catherine's power hung between them like a fragrance.

Ashleigh's determination to remain single and focus on service solidified. She belonged here. A place where she could vicariously cling to hope while pouring it into others. Heal the broken, when there was no healing for her. Comfort the dying, when comfort for her past and future fell limp and fragile. Purpose provided a substitute, even if a weak one. She could live life alone in the service of others. She had to.

She smoothed her hand over her linen suit jacket and scanned the room for Dr. David Ross.

"Well, well, if it isn't my long lost friend come to save the day."

Ashleigh turned in the direction of Jessica Ross' familiar voice. Hand to her hip and saucy expression fixed as if it hadn't changed from their last encounter eight months prior, she stepped forward from a row of cots. A few rebel strands of her blond hair sprang free from beneath her gray cap and waved around her face with the same twist of nonconformity as their owner.

Ashleigh found her voice. "What are you doing here?"

Jessica's emerald eyes shimmered with a love for life and a solid measure of mischief. "Checking up on you, of course." She wrapped Ashleigh in an embrace to chase away some of the weariness of the past week. Oh, the sweetness of friendship. "Actually, I work six months at the front, then six months off." Her grin perked with pixie flare. "They say it's for mental wellness, but since we know I've never been secure on that score, I tried to battle protocol."

It was beyond amazing how the bond of friendship gripped them as securely over eight months of time and distance as it had when they shared lessons side by side at university. The rigors and horrors of war hadn't affected Jess much and using her Father's connections in England placed her near the front lines.

"You? A rebel?"

"Yes, I know it's shocking, but someone needs to liven up the sticklers here in jolly old England." Her laugh bubbled warm and added another dose of peace to Ashleigh's world. "I suppose we'll be working together for the next few months, my friend." She winked. "Then I'm traveling back with Mother to the States to spend a few months at home." The light in Jess' eyes dimmed. "I hope to take care of her until the end."

"So the diagnosis is certain."

"Mother doesn't complain, so when her illness finally became apparent to others, surgery wasn't an option." Jess nodded with acceptance of the inevitable. "She'll be so happy to see you. I share your letters with her and she was praying to see you before—" She shrugged. "And I always love to see you."

"Getting to spend time with you *and* your mother will

be such an added surprise." Ashleigh gave a mental nod to Providence with a note to ponder on the perfection of God's timing. Almost as if He sent a firm 'no' to her notions of losing hope. Surely He wasn't *this* involved in her life – down to a detail with this perfection? But who else could plan so accurately? And the opportunity to bask in the presence of Vivian Ross, a woman as secure in her faith and love as Grandmama Dougall, brought more unexpected gratitude.

I will never leave you.

She paused on the thought, the added awareness of God's possible presence shook her.

"Since Mother took a ship over last week all the way from Warm Springs." Jessica frowned. "I mean, Hot Springs. People should never change the name of one's hometown. It's highly inconvenient." She waved the notion away with her hand. "Anyway, she's visiting and has been cooking for us. You will be our first guest, if you promise to come on Friday next. That's a whole week to garner enough excuses for me to combat."

Ashleigh covered her laugh to dampen the sound from her quiet surroundings. "That's wonderful." The longer she stayed away from her home until Sam's departure, the better. "I'd be delighted."

"Fabulous," Jess said with a soft clap of her hands. "Now, let's find David so you can have a proper introduction." She tossed a look over her shoulder as she turned. "Or whatever a proper introduction is to my mind. Despite Father's consistent coaching in English protocol, it's never stuck so well with me as it has David. He even uses the accent like a native."

At Jessica's familiar banter, the loneliness Ashleigh felt when she entered the hospital melted into … gratitude and questions. Was this another example of how God's hand brought sunshine as well as rain?

"David's started one of the first war hospitals in this area. We haven't seen a huge number of patients yet, but as the numbers increase in Italy or France, we're sure to get them. We've had some men come as much as a month after the actual battle, from Clearing Station to makeshift hospitals along the way, and finally, if they survive, here."

As she followed Jess between the rows of cots, listening to her rattle off about the rights of women, a smile warmed her to her soul. Here she knew the rules, understood the control and embraced it. Here she breathed in the need, offered answers, and accepted the questions she couldn't answer. She paused on the thought. Accepted the questions she couldn't answer? Like the myriad of 'whys' she screamed to the heavens.

They took a flight of stairs to the second level. Two halls split down each side of building with a row of offices in the center.

"David doesn't want to stop with only a war hospital, though. He has plans to create one entire wing as a children's wing and perhaps even develop a worthwhile hospital in these parts." Jess nodded to the left hall, dim and unused, a new glimmer in her jade eyes. "He was only waiting for the right incentive to get it started."

The thrill of a shared dream tickled with possibilities. A children's ward? Could she start her dream here? She took the stairs with a lighter step. "I have a feeling I am going to like this brother of yours."

Jessica's grin grew with hidden prospects. "Oh, I have high hopes on that score."

The joyful tickle took a downward spiral as Jessica's intentions bled into recognition. Matchmaking didn't fit her friend and poor Jess was bound for disappointment. Ashleigh prepared her best professional expression, stifled her emotions into their safe internal haven, and followed Jessica through an office door.

"Brother dear, I've found our wandering nurse."

A man in a white doctor's coat raised his head from his work at his desk. He shared the same green gaze as his sister, and moved it from Jessica to rest on Ashleigh. He held an air of the same quiet calm she'd sensed when she entered the building. His hair waved in a darker shade than his sister's, highlighting the paleness of his serene gaze.

He stood, soft smile forming, and rounded the table, hand outstretched. "Nurse Dougall, it is a pleasure." The deep undertones of his voice even coaxed a sense of tranquility. As Jessica hinted, his accent boasted more of their father's British influence. He took her hand, his smile growing with welcome. "I cannot express to you how glad I am to have your help here."

Ashleigh found herself smiling back at him without hesitation. "Thank you, Dr. Ross. I am happy to have the opportunity."

"You'll find that my brother, unlike me, has an amazing ability to make every soul he meets fall in love with him." Jessica beamed at her brother, admiration evident.

His gaze left Ashleigh's face and he turned a bemused expression on his sister. "I believe your praise is a bit extravagant, dear sister. I have yet to woo the affections of Lady Cavanaugh to my side."

Jess shrugged a grimace into place. "Please note, I said every *soul*, David."

"Careful." He dipped his chin, his tone holding more warning than his eyes. "We must remain indebted to our benefactress." He turned his attention back to Ashleigh. "As you can see, Nurse Dougall, not all siblings are alike."

She knew that all too well.

"I don't know, David." Jess patted him on the shoulder, their friendly relationship in direct contrast to her and Catherine's. "We're both hardworking, honest, have fantastic senses of humor."

"And at least one of us is modest enough not to admit it out loud."

Jess's grin turned to laughter and she squeezed his arm. "Ashleigh has agreed to join us for dinner next Friday evening, so you'll have a more relaxed environment to become acquainted. Especially after you work her through a first week." She shot Ashleigh a knowing look. "And if I know my friend at all, she'll want to take a tour of the hospital, coupled with a host of questions to ready her for her employment next week."

"Or immediately if necessary." Jessica's lightheartedness was already working its magic of loosening her own knotted emotions more readily than usual.

"Ah, an eager servant?" David's appreciative appraisal of her took her confidence up a few degrees. "I think you and I are going to get on quite well, Nurse Dougall."

The warm swell of a heartfelt compliment added another ounce of healing to her wounded heart. Yes, she'd found her place, her purpose. No need to mourn the loss of her heart.

Chapter Fourteen

As Sam walked through the village, alive with Well Fest festivities, the faint scent of violets on the breeze brought a smile. Holding Ashleigh in his arms, seeing the concern and love in her eyes, triggered memories of Queenstown – her gentle touch over his skin as she washed away the soot, their shared tears as they mourned the tragedy, waking to watch her sleeping across from him.

He pulled at the collar of his shirt and cleared his throat. His past with Catherine fell shallow and childish when compared to his sweet friendship with Ashleigh. Easy banter and mutual respect bound them, along with the stout tethers of a year's trials and the everydayness of good conversation. He just needed to convince her of the fact, to peel away her reservations to loving him.

But the transition from future sister-in-law to future-bride wasn't going to be an easy conversion. She'd withdrawn into her world of nursing and solitude, with the evening meal as their only time of easy conversation. For some reason whatever secret she guarded also kept her affections closed to him.

Women, girls, and children made up most of the occupants on cobblestone streets of the quaint village, enjoying the vendors and no doubt trying to distract themselves from thoughts of their young men scattered on the frontlines of France. And what about his home? Would the *Lusitania's* sinking pull America into the war sooner than later?

He scanned the crowd for Ashleigh, who'd disappeared into a toyshop with Stephen almost half an hour before, as he took opportunity to view some of the crafts and hand-fashioned jewels.

"Sam." Catherine moved toward him down the street, her black hair swept back, half-covered in a straw hat, blue ribbons trailing in the wind. He waited for some pang to remind him of his loss of her, but nothing happened. "I'm so glad to see you are still here."

Her cheeks blushed from the exertion in her speedy approach, heightening her beauty, but despite all the glamour of her appearance, her eyes looked sad.

"Are you all right?"

She smoothed a hand over her stomach and sent him a much-too-bright smile. "Yes, of course. I've only just arrived from London." She passed a hand over her eyes looked down the street. "Has everyone left you alone here?"

"Ashleigh and Stephen are visiting the toyshop so I'm investigating the local wares."

"How careless." Catherine moved close, sliding her arm through his. "If I were Ashleigh I'd take better care of someone as delightful as you."

He raised his brow, her declaration and past choices not matching.

She lowered her eyes and sighed. "Of course, it's taken losing your love to realize how dear you are. London and all of society's pretense proved the value of genuine affection." She squeezed his arm, and looked up at him, her expression thoughtful, and perhaps … authentic? "I hope you will not begrudge my poor use of your heart, Sam."

"We are still friends, Catherine. Always." He picked up a small portrait with a hand-carved embroidered wooden frame, surprised how easy he could release her. Their relationship had ended long ago, by her own hand. Why did she suddenly have trouble letting go? "Did you enjoy your trip?"

"Of course. Being in town is always such an adventure." She waved a hand toward the nearby building, her laughter as counterfeit as her smile. "Father would take us to the very same shop as children each year before Christmas so we could make our wish lists." Catherine pointed to the quaint brick townhouse beside the shop. "And over there is the home of Mrs. Linton." Catherine shuddered. "Governess number four, if I recall correctly."

"Number four?"

A playful glow lit the dimness in her sapphire eyes. "I've never been very good at following the rules, I'm afraid."

"Why doesn't that surprise me?"

Her lips slid to a pout. "Oh Sam, darling, you don't truly believe I was ever malicious in my defiance, do you?" Her frown deepened and she stared ahead of them. "That's what Mrs. Linton called it when I chopped off Ashleigh's hair."

Sam's breath burst out in a shocked laugh. "You cut off her hair?"

Catherine's feline grin returned. "A sibling bout of jealousy. Father bought bows for Ashleigh's Christmas present, the *best* types of bows, you understand. It was clearly unfair of him, especially when Ashleigh didn't care a whit for such things." Catherine moved close to his side again, gripping his arm into a sudden hold. "Oh dear, Sam. Here comes Drew Cavanaugh."

Sam followed Catherine's direction to a tall man with a fine hat and coat to match his polished expression. Everything about him blared self-importance, even down to his wrench-tightened walk. His gaze raked over Catherine in a way to claim ownership. She squeezed closer to Sam and offered him her most brilliant smile. "Never mind him, Sam. He's always causing a scene to gain my attention."

Never mind him? Impossible when the man's dark gaze preyed upon Catherine like a vulture. Even if Sam no longer had romantic feelings for her, he would certainly protect a lamb from the wolf when he could. Mr. Cavanaugh sauntered past them, slowing his pace to rake his gaze over Catherine's body.

Catherine shuddered against Sam's arm, watching Drew Cavanaugh's retreating back. "What an obnoxious man. Perhaps a good month fighting in the war would humble him a notch or two."

"I was under the impression most men of his age were conscripted earlier this year."

She lowered her voice to a whisper. "I happen to know that Mr. Cavanaugh was granted appeal of his conscription due to medical unfitness." Her grin spread wider. "He pretended to have a hearing loss in one ear and was released from the responsibility of war duty. So he spends his time spouting off that his contribution to the war effort of financial support is as beneficial as a soldier."

Catherine's intimate knowledge of Mr. Cavanaugh shouldn't bother him. News spread through this village with the speed of any small town in America, but her accusation bordered on treason. It wasn't surface knowledge. It was possibly dangerous, even illegal. And highly intimate.

Laughter pulled his attention away from Catherine and back to the toyshop front, where Ashleigh was speaking to some unfamiliar people. Stephen stood by her side, one hand in hers, the other wrapped around some sort of pastry. Cream framed his mouth and speckled his rosy cheeks. Almost three weeks after the tragedy of the *Lusitania* and the little boy's smile had returned in full bloom. Had his nightmares stopped too? Sam's hadn't. Even in daylight if he closed his eyes long enough he could feel the weight of water pulling him into the darkness of the funnel.

What caused Ashleigh's laughter? His gaze flipped to the gentleman who held her attention. A pointy edge slid right down the middle of Sam's well-placed intentions. The man offered a genuine smile and the woman to the man's right looked familiar. Blond hair, animated face? Jessica Ross?

No wonder Ashleigh laughed. Jessica's easy personality and jovial disrespect at society usually left him wrestling laughter too. The resemblance in the gentleman hinted that he was Jessica's brother, Dr. David Ross. The edge carved a little deeper. Sam might have liked him better if he'd been balding, an entire foot shorter, and a lot less interesting than he appeared to be.

"I see my sister has emerged." Catherine's voice iced over the words.

Oh yes, Sam saw. His vision became clearer and clearer. Now that everything was finalized with Catherine, he was ready to take hold of his relationship with Ashleigh with both hands. It *would not* be an easy sway to bring her heart to his. And she needed to know his sincerity - not a simple transfer of feelings from one sister to the next, but an awareness he'd been falling in love with her for months without even knowing it.

"Who might she have in her company, I wonder? I don't think I'm familiar with them." Catherine started for the small group. "I do love meeting new people."

Realization dawned with a solid dose of gratitude. Socialite Catherine Dougall was not the right person for him. His gaze focused on her younger sister. His chest expanded with purpose. A tedious handling of the situation pressed his impatience into submission. He had to tread carefully between the bond of sisters. Catherine's behavior proved her feelings for him never ran too deep. The understanding humbled him. He hadn't understood either.

Now? When he realized what love could be? Something much deeper than a superficial romance, heated kisses, or other's expectations. It emerged out of friendship, faith, and a commitment of two minds and hearts.

His smile grew with each step toward her. No matter how long it took, he would do everything in his power to win Ashleigh Dougall.

Ashleigh's smile stilled on her face. Catherine walked across the street toward them, with Sam close behind. Catherine's dress boasted some exotic designs of green, mauve, and pale blue draped in dramatic fashion and narrowing at the ankles. Dramatic was certainly an appropriate description for her sister all around.

And the afternoon had started so well. A carriage ride with Fanny and Stephen to the village, complete with a detailed conversation on how to approach Lady Cavanaugh about a location for the orphanage, an opportunity to purchase a few new clothes for Stephen from one of the shops in town with ready-made options, and a chance meeting with Dr. Ross and Jessica? All well, until now.

"Ashleigh, good day to you."

Her sister's treacle voice spooned out the words with false sweetness. Ashleigh met her fake smile with one of her own. "Catherine." She flipped her gaze to Sam, who effectively dashed her annoyance with a friendly wink.

"I see Stephen didn't leave the shop empty-handed." He nodded to the brown paper package in Ashleigh's hand.

"Those beautiful green eyes of his are quite persuasive."

Sam's grin spread wide, influencing her own.

165

"Ashleigh, dear, I haven't had the opportunity to meet these friends of yours, have I?" Catherine made no effort to hide her interest in David Ross. "Would you be so kind as to introduce us?"

Let the game begin. Catherine's need to draw any and all attention to herself. "Perhaps you remember Jessica Ross from her visits in Millington?"

Catherine's blank expression answered.

"Well, Jessica is a friend of mine from nursing school and this is her brother, Dr. David Ross, the lead doctor at Edensbury War Hospital and, subsequently, my new employer." Ashleigh gestured toward Catherine and Sam. "This is my sister Catherine, and our mutual acquaintance Samuel Miller, who traveled with me from Asheville."

A gentle smile broke onto David's face, a hallmark feature – though she'd yet to see much depth of feeling in him beyond the complacent expression. He maintained an element of control she'd never seen in a man. Perhaps the best word to describe him was calm. A pleasant contrast to her sister.

"Ms. Dougall is much too generous in her description of my station." He offered his hand to Catherine, then Sam. "Lady Cavanaugh is my benefactress, and most certainly the *employer* of the lot of us."

"You must be in good standing with Lady Cavanaugh if she supports you." Catherine's did nothing to hide her interest.

To David's credit, he seemed to recognize her intentions too. "I am merely her grateful, yet penniless beneficiary. Though, I can also claim her as my great aunt."

Catherine held her expression in check, but the gleam left her eyes. Ashleigh's shoulders relaxed. Surely the last thing the gentle doctor needed was a lecherous viper on his heels. She cringed at the bitterness in her inward rebuke.

Her sister was angry and deceitful, but nursing her own anger toward her wouldn't solve the deeper trouble of Catherine's heart. Whatever it was.

"And I'm afraid Aunt isn't as generous as we'd like. The hospital is in need of quite a few repairs and we can't seem to pay for enough help," Jessica added, propping a palm to her hip. "The woman is practically swimming in money but she doles it out like a miser."

"Sister." David's warning look barely quelled the irritation on Jessica's face, but she quieted. The two of them were quite the pair of siblings.

"I'd be happy to help with your repairs," Sam offered. "I'm here for several weeks and would enjoy the opportunity to keep distracted."

Yes, one of the many reasons starting the nursing job seemed so appealing.

David turned his attention to Sam with a nod. "Ashleigh told us of your travels. I am truly sorry for what you endured."

Sam took David's hand with new appreciation. "Thank you."

"And we'd be most appreciative of your help, should you have the time, Mr. Miller."

"I'll be happy to start as soon as I can, Dr. Ross."

"David, please." He looked to Ashleigh.

"And you could ride with Ashleigh into town whenever you wish to work, Sam." Jessica's hazel eyes glimmered with a hidden smile. "Especially in the evening drive home. It would be good company after our long days."

Ashleigh pelted her friend with a threatening look.

"That's a great idea." Sam's smile encouraged a warmth of tremors in her stomach.

"It comes as a surprise I've never met you, when I've

known of the hospital's existence for three months," Catherine interjected. "Do you not attend social events, Dr. Ross?"

"My occupation doesn't afford as many social outings as I would like. Today, Dr. Radcliffe from London has come to look over the hospital and has relieved me for the week. I take it as a much needed holiday."

"Well, I don't know if you should call it a holiday," Jessica interrupted and added one of her infamous eye rolls. "He's spent the first three days completing paperwork and writing letters for further support. Not my idea of a holiday at all."

"Unfortunately, supplies are needed as long as there is war." David's attention focused on Catherine, head tilted with interest. "If you are curious about the hospital, Ms. Dougall, I would be pleased to offer you a tour in hopes of encouraging your willingness to volunteer."

Catherine's eyes flashed wide. "Volunteer? At the hospital? What on earth could I do?"

"There are hundreds of simple tasks," David continued, nonplussed. "And if you have any of the intelligence of your sister, you will be a quick learner."

Catherine's mouth remained unhinged for a few more seconds. Yes, Catherine had a wealth of abilities and a quick mind, but interest? Not for serving up anything but her own comforts and self-advancement. David offered neither.

David's gaze flipped from Catherine, to Ashleigh, to Jess, his grin twitched with the knowledge of Catherine's shock. He saw right through her, but still gave her a chance to change. The thought humbled Ashleigh. Wasn't she always harboring anger toward Catherine instead of hope?

David gestured ahead. "I believe it's time for the well service. Shall we follow the crowd's lead?"

They moved along with the masses to the Brantwood Well. Hundreds of flower blossoms had been transformed into an archway over the rock well and created into a landscape-design of the hillsides surrounding Brantwood Lake. Above it the phrase, *I lift Up Mine Eyes to the Hills* and underneath the phrase, *Abide With Me.*

"What is this exactly?"

She wasn't sure when Sam moved beside her, but there he was, voice low and rumbling by her ear. Ashleigh glanced to her sister, who was focused on a conversation with Jessica and David. She swallowed the sudden tightening in her throat and tilted her head toward him, but kept her gaze fastened on the Well Dressing.

"During the Black Death water was thought to be contaminated - most water, in fact, except for some in this area. In gratitude for God's provision, even in the middle of such heartache, the people created these decorations for each well to celebrate God's protection. The flowers represent beauty and life, which is what these wells provided. It's been a tradition ever since."

His silence drew her attention to him.

His brow rose, and gentleness tempered the sparks between them like a soft whisper. "So even with trial, God is with us?"

She nodded, her voice closed with tears.

"You know, I think the *Lusitania* forced me to reassess a lot of things in my life." He cleared his throat, gaze roaming her face. "It could have been so much worse for us. God provided escape, even with the pain…through the pain."

His words struck a chord in her heart she wanted to ignore. A truth which resonated with Fanny's words from earlier in the week. Forgiveness? Healing? Protection even through pain?

"I have something for you," Sam whispered and pulled some paper wrapping from his pocket. "It's not much, but when I saw them in the shop an hour ago, I knew they were meant for you."

"For me?" Ashleigh looked from the package to Sam, who slowly unwrapped the paper to reveal two charms.

"You've lost so much. I thought...well...this was a way to start something new." He held his palms closer to her so she could get a better view of his gift. "Bring beauty back to something that was lost, maybe?"

Tears blurred her vision as she reached to touch the nearest charm.

"A horse?"

"Better to have one safely attached to your bracelet than to me."

She couldn't tame her smile. He hated horses – ever since one almost broke his jaw with its nose. Her fingers slid over the next charm. It was a pair of silver palms outstretched.

"Your hands." He gestured toward the charm. "The way you serve others with them."

A tear trickled down her cheek. "Oh Sam, I don't know what to say."

He bent his head closer. "Your expression is enough for me." He took her hand in his and deposited the charms into her palm. "But maybe it's a way to start over."

Start over? Could it really happen? Would God give her this chance after all? *Oh Lord, help me know what to do.*

With a little maneuvering, and Sam's help, she attached the charms to her bracelet and dangled it for full appreciation.

"Come." The priest from St. Andrews stood near the well, his white robe almost angelic. "Let us join in singing the hymn *Abide With Me*."

The singing began, slow and uneven, but soon blended together as the tune moved into the familiar.

Abide with me, fast fall the eventide
The darkness deepens, Lord with me abide
When other helpers fail and comforts flee
Help of the helpless, abide with me

Ashleigh looked up to see Sam staring at her, the words drawing her back to unspeakable questions of God's goodness and presence. He knew the terrors of night which gripped her. Healing? Yes, they both needed healing. Hers from a deeper, darker pain than the chilly Atlantic.

Anger shuddered with shame through her. *Oh, how much he'd stolen.*

Abide? Was she prepared to truly place those words into action? She belonged to Christ, but if he abided in her, could there be room for her hatred? The thought twisted a knot of uncertainty.

The next line tightened the knot. *Thou has not left me, oft as I left Thee?* But he had left her! In the darkness of her childhood, he'd given her over to a perverted madman.

I fear no foe, with Thee at hand to bless;
Ills have no weight, and tears no bitterness.

Her voice faltered, choked by truth and tears. Bitterness had been her constant friend for years, a sour pill to her sickness of her memories. And since the *Lusitania*, each reminder fed the malignant tumor of hate.

But was God here? With her still? Could he curb the sting? Triumph over this cancer to her soul. An inner glow begged to shine in her spirit. *Yes, He was here, pouring out His spirit through the words of this song.* He could restore what was lost, couldn't He?

Her gaze flickered back to Sam's, his attention still focused on her. She loved him. Her vision cleared. And that was something Catherine couldn't give Sam. *Her love.* Perhaps God heard her prayer? Could God subdue the tainted passions molded into her by her father's actions? She was helpless to her past, her father's vices.

But the song's refrain came again. She whispered it from her soul. *Help of the helpless, abide with me.* Could there be hope Sam would want her if he knew the truth? For the first time, hope for Sam's love bloomed amidst the brambles of her fear. Could love truly conquer the fear? Was she brave enough to try?

Chapter Fifteen

"I have a visit with Lady Cavanaugh on Tuesday regarding her property near the hospital." Ashleigh focused on Fanny's reflection in the mirror as Fanny made the bed, the woman's white cap attempting to keep some of the rebel curls covered. "Grandmama's support wasn't as much as I'd hoped. Her last letter held only half of what she'd mentioned before I left. It's going to take longer to become established at this rate, and who knows where I'll find suitable care for the children."

Ashleigh squeezed her eyes closed at the threat to her dream. Was it too big a dream? Too impossible? Perhaps she could reduce her hours at the hospital to care for the children. Her shoulders slumped. But she couldn't back out of her promise to David. Not when there was so much need.

Fanny paused in her work and looked up at Ashleigh's reflection in the mirror. "You're looking for someone to tend the orphanage? Care for the wee ones?"

"One diligent person to maintain the orphanage while I work should be sufficient for now. I'm only taking in a few children in the beginning, until we can secure a benefactor."

"I have someone in need of work, for tending the orphanage – and she'll do it for room and board," Fanny added, turning to tuck the bedcovers in for a neat, sleek appearance.

Ashleigh rubbed her forehead to ease the constant ache. Perhaps she'd sleep tonight. Sleep came in short supply since Queenstown. Catherine's return from London didn't' help either. She offered Fanny a tired smile. "Coincidentally, that's all I can afford at present."

"Then I have one for you." Fanny stood from her bent position over the bed and smoothed her hands down her apron. "My younger sister, Ruby."

Ashleigh turned from the mirror to face her friend. "The prostitute?" Even with her nursing experience, the word fumbled off her tongue.

Fanny's pert nod spoke of her confidence. "Desperate times forced desperate choices. She showed up on my doorstep three nights back, asking if I knew of anything proper and honest she could do. And she won't take handouts." Fanny's gaze fixed on Ashleigh. "A chance is what she's after. A solid chance to start over."

Start over? Ashleigh hesitated, weighing her response. "That's asking me to put my reputation on the line – not to mention the safety of the children. How can I know she's...trustworthy?"

Fanny's look turned intense, almost offended. No, how could Ashleigh ever question Fanny's intentions? She'd protected Ashleigh from her father as much as she could, even taking a beating on occasion, but offering the services of a prostitute? Or former prostitute? For orphaned children?

"Everyone needs an opportunity for redemption. To rise above their pasts, don't you think?" Fanny's gaze needled her into introspection.

News would spread in this small village and tainted reputations stained good intentions. Ruby's? Ashleigh's? If people knew of her ruined past, no one would want her taking care of children, orphans or otherwise. The sweet refrains of the MayFest hymn rushed to mind. *I triumph still if Thou abide with me.*

She turned back to her dressing table, the reflection of her dark eyes staring back in challenge. Her family lived a life of pretense. Her past stank of the scent. How was she

174

any different from them if not in the hardest places? If God did abide with her, if she had any faith in His control and love, how could she not respond with mercy and...hope. She'd promised him her life if He would save Sam – and He had.

"I would like to interview her first."

Fanny's expression relaxed. "I can arrange it for any time you have free, Miss."

Ashleigh took a deep breath and forged her decision deeper. "The sooner the better. If she can be here Friday afternoon, I will see her."

Fanny stepped close and placed her hand on Ashleigh's shoulder. "Would you be as gracious with your own past as you are with others?"

Ashleigh lowered her gaze and picked at the bristles of her brush. "I'm afraid to try, Fanny."

Fanny squeezed Ashleigh's shoulder. "Don't believe the lies. Don't allow your father to steal more from you, sweet child. Hasn't he stolen enough? It's time to let go and forgive."

Ashleigh shrugged off Fanny's touch, the fire hidden deep fueled to flame by her words. "Don't speak to me of forgiveness. I can never forgive what he's done. He was a sick and twisted man, with a heart of stone."

"You are right. He was sick and broken, in his mind and soul. The guilt of his poor choices forced his evil to the surface in ways no one could have imagined." She whispered out a soft Scottish prayer. "Ah lass, we all have the tendency to be as bloomin' evil as we can without God's work in our hearts."

"I could never be as depraved as him – and he doesn't deserve forgiveness or mercy from me – in life or death."

Fanny folded her hands in front of her and narrowed her eyes. "Do you remember living here as a child, when your grandmother oversaw the workings of the house?"

The sudden change in topic doused Ashleigh's anger. "Yes, of course."

"She would have a Christmas Party unlike any other seen in Edensbury. Ten times better than Crafty Cavanaugh. The whole place was alive with light and laughter. The first year I was here, I thought I'd entered Heaven when I walked through the door at Christmas."

Ashleigh narrowed her gaze, feeling the well-intentioned needling presence of a point mingled in with Fanny's tale. "Yes, it was marvelous."

"And everything in tip top order, make no mistake. Only the best of everything on display."

A grin soothed some of the previous tension on Ashleigh's face. "As generous as Grandmama is, when it came to her parties, she expected perfection."

Fanny's eyes glowed with her smile, a certain sign Ashleigh's response fell right into her plan. "That's right. Perfection. Nothing else would do, and the pressure was on to provide it." Fanny paced forward. "So what if I was placing settings on the table and noticed two sets of napkins, ones with mild stains, hardly noticeable except in the right light – and then others covered with gravy stains I'd not been able to get out. Which napkins should I use for my place settings?"

Ashleigh's jaw tightened. "Neither is appropriate. Grandmama would never condone napkins with mild or severe stains being placed at her Christmas dinner. You know—" Fanny's implication stole Ashleigh's words.

"God expects perfection for his Heaven and whether you like the sound of it or not, no one deserves his forgiveness or his mercy. Whether the sins are small or great, neither will do for His party in his House." Fanny took Ashleigh's hand in a gentle squeeze. "Your father doesn't deserve your forgiveness, that's a fact. But we don't deserve God's neither. In the light of his grace, we're all sick, broken madmen."

Ashleigh stared into Fanny's clear gray eyes, truth sinking deeper into the sponge of her conscience. She slumped into the chair, her thoughts wedged between pain and Fanny's words. Oh no, she didn't like it. Every aching ounce of grieving child within her screamed in protest.

"The very man who should have protected my virtue stole it? Where was God?" The words squeezed from her throat in a harsh whisper.

"Broken people do broken things, Miss Ashleigh. And their choices impact others. This world is a fallen place. But God lives among us. He's been with you all along. He gave you a Grandmama who would show you the love of Christ. He brought you to a place in America, free from the ill effects of your father's reputation here, so your family could start over. He sent Sam to you as a friend and protected you aboard the *Lusitania*. He's made you smart, compassionate, and strong. Who knows if your zeal to save the lives of others would have been so fiery had it not been for your solid knowledge of what it felt like to be wounded?"

Ashleigh panted against the sobs, holding them close. If she gave in to them, if she released her pain, what would be left of her? "But I can't forgive him. I don't know how."

"You start with prayer. A prayer for your father, and then you tell Sam the truth."

Ashleigh eyes grew wide, and she pressed her palm to her chest, breaths shorter. "No. No, I don't think I can. I would gladly give him my heart, but not the truth. If he ever looked at me with the same disgust as Michael..." Ashleigh voice caught, vision blurring. "No good man wants soiled material for a wife. I am used goods – as sure as your

177

sister."

"Each time you allow the past to hold your future, your father steals more and more from you. Your bitterness of the past and fear of the future stifles you and all your dreams. Tell Sam the truth and be done with this wicked speculation."

"Tell him the truth? I already struggle with these unwholesome desires for him. I crave his kiss. Dream about it."

"Dear child, those aren't unwholesome." Fanny knelt before her. "God made you with those longings for the man you love."

Ashleigh shook her head. "No, Fanny. When he's close to me, when he looks at me with this tenderness..." Her eyes squeezed closed and she pressed her fist into her chest. "An ache, a sweet ache of fire, burns here."

"Sweet heaven, Child, that fire is a part of God's plan too. If you let the desires consume you before it is time, then they can burn you, but the longing within you for him is a special design. God even talks about it in His Word."

Ashleigh tried to process the new information with the hateful beliefs she'd responded to for months, if not years. Could it be true? Could this desire be...from God? For Sam? She couldn't wrap her mind around it. Her parents never seemed to crave each other's company, let alone affection.

"If I tell Sam the truth, I risk losing his friendship along with his respect. If he knew?" Ashleigh shuddered. "Michael stripped me of the confidence. What if Sam rejects me too? I couldn't bear it, Fanny. Sam is my dearest friend."

"You're not giving Sam enough credit. He loves you and he's a good man." Fanny patted Ashleigh's knee and stood. "If you love him as you say, you'll tell him the truth and fear can't haunt you anymore. You have a choice. Take hold of your future or the past will take it for you."

Catherine couldn't curb her smile as she walked the hallway to her room. Her evening with Drew promised her prize drew close. Drew had asked her to meet him next week – for an evening at the theater. After his obvious slight in London, she'd thought her plans lay as dark and useless as their families dwindling funds, but his kisses in the alley of town reassured her. To give her such intimacy had to assure his affections, didn't it? Would he propose under the moonlit sky? As a Cavanaugh, she'd regain her family's standing in society, her mother's respect, and outshine her sister so much their father would smile down from heaven.

She deserved it for all her hard work, contriving meetings, sneaking Grandmama's money from letters meant for Ashleigh or the estate, paying the proper compliments where they were needed, giving up Sam. Her stomach roiled in violent contradiction to her near success. Sam's warning barbed into her conscience. *Lots of things that sparkle leave burn marks behind.*

What if Drew didn't propose? How could she secure his affection?

Catherine's footfall hushed against the worn Persian rug of the upstairs hall. One of the mercies of closing off the north and west wings of the house had been to move all the best furniture and tapestries to the east wing, but even those pieces spoke of their reduced circumstances. Her stomach curled along with her frown. No, her mother didn't deserve this – and neither did she.

Raised voices slowed her steps. She closed in on the door standing slightly ajar and made out Fanny's words. "In the light of God's grace we're all sick, broken madmen."

God's grace? Catherine rolled her eyes. Fanny spouted about little else, but God's grace hadn't served her at all. Stealing her family's fortune and her father's love. Besides, if God lived in the stuffy, emotionless church they attended, then she preferred to leave Him there. His heavy hand of judgment and joyless appraisal of the world didn't interest her at all, and talk of his love? No, God didn't want someone like her – and she certainly didn't want Him. Her brow perked. Unless He could give her Drew Cavanaugh or a new life.

Ashleigh mumbled part of her reply and Catherine stepped closer, listening.

"The very man who should have protected my virtue stole it? Where was God?"

The declaration sent Catherine's thoughts into a problem-solving frenzy. Man who protected her virtue? Fanny droned on something more about God and creating Ashleigh as someone special. She stifled her sigh to hear Ashleigh's response. "If he ever looked at me with the same disgust as Michael." A pause followed. "No good man wants soiled material for a wife. I am used goods – as sure as your sister."

Soiled material? Used goods? *Michael stripped me of confidence?* Catherine's eyes shot wide. That is the real reason behind Michael's betrayal? Ashleigh had given herself to him and he'd found her wanting. Catherine's grin inched up on one side. Her perfectly pure sister, a fallen woman? She licked her lips on the irony. Not even Catherine had gone as far as that. Close, but not all the way.

Years of living in her sister's glowing reflection, in hearing her mother's platitudes of Ashleigh's service and accomplishments, ground into a bitter trail of satisfaction at her newfound knowledge. Though an added sting of jealousy tripped her joy at her younger sister's intimate experience first, this little weapon of truth certainly wouldn't go wasted. If the need arose, and it probably would, she'd make wise use of her newfound knowledge to get what she wanted, or bring Ashleigh with her in the fall.

Chapter Sixteen

Ruby Ramsey possessed the same confident air of her sister and the same mop of auburn hair, but the wear of her choices marked deeper lines than her age suggested. She couldn't be over thirty. Maybe less, yet the pain and knowledge in those emerald eyes knew years of suffering. *One broken soul recognized another.* The woman's gray dress, frayed at the edges, hung loose around a frame too slender for a healthy person. Her high, angled cheekbones reflected hunger and the dark swells beneath her eyes, grief.

Ashleigh offered her hand. "Ms. Ramsey. Thank you for meeting with me."

The woman stared at Ashleigh's hand and sent a quick glance back to her face, as if to make sure Ashleigh meant it. Oh what shame she must bear.

Ms. Ramsey took Ashleigh hand in a stiff hold.

Ashleigh gestured toward a nearby high back. "Would you please sit down?"

"I'd prefer to stand if you don't mind, Miss."

Ashleigh nodded, taking her behavior in stride, but keeping a watchful eye on all the wordless expressions of Ruby's responses. Her pale face spoke of pain, physical pain, and she moved her body in a stiff manner – not the type of stiffness from confidence or pride, as she thought before – but of...soreness?

Nausea swelled at the thought of Ruby's reasons for soreness and a fresh wave of childhood memories nearly had Ashleigh excusing herself. Fanny's words carved a new challenge in her mind. If she forgave her father, would this constant fight against the past subside? Or at least …

lessen?

"Very well." Ashleigh took her seat behind the desk her father used to use, the irony not lost on her. In fact, the knowledge fueled her decision all the more to give Ruby Ramsey an opportunity. An opportunity to be seen beyond her past? "Your sister is a highly respected servant in our house, as well as a close family friend, and she has recommended you to assist me in the development of an orphanage. Is this your understanding?"

"Yes, Miss."

"It is a new endeavor and will require hard work, lots of hard work and patience."

The woman stood taller. "I ain't afraid of hard work. Been used to it my whole life."

"And patience?"

Ashleigh thought Ruby might smile but she squelched it – no doubt an expert at hiding her feelings. "I could use a bit of work on that score. I ain't got no patience for stupidity or harshness in adults, Miss, but for parentless babes, I have the patience of Job."

Stories of Fanny's childhood supported Ruby's comments. A father killed on the streets during a drunken brawl, a mother who gave herself out to men in order to purchase food for the children – and how she later died of consumption, leaving five orphans of various ages.

"I will need someone who can conduct care and business with the utmost discernment, discretion, and honesty. Are you prepared to leave your previous...employment and have nothing else to do with the patrons or facilities in which you..." Ashleigh groped for appropriate wording. "Conducted your business?"

"Completely and wholeheartedly, Miss." Ruby took a step forward, eyes agleam with hope, adding a touch of beauty to her hollow face. "I would like nothing better than to leave everything in my past behind and start brand new."

Ashleigh smiled. Ruby's determination matched hers. "Very well. We shall begin with a trial, of sorts." Ashleigh stood, the cool room adding a chill to the one inside her. "Should I call you Miss Ramsey? Or Miss Ruby?"

"I should like you to call me by my middle name, if you would. It might cause less of a stir, Miss."

Ashleigh's smile grew. Didn't Jesus give people new names when their lives changed? A new name – a new beginning? "And what might that be?"

"Kara."

"Very well, Miss Kara."

The woman almost smiled at the sound of her new name, and it made her look years younger–and healthier.

"We will begin work in the hospital's east wing until I have secured our own building. In the meantime, I will set you up with a room at the hospital starting this very night."

The woman's smile bloomed full and lovely, transforming her face. Ashleigh felt lighter at the gift she'd given. Hope dangled another fragile carrot before her and she chased it. She wouldn't be completely free until Sam knew the truth, but for now, she'd cling to what she had. Hope.

"I'm more grateful than I can say and I won't disappoint you, Ma'am."

"I wouldn't expect it. Now, starting tomorrow you will begin helping me ready the wing for our new charges. One of my nursing friends has spread the word of our new facility and I've already received a few letters from overcrowded facilities who need some relief."

"I can start today if I need to." Kara stood straighter.

Ashleigh rounded the desk and placed a hand to the woman's shoulder. Kara winced and pulled back.

"What is it, Kara?"

Her eyes grew wide and a red hue blotched under her golden freckled cheeks. "Nothin' to worry over, Miss. I have myself a new place now."

Ashleigh dropped her hand. "Show me."

Kara shook her head. "No, Ma'am. Ain't for the likes of you to see."

Ashleigh stepped closer, holding Kara's gaze. "I'm a nurse. Show me."

Kara looked to the floor and unbuttoned the top three buttons of her dress to allow the cloth to slide off her shoulder, revealing an upper portion of fresh, red welts.

"Oh, Kara," Ashleigh breathed and leaned closer to examine the wounds. Older scars zigzagged with the new ones, possibly from a belt or stick. Something whip-like, perhaps. "You've been lashed?"

"Tom didn't like my leaving the place." Her matter-of-fact tone chilled Ashleigh's heart, but she knew the steel of nerves. The necessary need to ignore 'feeling' to make it through another day. External scars for Ashleigh's internal ones. Oh yes, she knew the wounds of such reckless malignancy of soul.

"And I will keep you away." Ashleigh gently pushed Kara's blouse back up on her shoulder. "For a new beginning." She smiled. "Kara."

Ashleigh turned the corner of the hallway, arms laden with blankets for a few new arrivals in the hospital. Slowly soldiers trickled in, if they survived the train ride from the front. They formed a sad conglomeration of broken, beaten, and blind young men, lost, wandering, and waiting for the next transition. Melancholy seeped from the gray skies into the gray halls. *God, will you help them? Where is Your hope and light in these sad circumstances?*

But even in her makeshift prayer, her mind turned to

Kara and a whisper of something sweet offered a response. Hadn't she been an instrument of hope and light in Kara's life? Offering her a second chance? A new start?

She stopped in the middle of the hallway, staring down at the wooden floorboards. All this time she'd been waiting for hope to arrive, instead of recognizing it all around her. Within her. Suffering in the silence of her dark thoughts only kept her near-drowning in them, but what if...what if the desire for the orphanage, nursing, and the care for others were all part of a bigger plan God used to provide the one thing she ached for the most.

"You look like you could use a hand."

Sam appeared at her side, cap on, and grin sending her heart into arrhythmias. What a welcome sight. She couldn't get used to seeing him every day, watching him mingle among the wounded, helping where he could and disappearing to complete some repair. His whistle usually introduced his presence before he came into view.

"I don't know if you're the best help at the moment." She examined his body, dust and dirt powder his clothes from shoulders to kneecaps. "What on earth have you been doing?"

"Repairing the roof." He made a poor attempt at dusting off his shirt and then tugged a few of the blankets from her. "David really needs more help than I can give. It's a wonder there isn't a leak in every room."

"Well, he's certainly grateful for you. As am I. But you really shouldn't spend your entire holiday working."

He leaned close, the blankets separating them. "I get to see my best friend every day *and* help in the war effort? I think it's a formidable way to spend a holiday, don't you?" He removed his cap and scratched his head. "But I think I'm going to be late tonight. I want to finish the east side of the roof before I leave. It's going to take a while."

"Should I send Jackson with some dinner?"

"I'll eat something when I get back. There's no need to go to any trouble for me."

"Didn't you say I was usually up to some sort of trouble?"

He stared at her, his gaze softening in a way that made her believe he might…possibly…see her in a very different light? And if he did, what would she do?

Moans from the other room broke into the silence and Ashleigh sighed. So many hurting men, she didn't have time to fantasize over a daydream.

"You need more help. Four nurses aren't enough."

"We'll make do for now." Ashleigh shrugged and walked toward the doorway. "David has written a few letters to recruit more help, even women from the village are encouraged to volunteer. I tried to convince Catherine, but her interests are focused elsewhere."

"I never thought of her as similar to my mother, but I can see the path – the dangerous path my mother traveled. Catherine isn't who I thought she was."

He rarely spoke of his mother but the wounded boy she left behind when she abandoned her family years ago appeared on the hurt in his face. The little boy still sought answers. "I don't know what happened, Sam, but I…pray she keeps her head."

"I'm sorry to say this out loud, Ash, but I don't think your sister is using her head to get what she wants." He shook his head and sighed. "I can't believe I almost married her. Is that what happened to my father? He married my mother, oblivious to her true nature until it was too late?"

She hated how the truth unearthed in such a painful way. Poor, dear Sam. How could Catherine reject Sam, wound *him*, of all the men in the world? Perhaps Catherine's string of poor choice would teach her a solid

187

lesson of gratitude.

Guilt pinched a nerve. The last time Ashleigh had wished for retribution Michael went down with a sinking ship. No, she couldn't keep harboring resentment toward Catherine.

Oh God, forgive me. Forgive her? The thought stilled her and merged together with Fanny's analogy of the napkins. The ache deepened into throbbing pulse of awareness in her spirit. She needed forgiveness…as much as her wicked father?

Ashleigh flicked her attention back to the present. "I'm sorry, Sam. I know she hurt you. You deserve much better. Someone who will love you fully."

He didn't respond with words, but the softening of his gaze had her wondering about the direction of his thoughts. Fully? Her heart would love him fully. She looked away, too willing to fall into the madness of possibilities.

"Catherine has a strong will. She is going to do as she deems necessary."

He ran a hand through his hair, upsetting his curls. "Whatever the cost?"

"I hope not."

"A woman's reputation is sacred. Once stained, it's almost impossible to recover. She's playing a dangerous game."

Ashleigh squeezed the remaining blankets close to her chest, keeping her face as emotionless as possible. "I suppose even a stained woman needs the opportunity for redemption, don't you?"

He tucked the blankets under his arm and shot her an apologetic smile. "I'm sorry. I've turned the conversation in an unpleasant direction and that's the last thing you need in this place. There are enough worries within one ward of this building to last a year." He tipped his head toward the door. "Wanna see the garden benches I'm building for those convalescing so they can enjoy some fresh air?"

"You're building benches?"

"And a walking path with a railing so the ones who are blind can find their way." He'd always grown energetic with creativity – whether from wood working or photography, and the childlike giddiness was almost contagious.

"You're remarkable. Are you certain you can't stay for much longer? Forever, perhaps?"

His smile stilled and his eyes took on a look she dared interpret as interest? Attraction? She swallowed through her tightening throat.

"You never know."

She followed him to the door and tried balance the war of emotions at his words and glances. How would he stomach her stains? Even if she hadn't given herself away, the same corrosive loss tinged her past, her body. Would he reject her if he knew her reputation lay nearly as marred as Kara's? As she looked into those eyes she'd grown to love, a sliver of hope took flame. If she could trust anyone with her secret, anyone who would love her beyond her stains, if would be Sam.

Chapter Seventeen

Sam stepped out of the hospital, every muscle in his body aching from a full day of hard labor on the hospital roof. At least the soldiers would stay dry in their recovery –his consolation for the sore muscles screaming in his back.

He massaged a hand into his shoulder and looked down the street for a waiting car from Roth Hall. A cool summer breeze tossed loose leaves along the cobblestone, bringing a scent of wood-burning and frying bacon from the café across the street. Sam's stomach gave a responsive growl and he quickened his steps toward the Dougall car waiting up the lane. He'd only made it a few steps before the heady scent of lilac and a familiar laugh stopped him.

A couple stood huddled at the corner of a darkened alleyway, barely visible in the dim streetlamp. Sam turned his face away from the pair, uninterested in viewing the indecency, but the tenor of a familiar female voice slowed his forward momentum.

She laughed.

Catherine.

She stood too close to some man, his hands resting much too familiarly at her hips. Sam didn't stop to consider his choice.

He bolted forward and took Catherine by the arm. "What are you doing?"

He shot her a wilting look and pulled her away from the man he now recognized as Mr. Cavanaugh. "It's nearly nine o'clock and you're out on the streets alone with this man? In an alleyway?"

Catherine shook off his hold and turned back toward

Drew, only to see the man slithering back down the alley out of sight.

"Drew?" Catherine's voice disappeared into the shadows with Drew's retreating form. *Coward.* She blinked as if stunned and turned to Sam. Her red gown billowed around her like the blush he wished she had the sense to experience. She ought to be ashamed.

"No one was supposed to know we were meeting. Not yet, of course. He needs to prepare his family."

"Catherine."

His whisper drew her gaze up. "It's not what you think. He plans to marry me. He's told me as much. Promised, actually, and a Cavanaugh never goes back on his word."

"Get in the car, Catherine."

She hesitated.

"Now."

With chin up, she marched to the humming Model T and slid inside. Sam drew in a deep breath as he rounded to the other door, praying for enough self-control not to ring her stubborn neck. He slammed the car door so hard, Catherine jumped.

"We're ready, Driver."

The car rumbled forward. Sam kept silent until he thought he could keep his voice calm, and low enough the driver couldn't hear. She stared out the window, occasionally casting him a glance and then away.

Sam leaned toward her. "If Mr. Cavanaugh cared about you and your reputation, he would never ask to meet you alone in town at night. Those are not the actions of a gentleman."

"You're being ridiculous and antiquated in your prudery, Sam. The world is changing."

"Respect doesn't change, no matter how much the world does. No *gentleman* regardless of decade, would place a woman's reputation at risk."

"And who are you? My rescuer? Last I heard, you weren't interested in what I have to offer."

His jaw tightened. "As your friend, I take a continual interest in your welfare, Catherine. Our past, your choices, do not change that fact. Even if I must protect you from yourself."

Her gaze glistened in the moonlight and her smile turned feline. She slid close and pressed a lingering kiss to his cheek. "What a dear you are to worry about me so. Are you certain I can't give you a reward for your valiant rescue?"

He pulled back from her and stared down into her face. Clarity hit him like an anvil. Did she always use her body, her passions to sway men? Their shared kisses, their prolonged embraces... she'd used her emotions and body with him too. What had she already offered Drew? What was she doing? Somewhere behind the aspiring debutante hovered an insecure little girl. "Catherine, what are you doing?"

She flinched away from him as if she knew the direction of his words.

"A man should care for you to the point where you don't have to use your body to influence his decisions. He should enjoy talking to you, being your friend." His hand clutched hers and raised it to her face. "Or merely holding your hand. Mr. Cavanaugh is not treating you carefully, Catherine. He's not treasuring the person you are. Don't play this dangerous game."

"I *have* to do this." Her whispered singed the darkness between them. "You don't understand."

"No, I don't understand. Why should you have to throw yourself at men – or manipulate them into doing what you want?"

He tried to grab hold of little truths he could remember. Maybe rescue her from the choices which led his mother to ruin his father's life. He paused. But his father's life wasn't ruined. His heart had been broken, but his Father's strength came from something…Someone much greater than the circumstances. He'd forgiven his mother. Even, against Sam's wishes, responded to his mother's correspondence over the past year. How could he do that? What hidden power broke through the pain of betrayal and found hope?

His father's words broke into Sam's rush of confusion and settled around his heart.

When you recognize how much God loves you, it teaches you how to forgive. How to love beyond the pain. To see yourself as precious. I don't have to prove myself anymore. I can let it go.

The anger breathed out through his sigh. He softened his tone, searching for something important to say – to teach her. "You are worth much more than this choice. There is someone out there who will love you and take care of you without manipulation and secrecy."

"You're wrong, Sam. I don't have any other choices. Life hasn't dealt so favorably with my family to allow for such choices." She crossed her arms in front of her chest and stared ahead. "And I have no desire to hear of your pious resolutions. We're not in Asheville anymore and I've made my decision. One you can never understand."

Sam ran a hand over his face and groaned. He knew Catherine well enough to know when she set her mind to something nothing would stop her. Unfortunately, this choice might prove to be the first step to her losing a lot more than her heart.

†††

Roth Hall had always rested in the shadow of Edensbury Court and the massive reputation of the Cavanaughs. The grand home doubled the size of Ashleigh's family estate, and with the added property Grandmama had sold to the Cavanaugh's, it might even triple the size. Oh, what a sacrifice Grandmama made to keep the house intact.

The fact Lady Cavanaugh agreed to see Ashleigh so early was another benefit. It gave Ashleigh time to finish with her meeting and arrive at the hospital for her shift.

Lady Cavanaugh, in true countess style, sent a car complete with dour chauffeur. She snuck another peek at him from behind her windscreen, his expression as somber as the cloudy day. The car ambled down the Court's long drive, oaks lining the way toward the imposing gray house.

The chauffeur opened her door and she emerged, best hat pinned in place paired with one of her most high quality day suits, linen and lace, as a matter of fact. Grandmama would have approved. However, it was Lady Cavanaugh's approval and provision which provided the stamp of approval for her purpose with the orphanage, and would also afford support for other benefactors to follow her example.

And allow the orphanage to grow? Without the amount Ashleigh had expected from Grandmama, expanding the orphanage beyond the ten beds in the east wing of the hospital couldn't happen. She removed her motoring duster from her hat and took off her goggles then met the butler at the door.

"This way, Ms. Dougall."

He took her things with little ceremony and then Ashleigh followed the tall man through the reception hall. They moved through a maze of large adorned rooms, passed a massive spiraling staircase, until they entered a sprawling drawing room walled in with yellow paper. Windows lined one side, with dark drapes combating any faint light from the overcast sky. Each piece of elegant furnishing spoke of refinement and money.

An elderly woman, face as foreboding as the shadows in the room, sat perched on the edge of a chair, her gray gown in contrast to the sunny wall color. She stood and gestured to a chair with a slow sweep of her hand, her expression as welcoming as a thundercloud.

"Ms. Dougall." Her lips twisted into a knot as she spoke the name. "Do sit down."

Any confidence Ashleigh possessed fluttered directly out the window into the dreary day. She took her seat and offered her calmest smile. "Thank you for seeing me, Lady Cavanaugh."

She offered a ceremonial bow of her white head, face emotionless. "To be perfectly candid with you, Ms. Dougall, I only conceded to meet with you at the urging of my great nephew, Dr. David Ross. Otherwise, I have little to do with *your* people."

Ashleigh hands tightened in her lap. "My people, Madam?"

She looked down her nose and blinked. "The Dougalls have been a thorn in this family's side for decades. It was our hope you would stay in America and pollute that part of the world, but no. A year now, and the black ink of your family is already tainting mine."

The woman's dark eyes tried to force Ashleigh's gaze away, but she wouldn't flinch. "I have no idea to what you refer, Madam. All I know is at one time our two families were friendly and helped the people of Edensbury together. Grandmama even says—"

"Don't." The woman's harsh command slammed

195

Ashleigh's words to a full stop. "I will hear nothing of Emily Dougall."

"Very well." Ashleigh's own chin tilted up, hoping to display more courage than she felt. Her knees trembled beneath her skirts. When would the bitterness end? "Let us discuss the reason for this meeting. Your support would not be in favor of the Dougalls, but rather in the endorsement for destitute children of war – a most charitable contribution to the war effort, don't you think?"

"Do not peddle your lofty virtues here, Ms. Dougall. I have seen firsthand the playacting of your family passed down through generations, and I will not be swayed by your pretty face." Lady Cavanaugh dusted something off her arm, almost as an insult. "I admit I condoned this meeting out of respect for my great nephew. He holds you in high regard and assures me of your most honorable intentions."

"He is very kind. I do hope to help—"

"However, I will not be as easily fooled." She narrowed her eyes. "I wanted to make you aware, in person so we have an understanding, that I will not support any scheme of which you are creator. Your people are not to be trusted."

"On what basis? If your nephew, whom you respect, has no cause to question my motives, then why should you? I can't understand —"

Lady Cavanaugh came to her feet. "You impertinent young woman! How dare you question me? No doubt your purposes are—"

Ashleigh stood, readied to defend her position. "My purpose is to help homeless, parentless children. That is all." She would not back down from this woman's irrational fury, no matter how many rungs up the social ladder she lived. "I implore you, if your nephew offers his support, then it should at least cause you to examine me apart from this prejudice you have against my family."

"We have nothing more to discuss, Miss Dougall. If your sister, with her wild flirtations and disregard for propriety, hadn't secured my judgment, then your very appearance would have. I have no compassion for Emily Dougall." Lady Cavaugh's pointed her cane at Ashleigh. "Or her reflection. I have nothing else to give her. Good day."

The slap of her words sent Ashleigh into motion. Keeping her feet from stomping as she left the room and without waiting for an escort to the front door, she fairly ran down the hall. Within ten seconds she'd lost her way in the massive maze of a house, turning down one corridor and then another. *Oh Lord, please help me get out of this awful mousetrap.*

Voices emerged down the hallway, so she followed them. Surely one of the staff could give her directions to the front. Oh, if Lord Cavanaugh lived, his wife's actions would have shamed him. What arrogance and bitterness! Sour reputation or not, her family didn't deserve such severity. Clearly, the consistent rub of bitterness created a callous disposition. Ashleigh's steps slowed. Could bitterness transform her too? She didn't want to end up with such a heart.

She turned the corner of the hall and stopped just within the shadow, her breath coming to a stop in her throat. *Catherine?*

Her sister's disheveled appearance, not to mention how her body nearly wrapped around Drew Cavanaugh's, gave ample clarity to her sister's most recent occupation. Ashleigh stepped back into the shadow of the hall. Surely Catherine hadn't — she would never—but the way Drew Cavanaugh's hands flared down to Catherine's backside and the veracity of their kisses left little doubt. The blouse to her suit jacket hung crooked from misbuttoning and even the laces of her boots hung loose. Excused from dinner the night before? Ashleigh steadied herself with a hand to the wall. *Oh Catherine, what have you done?*

Could *this* be at the core of Lady Cavanaugh's hatred toward the Dougalls? Sam's words came back to her mind. What if he had married Catherine to find out she would only break his heart like his mother? A sudden swell of protection pushed her heart in Sam's direction even more.

She took a soundless turn back up the hallway into another corridor and nearly collided with a maid.

"I'm sorry, but could you direct me toward the front of the house? I believe I've gotten lost."

The maid's eyes gave a curt nod of understanding. "You'll not be the first, Miss. Follow me."

Soon, Ashleigh sat in the auto car on her way to the hospital, realization flushing shame into anger. Did Catherine always have to ruin everything, including her own life?

Chapter Eighteen

A movement out Sam's window caught his attention. Morning light filtered down to the dewy field and shone on Ashleigh's dark head as she walked toward the stables. Her riding suit conformed to her petite frame, highlighting a whole wealth of curves usually hidden beneath her skirts.

Ashleigh? His smile twitched in response.

Ever since Queenstown, his dreams shifted between dying screams and the love in her eyes as she warmed his frozen skin with her hands. Her friendship had eased into his life as gently as sliding his hand into hers to help her out of a carriage. Naturally. Effortlessly.

And just as easily it glided into something more. A sense of belonging he'd never known with Catherine.

Catherine.

He leaned a palm against the wall and sighed. What was she doing? Meeting with Drew unescorted at night? Engaging in who knew what in a dark alley? If anyone saw her, they'd think the worst, whether she'd acted on those assumptions or not. Maybe that was what had drawn him to her in the first place. Her desperate need of a rescuer. Someone to take care of her.

But he wasn't the man for her.

His heart belonged to someone else.

He grabbed his jacket from the chair and raced from the room. Jackson pointed the way to the stables, a hint of a grin donning his normally emotionless expression. Sam may not be meant for the life of valets, butlers, or horses, but he was beginning to understand what part of this world *did* fit – and he was going to make sure he didn't lose her.

He entered the barn and breathed in the full mixture of

hay, dust, leather, and something else he couldn't identify. His one and only experience on a horse left him on the ground in a heap of dirt, tears, and nursing a broken arm. The animals were beautiful and amazing...from a safe distance.

Ashleigh stood in the middle of the stable, hands gliding over the cinnamon-colored coat of a horse. Her beige riding breeches clung to her curves. The cool morning suddenly scorched with summer heat. Long gone were the "little girl" thoughts, replaced by a real attraction – and something much deeper.

Love.

He'd told her in Queenstown, but she heard it from the lips of a friend, not a man ready to win her heart. It was time for a change.

She rested her cheek against the animal's neck, eyes closed. Her pinned back hair highlighted her long neckline. The slightest hint of a smile eased onto her lips, like hugging the stinky horse was the most pleasing experience she'd had in a long time.

Sam held a grimace in check and rolled his eyes. Hugging a horse? The way her hand smoothed over the animal's skin drew his attention to her fingers and his mind spiraled back to Queenstown. A vision of her touching his face before boarding the lifeboat blazed a hot line of awareness across his skin. He practically felt the warmth on his cheek even now. Why did she have to caress a horse like that?

Clearly, he was going mad. Jealous? Of a horse?

Ashleigh opened her eyes and caught him watching. Her pale cheeks flushed with an attractive pink to match the tint of her lips. "Good morning."

"I saw you walking to the barn and thought I'd check on you."

She brushed a long stroke across the horse's body again and tossed a grin over her shoulder. "To make sure I was keeping out of trouble?"

His breath staggered as if he were a schoolboy enamored by a pair of fine eyes. Maybe he was. He swallowed hard and broadened his smile. "I don't attempt the impossible, little girl."

"I see your mischievous streak has returned with wit clearly in place."

"Actually, we didn't get a chance to talk yesterday. You had to stay late at the hospital and David had me digging a ditch out back." Sam rubbed his aching shoulders to encourage a sympathetic smile from Ashleigh's rosy lips. "How did the meeting with Lady Cavanaugh go?"

Her expression told the story.

"Suffice it to say, Lady Cavanaugh is neither as kind nor obliging as her husband." Ashleigh continued giving long strokes to the horse as she spoke. "There was some sort of rift between her and Grandmama. Without her dear husband around to check her, I'm afraid it's a lost cause."

He stepped closer, wondering if she'd let him hold her. "I'm sorry, Ash. Are there any other options?"

She sighed and tilted her head to look up at him, a stray curl slipping free from under her hat. "Nothing in the short term. All of the other options will require time and letters to determine what sort of support or housing on which we can rely. I can't help but wonder about those poor children. I've already received two letters from orphanages begging for a place."

"There has to be something we can do to help them."

She stared at the horse, brow pinched. "I'm not certain of an answer right now. That's why I came here to think and…pray?"

He placed his hands on her shoulders, turning her to

face him. "What can I do? Point me in the direction and I'll do it. These children need someone who can take care of them, and I can think of no one better than you."

"You're very kind, but I simply don't know. I plan to discuss it with Rev. Reynolds in a few days, but otherwise your care and friendship will be the perfect balm for my disappointment." She gestured toward the horse, a warning light in her eyes. "And...riding is even better with a friend. Feeling adventurous today, my dear Sam?"

He looked from her grin to the horse and comprehension crawled forward, along with a healthy heat in his neck. "Um...no." He waved the idea away. "You have my full friendship, but riding? I'm no horseman."

"Come on, Sam. It's refreshing and energizing. And it would do us both good, you know. I shan't have many more days of leisure as the hospital needs grow and you'll return to America soon."

"I don't have the best history with horses."

"Well, they are quite large and fast, but you were only a child last you rode." She slid the bridle over the horse's head, her mock frown twitching. "I can understand why you might be afraid of them."

He narrowed his eyes and moved forward a few stiff steps. "I didn't say I was afraid."

She blinked, wide eyed. "No, of course not. Merely cautious, is that it?"

His grin inched wide at her faux innocence and he examined the massive horse from a fresh perspective. Ride? At eight, he'd made a promise to himself never again. But that was a long time ago. Maybe another try?

"Where's the knob thing for your reins?"

She glanced up, bobbing her attention from his face to the saddle. "The knob thing?"

He waved a hand toward the front of the saddle,

stepping closer to the intimidating animal. A breeze brought a hint of violet and he narrowed the gap between them even more. He'd always preferred the smell of violets to horses. "The hook-like point at the front."

Her teeth skimmed her bottom lip, pinning her smile. "This is an English saddle so it doesn't have a horn."

"Oh, right." He shrugged to hide his embarrassment. "When in England…"

"I do wish you'd join me. There's no one I'd rather spend time with than you, my friend."

Those eyes. Her entreaty. How could his childish fear compete? "I don't know."

"I assure you. Quitters never win."

Oh, no she wouldn't. "Quitter?"

"You'll fall in love with it, I assure you."

"Fine." He raised a finger. "But only this once and a short ride."

Her nose-crinkled-grin of sheer pleasure had him questioning why he hadn't agreed sooner. Or more often. Or when she rode at the Morris' ranch back home.

She handed him the reins of the horse. "Hold Shakespeare while I tack up Sugar for you."

"Sugar?" Somehow his manhood seemed in question.

Ashleigh seemed to read his mind. "She's a sweet horse for sweethearts."

Her wink caught him off-guard and spiked the attraction, but he didn't have time to sift through a clever retort. She brought an intimidating-looking black mare around and the eight-year-old within him took a step back.

"Oh, Sam, you don't have to go if you don't want." Her face sobered.

"I'm not a quitter."

"No, you're not." She looked at him, eyes growing intense. "Only with horses."

He almost reached to caress her cheek, but she blinked out of the stare. "Do you remember how to mount?"

"That's the only thing I remember, except for the falling part."

"Well, I pulled the girth tight, so *this* time, the horse won't fool you. It is quite a long distance from the back of horse to the ground, isn't it?"

He ran a palm over the smooth skin of the horse's neck. "Especially when you're eight years old."

She cringed, but kept the teasing glint. "Are you certain you're ready?"

"Certain?" He peered over the horse's back at her. "No."

"Oh, well." She hitched a shoulder. "I'll accept respectful fear and friendly coercion as proper readiness."

He chuckled and then needled her with a warning glance. "Just one thing. No racing, little girl."

Her eyes grew wide, palm flattened to her chest. "Oh Sam, I never race." She turned to Shakespeare with a murmur he barely heard. "In public."

He groaned. Yep, he was in trouble--in the best possible way if his pulse had anything to say about it. And spending this time with Ashleigh, out in the sunlight, would be a happy distraction from the ache of loss and tragedy still permeating his solitude and dreams. She understood. He recognized the grief in her eyes when she'd stare into the distance. He knew her thoughts turned to murky water and fading cries.

With a deep breath, he focused every muscle on a fluid movement from the ground to the saddle. He hit his mark, the experience much easier than he remembered. Maybe growing two feet and twenty years made the fear a little smaller too. He could handle this. Tall. Brave. Strong. He almost felt heroic – a definite boost in confidence.

"Nice work. You mounted like an expert."

She looked up at him and he breathed in the pride from her smile.

"Now, are you ready for the difficult part?"

His pride faded like dying daylight.

She laughed. "I'm teasing. Sugar will do all the work. You only need hold the reins." She rested a hand on his leg, unaware of its effects shooting over his skin. "And relax. You are not going to make for an easy ride if you keep your body tense. There's no need to be nervous."

"What if I *am* nervous?"

"You're an expert actor, my lord." She swept low for an impressive bow, and then with beautiful fluidity mounted Shakespeare, topping off her mount with a pointed look in his direction. "Pretend you aren't nervous."

Sam grunted his response and ignored the way her body hugged the saddle. Sugar's easy stride followed Shakespeare's lead out of the barn and into the countryside. Vast and open. *Plenty of space for a run.* Sam's stomach snagged on the thought. *Don't think about it. You're doing this for Ashleigh.*

They rode down a well-worn path from the stables, a comfortable silence humming between them with the chip-chip of morning birds. Sam studied Ashleigh's profile, admiration expanding his chest until he thought it might explode. He'd only begun to see the strength housed within such a delicate and beautiful frame. Would she love as fiercely as she cared for the needs of others? So good and beautiful and pure. He could take care of her until the shadows left her gaze, until she smiled with abandon, until she grew old in his arms. His dear friend forever.

She caught him staring and sat up straighter, tossing an uncertain look over her shoulder. "You're riding like an experienced horseman, Sam. It's not as bad as you thought, is it?"

He nestled into the saddle with a bit more ease and loosened his grip on the reins. "You were right. It is relaxing and…" He held her stare. "Beautiful."

A rush of pink flooded her cheeks as the intention of his words became clear. She looked away first. "Spring and summer are lovely times of year here."

Sam followed her gaze to the scene ahead. A majestic line of firs and cedars were sketched against the horizon of pale blue sky framed in by emerald hills splashed with sunlight. The colors breathed of sufficient rain and rich soil, complementing the sky with perfect hues. God was truly the best artist.

The thought struck him with a sense of wonder. The great open field, the beautiful countryside, the camaraderie of a friend. This was home to him. The freedom of enjoying the grand simplicity of nature. A cool breeze brought an unfamiliar and sweet scent with it.

He took in a deep breath of the air. "What's that sweet smell?"

Ashleigh nodded ahead of them to a field of yellow and red flowers. "Poppies."

"Poppies?"

"They always seem so alive and they're extremely resilient flowers, able to survive many things other flowers cannot."

"Like you?"

She laughed. "Me?"

"You've been able to survive so many experiences few could."

"We both have."

Her gaze stayed in his longer this time.

"Are you still having the nightmares?"

She drew in a deep breath and closed her eyes, lifting

her face to the sky. "Sometimes. And Stephen will occasionally, but they're less frequent. And you?"

"The same. I've kept up with some of the news out of Queenstown."

"So many bodies were never recovered." She turned her head, dashing away tears she didn't wish him to see.

Silence paid the loss homage.

"Thank you for taking such care of Stephen."

Her tear-stained smile bloomed. "Caring for him has been a pleasure. Hopefully, he will be the first of many children who can find a safe and loving place here."

She looked back to the view. He followed.

"This countryside reminds me of home. I wish I had my camera so I could capture it."

"Yes, I wish you could too."

"After all that's happened, I've realized what's important. That life and...love should be cherished."

Her mouth dropped open. Her chest pulsed into a faster pace with the surprise in her breaths. As if choreographed, their horses moved closer, bringing her walnut-colored eyes into clearer view. She shifted under his gaze, and he knew she was trying to maintain composure. Did she feel the same pulsing energy swirling between them as certain as the new electric street lights on Main Street in Millington?

A sudden movement blinked into Sam's periphery – a dart of fur speeding across the path in front of him from the tall grass at his right. His body clenched with surprise. Sugar reared back, whinnying out her surprise and sending him off balance. He shouted his surprise and dropped the reins. Without another hesitation, the terrified horse took off in a dead run. *Perhaps 'dead' wasn't the best descriptive, especially since his life started to pass before his eyes.*

Sam's expression sent a rush of awareness over her skin, trembling to life the hope from a few days ago. The same expression of…attraction darkened his aqua eyes. Could it be true? Could something beautiful and real surface beyond her doubt, her fear? Was he talking about her?

She broke the hold his gaze held on her thoughts and turned back to the horizon, pulse pounding a trepid rhythm in her ears. Why was she taunting those paper-thin hopes? But her attention came back to him. The look glowed with more promise. How could she give into it?

A rabbit from the underbrush rushed across their path, shocking her from contemplation and tightening her hold on Shakespeare. He took a few steps back then stilled, but Sugar panicked and took off in a full gallop, Sam hanging on for dear life. *Oh heaven help her! He'd never trust her again!*

She dug her heels into Shakespeare's sides and urged him after the desperate duo, their pace and path leading straight for Brantwood Lake. Ashleigh leaned in, Shakespeare's black mane whipping against her face, the scent of him rich and familiar. She moved with him, control and strength a byproduct of years of riding. As pretentious as everything else was in her world, this complete abandon and speed fed an ache restricted like the confines of a corset.

The lake emerged from over the next hill. Sugar didn't seem to notice, her pace not slowing. Sam's saddle slipped to the right, his grip and scream encouraging Sugar's panic.

So much for keeping Sugar's girth tight. Sneaky horse. Would she catch Sam before the saddle slipped him over the side and Sugar trampled him? Would he crash into Brantwood? A whoosh of dread catapulted her back to the *Lusitania*, leaving him behind, knowing he might be among the many dead.

She closed in, trying to mentally calculate how much time she had before they reached the lake. Sam's saddle slid further to the right, the reins flapping free to his left and his arms clasped as far around the horse's neck as he could get them. *Poor man.* If he survived the ride, he'd probably kill her.

The lake glittered nearer, Sugar in a blind run. Ashleigh rode up to Sam's left and reached for the loose reins. The leather flipped away. Sam had his eyes pinched tight, but at least he'd stopped calling for help. Shakespeare caught the gist of her request and followed the tilt of her body, edging closer to Sugar. Her fingers slipped over the reins on her second attempt, but then fluttered away before she could grasp them. The lake was seconds away. With a last attempt she snagged the leather and jerked back with more force than she'd intended.

The scene slowed horror by horror. The horse slammed to a stop, hooves burying into the rocky beach until he was chest deep into the lake. Water rained around him in fury. With choreographed style Sam rose into the air over the head of the horse, turned a flip, and landed in a massive splash on the other side.

Ashleigh stared at the waves in the place he'd landed, a circle of ripples the only indicator he broke through the surface. Complete shock locked her movements. Where was he? How could she find him under the murky lake?

Sugar's whinny shot her into motion. She slid from her saddle and ran into the lake. The cold water poured over her boots, seeping calf-deep. She scanned the surface, moving further, hands slicing into the depths in an attempt to find anything resembling an arm or leg. The icy water seeped into her breeches, shooting a residual chill up her spine.

Oh God, help her.

"Sam!"

If he landed head first, it could kill him. Hitting at the wrong angle might break a bone. She moved deeper and drew in a quick breath. The water soaked through her shirtwaist and shocked another shudder to her system. "Sam!"

Oh dear God, not another watery grave.

All at once, something tightened around her ankles and pulled her off her feet. She reached for a handhold, but the water sliced through her fingers like air. The chilly lake caught her in mid-scream as her head plunged beneath the water.

She fought to the surface, but strong hands supported her around the waist, bringing her to a stand on the muddy lake floor. Familiar laughter trickled through her water-soaked hearing. Relief poured through her at the rate of the water streaming down her face.

"You know you deserved that."

Ashleigh wiped her vision clear with her saturated sleeve and shot Sam a glare. "I did not." She splashed a wave of water right into his grin.

He pulled her into his arms to stop her splashing, his brow raised in accusation from beneath a halo of dripping ringlets. "Fall in love with it?" He shook his head and water spun from his blond curls. "There is nothing lovely about watching my life flash before my eyes."

She shrugged and lowered her gaze to keep it from getting lost in those familiar eyes. The warmth of his body pressed into her damp clothes, urging her to snuggle in a little closer. She stilled the impulse. "I suppose you got the worst over now. There's nothing left but enjoyment." She tried to turn, but with water wrapped around her legs, the weight of her soaked clothes, and Sam's palms molded to her shoulders, she could only stand there – trapped in front of him.

"I'm not getting back on that horse, little girl."

He made an exaggerated gesture toward poor Sugar, but the mirth in his expression defied the storm cloud of wrinkles on his brow.

Her pulse continued a steady climb in her ears. Near-death experiences coupled with dramatic reunions seemed to be their pattern, of late. Each one somehow drawing her heart closer and closer toward him.

She dragged her gaze from his and cupped her hand over her eyes as she examined the mid-morning sun. A whole host of tingles joined a shiver across her skin, but they had more to do with Sam's touch than the chill of the water. "It will take us two hours to return on foot."

"I think that's the least you owe me after all the trouble you've caused with that *sweet* horse."

"Trouble I've caused?" She caught the playful gleam in his eyes, bluer from the brilliant colored sky behind him. A smile wrestled for release. Safe. He was safe. She couldn't imagine losing him, or letting him go. There was no other man for her but him. "I suppose you *are* right, as usual. Perhaps we can try again next week."

He grimaced and stared down at her, his gaze a riddle of unreadable emotions. "Not on your or my life, Ashleigh Dougall." His voice closed to a whisper. "But mostly mine."

"Don't be dramatic."

His brow tilted along with the corner of his lips. "Dramatic? Don't you think this scene resembles more of a comedy?"

"Now, but not when you were flying to your death. I couldn't think of losing you again."

The comment slipped out, unguarded. Their faces

hovered inches apart, his warm breath against her face ramrodding a strange collision of internal heat and external chill of seizure-like proportions. She shuddered and his arms tightened around her, drawing her closer. Warmth spread from his body into hers and branched out across her skin.

"You know, I'm a big fan of comedies and…romances."

"Are you?" Her questioned breathed out, almost silent.

His gaze roamed over her face, a sweet caress. Love lingered in his gaze. He reached up to touch her cheek, soft and warm against her skin. She held her breath, half fearing, half-hoping. Was this all a dream?

She swayed forward, toward the lemon-tinted air. An overwhelming curiosity about his lips kept her focused on them a bit longer than any stare outside medical necessity, but they were suddenly magnetizing. Had Fanny been right? These feelings were natural? Even good? She could almost drown in the wonderful warmth of them, the anticipation…the hope. All of her tensed emotions came unloosed by his tenderness. Would he kiss her?

Sam held her close, marveling at the perfect opportunity. Those beautiful pink lips parted, pumping shallow breaths against his neck, and her eyes searched his, uncertain, amazed, wondering. She revealed her love for him in those words, *"I couldn't think of losing you again."* Unraveled waves of damp curls poured over his palm against her cheek and her nearness worked its magic to loosen his tongue. "I am, especially romances that start with friendship and…um…frog gigging."

A snicker split her tempting lips into a smile. "Sam Miller," she whispered his name, drawing him even closer into violet sweetness and walnut-brown eyes. "You're the only man I know who can make the word frog gigging sound romantic."

"It is." His fingers trailed a gentle line down her cheek. The touch of her skin fueled sparks up his arm with the promise of something remarkable. "Only the truest romances start there."

She studied his lips now, chest pumping a shallow rhythm of breaths like his. The culmination of shared pain, lasting friendship, and the aching patience in a long wait drew them toward each other. Maybe even a gesture from God's hand gave them a final nudge.

Ashleigh peeked up at him, their noses almost touching. Her gaze asked the question before it met her lips. "Sam?"

He knew exactly how to answer her question. He cradled her face between his palms, and held her gaze until her eyes closed in acceptance and her smile spread with welcome.

His mouth touched hers. Warm and sweet poured through him, stirring more than fire, but a sense of coming home. He drew back only to return and take another taste, an innocent and satisfying savor. She sighed into him, and he pulled her closer, more secure. Her body settled against his chest, one rhythm of heartbeats. This was where he belonged, kissing his best friend and falling in love all over again.

One of his hands left her cheek to slide across her loose hair, cool and soft between his fingers. Her palms trailed over his shoulders, apparently enjoying the discovery as much as him, and her fingers knotted into the damp hair curled at the base of his neck, shocking a tingle across his scalp.

He pulled back, his thumb smoothing across the soft folds of her bottom lip. "I've waited a long time for that,

Miss Dougall."

Her eyes remained closed. "As have I."

"I don't know about you, but it certainly exceeded my expectations."

Her gaze flickered to his. She placed her palm against his cheek. "I never thought we could...I only hoped."

"And now we might have a bit of a dilemma."

She frowned. "Can't we return to simple and straightforward? It sounds so much lovelier."

He kissed her again and leaned his forehead against hers. "Simple may be in the future, but right now I have a sneaky suspicion Catherine isn't going to approve of our mutual interest."

Ashleigh's gaze sobered. "Particularly since it involves me."

The tension he'd seen during his visit didn't sit well with Ashleigh's future. "Maybe we should keep our complications secret for now, until closer to the time I leave?"

Her smile returned and he rewarded it with another kiss, drawing a sigh from her. "I think we're fairly good at managing secrets, don't you?"

"Are we?" He pulled her to his side and helped her to the rocky beach. "How long have you known?"

She lowered her gaze, the soft flush returning. "Since we boarded the *Lusitania*." Her expression turned apologetic. "I think it had been gradually growing for a long time, but I became aware of it then."

"You *are* good with secrets."

The light in her eyes dimmed. Her brow puckered. "Only when I have to be. You didn't belong to me. I couldn't act on my feelings. I wouldn't have jeopardized your heart or even Catherine's. But now—"

Sam wound a strand of her hair around his finger.

"Now?"

"Now I have a beautiful secret."

He took her hand from his cheek and placed a kiss on her palm. "How could I have been so blind? Why did it take so long to see you?"

The impish glint returned. "Well, Mr. Photographer, maybe you only needed the right focus."

He kissed her charming grin again. She gripped his shirt and encouraged him to linger. Their warm mouths sent a stark contrast to the cool dampness of their faces. She tasted sweet with the slightest hint of syrup from breakfast. Yes, his view had been out of focus for a while, distracted by periphery. Not anymore.

She stepped back, palm pressed to her chest, and moved with unsteady gait to the horses. He followed with a lighter step, a notch of pride in his kiss' effect on her.

"Let's walk, my dear friend." Her words came breathless, raw.

He snatched her hand and pulled it to his lips, warming her wrist and breathing in the fresh scent of violets. "Seems a shame to suddenly feel all this freedom inside and not be able to express it."

She sighed. "As long as we both understand the freedom of it, then I don't care if anyone else knows."

"For now, but as soon as I can I'm going to shout it from every cobblestone street in Edensbury."

He braided his fingers through hers and they each grabbed the reins of a horse, giving a reluctant tug back to their world of pretend. "Come on, my kissing friend, let's get you home and dry."

Her face brightened, nearly glowed. For him.

She gave his hand a squeeze before letting go. "I must say that ride was the single most terrifying and rewarding I've ever had in my life. I can't even think of a Life Saver

215

to describe it."

"Ash-honey, I think we might need the whole pack of colors for that one." He jammed one hand into his pocket and held the reins of Sugar, the rebel, with the other. Clamping his lips tight against the impulse for a victory cry of joy, he determined to keep their secret safe--for her sake. Even if he had to avoid Ashleigh and her lips to do it.

Chapter Nineteen

"You've just given this woman a lot of information in a short amount of time." Jess replaced her blood-soiled apron with a clean one and adjusted her white cap. "You and Sam have a secret romance?"

"Shh…" Ashleigh shot her friend a sharp look in an attempt to curb her volume from the wounded in the room behind them.

Jessica's frown emerged from behind Ashleigh's palm, but it didn't match the twinkle in her eyes. "This demolishes my poor attempt at matchmaking, I assume."

Ashleigh shook her head and turned back to the fresh set of aprons on the table before them. "You would focus on your matchmaking scheme first, wouldn't you?" She tied the apron tight. "When there is Lady Cavanaugh's rejection and Catherine's—"

"Power hungry lusts?"

Ashleigh slit a glance to the doorway to make sure no one was near enough to hear. Cora and Rachel, the two newer nurses, kept open ears to gossip.

"It's not as if people don't already know about your sister." Jess rewashed her hands in the basin of clean water. "Catherine's been living in Edensbury for a year. Her reputation keeps the local newsmongers quite happy."

Ashleigh closed her voice to a whisper. "You think the general public knows she's sleeping with him?"

Jess dried her hands and stepped aside so Ashleigh could have access to the basin, her golden brow sliced to an arch. "She's known throughout the village as a notorious flirt."

A slight pang stung for her sister. Even after all the

years of anger, watching her make these choices was like watching a…torpedo hit a ship. Disastrous. "Catherine's behavior only fueled the flames of Lady Cavanaugh's hatred for my family. What is she doing?"

As they passed the doorway, Ashleigh caught a glimpse of Sam, sleeves rolled up to his elbows, toting several pieces of plywood. He nodded as he passed and topped it off with a wink. Ashleigh tried to tame her smile but failed miserably.

"Oh yes, this secret will never get out." Jessica rolled her eyes and turned toward the room of wounded. "Please, don't resort to acting in those new moving pictures, Ashleigh. You'd never succeed."

Ashleigh's warm cheeks cooled with the awareness. What would happen if Catherine found out? Weren't there too many secrets already? In her sister's anger-laced, volatile state, what might she do? Did she harbor the same dark past as Ashleigh did at their father's hand?

She came to a stop at the end of a bed and decided to return the topic to less terrifying places. "I've never understood your aunt's feelings toward my grandmother. Grandmama is the loveliest woman in the world. I can't imagine her offending anyone."

"Aunt Maureen has hated your grandmamma ever since she learned that Uncle Jeffrey wished to marry her first. When Grandma Dougall graciously turned Uncle Jeffrey down for Lord Quinley it took my uncle two years to recover. Aunt Maureen will never forget it. Your family's decreased circumstances and Catherine's behaviors are more socially acceptable excuses than Aunt Maureen's childish jealous." She nodded toward the patient in the bed, and raised a brow. "Redressing?"

Ashleigh focused on the twenty-four-year-old amputee and nodded, stepping to one side of his cot. Poor man. Perhaps he'd be one of the lucky few to recover sight after gas exposure. The red splotches emerging from beneath the bandage on his face gave no reassurance.

She grabbed gauze from the nearby table and turned to Jess. "But that was more than fifty years ago."

"No one can hold a grudge as well as Great Aunt Maureen." Jess grasped the man's soiled stub as Ashleigh unwrapped the new amputee's old dressing, the fresh scent of blood a commonly sad occurrence with these young men. Moans created background noise. "She hasn't spoken a word to me since I degraded the family by serving at the front. Saving wounded and dying men isn't proper for a woman of my pedigree." Jess's wink added some levity. "I've probably lost what little money she planned for my inheritance." She placed a palm to her chest and feigned a frown. "What a disappointment."

"Do you think she suspects the…intimacy of Catherine's behavior? It could ruin our family even more."

"Or Catherine's grand designs," Jess added, blond brow lifted. "But it wouldn't be all that flattering for the Cavanaughs either. Catherine doesn't meet family status, even with the pedigree, remember."

"Then why would Drew make the effort if he had no intention of marrying her? What could he possibly gain?"

Jess's expression answered the question.

"And Catherine is desperate enough to—"

"Do anything?" Jess finished. "Seems so, but money or status isn't worth her honor, and Drew isn't either." Jess focused her attention on the sleeping soldier's pale face and pushed her fingers through his damp hair. "Cousin Drew gives up his virtue, while these men give up their extremities and lives for the Cavanaughs to maintain the lifestyle they enjoy? This war will change a lot of things." Jess cast a knowing look to Ashleigh. "Starting with this blasted social arrogance, I hope."

Ashleigh ached for the loss her sister's misplaced intentions brought. What would make Catherine so desperate to willingly and blindly give one of the most intimate parts of herself? "So he have no intention of marrying Catherine?"

Jess tossed a towel over her shoulder as she grabbed a new pin to hold the gauze more securely. "As the heir, he wouldn't waste his prospects on your sister." She shook her head and handed the pin to Ashleigh. "Catherine is as much a pawn to Drew as Sam was to her. I just hope she realizes it before something worse happens. She's playing a losing game."

Ashleigh pulled the blanket up over the young man and offered a simple prayer against infection as she tucked the blanket around his chest. Abide with him? Yes. Please, God. *And be with Catherine.* She paused. When had she started praying so naturally again? Let alone for her troubled sister? She sighed. Perhaps her heart knew a lot more than her mind understood. She thought of Sam's sweet kiss and smiled. Perhaps following her heart over her head wasn't such a bad idea some times.

"Jessica told me of our aunt's refusal." David tapped a finger over his frown, his green eyes fiery, showing more emotion than Ashleigh had seen since meeting the gentle doctor. "And Sam was quick to share your plans to seek another place."

"I only hope to find a solid benefactor and someone who is willing to offer suitable lodging." Ashleigh sat across from David's desk watching him pace behind it. "A few more months, at least?"

He stopped and sent her the intense stare of his. "Why not stay here?"

"Here?"

"I was quite serious about using the East Wing for the orphanage. Sam could transfer his efforts to those repairs and perhaps I can use my charm." His eyes took on a gleam she'd never seen before. "To obtain extra funds for unspecified support to the hospital building. Appropriating some of those monies to help orphaned children might increase her appeal to the villagers, whether she recognizes it or not." He almost grinned. "She'll be shocked at her own magnanimity."

Ashleigh laughed and shook her head. "Are you certain?"

"Come now, Nurse Dougall. You have known me several weeks now. I am quite serious in matters of care for the wounded and destitute, you can rely on that." His smile unfurled unexpectedly, like a little boy who'd received his favorite gift. Maybe he did have a little charm and fire underneath all his quiet strength. "What supplies will you need to begin?"

Ashleigh stood slowly, searching for her voice. "I…I'm overwhelmed."

"Serving the broken and dying, watching the pain in this everyday battle for the next breath, makes one fight harder to bring life and healing to those we can." David stepped close, giving her elbow a gentle squeeze. "I will make certain you have what you need, as far as I am able."

There was an intensity and vibrancy in his emerald eyes, passions and energy cloaked behind the calm demeanor of a physician. No, Dr. David Ross was not all he seemed. "You're certain the children will not hinder your work with the soldiers?"

David's smile softened. "If anything, the children might be a hopeful addition to the lives of these men. And there is corridor separating the East Wing from the main hospital as well as its own entrance and garden – to which you will have easy access for recreation. It's an easily solution and I wish I'd thought of it sooner."

"Thank you, David. Thank you for your kindness and service."

A glimmer of mischief flickered across his expression before it disappeared. "I'm not as magnanimous as you think, Nurse Dougall. I want to keep you. It is rare to find a theatre nurse with the expertise, skill set, and compassion you possess. If housing the children here will keep you here, I am pleased to offer."

"David, I finished building the storage shelves—" Sam came to an abrupt stop in the doorway, his gaze shifting between Ashleigh and David, then to David's hand at Ashleigh's arm. "I didn't mean to interrupt."

Ashleigh stepped toward Sam, David's generous news brimming her smile. "Oh, Sam, it's no interruption, it's a celebration."

"Celebration?" The wariness in his gaze dimmed a little.

Was he jealous? A little shiver of delight tipped her smile broader. No one had ever been jealous of her. She took another step forward, holding his gaze. "Dr. Ross has offered the East Wing of the hospital as a place for the orphanage."

"Perhaps you could take your service and energy to that end until you return to the States?" David added, nodding toward Ashleigh. "Since you both are such good friends, and have hearts for service, I'm certain you can come up with the best plan for repairs." David's gaze measured them. "And with your mutual interests, it shouldn't be a hardship to spend time together."

Heat drained from Ashleigh's face. Did David know about their relationship? She dared not look at Sam, but his ready response drew her attention up.

"That sounds like a great idea, David." Sam offered his hand, a glint of humor in his eyes. "And if there are other ways I can help with the hospital repairs, I'll alternate my time." His gaze dipped to Ashleigh's. "I'm at your disposal."

Her breath lodged in her throat and wrapped around a need to laugh. She barely kept control. "Fantastic news, Mr. Miller. I only have you for a few more weeks and I'll use every ounce of your talent and energy to get the East Wing into shape for our little lambs."

"Little lambs?" David's smile faded but not his teasing tone. "Ms. Dougall, from my limited experience with children, 'lambs' wouldn't be the descriptor I'd choose." He inclined his head. "But I've seen you calm the most disgruntled patient of mine without so much as raising your voice, so I have great faith in your ability to...tame lambs."

"Lambs might have been an inaccurate word choice." Ashleigh laughed. "And though I'm a firm believer in miracles, Dr. Ross, a certain application for Ralph Pennington does leave me wondering at my skills. The eight-year-old has been removed from two previous homes and is on his third."

"More adventures for our flock of injured soldiers, a few lost and rambunctious lambs."

"You may need to invest in a lion tamer from Barnum and Bailey's Greatest Show on Earth, Ash," Sam said.

"You fellows are a hilarious duo, aren't you? If the circus is in need of a few more clowns, perhaps I'll know where to recruit." She shook off her smile and leveled Sam a look. "For now, Mr. Miller, let's go see what work is to be done in the East Wing."

Chapter Twenty

Catherine joined them for dinner, pale and quiet. Though every piece of her ensemble boasted of elegance and sheer beauty, something was wrong. Her sister walked with a veil about her, and despite the rift between them, Ashleigh mourned for her. The price her envy cost. Catherine had remained absent at meals for a week, since Lady Cavanaugh's, and Ashleigh was fairly certain she knew why. In the morning light of her rash choice, she recognized her mistake, a decision she couldn't absolve. She'd gambled and lost.

From the look of contained rage straining the contours of her perfect profile, Catherine hated the effort of coming to dinner. There glowed a dangerous desperation in the fiery light of her eyes, a near-panic. Even the natural workings of the dinner service moved with an effort to keep the strain from breaking.

Ashleigh hadn't seen her sister in three days. Repairing the East Wing of the hospital, paired with her nursing responsibilities, monopolized much of her time. Working alongside Sam proved an easy chore, especially when he nipped a kiss here and there. She'd done well to push her guilt and fear away and live in the joy of their new romance, but in the quiet of night – she wondered. As their kisses grew in intensity so did the fire in her chest. Was it a normal feeling for women to experience with the men they loved or was it a disgraceful byproduct of her father's misuse? She craved Sam's touch, longed for his embrace to last a little longer each time. How could she know if the debauchery of her past incited a darker fire than her natural inclination?

"You are ill, Catherine darling." Mother's strident voice searched for a note of command. "You must eat something."

"I am not ill." Catherine's tone raked over the words like a hiss, her palms splayed against the table as if to keep balance. "And I do not wish to be told what I should do."

Mother didn't as much as blink, but continued carving the ham on her plate. "I assumed the news would have made you ill. I know how you fancied Mr. Cavanaugh."

Ashleigh looked from her mother, who proceeded to take a bite of ham as if nothing was amiss, and Catherine, whose scorching gaze hinted at a mask for tears. Red-rimmed eyes blinked, then narrowed with blame. "What have you heard?"

Marion Dougall lifted her eyes and finally seemed to notice she'd captivated the attention of the room. "Mr. Cavanaugh's engagement to Lilith Parker, Lord Devin Parker's eldest daughter." She returned to her ham, nonplussed. "It's been all over the village."

"That can't be right." Scott's frown wrinkled with the effort to make sense of situations in the realm of society. His intrigue in the realm of the elite was about as intact as Ashleigh's. "I thought Mr. Cavanaugh had his sights set on Catherine. He visited enough over the past six months to make anyone think—"

"It seems, dear brother." Catherine seethed through clenched teeth. "Mr. Cavanaugh has lost interest in what I can offer him."

Catherine's gaze flickered to Ashleigh's and locked. Even with an effort to keep her expression neutral, a growing suspicion that Catherine recognized Ashleigh's knowledge of her fall thrummed to her pulse. For the briefest moment, hurt pooled in the dark blue of Catherine's eyes, then dwindled like fading daylight.

"You can't really blame the young man, Catherine," her mother continued, obviously unaware of Catherine's crest toward an eruption. "He is to inherit the Cavanaugh fortune. It is his duty to marry for—"

"Prestige, money, influence." Catherine tossed her napkin on the table. "I know. And we have none of it, not from want of trying to secure it either – at least from *this* Dougall."

"And what is that supposed to mean?" Scott leaned back in his chair and crossed his arms.

Catherine shot the full fire of her blame to Ashleigh. "You could have helped your family, couldn't you? All the time you went to college, studied, took care of poor orphans and the worthless sick in Asheville – you could have been looking for a husband who would rescue the reputation of this family, but no, you chose other people over our needs. People you didn't even know."

So this was the reason for Catherine's venom toward her? She didn't think Ashleigh cared enough for her family or their reputation? Ashleigh had never been one to coddle to status envy, but she hadn't neglected her family, had she?

"Catherine, stop being cross. Drew Cavanaugh's choices have nothing to do with Ashleigh." Mother took a drink and dried off her lips before continuing. "And it isn't as if all is lost. Lilith Parker is a sickly, weak young woman with a temperament as sweet as a lime. Many wealthy aristocrats choose to support women with more…stamina for their private lives."

Mother's full implications shocked quiet across the room. Even Catherine stuttered her words. "Do you mean I should become his…mistress?"

"Many men of rank and title hold mistresses nowadays. The women are paid handsomely for their services and *some* held in high regard. It is a more common occurrence than you realize and holds some banner of acceptance in society."

"Mother." Ashleigh dropped her spoon with an uneventful clink. This sort of conversation? And at the supper table in full hearing of the staff? "Catherine hasn't lost her self-respect."

Her mother shrugged. "You should not be surprised at the way of the world, Ashleigh. You are arms deep in the cruelest part of it at the hospital. It is the way of things."

"Though my lack of virtue may be common knowledge, unlike *some* people's--" Her gaze locked in on Ashleigh's as she stood from her chair. "I still have morals, Mother, *and* expectations. No matter what you may think." She looked back at her mother. "A man will love only me, or not at all. That includes Drew Cavanaugh."

Catherine's gaze shot darts at Ashleigh until she'd exited the room. Without a doubt Catherine was angry, and most likely felt rejected, but there was something else in her gaze. A look to make Ashleigh's hope shudder.

"Must you move to the hospital *now*?" Sam hated the complaint in his own voice. Seeing Ashleigh every day, catching glimpses of her first thing in the morning or last at night even in secret, had become a welcome routine. Their regular conversations and hidden kisses came as expectant as breathing each day. "I'm only here one more week."

Ashleigh offered him an apologetic frown as she placed Stephen into Fanny's arms in the motor car. "We have three new children arriving in two days. Kara will need my help."

As she passed him, he stopped her with a hand to her wrist. Her body bounced against his and he steadied her with tight arms. Oh, she fit so well there. "Is there an extra room at the hospital for me? I could help David. Carry people? Supplies?" His gaze pierced her with deeper meaning. "Anything to stay close to you."

Her hand came up as if to touch his face, but she caught it. Each day proved a greater battle of impulse over expectation. Touching her, showing his affection, came too easily.

"We could certainly use your carpentry skills," she offered, nudging his wounded pride with a smidgeon of hope. "There are so many repairs needed to the East Wing so with your work there *every* day, we should still have some time to visit." She lowered her voice. "And I could come for dinner here every evening."

Her dark gaze roamed his face, sweet care and admiration as tangible as if she'd kissed him. No, she didn't want to be parted from him either – but the needs of others came first. He hoped the smile on his face conveyed the spectrum of affection pressing in on his chest. "I love you."

Her eyes rounded and her bottom lip quivered open. Tears pooled in the depths of gold and brown. "Oh, Sam." She narrowed her gaze but couldn't cover the hint of pink in her cheeks. "How dare you make such a declaration while we're standing in the middle of a group of people and I cannot properly reward you?"

"Well, the thought of your reward will have to do for now."

Their gazes held and the pink in her cheeks deepened.

"Ashleigh," her mother called from the doorway, proceeding in a frantic walk toward the house, her usual manner. "You must be sure to come for dinner each night, as promised."

Ashleigh's gaze flickered back to Sam's. "I was just sharing that bit of information with Sam."

Her mother skimmed over her simple day-dress and sighed. "If we were only the family we used to be, you wouldn't feel reduced to wear such simple gowns."

The effort it took for Ashleigh to draw her attention away from Sam expanded the warmth in his chest.

"In all honesty, Mother, it has been my sheer pleasure to keep my nurse's uniform on for an entire day instead of changing clothes three times to fit the demands of mealtime or certain activities."

Her mother's chin raised and she pinched a frown. "When I was young and on my father's grand estate, we changed clothes no less than five times per day and found pleasure in the employment. It was one of the privileges of the upper class and we took pride in our station." She lifted an accusing finger, but her voice broke. "You...you should remember of which stock you came. Of your pedigree."

Ashleigh walked to her mother and took her in her arms. "I meant no offense." Ashleigh met Sam's gaze, her smile sad. "Our worlds are different, Mother. Neither better nor worse." She stepped back. "But this world is changing...and we must change with it."

Sam rode with them to the hospital, taking the back entrance to keep Stephen from seeing the wounded in front. A young woman, auburn hair a match to Fanny's, greeted them at the door, the resemblance enough to alert him that she was Fanny's sister, Kara. She looked the part of a nanny, or at least what he'd imagined English nannies to be: high-collared dress, tight bun, and white apron in place.

It took only a few trips to unload Ashleigh's and Stephen's things into a small apartment on the second floor. The rooms were a far cry from the giant spaces of Roth Hall, but as he watched her place some of her belongings among the plain and practical furniture, he knew she didn't care. How could he have thought his life would fit with Catherine's?

He stepped out into the hallway while Ashleigh put away her clothes and Fanny saw to Stephen's needs, offering Kara a smile as she passed with a tray of tea. "I think you and Ashleigh are going to have your work cut out for you with three new children arriving tomorrow."

She offered a curt nod. "I understand children who need love. Fanny and I have had our share of it first-hand, and it will be an honor to give them back some of the good we got from strangers."

Sam's grinned stretched. "With Ashleigh's passion, you're bound to have all twelve beds filled within two weeks if you're not careful."

"Fanny's always spoke highly of her, ever since she started working for the Dougall's all those years ago, and I admit there's none like her, sir." Kara's smile brightened and years dropped from her. "Any man would find himself blessed beyond his purse with the likes of her."

"I think you and I are in full agreement, Miss Kara."

"She works like a soldier and she's got a heart of gold. I owe her my life, and that's the truth. Saved me right out of my circumstances. I'll work for her until my dying day out of pure gratitude."

Sam surveyed her, taking in her folded hands and quiet demeanor. "Ashleigh's always been one to rescue people. You should have seen the collection of stray dogs and cats she tried to hide from her father when she was younger." He chuckled. "But she always found a home for them once he discovered her secret zoo."

"Aye, rescuer is a good word for her. That's what she did for me. Took everything in me to break free of him and run off without no place to go but to my sister." Kara shook her head, chin wobbled for a moment, the only sign of her struggle. "And I wouldn't take handouts, but I couldn't go back to my life of sin. I'd have starved first."

Sam steadied his expression even though curiosity burned a fire of warning in his chest. Life of sin? Surely this quiet woman couldn't mean what he thought. Ashleigh wouldn't hire a woman with a questionable reputation to work with homeless children, would she? A woman with a disreputable past had no place with vulnerable children.

"How did you get away?"

Her gaze shot to his, determination marking her stare. "God found me right in the middle of the brothel and told me to leave. I didn't know how I'd get my next meal or my ride to Edensbury, but I knew He didn't want me in that horrible life no more, so He'd take care of the food and the ride."

Her matter-of-fact declaration and confirmation stole Sam's calm. "And Ashleigh knew about your past when she hired you?"

The kindness in Kara's eyes flicked to fire. "I don't lie." Her voice remained much calmer than his. "Miss Ashleigh trusted me with a second chance. Ain't nothin' sweeter in this life than someone trusting you with a second chance. God's done that for me and He's used Miss Ashleigh for it. I'll take it."

"I bet you will."

Her eyes narrowed almost imperceptibly. "I don't expect everyone to understand, Mr. Miller. If you ain't never realized you needed a second chance, you can't understand the gift of one."

Her direct stare fueled his anger even more, but she spoke before he could. "Will that be all, Mr. Miller?"

"Oh yes, Kara. That is all."

Ashleigh stepped out into the back garden of the hospital. All her efforts to ready the walled-in parcel as a play area for the children bloomed about her in the form of a small fountain and budding lilies. Benches were scarce, but perhaps she could convince Sam to add one or two more, then she could sit on one and think of him when he was gone.

A lone bench nestled under a sprawling oak. Its rambling branches cast a lovely shade over the seat, as she'd hoped, and held the object of her search. Sam bent forward, hands folded in front of him and elbows resting on his knees. He'd told her he loved her. Not as a sister or friend, but as a man to a woman. *He* loved *her*. The notion pulsed a wonderful tingle through her and gave her added courage to open up her past to him. They knew each other, and loved each other well enough to weather her father's sick mistreatment. Sam would love her anyway. He would understand.

She walked a little straighter, confidence building with each step. After all, the atrocities hadn't been her fault. God was with her. He could make her whole, as He promised. Her past didn't have to rule her future, and in the light of Sam's beautiful love, he would recognize her as an innocent victim.

"I see you're making wise use of our one bench in the garden."

His gaze remained fixed on the red-hued horizon over the wall, and her steps faltered. Something was wrong.

"Do you remember the story of how my father met my mother?"

A dark undercurrent carried his unexpected topic of conversation. She eased herself down on the bench beside him, confidence dwindling a little. "I believe so. He rescued his brother from entering a brothel, and met your mother there?"

"She'd only been there for a week, so she claimed."

His tone sharpened with anger. "Sold to pay off her father's debts."

"Oh, how horrible."

"Yes, it is horrible." His frown twisted with disgust. He looked down at his clenched hands, his jaw tightened. "Because it tainted her forever. Some say that once a woman is…misused she can never carry on a normal life again. Those desires lurk underneath, waiting to find a way out."

Ashleigh drew back as if burned. He knew. Oh know, someone else had told him. "And you think those people are right?"

He slammed his fist against his leg and stood, ramming a hand through his hair. "That's why she left Father. She craved something more…and ran off with the first man who would give it to her." He turned his gaze back to Ashleigh, eyes burning like blue fire. "They'd carried on with their relationship for months before Father found out. Her past life came back to steal her present and Father and I suffered for it."

Ashleigh pressed her back against the bench, breath thrumming shallow with her heartbeat. For years she'd watched him struggle with the wounds from his mother, seen him bury his anger deeper and try to ignore it, but the heat of it surprised her as it rose to the surface. Her courage trickled to nothing. "I don't think that's true for every woman, Sam."

"Clearly." His gaze pierced her. "You've hired one of her kind to take care of needy *children*."

She replayed his words to find their meaning and released her kempt air in a quivered sigh. *Kara.* He'd found out about Kara's past, not hers. "Her kind?" Relief hardened into a defensive shield as she stood. "I'd hire any of *her kind* for the quality and patience I've seen in her work." Ashleigh gentled her voice. "Kara is not your mother."

"Your compassion is blinding you, Ashleigh. I don't know if a woman like that can ever be truly reformed."

"And your bitterness is blinding you from seeing what God can do for a person who desperately needs forgiveness." Her own words surprised her. The faith behind them. Perhaps she'd not left God as far behind as she thought. Perhaps *He* was constantly reminding her, pursuing her. Never letting go.

Sam stepped close, gaze dark and face rigid. "Not everyone is as innocent as you, Ashleigh. Not everyone holds the same sweetness. And not everyone can be rescued. Some people are broken beyond repair."

She refused to back down to him, to agree with him. Every hope in her future depended on standing up to his false assumptions and unyielding prejudice. Her soul trembled with the need to fight. "I can't believe that, Sam. I *won't* believe it." She pinched her hands together to keep them from shaking, begging the cool calm of her emotionless blanket to come, but it wouldn't. She'd opened herself up to so many feelings for him; she couldn't hide. Her heart was at his mercy, bare and begging. "If God is anything else, He is a rescuer of the lost." Ashleigh pointed toward the hospital. "Kara Ramsey has shown nothing but the utmost virtue and kindness since I employed her. I've watched her with Stephen and even sent letters to people who knew her before she was *forced* into prostitution. She is not—"

"Forced?" he scoffed. "I think a woman can choose whether to give herself to a man or not."

He would despise her if she knew the truth. Just like Michael. The veil of unfeeling dropped over her, weakening their bond. Anger cooled to ice in her veins and her words softened to cold monotone. "Perhaps you've never been broken – never felt beyond hope, so you wouldn't understand."

"My mother's excuse was a ruse. These women chose their paths. They deserve their judgments."

The hardness of his words fueled her anger even more. She trembled with a need to prove him wrong, to shake him out of his arrogance. *God, help me.* "What of the...the Samaritan woman?"

"What?"

"And the woman caught in adultery?"

He stepped back from her, shaking his head. "What do they have to do with—"

"Did Christ show them mercy or wrath?"

"We're not talking about them."

"Yes, we are. Women *like them*, who needed more than a hard hand and a harsh word." She pressed her fingers into her forehead, heat rising into her face. "God help us, Sam, if His hope and grace stopped with only the perfect, good, and healthy. Who is in need of healing and grace more than the wounded, sick, and dying?" Then the thought came to her, the realization. "Have you ever been broken? Ever cried out for a wholeness you craved like one more breath?"

"What are you talking about?"

"Have you ever yearned for one thread of hope when there seemed to be none?"

"We're not speaking of Kara anymore, are we?" His gaze turned wary. "Catherine?"

She ignored his question, pushing forward with her argument. He needed to understand – their future hung on it. "You can't know how much you need grace, until you think there isn't any hope. God doles out judgment, but He reserved it for the self-righteous."

Sam's eyes widened at her clear accusation, but she would not back down.

"He showed mercy to the broken." Ashleigh took a deep breath and pressed her point. "Kara has been broken, but not as you think. In your haste to pass a verdict, you've failed to find out the full truth. She offered herself as a substitute for her younger sisters. They were going to take one or the others. She shielded her sisters to save them."

To his mule-headed credit, a hint of regret broke onto his countenance.

"But even if she hadn't, God is still bigger than her poor choices or her stains." Her words quelled to a whisper, truth dawning. "Larger than the ones others forced upon you too. Everyone needs redemption."

His brows wrinkled and he shifted his weight, gaze taking on less fire and more concern. Perhaps he would listen. "Ashleigh? What are you trying to tell me?"

"Be careful how quickly you wield judgment, Sam."

His hands cradled her shoulders, gaze searching. "What is it? What's happened?"

"Ashleigh!" Jess ran from the doorway, blood splattered across her apron and eyes wide. "We've had our first delivery of soldiers from the Britain's offensive. Quite a loss, and an unexpected…miracle in the middle of it all." She pressed a hand to her cheek and settled a sober gaze on them. "You need to follow me." She stopped in mid-turn and looked back, complete helplessness in her expression. "You too, Sam."

Sam kept at her heels as they weaved through the corridors of the hospital toward the front room. Just before entering, he grabbed Ashleigh's hand and squeezed it, pulling her to a stop outside the door. She looked up to see an apology etched in the lines on his face.

"Ashleigh, we need to finish this conversation." He

pulled her close, a plea in his voice. "I don't want this between us. Whatever your choice with Kara, I love you."

But not if he knew how similar she was to Kara. She stifled the burn of tears and forced her words out on a whisper. "I love you too, Sam. No matter what happens."

His sad smile reframed his apology. She squeezed his hand back and sped to catch up with Jess, holding to a fragile string of hope that a long discussion and honest explanation might clear up his doubts. He might be hard-headed, but he wasn't unreasonable, and she'd hold out every last ounce of hope that reason would triumph over prejudice and stubbornness.

"I wasn't certain at first, because it seemed impossible," Jess said as she led them at a frantic pace down the corridor to the main ward.

"What are you talking about?"

"It's unbelievable." She shook her head and pushed through the doors of the ward, offering them an uncertain look over her shoulder. "But even all beaten up and bleeding, I recognized those green eyes."

Ashleigh tripped forward and Sam caught her arm.

"Said he was found on a fishing rig and brought to shore." They weaved between the cots, moans and the smell of morphine mixed with dried blood almost overpowering. "Then he must have wandered around in a haze, lost his direction and will to live, until he got caught up in the fighting. That's how we have him. It's the most bizarre case of lost and found I've ever seen."

Jess's words clicked slowly, piece by impossible piece, until she stopped in front of a cot. "I told him I'd find you." She shrugged and peered over Ashleigh's shoulder so her gaze could include Sam. "Both of you." With a helpless lift to her arms, she nodded toward the cot.

Ashleigh focused on the man lying there, taking in the

wrapped left thigh soaked with blood, the cradled left arm, and a scraped raw left side of his face. Matted brown hair flattened to his head by the usual trilogy of blood, mud, and sweat. Then, her gaze found his. His eyes focused on her, recognition coming slow, before tears fell down his mud-streaked cheeks.

"Ashleigh." His scratchy voice whispered the word, almost a prayer.

She stared, frozen in place by sheer astonishment. Whether from compassion or the weakness in her legs, she knelt by the side of the cot and worked a strained voice through a tightened throat. "Michael?"

Chapter Twenty-one

Seven weeks since the *Lusitania* and Michael was alive? She tried to speak, but the impossibility of it stripped all words. He shouldn't be here. Alive. There were too many questions for answers right now, but one thing was certain – the sorrow in his eyes pushed past all the anger she wanted to unearth.

What had he suffered in the last seven weeks? His raw physical pain told a story his raspy voice wouldn't allow at present. Sam knelt beside Ashleigh, the wonder and astonishment on his face a mirror of her heart.

"Hey, friend."

Michael looked over at Sam and another sob shook his shoulders, his absolute brokenness merging in the tears on his face. "So sorry."

One of Sam's hands warmed Ashleigh's back, the other covered Michael's good arm. "I'm just glad to see you alive." Sam's voice broke and nudged the tears loose in Ashleigh's eyes. "I'd never want to leave with last words like ours again."

Ashleigh stood and took a sponge from the basin nearby and gently dabbed at the wounds on Michael's face. She needed to keep her hands busy, keep her emotions under amiable control – but this unexpected resurrection frayed her abilities. How? Sam offered her a soft smile, his own tears visible and tender, emerging as the gentle-man she loved, not the hardened one from outside.

Michael's hand clutched at Sam's. "Forgive me." He turned his head to Ashleigh, gaze imploring to her soul. "Forgive me?"

The request stung like alcohol, burning open years of

wounds and thousands of excuses. Her father's face emerged unbidden. Forgive? A wave of nausea turned her face back to her work. Hands steady, heart erratic. How could she? After all he'd said, after the promises he'd broken. *Broken?* The fresh argument with Sam wedged a shaft of light into her bitterness, urging her to replay her own words. *What God can do for a person who desperately needs forgiveness? He is a rescuer of the lost.*

"How did you survive?" She focused on the bandage around his leg and began to carefully unwind it. His request still reverberated in her chest, beating for an answer. "So many died of exposure, and we couldn't find you in Queenstown."

He closed his eyes a moment and she thought he'd fallen asleep, but he rallied when she moved his leg to finish unwrapping. "Swam. Drifted. Fishing boat found me. Can't remember days. Almost died."

"It's a miracle." Sam patted his good arm, still amazed. "Why didn't you try to find us?"

His breath hitched with a sob, and sorrow as tangible as the tears in his eyes contorted his raw features. "Why come to you?"

The simple question broke through her resolve, her hard-earned bitterness, and she leaned close, barely able to voice her words. She took a cloth and wiped at his grimy face. "We spent days trying to find you."

"Searched for me?"

"Of course," Sam added, but Michael's eyes never left Ashleigh's face. "Like I told you onboard. You could have come to me." He tossed Ashleigh an encouraging glance. "To us."

"Lost everything. My wife. Self-respect." His voice broke. "My son."

Ashleigh's gaze shot to Sam's. His eyes grew wide,

realization dawning in those beautiful blue depths. Here was something she could do for him. To show she cared. It wasn't as dangerous as forgiveness, but it was something. Adrenaline pumped through her chest. "Michael, Stephen didn't die."

Sam continued the story. "Ashleigh saved him."

Michael's gaze dodged between the two of them, processing slow.

"He's here with us." Ashleigh smiled at the comprehension dawning on Michael's face. She looked back to his wound, forgiveness playing tag with her own need for justification. "Once you are able, perhaps we can secure you a room near him."

Ashleigh sponged down his wound, keeping her attention away from his face, but his sob brought her back to him.

"Don't deserve it." He shook his head. "God shouldn't give." His watery gaze found hers and eradicated resolve. "Kindness from you. Not after all I've—"

"I forgive you, Michael." The words slipped out on a whisper, but he heard them. So did Sam. He was too close not to hear them.

Her body tensed with the sudden recognition of what she'd done – what she'd said.

"How?" He searched her face.

Heat crawled up her neck and rested on her cheeks, but she couldn't leave his gaze. "Because we all need second chances." She glanced up at Sam, begging for him to listen and understand. "We all need forgiveness."

"Thank you." Michael covered her hand with his good one. "Needed to make things right." He rested his head back on the pillow. "Irish showed God's love. To me."

"It's an amazing story." Sam stood, curiosity flicking from Michael's face to Ashleigh's. "And you have a great lot to live for, friend. You have Stephen." Sam pressed a hand to his chest. "And you still have this family." He looked back to Ashleigh. "We plan to help you heal."

"Exactly." Ashleigh finished bandaging and skimmed the room.

Some soldiers leaned against the wall for support, a few took up space on the floor near occupied beds. And there were more being ushered or carried inside the front doors as they spoke. She turned to Sam. "Perhaps we could move Michael upstairs and free up a bed. There's no reason, with your help, we can't treat him there." She tried for a smile. "You might get your wish after all, Mr. Miller, and be Michael's roommate for the next few days."

Sam's smile outshone his curiosity. "I think I can handle it fine, Nurse Dougall." He gently nudged Michael's good shoulder. "And once you're up on your feet, Ashleigh has some work we can do together. Like old times."

Ashleigh caught the frantic look in Jessica's eyes as she passed the cot and gave Michael's wounds another quick scan to ensure he was stable. "I am needed with other patients." Ashleigh nodded to Michael. "Sam will find me if you need anything."

Tears seeped from beneath Michael's closed eyes. "Already met my need." His gaze opened to hers. "Thank you."

Ashleigh walked to help reset the broken bone of a soldier nearby, a strange, new lightness in her chest. A curious freedom accompanied her steps. She glanced back at Michael. Sam leaned close to hear him talking, and the feeling lightened even more. The heaviness of her anger, the edge of her hate, had disappeared with a single moment of forgiveness?

Would it be true for others in her life? She stiffened.

Forgiving Michael was one thing. Forgiving her father required surgical tools to dig at the center of her soul. His sin attached to her life from early childhood and spread like a cancer to her thoughts of love. How could she ever forgive him – even if she wanted to? It was impossible.

Ashleigh walked upstairs long enough to grab a bite of dinner and check on Stephen. Another day of solid work, the onslaught of wounded left no time for anything but bandaging, cleaning, sewing, and…saying goodbye. Three deaths since the arrivals that morning, and if her instincts were correct, two more would follow soon. Traveling from the front to local hospitals proved to be the death of many, but remaining at the Casualty Clearing Stations kept the severely wounded in constant proximity to disease and danger.

There were no easy answers or solutions. A majority of the men from the Somme Offensive were young, barely in their twenties. One wounded doctor didn't even live beyond the threshold of the hospital door. David mentioned a possibility of over thirty thousand casualties on the first day.

Her body ached to sit for a few minutes, even more than her stomach grumbled for food. Stephen's giggle boosted her energy as she came to his door. She peeked inside to see Sam lying on the floor and Stephen sitting on his stomach, as if riding a horse. Sam tickled Stephen's belly until he fell off and then climbed up again. The sight found residence in her hopes, encouraging a daydream of her own. A little house in the country, a baby in her arms, and Sam's kiss.

The thought of his kiss warmed her from her ankles up. His look and touch held a familiarity and depth which surged far beyond simple attraction, but brought her home.

A good home. A place where people lived in safety and love.

Sam sat up and saw her standing in the doorway.

"Hi there, my sweet friend."

She leaned her head against the doorframe and stared at him. His grin tipped to lethal proportions and her heartbeat stuttered in reply. Love shone unhindered in those beautiful blue eyes, spotlighting on her. *Her?* It still seemed like a lovely dream. And now, with Michael's return, even more of her life drifted into a sweet place of hope and possibilities. Ashleigh would have her future. Stephen would have his father.

Sam loved her. Thoughts of their previous conversation crowded in on the gentle swell of peace. Could his prejudices about a woman's misuse be applied to her? She had to tell him. Didn't she?

The truth had a frightening way of arriving when least expected – and she didn't want that sort of surprise.

He snatched Stephen up into his arms and walked over to her. "You've had a long day."

"And hard." She smiled and ran a finger over Stephen's cheek. "But good surprises too."

"Definitely. Michael should be moved today?" Sam cupped her cheek with his hand, trailing a thumb over her cheekbone. She closed her eyes, almost lulled to sleep by his touch while standing up.

"Mmhmm. Fixed up the room at the end of the hall for you."

His strong arm came around her. She smiled and leaned against it, lemon a welcome scent from the morphine and blood combination of downstairs. Stephen's excited chatter hummed away the echoes of moans and dying breaths crowding her head. Nursing school and the hospital in Asheville had given her solid experience, but nothing like the traumatic wounds of war.

She pressed her head further into Sam's shoulder and soaked in his warmth and strength. He knew her better than anyone besides Fanny and Grandmama. Surely, he would love her beyond a violation she had no power to control.

"Will you have a chance to rest?" His words vibrated through his chest to her ear, drawing her closer. Oh, how she could revel in the feel of him, in his voice and scent.

She kept her head nestled in the crook of his shoulder, eyes closed. "I'm not certain. New patients keep arriving by the hour."

His arm tightened. "You can't work if you can't keep your eyes open." He pulled back, searching her face. "And you *have* to be hungry."

She squinted up to him. "I am pretty hungry. Did Kara leave anything for me?"

Sam steered her to a chair by the window and urged her to sit. "I'll be right back."

The soft folds of the chair welcomed her with the magic of a pillow. "You don't have to hurry."

"No trouble at all, my kissing friend."

Sam's gentle voice sounded far away, but Ashleigh's eyes wouldn't open to ascertain the exact distance. Darkness closed in with the familiar scent of lemon nearby.

Ashleigh's pale face told the tale of her exhaustion. Just the small glimpse Sam took while visiting with Michael had his stomach in knots. Bloodied arms, scarred faces, missing limbs...and pain, or worse, vacant expressions where life seeped to a close. She'd barely sat down in the chair before deep breaths confirmed his suspicions. Asleep – already.

She was stronger than he. Within her willowy frame beat a resilience and compassion great enough to individually treat every one of those patients, if her body could hold out. He snatched up Stephen from the floor before the toddler climbed into Ashleigh's lap and headed into the hallway in search of Kara.

It was a good thing they were moving Michael so he could get his first glimpse of Stephen since the sinking. *And* Sam could spend his last few days trying to help Ashleigh prepare. He'd completed one bench for the children's play yard and made a few repairs from water damage, but after a good assessment of the old building, there was so much more to do. He still needed to add a swing for the children and firm up the rock wall surrounding the yard.

Ashleigh assured him Michael's arm would heal, but his knee might leave him limping for the rest of his life. Limping was better than never walking again. With Michael's past experience at his father's furniture shop, he possessed a solid skill set and he'd always been more charismatic than Sam. A regular salesman.

His stomach screwed tight for a second at the thought of Michael and Ashleigh being in such close proximity while he stayed across the ocean. It was a sensible choice. Michael couldn't take care of Stephen on his own, and the boy already built a bond with Ashleigh, Kara, and Fanny. Michael could heal, work, and reestablish his relationship with his son.

And Ashleigh would wait for Sam.

Like he'd hoped Catherine would do.

He firmed his chin and nodded. This was Ashleigh. Doubt seemed out of place when paired with her.

He met Kara coming up the stairs with a tray in hand. Her gaze flickered to his and then back to the tray. "I saw her come past and thought she'd need something."

"Thank you, Kara." His words crept out in a stiff reply. A part of him knew his reaction was stupid, laced with a shellac of bitterness, but a well-worn path of anger burned deeper. Years of whispers about his mother's choices, teases from boys at school, and grim-locked expressions of adults whose conversations whispered of his father's ignorance in marrying a fallen woman brought a barrage of mistrust. *Once a fallen woman, always a fallen woman.*

Watching the brokenness of his father, hearing his sobs in the middle of the night when he didn't think Sam heard him, solidified a promise to himself to find someone. He'd refused to write his mother a year ago when she began a correspondence with his father. Refused to hear his father's gentle plea to forgive or questions of his mother's reformation.

Once a fallen woman...

Kara stared at him, almost challenging him with an upturned tilt to her narrow chin. Her clear hazel eyes pricked his conscience, a barb of discomfort to his preconceptions. "She'll listen to you, Mr. Miller. She needs to eat and rest."

Sam battled the softening around his heart. "I will make sure to do that."

"Then hand over the lad." Kara raised her copper brow.

Sam's hold tightened on Stephen and he looked down at the food, Ashleigh's pale face resurfaced in his thoughts.

"You can't hold both, Mr. Miller. You going to have to release one or the other." The look in her eyes suggested she held a deeper meaning behind her words.

Sam groaned and with obvious reluctance, he gave Stephen over to Kara and took the tray.

"We'll be in the extra room getting it prepared for you and your friend." Kara nodded to him, but offered a brilliant smile to the boy.

It transformed her face. Stephen put his little hands up

to her face and gave her a resounding kiss on her cheek. She chuckled and kissed him back, walking with a little bounce to the room at the end of the hall.

He looked away, his will weakening a little from the scene he'd witnessed. No. He couldn't soften to a woman like Kara, because then he'd have to admit his mother could change. And that wasn't possible. Betrayal's familiar groove had a direct line to his heart.

He slipped into the room where Ashleigh slept, leaving the door open to ward off impropriety. It was no hardship to watch her sleep. Even with her hair pinned back in her nurse's cap and the dark shadows under her eyes, she looked beautiful. But she needed to eat. How long had it been? Breakfast, where she'd rushed through a muffin before she was called to surgery?

Jess' usual energy waned too, showing her wear from the ceaseless work. With only four or five nurses for hundreds of soldiers, they'd never find rest. Sam shifted the tray to one hand and knelt close, placing his palm over her hand. Her lashes, long and dark, fluttered open and her gaze locked with his. Warmth welled in his chest. *His Ashleigh.*

"I'm sorry to wake you, but I know you're hungry."

She took in a deep breath and blinked open her eyes further, her smile soft and sleepy. His gaze dropped to her lips and his pulse drilled to a faster speed. Why had he worried about feeling attraction for her? It was a seamless expression when love was involved. The strong urge to protect her had him bringing the sandwich closer.

"I don't know how long before you have to go back."

She sat up straighter and looked at the sandwich. "Not long, but I'm so glad I get a chance to see you." Her tired gaze flickered back to his. "I've missed you."

He wedged closer, setting the tray on her lap to free up his hands to cup her face. Her gentle smile welcomed him to take a taste…and not of the sandwich. The impact rippled all the way through his body. His fingers eased over her skin to palm the back of her neck, savoring delicacies in her warm lips and eager response. Her slight moan encouraged him along and her fingers threaded along his ear into his hair, bringing tingles to life on his scalp. She allowed him to lead, which unearthed a whole new trail of emotions. Keeping her safe, happy, and loving her until she gasped and smiled. Oh yes, he was ready for it all.

He pulled back a few inches, her lips flushed from his kiss, and her dark eyes glowing. His thumb caressed her cheek and touched the corner of her drowsy smile. "Is help coming for you and Jessica? Some kind of relief?"

She pressed her eyes closed for another second and took a piece of buttered bread. "There isn't money to pay for help, but David has encouraged a few women from the village to volunteer their time. I think if we had women who would write letters for the men, or talk with them, or take down their names or make simple arrangements to prepare for surgery, it would relieve some of our responsibilities." She took a bite and sighed as if the task was enormous.

"Is there any other place to go for help?"

Ashleigh raised a brow. "Anyone with a pulse and a willingness to work can serve. We can find something for them to do." She shook her head and took a sip of tea. "And I only have Jessica for one more week before she returns to the States with her mother to…ease her passing."

Sam knelt back down and studied the ground. Surely there had to be a way to bring more workers. But what women did he know in the little town of Edensbury? Who could he recruit? Fanny? He drew in a cautious breath. Catherine?

Ashleigh took a few more bites and stood. "Thank you,

Sam."

"You haven't rested enough. Can't you stay a little longer?"

She looked at the stopwatch in her pocket. "I have an amputation. Jessica managed the last one, now it's my turn." She set down the tray and reached up to touch his cheek. "I'm sorry."

How could he complain when she was saving people's lives? He slipped his arm around her waist and she shifted her weight into him, resting her hands against his arms. "Our stretcher bearers are going to move Michael up to the room tonight. Are you certain you don't mind keeping a watch on him?"

He kissed her long and sweet, until thoughts which required a golden ring on her fourth finger began to invade his mind. His grin tipped up at the thought.

"Why do I suddenly have the feeling you are not thinking of sleeping in the same room with Michael Craven?" She grinned and moved her hand from his cheek to his hair.

He snuck another kiss, drawing a sigh from her as they pulled apart. "My thoughts weren't fit for sharing until…um…later."

"Later, is it?" She stood on tiptoe and gave him a gentle kiss. As she stepped back, out of his arms, her hand lingered in his. "Sam Miller, I'm looking forward to later."

Chapter Twenty-two

Sam would never forget the look on Michael's face when he saw his son again. Complete joy and gratitude. Stephen responded more cautiously, but within an hour he'd crawled onto Michael's lap to have a storybook read. After a lifetime of Michael at his neighbor, and almost a year of his absence, the tender moment began the journey of healing for their friendship. Michael wasn't the same. Along with the wounds, there was a deep sense of humility and gentleness his friend had never possessed.

Loss and pain carved new attitudes for people, and Michael's transformation revealed change at the soul level. When he spoke of the family who nursed him to health, their faith and love to him, his eyes shone with hope. God's hope. Michael's life, his outlook, had changed. It urged more of Sam's own contemplation.

But Michael's new peace didn't steal his moans in the night. Ashleigh had warned Sam of Michael's nightmares, probably similar to the ones they both understood. Coupled with his occasional moans of pain, it left Sam's body weary by morning. But every sleepless minute was worth it to see his friend's eyes light up when Kara brought Stephen back into the room after breakfast.

He wasn't too certain he had the energy for his morning task, though. He offered a quick prayer of help before he entered Roth Hall. Jackson greeted him with a letter in tow.

"This arrived for you this morning, sir."

"Thank you, Jackson." Sam tucked the envelope into his jacket pocket, focused on his goal at hand. Persuading Catherine to volunteer at the hospital. Perhaps he'd begun to place too much faith in miracles.

He found her with her mother in the drawing room.

Sam shortened the pleasantries to address the problem at hand – the need for more assistance at the hospital.

"I'm not very good with sick people." Catherine looked up from the writing desk, pages in hand. "Besides, our aunt has just invited me to London next week for a visit. It seems the Zeppelin raids have stolen most people from the city and she finds herself quite lonely." Her grin turned playful. "Doesn't that count as my war effort?"

"I can't believe you'd wish to visit her, lonely or not." Mrs. Dougall scowled, book in her lap, but not one hint of interest in reading it since Sam's arrival. "Zeppelin raids? Frightful."

Frustration brewed to the top of Sam's self-control. London trips when men were dying in a hospital ten miles away? He turned the full fire of his gaze on Catherine. "You are a strong, smart woman. You have the opportunity to serve these men who are defending your home. Can't you spare an afternoon? A few days?"

Catherine rested her chin on her knuckles and stared at him. "You actually think I could be useful?"

"Of course I do. Prove it to yourself, if nothing else."

Her brow furrowed and she continued to stare at him. Did his words penetrate through her façade to her heart? Surely she had a conscience beneath all the playacting. The failure of her plan had taken its toll with her own dark eyes and pale complexion. He'd known her a long time, seen her way of easing people, her quick mind. Couldn't she put it toward the benefit for others than herself?

"Let Dr. Ross know I will come two afternoons a week." Catherine turned to her papers. "And I'll write to our aunt that I will delay my visit for a few weeks, until the rush of this offensive dies down."

Sam decided to hold his tongue and not elaborate on the fact that from all accounts, the Somme was far from over, let alone the war. At least she'd agreed. His faith in her buoyed back a little. "I'll be happy to let him know. I'm sure both he and your sister will be appreciative."

Mrs. Dougall waved a hand in the air. "She has no place in a hospital with dying soldiers."

"We can find a place for her away from the worst of it, if necessary." He focused on Catherine. "You are strong, Catherine. One of the strongest, most determined people I know." And she'd do anything to get what she wanted, so maybe if she focused her energy on helping others, miracles might follow.

"Strong?" Her laugh hollowed and she pressed her hand to her stomach. "At present, I don't feel well. I'm going to my room."

Sam followed her into the hall. "Thank you for agreeing to come."

"Aren't you afraid I'll use my feminine wiles to make poor influences?" she challenged him with a raised brow. "Lead good men astray?"

He took her arm and stopped her from stomping away. "You are much more than those rumors, and you have the chance to prove it now. To stand up and be the person I know you are."

"If you had such faith in me, you would never have abandoned me."

"You called off the engagement, Catherine – and then you tried to use our friendship to attract another man." Her glare ignited his frustration even more. "Why do you feel this need to make these wrong choices? I've seen compassion and determination in you. Goodness. You aren't desperate. You can choose to be honest - To be as good and dedicated as—"

"As my perfect sister?" Her blue eyes narrowed with a dangerous glint, her palm pressing more tightly into her stomach. "My wholesome, sweet, *innocent* sister?"

"This isn't about Ashleigh."

"Oh, I think it's been about Ashleigh a long time." She stepped closer, gaze fastened on his. "When did she start moving her way into your heart? Last month? Last year?"

He shook his head and walked around her toward the door. "I'm not going to satisfy your question with an answer. There are wounded soldiers and hardworking nurses who need extra help." He turned, pointing a finger in frustration. "I don't know what it is between you and Ashleigh, but it seems you're the only one holding this secret grudge."

"Me?" Her hand flew to her throat in mock shock. "Oh, not only me, my dear Sam. Ashleigh's good with secrets too. Very good, in fact. I wouldn't wonder if she's a far better pretender than I am."

A sliver of fear slid from her words to his heart. Hadn't Ashleigh said something about keeping secrets? "There's no need to turn this into a way to slander your sister." He raised his palms and backed away. "I thought you might be the type of person who would agree to help for the right reasons. I was wrong."

Anger lit her expression, but her smile slithered into place. "Oh, you're wrong about much more than you think. Did I hope to marry Drew Cavanaugh? Yes, I did, and to my eternal regret, I used your affections and lied about our relationship to spark his jealousy. There, I've admitted my flaws." Her smile grew, a hidden message striking at his confidence. "Now why don't you get my sister to admit hers? To tell you of her little indiscretions which shoved her fiancé into the arms of another woman?"

"I knew you were desperate to win Drew's attention,

but I didn't think you were mean spirited too." He turned toward the door, wearier from this conversation than he'd been after a night of Michael's nightmares. He'd been foolish to come.

"Aren't you even a little curious why Michael left her?"

"Obvious." Sam kept walking. "He had a son."

"And he'd slept with Ashleigh."

Her declaration stopped him in the doorway. He fisted his palms at his sides and slowly turned. "Why hate her enough to start this lie?"

Catherine laughed. "Lie? Why don't you ask her? She's not the innocent puritan you've placed up on a pedestal. Evidently their affair eventually turned him into the arms of his previous romance. Ashleigh was a disappointment of some sort. Why didn't he merely tell Ashleigh about Stephen, knowing my dear sister's affinity for children?"

"Maybe he was ashamed of his actions."

Catherine clicked her tongue in mock comfort. "You know Michael. So confident and self-assured. He could have swayed her with his charm to get her to forgive him." Her grin returned, dark and much too happy for the conversation. "I heard her confession. Maybe Michael was just like you." She stepped close and pulled at his jacket, her gaze examining him with a hint of triumph. "He thought Ashleigh would be different than the others, but to his dismay--" She offered a mock pout. "--she was like the worst of us. Desperate for love. If you doubt me, ask her."

Sam couldn't imagine the bitterness which would force Catherine to such a ridiculous accusation. It was beyond comprehension, even if a question stirred between the lines. Not Ashleigh. "I wouldn't disrespect her with the attempt." Sam opened the front door.

"Haven't you wondered at her secret? The thing that keeps her cautious. The one fear to wake her up at night. It all finally made sense. Who knows how long she's grieved over her choices, knowing it would ruin her?"

Ruin her? Past conversations with Ashleigh rushed into the light.

"I can see the truth eating away at her like a cancer."

Her words on the *Lusitania* struck him in the heart and opened the door for more doubt. Cancer? *The only way to fix it is to place it in the past.* Isn't that what she'd said? *Some things can't be fixed.*

No, he wouldn't fall into Catherine's trap. Right now Ashleigh needed him. In two days, he'd be on his way to Liverpool to board the *Saxonia* for his trip home.

"Good-bye, Catherine. I hope after you think about how you can serve others, you'll reconsider volunteering your time at the hospital. Good men could use your kindness, assuming you still have some to offer."

Her eye grew wide and he cringed at the hurt which followed her shock. She'd played enough games with him, but to turn this into a slanderous tale to hurt Ashleigh was beyond a game, it was malicious. He cringed. And to think if he'd married Catherine his life would have resembled an emotional yoyo. Thank God for rescue!

He sat back in the car as Marsh started back to the village. An adjustment to his jacket reminded him of the letter in his pocket. He pulled it out and grinned – a missive from his father. Good thing it arrived today instead of tomorrow, since he'd have been gone from Edensbury by the evening for his journey back to the States.

He flipped over the envelope, his father's familiar handwriting almost as comforting as the man himself. A few lines down at Sam's breath hooked tight in his chest. He sat ramrod straight.

Your mother arrived three weeks after you left. Three weeks? Which meant she'd been in the States for a month and a half. Why hadn't his father told him? *She was concerned for your safety after hearing the news of the ship.* Concerned? She'd never been concerned about him. If she had been, she wouldn't have left him for a piece of scum from her past. *She is a changed woman, Sam. Pray before you come. Pray diligently that God will open your heart to forgive her. For my sake, as much as hers.* His sake? Why would he want Sam's forgiveness for his mother's abandonment? *She has become the woman I'd always prayed she'd become. Time and pain have made us both better than we ever could have been before our separation.*

A nail of heat bolted into his chest. His father wanted to reconcile with her. He as much as wrote it. Impossible. Was there no woman in the world who wasn't out to manipulate her way into a man's heart? His hopes clung to Ashleigh. At least there was one. No matter what Catherine said.

"I can't thank you enough, Ashleigh," Michael repeated for the third time in as many minutes. His pale green eyes stayed red-rimmed from his easy tears, but at least each day saw fewer and fewer of them. It would take years for her to get accustomed to this humble, gentle man who used to flaunt his pride like a British flag.

She'd finally managed to get him up in a chair for an hour, a good sign of healing. "I think it's certainly sufficient for one morning." She teased a grin out of him. "You should have most of your strength back in your right hand within a few weeks."

"Then I can start helping out more around here." He scanned the room. "Sam's told me a little about some of the needs."

"We will be grateful for the help." She slipped back his shirt collar and checked the cut he had from collar bone to shoulder. A slice of a bullet? Or a piece of debris? "This is healing nicely, but I'm afraid it will leave a scar."

"No matter." His gaze focused on hers again, intense and earnest. "You look tired. Are you getting any rest?"

She rocked back on her heels, the change in him unnerving at times. Past experience hadn't prepared her for his tenderness or interest, not to mention the fact she still marveled at his survival. She didn't even know him. Not *this* Michael. "Perhaps once the influx of wounded passes I can rest, but right now it isn't an option. I've even had to postpone the arrival of new children to the orphanage because I have no time to help Kara."

His dimpled grin peeked forward, a reminder of the Michael she once knew. "She seems capable enough."

Ashleigh pushed against the arm of his chair and stood. "Without a doubt, but she is still human – and she isn't a carpenter, though she's tried a few times."

"Whatever you need, all you have to do is ask." He grabbed her hand. "I can't take back the horrible way I've treated you. I can never repay your compassion to me." A gentle squeeze punctuated his words. "But you saved my son; you've taken care of me and forgiven me. I will do anything I can to help you."

She paused her reply, resting her hand in his. Was the poor man trying to earn the forgiveness she'd already given? Did the burn of unforgiveness really appear as unrelenting at the look in his eyes? She didn't want the ache of bitterness toward him in her heart anymore, for him or her.

Ashleigh knelt back down and stared up at him. "Michael, you don't have to keep trying to earn my forgiveness."

His eyes grew watery again, but his smile remained intact. "I'm not. I'm thankful you forgave me and I want to give something back, not earn anything." He shrugged. "The family who helped me after the *Lusitania* reminded me of what Sam's father used to say to me when I mess up with him. When you realize you've been forgiven of much," His gaze grew more intense. "your natural response is to love much."

Abide with me. The call surfaced from deep inside, like when Michael first requested her forgiveness. God's voice, a ceaseless call to release her pain and anger about her past to him. But how could she? If she forgave her father, wouldn't it be like condoning what he did? She'd held on to her hate so long, if she let go of it, what would take its place?

He watched her, almost as if he knew her thoughts. She shuddered and pulled her hand free, drawing in a breath and averting her gaze to the gauze on his forehead. "Let me see to your wound here and then I must return to the hospital."

He placed his head back against the chair as she leaned over him, his eyes closed, which was good. Any more piercing looks might very well have had her in tears. The request quaked through her spirit, springing open doors of questions. Forgiving Michael was one thing. Forgiving her father was…impossible.

Chapter Twenty-three

Sam peered into the room to see Ashleigh's fingers smoothing back Michael's hair. Her nearness to him, and the way he watched her, shot blinding pain and banged open the floodgates of doubt Catherine stirred. Surely Catherine was wrong. She had to be.

The thought drilled an ache in his chest. If Ashleigh had given herself to Michael while they were engaged, the knowledge of it would shock his opinion of her, of course. Then keeping it a secret?

He pressed his palm into the doorframe. Deception? Like Catherine and his mother? Oh, the news of his mother's presence in Millington raked over his nerves like a saw on wood. He already wanted to hit something – and protect his father from the effects of a false woman. He stared at Ashleigh, her care evident from the gentleness in her touch against Michael's skin.

False woman?

An ugly fire burned up through his chest, tainted with the smoke of jealousy. If Michael had never returned...

The thought pierced his conscience with the pain of a hot iron. How could he even wish that?

Her face stayed only a few inches from Michael's while working closely with the bandages on his chest. He could probably smell the scent of violets on her skin. Did she smile at Michael the way she did with him? Did she still feel attraction? Would their intimate experiences together draw them back to each other in ways with which Sam couldn't compete?

And shouldn't have to. His chin tightened. He loosened his shoulders and sighed. Catherine's accusations were fraught with questions and lies. His gaze zoomed back in on the couple by the window. Her gentle smile, his blatant adoration, and Sam's stomach knotted all over again.

Michael saw him first, his grin spreading wide with welcome. "Was your trip to Roth Hall successful, friend?"

Friend? Yes, he was renewing his friendship, not trying to find another reason to fan suspicion. "A little. I secured two afternoons a week from her."

Ashleigh's brow crinkled. "You talked to Catherine about helping here?"

He forced himself to keep his mind focused on her face, but his thoughts spun in worry. Did she freely give herself to Michael or did he take what he wanted from her? The secret she harbored on the *Lusitania* certainly haunted her. Was she sorry? Did she enjoy being with Michael, gasping to his kisses?

Sam clenched the thoughts to a stop and hoped he smiled. "It took some convincing, but I think she means it."

Ashleigh tilted her head with her grin. "Did you have to resort to blackmail, jealousy, or charm?"

"Come on, Ashleigh, you don't think Sam has that much charm, do you?" Michael laughed, and then grabbed at his side to brace the movement against his fractured ribs.

Ashleigh's gaze never left Sam's, and the light in her eyes brightened with affection. "I'm certain he does."

Catherine had to be wrong. Maybe he could let the doubt go. Pretend Catherine never said anything. Close the thoughts away with a myriad of other memories from his mother. His blood ran cold. *His mother.* The woman who thought she would woo her way back into his father's life. Ashleigh wasn't like her. She truly cared for him. He could see it in her eyes, but what if, over time, her connection with Michael overrode her feelings for him? If she went back to her first love because of the draw of that physical connection?

"Are you well, Sam?" Ashleigh stepped forward, studying his face from forehead to chin. "You seem concerned."

Her honest perusal gave no hint of anything but care. How could he even suggest Catherine's words to her? "Conversations with your sister have a tendency to be challenging."

"No doubt." Michael closed his eyes and leaned his head back on the headrest of the chair. "I'm exhausted just thinking about it."

Ashleigh knew him too well to take the bait of distraction. "Would you help me bring lunch in for Stephen? Kara had to go shop for more supplies."

He looked beyond Ashleigh to Michael, searching the room for a reason to stay behind, but she caught him. She nudged him as she passed on her way to the door. "I could use your assistance, Mr. Miller."

"Of course." He braced himself as he followed her into the hall.

She'd pick it out of him with the pain and prodding of an operation, no doubt. He rubbed his hands against his thighs to quell the sweating. What could he say or do? Her past may have been in the past, but it impacted her future – their future. He cast a look back over his shoulder where Michael rested. He'd take care of her much better now – and she loved Stephen like he was her own already.

Blast! He didn't want to even consider it.

She led him into the small dining room nestled at the farthest end of the hall from the bedrooms and listening ears. Yes, she knew something wrong. Smart and beautiful.

Closing the door behind him, she turned, crossed her

arms, and stared up at him. "Whenever you're ready."

Maybe he could get out of it, or distract her? "I received a letter from Father before I came here. It's about my mother."

She stepped forward, her palm on his arm to comfort. "Is your father all right?"

Sam ran his palms down her arms, relaxing his tense face. "He's fine, for now." His smile tightened at the thought of his mother. "My mother arrived in Millington about six weeks ago."

"Your mother?" Ashleigh's mouth dropped open. "Why?"

Sam turned to pace the room. "Evidently she was concerned for my welfare when she received news of the *Lusitania*." He looked to Ashleigh, bitterness a sour taste. "Or so she says. It seems she was only trying to find an excuse to win over Father."

Ashleigh released a slow breath and shook her head. "What a shock. I'm so sorry, Sam." She approached him, her touch stopping his movement. "Is there something else?"

He drew in a shaky breath at her touch, trying to fight against the doubt nudging a kink wider. "I need to see Father. I plan to leave this afternoon."

His gaze flickered to hers and away. Silence deepened the uncertainty.

"What else is wrong, Sam?"

Her sweet voice pierced his conscience. He slid his gaze to hers and attempted a shrug. "Conversations with Catherine haven't been pleasant lately, that's all. She had a lot of things to say I didn't like hearing."

Her brows rose, but she didn't step back, only lowered her hands to his chest. "You'd best get it out in the open so we can disperse all doubt, or it will be between us. And I don't want anything between us."

Her words pricked at his concern, gaze focused on hers. "Neither do I. Ever." He tried to curb his doubt with a caress to her cheek. "Catherine seems to think she knows why Michael left you – even the reason for your private discussion aboard the *Lusitania.*"

Ashleigh's breath caught. Her face paled. "What?"

Her reaction fueled his apprehension. "She talked about certain...instances in your past that...influenced Michael's decisions." Heat rose into his face. "Instances of an extremely intimate nature."

She stumbled back from his touch and balanced her hand against a nearby chair. "How did she know?" Ashleigh's whispered word secured the worst truth.

Catherine hadn't been lying.

He shook his head to clear it of the vision his brain immediately concocted of her and Michael together...intimately. It couldn't be true. Not Ashleigh. "It can't be true." The words wrenched from him. He paused, trying to sort it out. "That you've been...In your past you've...you're..."

"Not as pure as a woman should be for her husband?"

Her declaration hit him like a fist. "It's true?" He slammed his palm against his chest and retreated another step. "Why didn't you tell me?"

Sorrow so tangible he could feel it in his heart softened her gaze. A jagged veil of self-control kept him from trying to comfort her as he always had. How could he move beyond this? Michael was here. Alive. And she'd *been* with him.

"I was trying to find the courage. I should have, but it's not an easy conversation."

"I can imagine." His jaw worked, tightened. Catherine's phrase burned into his conscience. *She might be a better pretender than me.* Fooled by Ashleigh too? It can't be. "Did you plan to tell me before...before it was too late? Before I'd have a chance to choose whether I wanted those visions in my mind at night with you or not?"

She winced at his words and an added slice of pain coursed through him. He hurt for her, he hurt for him...he ached for them, and the future he couldn't even see anymore. It was too much to process at once. Too much to try and sort out between his mind and his heart.

Her lips wobbled, steadied, and the China doll emerged. "No one should have those visions in their heads. I would have told you."

The bond between them weakened with the light in her eyes, and a fire of anger burst through his veins. His emotions had been stretched from one side of the Atlantic to the other, by two sisters? Who could he trust right now? One lied to him so he'd stay with her, the other kept the truth from him for the same reason? Two sides of the same coin-- and both proving he was an idiot.

The doubt in his gaze seared worse than his words. He'd never doubted her. The link between them split wide a knee-weakening wound. She gripped the nearby chair. "I'm sorry you found out this way."

"I'm not sure there is an easy way." His gaze found hers, intense, almost...angry? Oh yes, blue steel. She'd lost him. Tears burned for release, but she kept a paper-hold on them. "Wait, is that what you meant by your home being a houseful of actors? Everyone pretending?"

Her spine stiffened. "I never pretended."

"Are you sure about that? You always seemed so innocent and pure."

Her sigh made a jagged release as she kept her gaze from the betrayal in his eyes. A hollow cavern of need and hurt opened wide in her soul. "I tried to tell you in the garden, but you'd learned of Kara's past and—"

"So that's why you took her on? To justify your past?"

Her gaze shot to his, fury and pain lighting a fuse. "I don't have to justify my past to you, Sam. It's beyond words for justification. You have no idea." Her voice broke on the words and she took a deep breath to continue. "But I do believe in second chances and…forgiveness." The admission rocked her spirit with acute truth.

"You just admitted to it and you're implying that I'm being harsh? Friends share secrets with each other, Ashleigh, especially when marriage might have been in the future."

His statement closed off her last sliver of hope. Words, feelings, emotions all crashed together with the same massive loss as watching the *Lusitania* sink beneath the waves. "I have never lied or misled you. I only hoped for more understanding from you, as my friend."

"More understanding?" He shoved a hand through his hair then slammed that palm against the wall. "I can't understand it, Ashleigh." His gaze scoured her. "You led me to believe… I thought…"

"I'm sorry, Sam. You've made your judgments." She drew in a quivering breath, the tears breaking through her resolve, as Sam's love had done. "And I am found wanting."

He stiffened, his expression twisted with an inward struggle. If his soul ached anything like hers, if their friendship had meant anything to him, then his pride and his heart battled a fierce operation. His love wasn't enough to overlook what her father broke apart. How could she have been so blind to believe it possible?

"I can't stay here." His words caught and he moved toward the door, stumbling. "Catherine tried to emotionally manipulate me, but I never thought you would stoop to such a level." He had the decency to look sorry for his previous statement, but continued to back away, palms raised. "I don't know what to do about this. I can't even think straight. It's changed everything. "

Tears rushed warm down her face, unchecked. Every piece of her well-honed protection shattered from his rejection. Hope's fragile thread sliced free. "Yes, it has. I'm so sorry, it has."

He stumbled into the doorway, bracing a hand to the frame, his expression faltering between hard and helpless. "My father needs me." He swallowed, a sheen of moisture glistening in his gaze. "And I can't... I don't know..."

"Godspeed, Sam." She would say it so he wouldn't have to. *Good-bye. Farewell. As you take my heart with you.*

His gaze locked with hers, time froze a picture, neither able to change the truth wedged between them. "Ash?"

His jaw pinched tight and he rushed from the room, the door slamming behind him. Her knees buckled. She collapsed to the floor, covering her face and crying out for an answer. *God, where are you?*

Chapter Twenty-four

"Whoa there, friend." Jessica stilled Ashleigh's arm as she jerked some scissors from her surgical tray. "Do you want to talk about which Hun you're fighting today?"

Ashleigh sighed in frustration. Nursing added a welcome distraction for the last forty-eight hours where she hid her pain in helping others. The distraction worked in the past, all through her training and even in the care of her father, but now – it wasn't enough. Once the tears started, they broke free. Keeping away from Fanny's watchful gaze proved beneficial, but working alongside Jessica made pretense impossible. She couldn't maintain the façade.

"I'm tired. It's been a long two days."

Jessica pried the scissors from Ashleigh's hands and then pointed them at her. "Well, if you work through breaks and rarely sleep, *Nurse* Ashleigh, it's a common physical side effect."

Ashleigh stared at a scalpel newly washed, unable to reply.

"Right." Jess' lips pierced closed and she nodded, the scissors tapping against the surgical tray in an annoying rhythm. Thankfully, she tossed them down and grabbed Ashleigh by the arm, nearly dragging her from the room.

"I have surgery in fifteen minutes, Jessica."

"All the more reason to share your troubling thoughts before you remove some poor man's wrong leg."

Ashleigh looked at her, horrified.

'Oh, good. I got your attention." Jess's cocky grin bloomed. "And distracted you." She pushed Ashleigh into the storage closet across from surgery, and slammed the door behind them.

"Are you senseless?"

"We've already established my mental health issues." Jess flipped on the dim electric light and crossed her arms over her chest. "Now it's time to talk about yours."

Ashleigh tried to push past her, but Jessica blocked her way. "Nope, I won't let you wallow in your own trouble without healthy redirection. You're not getting out of this closet until you share. I'm only here for four more days, Ash. It's more than missing Sam." Her gaze softened. "Let me help carry this burden with you."

Jessica's open arms broke Ashleigh's tenuous hold on her tears. Ashleigh walked into her hug and held tight, shaking with a fresh wave of deep sobs.

As weeping subsided, Ashleigh heard Jessica's whispered words. *A prayer.*

"Dear heavenly Father, I don't know what weight presses upon my friend, but I am certain of your love for her."

Abide with Me. The still, soft voice reminded her and a sudden realization saturated Jessica's uniform with more tears. Ashleigh wasn't sure if she'd expected lights from Heaven or a crash of thunder to prove God was with her, but in the subtle sweetness of Jessica's care, she felt Him. As real and warm as the arms holding her, His presence pushed against the hurt and fear, until it consumed her with blinding truth.

I am with you.

His words from a childhood memory poured like salve over her wounds, filling them with a mixture of assurance and peace. Jessica's hands suddenly became the hands of God, bringing comfort. Was that how He worked? People throughout her life showing His fingerprints?

Grandmama's continual wisdom and peace. Fanny's guidance and convicting nudge to make her see beyond her pain? Jessica's friendship? Michael's reformation?

Tears of hope and gratitude mingled with the harsh sting of loss. Ashleigh took a deep breath and stepped back, and through her broken voice she told Jessica what had happened, her entire past.

Jessica ran a hand across her face and released pent up air. "Oh, Ash." She shook her head and pulled Ashleigh back into her arms. "I am so sorry."

Ashleigh nodded against Jessica's shoulder. "I never prepared myself for the hurt." A sob shuddered over her shoulders. "Or the loss."

"It's betrayal." Jessica bit down on the words, teeth clenched and brows pinched. "I just can't believe Sam responded this way."

"Can you imagine the images in his head?" Ashleigh cringed and pressed a palm to her queasy stomach. "Oh, what he must have thought of me! The look in his eyes—"

"Something feels wrong about his response, though." Jessica raised a palm. "Are you certain Sam knew about all this? He may be hard-headed, but he isn't unreasonable or compassionless."

"This goes well beyond his head. I've broken his heart." Ashleigh's voice hitched again and she wiped at a new rain of tears.

Jessica shook her golden head again and grimaced. "Even if it made him cringe, your friendship alone should have shook out some comfort. He can't be as heartless as that. *No one* could see this as your fault, especially him. Something isn't right here."

"What do you mean? He spoke of my past. And the look on his face showed utter mistrust. He spoke of Father—" Ashleigh stopped, gaze darting to Jess'. "He never mentioned Father, but it was implied."

Jessica's lifted brow contested her diagnosis of the

problem.

Ashleigh stepped back, replaying the conversation in her mind. "To what else could he have referred? It is the only logical answer."

Jessica's expression turned pointed. "Ashleigh, we're talking about a man here. Logic has very little to do with it."

Ashleigh almost smiled. "I have no doubt of Sam's manhood." A fresh rush of warmth at the thought of his kiss nearly choked her words. "But who could stomach the picture I presented to him? I cannot blame him for his reaction, I hoped for something different."

"You're being much too nice to him." Jessica crossed her arms again, eyes narrowing. "Don't you dare take responsibility for his reaction. Your father's choices were sick. Sam's decision was wrong, and you are not a victim unless you choose to act like one." She sighed and raised a pointed finger. "Let's find some answers once and for all."

Jessica's words, no, more like commands, brought strength to Ashleigh's spine and a little lift to her smile.

"We need to discover exactly what Sam knew so I can decide whether to perform a lobotomy on him or not."

Ashleigh shook her head but welcomed the smile. "I think that might be a bit extreme."

Jessica waved away her words. "You're right. His behavior is indicative of a previous lobotomy, poor man." Jess's gaze shot Ashleigh a challenge. "There's only one other person in England who knows what happened in that conversation."

"Catherine."

Jess' lips pinched and she tucked her chin in a nod. "I think you and I just switched our break times. I'll take the surgery. You take Catherine." She opened the closet door and stepped out, tossing a look over her shoulder.

"Needless to say, my work will probably be less painful and more productive than yours."

Catherine sat in the garden, her gown the oriental style and embroidered in purple and gold. She appeared as an exotic and intriguing fixture among the rainbow foliage of summer, almost approachable and sweet, but Ashleigh knew the truth. Every conversation and scene of their relationship for the past fifteen years was tinged with the heat of Catherine's hatred. It was a disease without etiology. A wound with no cause.

Or no known cause.

Catherine looked up from her musings, the cloud-cloaked sunlight highlighting her pale face. She didn't look well, but her feline smile curled for battle nonetheless.

"So you've come for a visit, sister dear?"

Ashleigh had wondered if Catherine guarded the same hideous secret, too afraid Catherine might one day turn her knowledge into a weapon. As she had. Instead of weakening her resolve with shame, the thought fueled new energy and defense. Fanny's words clicked into place. It was time to reclaim one part of her future. *Herself.*

"We need to talk."

A faux look of surprise dawned on her face, eyes glittering. "Our discussion wouldn't have anything to do with Sam's stealthy escape from our home yesterday morning, would it?" She rested her chin in her hand on the decorative table in front of her, adding another flutter of eyelashes.

"I have only come for answers, not an argument." Ashleigh's hands clamped in front of her and a firm fire of determination forged each step closer. "What exactly did you share with Sam?"

Catherine leaned against the bench and rested an arm

leisurely along the back of it. The very portrait of a modern woman, without the popular bobbed hair. Her broad brimmed white hat in stark contrast to her raven hair tilted at a fashionable angle and shadowed the right part of her face. A smirk surfaced in that shadow. "You're always spouting off about my need to be honest and forthright. To shun deception." She ran a finger down the right side brim of her hat. "I was merely following your moral platitudes. I would think you'd be proud of me."

Heat curled a fiery tangle in her stomach. "Since you're suddenly on a path towards righteousness, let us clear the air, shall we? Why do you hate me so much?"

"Honesty? Is that what you really want?" Catherine laughed and stood, slow and deliberately, her gaze never leaving Ashleigh's. "You're a clever girl, I'm certain you can sort it out." She walked a circle, a she-cat on the prowl. "All it took was perfect timing, a dash of patience, a lifelong desire to see you rejected by someone you love...in the same manner Father rejected me."

Ashleigh spun to face her. "*Your* rejection?"

Catherine stepped close, sapphire eyes aflame. "Don't pretend you understand my pain or are ignorant to it." Her brow rose, pleasure humming in her words. "Your intimate relationship with Michael provided the perfect picture to Sam of what you really are. You call me a pretender? Were you hoping Sam would never find out about your loss of virtue to your fiancé? Michael's arrival couldn't have been more opportune."

Clarity stung revelation into full view. Thin breaths barely gave oxygen. "Michael?" Ashleigh slid her fingertips across her forehead in a vain attempt to gather understanding. "You told Sam that I had been intimate with Michael?" Ashleigh replayed their conversation again. No mention of her father. The 'visions' he abhorred were thoughts of her and Michael together – especially as she was taking care of his friend? *Oh, Sam.*

"Does the truth sting?"

A lifetime of answers clinked into place. Sam's vehement response. Catherine's long-standing hatred? Her dogged determination to save the family 'name' no matter the cost. "You think Father rejected you?" The words crawled out of her with slow comprehension. "Because of me?"

A frost of tears brimmed in Catherine's eyes. "You stole all of his affection. He spent secret time with only you, bought you special gifts, called you his 'little darling'." She spat out the endearment. "He loved you best and left nothing for the rest of us. No matter how hard I tried to prove myself, to break your bond, he always found you. Even to his dying breath, he called for you at the end. Not me, or mother – but you."

Ashleigh closed her eyes with a sigh. A boulder of misconceptions forged from years of bitterness rolled from her heart. And a brief wave of relief breathed out along with clarity. Catherine had never been contaminated. Her gaze met her sister's. Or not in the same way Ashleigh had. Hatred from a lie had twisted her perceptions and robbed them of their sisterhood, but she'd never known the hateful scorch of his lusts. "I wouldn't wish for our father's brand of affection if I were you. What he took from me can't be repaid by any number of gifts or time."

"There you go, trying to lessen the blow of his rejection. How could you know what it felt like to have your own father prefer one child over another, and me the eldest?" She pointed her finger. "I've tried everything to prove my devotion to this family, sought a connection with one of the richest men of our sphere to save our reputation, even given up my…" Her voice caught, but she snarled through it. "And you try to placate me with an ominous excuse?"

"Let me explain what Father's definition of care looked like, then you can decide whether your jealousy and hatred has been worth the cost." Ashleigh lowered her hands to her sides, gaze unswerving. "Michael didn't take my virtue. I've never *given* myself to any man. This idea you've fashioned about our father? This notion you've nursed into a burning hatred is built on a sham."

Catherine's smile coiled to a snarl. "I know what I saw, what I experienced."

She had no idea of the nightmare fingering through the shadows of their house, the specter she was about to unearth. Ashleigh's scars took the form of their father's physical betrayal, his duplicity a sick fragrance in the air of her childhood, but Catherine held scars too.

Betrayal scarred Ashleigh. Rejection marked Catherine. Oh, the tangled web her father spun for them all.

"Let me remind you of what you saw." Ashleigh's kept her voice soft, the truth's pain clear enough without the added harshness of volume. "I was eight. You were eleven. I walked in on you and father in the library right after the dinner meal."

The fury in Catherine's eyes merged with confusion and as the memory awakened, fear paled her face. Her lips shaped into an 'o', as if to say something, but no words formed. Her usual verbal fight fled with a sudden rush of air. A swell of compassion drew Ashleigh closer. She knew the memories she'd extracted–memories buried under years of denial and hate. *Please, God, let it have only been me.*

"I came into the room and Father had you in a corner."

Catherine's sharp intake of breath paused Ashleigh's

words a moment.

"I pulled him away from you and asked him to come fix a puzzle Scott had broken. Do you remember?"

Her wide-eyed horror answered with vivid clarity, she stumbled back onto the bench.

"As I look back on it now, with years and painful experience as my measure, I recognize his intentions for you, but as an eight-year-old, his hovering against you and his brusque command to leave held no meaning. I simply wanted his help and in asking for it, I took your place of his misplaced and…" Ashleigh shivered. "Horrible passions."

"I…I can't—" Catherine pressed her hand to her stomach and focused on some unseen image ahead of her.

"It was the same time Father's financial choices began to shadow our family." Ashleigh released a long breath, tears gathering a knot in her throat. "Hindsight brings all sorts of clarity. At the time, Mother rejected him, shutting herself away for weeks. And somehow in the middle of his despair he turned to a more base release for his frustrations."

"He…he wouldn't." Catherine blinked, the battle for understanding, for comprehension of something so depraved a difficulty for anyone, let alone a daughter of her father.

"His sickness arose in his most desperate time. Isn't that when our true nature shines? In our greatest helplessness? Father found a child who had no idea what evil she'd uncovered with the simple request for help and attention. What he'd intended for you, he turned onto me."

"You have to be lying," Catherine whispered, her fingers clawing the arm of the chair. "What you are implying…what you are saying…"

"I know it's difficult to believe. I wish it wasn't true. Oh, how I wish it wasn't true." Ashleigh lowered to the bench beside her, but Catherine pulled away, a frightened child surfacing into adulthood. Somehow, seeing the shared wounds weaved a fragile bridge of connection with her sister she'd never known. Her false assumptions, her injured heart, stemmed from a lie which evolved into her hatred and even her obsessive need for attention. "Catherine, think about our childhood. How often did you find me weeping? Or hiding? Or seeking places to withdraw from the rest of the family when he was present?"

She shook her head, lashes fluttering with pinpoints of tears. "You wanted to make Father look for you. It was your way of getting his attention. It can't be—"

"My prayer for you..." Ashleigh almost reached to touch Catherine's arm, but placed her hands in her lap instead. "...for us, is that we'll see our past for what it truly is. That you will push aside your anger long enough to recognize I'm not your enemy or your competition. I never have been."

Catherine stared at her, eyes red-rimmed and haunted. She clutched the top of her blouse in a fist. "How long?" Words squeaked from her. "*If* this story is true, how long did it last?"

Ashleigh stood, exhausted from the effort to control her emotions, to defend her actions. "Eight years, until I was old enough to fight him back and win."

Catherine gaze distanced into a memory. "The cut on his cheek?"

Ashleigh nodded, truth burning a painful path from the lines on Catherine's perfect brow. "I fought him and broke a mirror in my room. With one of the shards—"

"You stopped him." Catherine looked up. Her breaths pumped shallow.

"He never touched me again."

Catherine's expression pearled to vacant. This news

277

redefined her world, her anger, and would take time to process. Maybe months or years. But could God use this horrible mess to restore a long-lost relationship?

The conversation, an autopsy of her past, left Ashleigh internally beaten and bruised. The newfound sense of God's presence comforted the ache of Sam's absence and poured an overshadowing of grace against her undercurrent of pain. Severing him from her life left an internal bleeding of regret and loneliness she'd never imagined, and an ever deeper need for her Heavenly Father than she'd ever known. *God, please replace this emptiness with You – and be enough for me...* She glanced back at Catherine. *And my sister.*

Chapter Twenty-five

"If you walked into the hospital right now not one soldier would recognize you."

Ashleigh stood by the doorway with Jessica, her pale green travel dress a direct contrast to their usual gray-blue nurse's gowns. And her typical white nurse's cap did little to bring out the jade in her eyes as much as the green, broad-brimmed hat she wore for her train ride to Liverpool.

Jess grinned and touched the tip of her hat. "Until I open my mouth and set one of them back on the straight and narrow. Then they'll know exactly who I am." A frown pulled at her brow. "I hate to leave you here with the bulk of this responsibility. When is Louisa supposed to arrive?"

"Next week." Ashleigh refused to ponder Jessica's absence. On the heels of Sam leaving, the realization nearly broke her heart all over again. "I believe David mentioned Tuesday."

"Tuesday it is." David nodded as he walked up to his sister and gave her a peck on the cheek. "I had to wish safe travels once more." His normally calm voice held the slightest shake. "I can be home in less than two weeks if necessary."

Jessica's expression firmed with the look in her eyes, strong. "I will send a wire. From the progression so far, I'm expecting three months, perhaps, if God allows." She cleared her throat. "I'd be perfectly content with a good, old-fashioned miracle too."

David's palm glazed Jessica's shoulder in a gentle sweep, the look on his face conveyed more feeling than Ashleigh had ever witnessed in him. His green eyes focused. A powerful intensity, magnetic and energetic all at once, created a fascinating play on the chiseled lines of his face. His usual serenity fell away in contrast to a potency of emotion equal to Jessica's unending boasts. Breath stealing.

"I love you." He cupped both of her shoulders. "And will pray for you every day."

The earnestness in each syllable reverberated to Ashleigh. Underneath his calm demeanor beat a passionate heart. Jessica's zeal burst out of her on a regular basis in her dry wit and furious work ethic, but David's simmered beneath the surface, rising when necessary. Would Ashleigh's faith, her passion, grow to be like theirs?

He gave Jess' shoulders a squeeze. "Whether His miracle is of this world or the next, let me know when you need me. I will do all I can."

Jessica took his face in her hands, kissing his cheek. "Be careful."

David nodded, his expression returning to its usual calm, except for a residual spark in his eyes. "And you." He turned, passed a gentle smile to Ashleigh, and disappeared into the front room.

Jess turned a watery gaze on her, smile hitched in pixie-style. "Are you sure you want to spend your time convincing Sam when such an impressive, not to mention handsome, man walks the halls of this hospital as single as a solo?"

Ashleigh's smile fought against her heartache, and won. "Tempting, but my heart is holding out for a more stubborn fellow, I'm afraid."

Jessica's brows shot high. "Oh, don't let David fool you. He's as stubborn as Grandma Dougall's posture." Her wink tickled another grin. "But in matters of the heart, I think *you* might be the champ."

Ashleigh worried her lip. "I'm praying for…a miracle.

For you, and me."

Jessica angled her head in challenge. "When I arrive in Asheville, do you want me to find him and slap him? I'd gladly oblige."

Ashleigh shook her head and laughed. "I think it's time for me to sort out what God wants for me. If it's Sam?" She swallowed down a lump of fear. "Then I wouldn't complain, but he needs to know the truth, and then make his decision free of any reservation."

She placed an envelope in Jess' hand, reluctant to release it.

Jess raised her brow.

"If you have opportunity, would you give this to Sam? It…it explains everything."

Jessica pulled the envelope free and pointed it at Ashleigh. "It's the one way to clear all doubt."

"Exactly." Ashleigh threw her arms around her friend's shoulders and barely stayed her tearful appreciation. "I love you."

Jess sighed into the hug. "I can't promise I won't try to slap some sense into him too." She drew back enough to prove her sincerity with a pointed look. "Literally."

A few tears spilled over. "If it would work."

"If it doesn't, you don't need him anyway." She lowered her voice to a whisper. "And I have a very eligible brother who would make a fantastic alternative."

Ashleigh took Jessica back into her arms. "I am going to miss you beyond words. You can never know how much I love you."

"Oh yes, I can." Jess hugged back. "The next time I really need you, I'll find out."

Sam's conscience ate a hole into his well-coaxed anger all the way across the Atlantic. Lies by omission were just as wrong as deception, right? Ashleigh's deceit was as contemptible as his mother's or Catherine's, wasn't it? Memories from his time with Ashleigh aboard the *Lusitania* resurfaced and plunged him into more doubt. She'd loved him, hadn't she? He'd known no greater friend, not even in Michael. Every selfless act she'd offered, every tender word? She'd attempted to keep him at bay, he'd seen it.

What could it all mean? How could he move forward with the knowledge of her intimacy with Michael?

He groaned, tired of sleepless nights, tossing between prayers and anger. And sun-soaked days aboard the *Saxonia* filled with Scott's clear admiration of his sister. He didn't want to hear about Ashleigh's virtues. He wanted to let the anger seethe and harden against the pain knifing through his chest at her absence.

And then there was guilt. He should have gone back to her. Ten years of friendship deserved an explanation, if nothing else. He squeezed his will against the compassion. Wasn't she just like his mother, though? Whether the need had been to use him to make another man jealous, or keep the truth hidden so she wouldn't have to feel the sting of rejection, it all came down to one thing. Self-seeking deception.

Maybe getting back to work in the furniture shop was exactly what he needed. His father's quiet life. The consistent reward of hard work. And a long walk into the mountains. He groaned. No, the emptiness in his chest had an Ashleigh-shape to it no one or nothing else could fill.

After taking Scott to Grandmama Dougall's home, Sam directed the hired car up the road to his. His father's occasional mention of letters only triggered more anger. His mother's betrayal burned with more raw emotion since England. If he remembered correctly, her husband had died some years back, evidently freeing her to come seduce his father. Heat rifled a fresh wave up his spine. He would not let her hurt his father again.

Before the motorcar puttered to a stop, Sam had the door open, foot dragging the dusty drive. He jumped from the seat, grabbed his luggage, tipped the driver, and left his trunk where it fell. His father was probably exhausted from having to put up with her presence. Surely he couldn't have meant the words in his letter. A second chance? Not for her.

A sweet sound of a woman's laughter drifted with the scent of dogwoods on the warm summer breeze. It came from the other side of the house, where the old rock wall wrestled ivy and rose bushes to frame a little garden. Everyone who knew his family called it Abram's Garden, because of his faithful tending. Not even Biltmore, with its architecturally designed grounds compared to the simple beauty of his father's garden. Rose scent emerged as he rounded the corner of the house.

A chink in the stone wall gave him a small lens to view the occupants. Sitting on a bench *he* built, his father entertained a woman, face turned away from his view. Her hair shone the color of oak-finish, the same hue as his own, and knotted at the back of her head. His mind fought the recognition his heart made. His father was a reasonable man. Not prone to sudden emotional decisions – especially with a woman who threw commitment out with the slap of a year-long affair.

The look on his father's face brought Sam's hurried steps to a stop. *Pleasure.* He hadn't seen a look of such joy on his father's face in years. The image should have heartened his own happiness, but for the woman who influenced it. *Unbelievable.* He would *not* see his father wounded again.

The woman turned her face toward him, then, eyes

sparkling in mid-laughter, and he tensed all over. Time had placed lines around her eyes, but she appeared unscathed otherwise. Probably even considered attractive by some. And just like Catherine, she was using her beauty to railroad a good man.

Rosellyn Miller returned without one scar, but he'd be sure to remind her of the ones she left behind.

He released a rush of air through his nose and pushed his way through the garden door. Both faces looked up as the door crashed open. Father stood and stepped forward, arms open and eyes wide. "Ah, you've arrived." He grabbed him so firmly it distracted Sam from his anger for a second. "I'm so glad you are safe."

Rosellyn came to a slow stand, her hands twisting in and around each other. Was she plotting how she'd sway Sam like she'd obviously done to Father? Well, he'd learned his lesson. He wouldn't be fooled again. Sam stepped out of his father's arms and gestured to Rosellyn.

"What is she doing here?"

Father's smile fixed and he nodded. "It's a long story. Would you like to sit as we explain?"

"We?" Sam stared at Rosellyn, who had the fake decency to glance down. "There is nothing I need to hear from her."

"Sam." His father's tone held a slight reprimand. Sam's anger rebelled against it. "As justified as your feelings are, she is my guest and will therefore be treated with respect."

Air burst from Sam's lungs in shock. Respect? How could father bear to look at her, let alone *laugh* with her in the garden? He looked from his father to Rosellyn and back, his pulse pumping a rapid drumbeat in his ears. "Then I will come back later, when I won't be a threat to your *guest*, because there is no way I can show respect to someone who betrayed her family and then abandoned them."

"Samuel Miller, you will not—"

"Abram." Rosellyn's soft interruption stilled his father's rebuke. "He is right. I've done nothing to earn his respect, only his hatred." She picked up her parasol from the bench and walked toward the house. "You've had more time to adjust. I believe your conversation would be best suited without my presence. This is Sam's home, not mine, and he should feel the freedom to speak however he needs." She passed by him, her gaze flickered to his, a flash of gold, her voice almost...gentle? He tensed at the thought. Catherine's had been too.

She disappeared through the garden gate, a cane at her left barely noticeable but for the awkward limp. Sam released the breath he was holding, and the vice grip on his bag. His case fell with a quiet thud to the earth.

Father stared at the closed garden gate for a moment and then turned back to the table set with sandwiches. He'd entertained her, and from the look in his eyes, he had...feelings for her. Sam's stomach revolted. How could he? Well, Sam had a few feelings for her too, but they involved more of her leaving than staying. Was it a curse that smart men were idiots around beautiful women? He certainly felt its truth, all the way to his broken and confused heart.

"Would you like to sit down?" His father's words jarred Sam back to attention. He followed his father's gesture to one of the rod-iron chairs around the table. "I can imagine you're hungry after your trip."

"What is going on here, Father? I leave for twelve weeks and come back to find my mother courting you in the back garden? If I recall, we never wanted to see her again."

"*You* never wished to see her again, Sam. A sentiment I shared with you for a while, until God healed my heart, as I pray He'll do for you. Things have changed and—"

"Yes, it is clear things had changed."

"And I think you need to hear the entire story. I'm not expecting you to like it. I'm only asking you to listen." His father's expression commanded attention. "And then pray about the appropriate response."

"Appropriate response? Given her treatment of us, I think my response was well above appropriate. Since when has she deserved anything better?"

His father's gaze drilled into him. "Since God is her judge and not you."

His father's intensity shocked Sam to silence. Few instances rattled his father's calm, and his adamant defense of Rosellyn Miller seemed wrong. Illogical. Yet his father was a good, solid, smart man. Methodical yet compassionate. Perhaps too compassionate? A genetic trait passed down to Sam, evidently.

Father ushered Sam to a chair. "You know I love you. You have been my focus and the biggest part of my life for over fourteen years. We've comforted and encouraged each other through many things, as we will continue to do." He offered a small smile, as if reading Sam's doubts. "I've not been swayed by any of her feminine charm. She didn't come here for a relationship. She came here for you."

"Me?" Sam laughed. "I can't believe that. If she'd cared anything about me, she wouldn't have--"

"That was a long time ago – and nearly a lifetime of change has happened to her since then. Your anger froze at fourteen years old and has never moved or softened, though situations, time, and circumstances have. What your mother did was wrong. She will admit it fully and with great regret, but if you look a little deeper, you'll see she's

286

not the same person."

"I don't want to look deeper." Sam crashed down into the chair with a moan. "I don't want to see her at all."

"I've had four weeks to get used to her presence, but I understand your bitterness. When she first arrived on my doorstep, I didn't want to talk to her. The letters we'd shared at a safe distance from my pain had given me a small hint into her harsh life in Chicago."

"I'm certain her stories were heart-wrenching." Sam's words tasted of sarcasm.

"She was forced to see her choices and suffer the consequences. She needed forgiveness. As sure as a sick person needs medicine, she needed forgiveness."

Sam nursed his pride, inflaming his bitterness a little. "Forgiving her doesn't mean renewing a relationship."

"Not completely. And we are a far cry from rekindling our relationship. It's like meeting a new person." His gaze focused on some distant scene. "The first two years after she left, I hated her. After a sermon particularly bent at forgiveness, I started praying God would help me pray for her. Then my prayers became less anger-driven and more sincere. When her first letter arrived last year, it was clear she wasn't the same woman I once knew. I had no intention of being with her, but when she arrived...slowly God opened my heart to her. As I wrote to you, she'd become the woman I'd always prayed she would be."

"Couldn't she have sought your forgiveness in a letter? Why did she have to come all the way over here to see you face to face? Money?"

"The Lusitania initiated her visit, but my forgiveness encouraged her to remain." His father sat next to him and tilted his head, considering the accusation. "I thought about money at first too, but the truth is her husband did one good thing for her. He left her with a considerable fortune upon

287

his death for the care of their son, Clark."

Sam leaned forward, his curiosity perking a little. "She has other sons?"

"Not anymore. Clark died three years ago trying to save his little sister's life. Only a year after his father passed on."

Sam rubbed his chin, digesting the information, trying to remain indifferent.

His father continued. "Mr. McCoy was a violent man who took out his anger in small and large degrees on your mother. She lost three babes before they were born because of his hard hands and subsequently broke her hip." He gestured toward the way she'd disappeared. "Which is why she uses a cane."

Sam braced himself against the grief on his father's face. His mother made her choices, as sad as they were. Shouldn't he be glad for her pain to provide some sense of retribution?

The very thought cracked the edge of his resolve. He'd seen children die. All ages, sinking with a massive ship into the frigid Atlantic. The sorrow ingrained on each memory of the *Lusitania* along with the plaintive cries of hundreds and the ominous silence that followed. She'd lost three children at the hands of her husband, and the other one?

Sam closed his eyes and released a long breath. Praying for a hint of his father's calm and reason. "And you think all this is true? That she's not making it up to influence you?"

"She has a few pictures, but I didn't need them. The pain is clear. Fiona confirms it too."

"Fiona?"

"Your sister. She is eleven."

Sam blinked. "My sister?" Comprehension unwound. Of course, if his mother had children, they would be his siblings.

"She's the only one to survive of the five children from your mother's marriage to Mr. McCoy." Father's lips tilted in a small smile. "You will love her, Sam."

Sam placed his head in his hands, thoughts reeling against feelings; assumptions and pain vied for understanding. "I don't know what to think. How can you push away all those wrongs and years of loneliness and bitterness, to let her in?"

"By recognizing I was as much in need of grace as she." Father placed his palm on Sam's knee, a comfort from years of camaraderie. "Do you think my years of hatred, wishing she was dead, were right either? Now to know what wounds she's suffered, and by her own choices, grieves me for her. She doesn't only harbor pain, but guilt too." His stare needled Sam's conscience. "There are so many scars."

Sam stood, his father's gentleness and call for grace rubbing like sandpaper against his wounds. "This is too much, Father." He jabbed a hand through his hair, the throbbing in his head now keeping time with his pulse. Ashleigh came to mind and he ached worse. "Will I have to see her? Talk to her?"

Father lowered his head, braiding his fingers together in front of him. "Only by chance if you wish, but I hope in time you will try, if nothing else for my sake. And Fiona's. She can't wait to meet you."

Sam pinched his eyes against the pain in his head and his father's magnetic pull. He'd do anything for his father...*almost anything*. Reconciling with his mother pushed their relationship to its borders. "I... I need to go for a walk."

"The footpath to the falls might be a good direction. I cleared it off a few weeks ago."

Sam jammed his hands into his pockets and nodded, starting in the direction of the familiar path up the hillside. He swung wide the garden door to leave.

"Sam."

He turned to his father's call.

"I love you, son."

Sam swallowed hard and nodded. He nearly ran from the scene, taking long strides toward the tree line. His chest collapsed with a sob as the burning in his eyes turned into tears. He walked faster, if in an attempt to outrun his anger or sorrow, he wasn't sure. Higher he climbed up the trail, stopping midway to look back over the houses below.

The Blue Mountains framed the horizon, highlighted by the orange haze of sunset. Grandma Dougall's gray Victorian, a classic beauty, nestled among the hillside. He needed to see what Ash thought. Bathe in her friendship and comfor—

Reality broke in. When he'd left England, he'd not only lost his future bride, but his best friend. The pain doubled him over and he crumbled to the ground. *Oh dear God, help me. What am I supposed to do?*

Scenes from his last few days with Ashleigh crowded into his aching skull. Kisses and conversations. Looks and touches. Celebrations and pain. Besides his father, she'd been the closest person to him during the past year, and now?

He couldn't have misread her. The hurt in her eyes when he'd left her at the hospital knifed fresh pain and tears. Extreme stress would have brought out the lie at some point or other, but she remained consistent. Loving him with her actions and words. His chest pinched tight at the thought of her kiss and the vision of her kissing Michael in a more intimate way.

She didn't love Michael. He was certain.

But could he love her even with the knowledge of her past with Michael in his head? Was it truly in the past? His pride hammered a pounding 'no', but his heart, his spirit cried a very different response. He was utterly lost in the madness of all the broken pieces and scars.

If God is nothing else, He is a rescuer of the lost.

Hadn't Ashleigh said that? He closed his eyes to remember. *Everyone needs second chances.* Yes, she'd said that too.

His heart cracked with pain between longing for her and fear of giving up this hardened hate for women like his mother. *Second chances?* He'd tried to do things the right way. Make the right choices. Treat people with respect and honor. But here he was, weeping in the dirt on the side of a mountain, alone.

He looked ahead to the horizon, a masterpiece of orange, yellow, and red hues. No, not alone. Could God make sense of this catastrophe and the blubbering of a confused man? He leaned forward, bracing his elbows on his knees and stared at the fiery sky. There was only one way to find out.

After too long trying to sort things on his own, it was past time to ask the One he'd cried out to for years. Guilt riddled a path to the rest of his emotions. Was that all God was to him? Is that the only time he sought Him, when he couldn't fix things on his own?

His spirit cried an answer to drive the guilt a bit deeper. Something…no Someone needed to rescue him. In the silence of the rustling leaves, surrounded by the sweet scent of dogwood blossoms, Sam opened up his heart and his future to His Father. He was lost – and needed a rescue.

Chapter Twenty-six

Ashleigh rubbed the back of her neck after a long day bent over wounded soldier. Five surgeries and an influx of new wounded kept her working back to back the entire day. She couldn't complain. David worked as hard as all the nurses, barely stopping for a meal. His steady voice and assertive command of stressful situations settled on people, including her. He maintained perfect control, almost too well. His emotions never flared to anything beyond…pleasant.

The workload hadn't slowed since the first soldiers arrived, and a part of Ashleigh was grateful for the distraction. Her heart went out to many of the poor fellows, stuck in thin-mattressed-cots for long days. She'd entertained the notion of visiting Lady Cavanaugh again, if nothing else to tell her of the work of other great ladies who took much better care of the wounded. But at least Lady Cavanaugh had provided sufficient funds for a proper Surgical Theater, instead of operating without appropriate supplies.

And Catherine? Her presence in the hospital over the past week afforded an unusual combination of uncertainty and hope. If guilt spurned her to move among the wounded masses, then it was the best use of guilt Ashleigh had ever seen. On occasion she would catch Catherine watching her, an unreadable expression on her pale face.

They'd barely spoken, unless to assist patients. The worst had already been spoken. Their father was a monster, their childhood laced with lies.

Yet along with the horrible truth came a softening to the relationship with her sister, but what about Sam? God's comfort tended her wounds, but failed to quell the festering ache in her heart. Work helped. The children comforted and distracted her, and seeing Michael taking responsibilities of carpentry to earn his board added a dose of contentment, but her heart longed for Sam. The taste of his love ruined her to the option of anyone else.

She mentally forced God's truths to her mind – an arsenal to combat the ache of her shame, the emptiness of her loss.

Laughter cascaded down the stairwell from above and lured her for a lunch break and visit. Caroline, a seven-year-old girl just arrived from Manchester, held a ball. Her dark hair, cut short from her previous placement, hung round her face in ebony ringlets.

With her tongue clenched between her teeth, she rolled the ball down the hall. Ashleigh hurried to the top of the steps in time to watch the ball knock over three of the five milk cartons lined at the other side. Michael cheered from his place by the cartons, Lance, a five-year-old at his side. Eight-year-old Charles waited for his turn after Caroline, their oldest orphan at ten. Kara sat in a chair by the far window, rocking Edith, Lance's baby sister, both left without family after a London Zeppelin raid.

"Nice, Caroline. You might end up as a professional bowler with rolls like that." Michael's encouragement brought a bright blush to the girl's cheeks. Poor thing knew little of such affection.

"Wonderful shot," Ashleigh added coming among them. "I think you might be a natural."

Caroline's smile widened to reveal some missing teeth. "Thanks, Miss Ashleigh. I'm even better at baseball."

Ashleigh met Michael's gaze and they shared a smile.

"We'll have to plan a showing in the back garden later.

What do you say?"

"I can play too," Charles added.

Ashleigh brought her hands together in a single clap. "Sounds like an excellent plan."

"Miss Ashleigh, might I have a few words with you?" Michael tilted his head toward the small dining room.

Ashleigh led the way into the room and Michael followed, cane in hand. "I didn't want to mention this in front of the children, but I finished the bunker in the side garden."

She nodded and fought a chill at the thought of one of the monstrous airships making its way this far north of London. "It's unlikely the Zeppelins would come to our town, isn't it? We have no prize to offer them."

"I think fear is their prize, and they can encourage it in any town. I'd rather be prepared."

"Of course." She patted his arm. "Thank you for taking care of it. I pray we never have need of it."

He ran a palm over his face and sighed. "Me too." His grin quirked. "Perhaps, after the war, we can dig it out and build a swimming pool. I tried to convince your grandmother to do that in her backyard, do you remember?"

Ashleigh crossed her arms and chuckled at the thought. "You tried to convince Grandmama of quite a few schemes, if I recall. You and Sam kept a ready set of adventures on hand, I believe."

His gaze sobered. "Any news from Sam?

"No, I can't imagine I'd hear anything so quickly. It's only been a few weeks, and with mail as unpredictable as the war, I doubt I'll hear anything soon." She sighed. "If at all."

Michael leaned against the wall, removing extra weight from his weak leg. "He's stronger than I was, Ash.

I was arrogant and prideful. If I'd had an ounce of the awareness I have now, nothing could have kept me from loving you all the days of my life, but it took the *Lusitania* and this--" He gestured to his leg. "--to humble me and show me what really matters. Faith and family."

"You'd have loved me?" She angled a brow at him, the heat of challenge rising into her voice. "Even with my past?"

His gaze never faltered, not even a flinch. "We all have a past." Sadness quieted his voice. "It took losing everything to realize it. God knew how stubborn this head was." He tapped his forehead. "He had to use extreme measures to get through to me."

She smiled, still in awe at the person he was becoming. Strange to feel freedom talking to a man about her past and not suffocating from shame.

Michael leaned closer, tenderness and understanding softening his features. "You're not the person your past whispers to you. That's what the family who rescued me told me. And I have a feeling you've been carrying around your father's disgrace a long time. No matter what you yelled at me on the *Lusitania*." His smile sloped and he touched her arm. "I think it's time you started seeing yourself like I do, or even better, like God does. Not what's been taken from you, but what's been given to you."

"And what is that?" She shifted a brow and glanced around the room. "A leaky building, a hospital full of wounded soldiers, and a friend who lectures me?"

"I was thinking more along the lines of all the things you have here, the beauty and strength." He tapped her chest and then waved to the children in the hallway outside. "And there." His green-hued gaze locked with hers again. "And thank you for calling me your friend."

And he was. Forgiveness was a powerful thing,

dissipating her anger toward him and rekindling a sweet friendship, must sweeter and more genuine than before. Her mind turned to Sam. Would he ever accept her, flawed, bruised and all? She wanted the same freedom with him – to be accepted…loved by the man she loved most in the world.

Hope whispered its song again. She snatched at the melody. Michael's words forced her to listen. How did God see her? Even with her horrible past and the anger she'd harbored towards Him, He loved her – completely. *As she was.*

"Thank you, Michael." She grabbed to the sliver of hope and held tight. "I pray Sam comes to the same realization, without having the inducement of a near-death experience."

Michael nodded. "Me too, Ash. Me too."

Sam stepped from the car and stretched out his back. He'd spent the last week from dawn until dusk at the furniture shop, trying to work out his frustrations and sort out all the insanity of his life. But above all to avoid seeing his mother. It had worked for the most part – only catching glimpses of her as he passed Grandmama Dougall's. She would raise her palm in welcome, expecting nothing, and each time he focused on making it to his home without acknowledging her presence. And his father told him he'd wait until Sam was ready to talk.

As shock and anger tempered to grief, he wasn't sure he'd ever want to talk to his father about it. He'd written to Ashleigh earlier in the week, attempting to bridge the chasm between them. But where would it go from there? Their relationship had shifted like the sea, hadn't it? From friendship to romance to… He groaned. What? He was only certain of one thing. He *missed* her. Her laughter, her camaraderie, her tenderness. Air stuck to his lungs like trying to catch a breath after smelting an iron backing to a chair. He *needed* her.

A movement of white and blue from down the hill caught his eye and brought his feet to a stop. A young girl sped from the back of the house up the hill. She wasn't running directly toward him, but to his right, taking a path to the forest tree line. A few times she glanced behind her, as if she thought someone might be watching her, but otherwise her feet made no attempt at a detour. She bounded forward like an animal of the forest, golden hair trailing in long waves.

Sam's grin started before he could stop it. Was she his little sister? Fiona? He'd imagined a prim and proper little thing, but the golden-haired runaway didn't appear to fit the description. A few times throughout the last week, he'd allowed himself to wonder about her – curiosity tugging him to peek at Grandmama Dougall's house each afternoon to catch a glimpse.

She could be some haughty, spiteful child molded in his mother's image. Letting another person into his heart, especially one of the female variety, took risks. He hesitated a moment and then stepped toward the hill in time to see her start climbing a tree. His grin twitched a little wider. And just maybe he'd get along with her fine.

He strolled down the hill, hands fixed in his pockets and guard up, whistling a tune of his approach. As he neared, he shaded his eyes from the late afternoon sun and looked up. She was waiting, golden-gaze fixed on him. She swung a branch lower, her white tights showing off trim legs and black boots.

She wrinkled up her freckled nose, surveying him. "Are you my brother?"

Sam tilted his head to examine her right back, enjoying

the game. "That depends. Are you Fiona?"

Her eyes lit and she nodded. "You look like me."

He let her words sink a little deeper, and it didn't hurt as badly as he thought it might. "And you are quite the tree climber."

She shrugged, looking to the treetop and back. "I always tried to keep up with my brother, Clark." Her chin turned a proud tilt. "He took care of me, you know. That's what big brothers do."

A sudden protectiveness squeezed Sam's chest. It was a new thought, but not foreign. He'd felt like a big brother to Ashleigh and Scott for a long time, but here was a blood-sister. From the spark in her eyes, she didn't seem in need of protection.

"I see. And what did you plan to do up in the tree?"

Her hair spilled over her shoulders as she stared down at him, a mischievous grin perched on her lips. "I was trying to hide from Mother long enough to sneak up a good tree." She lowered her voice to a whisper. "She's terribly fixed on seeing me refined."

His heart warmed even more to this bright-eyed spirit. He worked up an appropriate grimace. "That sounds awful."

She rolled her golden-hued eyes. "You have no idea how awful. She is determined I shall not fall into sin as she did, but I have tried to explain how climbing trees and fishing have very little to do with sins. I've not heard Father McClay mention one of them from the Bible."

Sam laughed. She reminded him, with all her determination, like another little girl who used to fish and climb trees. A little girl who grew up to steal away his heart. The ache resurrected with full potency.

"Well, as I understand it, some of Jesus' best men liked fishing."

She snapped her fingers, another contradiction to a refined lady. "That's exactly what I told Mother. And there was a short man who climbed a tree. The only reason Jesus told him to climb out of the tree was to go fix supper, not to make him more refined. He changed them all on the inside, where it counts most."

"I believe you have a clear argument."

She studied him a long time. He shifted his feet under her honest, umber gaze. "You don't seem unpleasant at all."

"Unpleasant?"

She nodded, brow crinkled. "You haven't even tried to come meet me yet, and you've been home over a week."

Sam rubbed the heat of embarrassment crawling up the back of his neck. "There isn't a simple explanation."

"You know what." She shimmied down the tree like an experienced tree climber and propped both hands on her little hips. Did girls really start bossiness this young? "You just need to stop being angry with Mother."

Sounded simple when she put it that way.

"If you don't I'll never have *your* father as *my* father."

A shocked laugh shook Sam's shoulders. "You want my father for your father?"

She looked at him as if he didn't have a brain in his head. "Of course, I do. He smells like lemons." She sighed. "And I love lemons."

Yes, she was *his* sister.

"And he has a pleasant laugh."

Sam's grin stretched broader. "So a good father should smell like lemons and have a nice laugh?"

"Well, of course. It's what I prayed for." Her eyes widened. "And his kindness. He's not tried to hit me once, not even when I fell on one of his new chairs in the furniture shop and smashed it to bits."

A ribbon of fire exploded in his chest. Hit her? Who would ever stoop so low as to hurt a child? As horrible as the loneliness and rejection felt after his mother left, he'd always had the solid love of his father.

"No, my father would never hurt you, Fiona."

"And he's not hit or screamed at Mother, even when she did some very bad things to him. His voice is soothing, like a bubbling brook. I think a good father should be kind, don't you?"

"Most certainly." He crouched before her, watching the animation of her expression shift. Oh, what had this little girl known? Pain at such a young age. Wounds he couldn't comprehend.

Her grin crinkled her nose again. "Mother keeps smiling the joyful smile all of the time."

"The joyful smile?"

She studied him again with a puzzled expression, sunlight glinting off her hair. A place in his heart opened up for her. A sister.

"The smile of your whole face. The kind that makes your eyes light up and warm the person next to you." Her golden brows shot high. "You're wearing one right now."

"Am I?"

She winked and he embraced the immediate love for her. "I think you'll do just fine as my older brother." She measured him with another long look. "We only need to have you stop being so angry with Mother."

"Fiona," called a voice from the house.

Fiona lips twisted to a pout. "It's Mother." She stepped past him and stopped. "I'm sorry she was a bad mother to you. She told me she left and it hurt you, but she's not a bad mother now." Her expectant look demanded his attention. "God has such a big world with so many people, I don't suppose all of them will take the same road to get to Him. I'm sorry Mother's road took her away from you to find God, but it brought me about, and I'm fairly glad to be alive."

"Fiona."

The call nudged her a few more steps away. She walked backwards to keep talking, her hands dancing in the air as she spoke. It was pretty clear she liked talking, and he didn't mind listening. "And I should like having you for a brother. Carl's been in heaven for two years now and I'm in desperate need of a brother again."

His mother's choices led her to a harsh life, one littered with unimaginable grief. Could the loss, the ache, have changed her as it did Michael?

"I hope you will stop being angry with Mother and give her a second chance." She offered him a deep curtsy topped with an adorable smile. "Nice to meet you, Sam."

She skipped off in the direction of Rosellyn, who stood in the back garden of the Dougall house, shielding her eyes from the late sun. She took Fiona in her arms and ushered her to the house, hesitating a second before entering. With a slight lift of her hand, she waved.

He offered an easy nod, keeping his hands in his pockets. A *second chance?* Ashleigh's face came to mind.

His pulse jerked to a faster beat. All of her compassion and tenderness with him. Their teasing and conversations. Had he thrown it all away over a stint of jealousy? And he didn't even ask her if Michael had stolen her virtue, or if she freely gave it. Hadn't she hinted to having something taken from her when they spoke in the garden about Kara?

What had he done! His pace turned into a run. He'd write her again tonight, maybe even send a wire when he was next in town. Find a way to reopen their communication. Her response would direct whether he needed to entertain insane thoughts about another

Transatlantic crossing, or painfully sever their tie. The thought pierced him. He'd rather have a broken Ashleigh, than no Ashleigh at all.

Darkness wrapped around another day of work and the hospital finally lulled into its evening hush. The sweet scent of magnolias hitched aboard the early September breeze as Ashleigh stepped out into the garden. A few loose strands of hair blew across her cheeks, blessing them with a refreshing violet touch after the stench of the operating room. She had no room to complain.

Thanks to the begrudging, yet generous gifts of Lady Cavanaugh, David's operating theatre was in top order with the most up-to-date supplies, but the needs remained staggering. Soldiers came with gas blindness, various grades of amnesia or disorientation, gangrene, respiratory troubles and many other illnesses. The list drew out in a long blend of various difficulties these poor men would probably keep for the rest of their lives.

The reality of God's closeness provided a cloak of comfort, even three weeks after Sam left with no answer. Grandmama's letter had arrived two days earlier and provided insights into Rosellyn Miller's return, so there was a good chance Sam had little energy or time to put his mind to her heart – or at least she kept comforting herself with the thought. But hope's thread frayed with each passing day.

Grandmama's letter offered words of love and peace which encouraged Ashleigh's newfound faith of God's nearness. *He* would have to be enough. Perhaps God's dream for her never included a family except for those who had no other. She glanced back at the stone walls of the hospital to the East Wing, the lantern light from the boys' bedroom dimming.

Four children arrived two weeks ago, giving Ashleigh another distraction from the ache Sam left in her heart. The older girl skittered around, fearful of any loud noise. She'd lost her mother in a London raid and her father on the front lines. Her little sister, barely five, danced about in a fairy world – perhaps protecting her from the hideous truth of war. The two boys came, rowdy and curious, but desperately seeking affection. Michael's charisma proved the perfect match for these lost little boys, and his humility calmed them. He and Kara practically ran things on their own, especially with David's need for her in the hospital – especially since Jessica's departure.

Fresh light streamed out from the doorway and Michael's silhouette moved forward. The moon's radiance shone bright and full against the garden shrubbery. He limped ahead, weight steadied against his cane, but his movements more fluid than last week. She knew a year ago he would have rather died than live life as a lame man, but he carried his weakness with him now as a banner, almost. Just this week he'd told her his leg reminded him of how much he must trust in Christ for strength instead of himself. Was God changing her in the same way? Creating trust?

Ashleigh hugged herself and smiled in welcome. "I needed a bit of fresh air before turning in. Aren't you exhausted after managing the boys for three hours this afternoon?"

Michael shrugged. "It was good for me. Stephen loves playing ball with friends." He pointed toward the bench with his cane. "Care to sit for a spell?"

She lowered herself, resting her wearing legs. It wouldn't be wise to sit too long for fear of falling asleep. Even now her eyes drooped under the long hours. "Only a few moments. I need to make certain Kara doesn't need my help."

"Kara is fine. She could take on the entire hospital by herself, I believe." He settled next to her, waving at the space between them. "To guard both our reputations."

She laughed at his teasing grin. "Well, we wouldn't want to tarnish them, now would we?"

He stretched out his legs and lifted his right to cross over his left. "Speak for yourself, friend. I'm taking God at His word that all things are made new." He braided his hands behind his head and leaned back. "I'd like a clean start in the right direction."

She looked over the dark horizon and breathed out a long stream of air. "So would I, Michael." It sounded like a lovely dream.

They sat in amicable silence, the breeze shuffling a few fireflies through the night and ushering the sweet scent of earth and roses.

Michael suddenly sat up straight and turned toward her, minding a careful movement of his right leg. He opened his mouth to speak, and then stopped to study her face. His hesitancy tightened her spine in warning, but she wasn't certain why.

"An idea just came to mind. It's probably a bad one."

Ashleigh felt both of her brows lift with her smile. "I feel duly warned."

His expression turned serious. "You know all about my past."

"Yes." The word formed slow and deliberate.

He drew in a deep breath, keeping his gaze fixed on hers. "And I know all about yours."

She grimaced and nodded.

"What if—" He looked down at her hand resting on the bench between them. "If Sam doesn't respond, Ashleigh. If he doesn't—"

"I can't think about that yet, Michael." She shook her

head and fisted her hand into her lap. "Not yet."

"I understand, and I won't push anything until you're ready, *if* you ever are." He covered her hand with his. "But know this. You don't have to be alone. If I get another chance, I'll love you the right way."

She drew her hand from beneath his. The very thought pulsed more pain and longing against the heartbreak Sam left behind. "I can't give up on him, Michael. I love him."

Michael's smile softened. "I know you do. Lucky guy." His gaze moved from her face to focus on something beyond her. "And I hope you both have—" His smile froze and a look of horror dawned on his moonlit face.

"Oh no."

A noise like thunder rumbled over the fields. Ashleigh turned in the direction of his stare across the vast countryside to a glowing ball of fire in the distance. Another explosion rocked her confusion, with the soft light of the moon clearing up any doubt.

Hovering in the night sky, a gray mass of German tyranny, flew a Zeppelin airship.

She jumped to her feet. "No. It can't be coming for us. Not here." Its nose pointed directly at the hospital. "We're a town of civilians."

Michael grabbed her arm and pulled her toward the hospital door, limping at his fastest pace. "Nurses help British soldiers, farmers provide food for them, and the elite in country houses fund the war effort. From the Huns perspective, there are *no* civilians."

Chapter Twenty-seven

A loud whistle sounded from behind as Michael pulled her through the doorway. Another explosion followed, closer this time. Shafts from the search lights glared across the field outside and a siren sounded from nearby, piercing the night sky like the wail of a child. Ashleigh and Michael met Kara on the steps to the second floor, each girl at her side.

"I am taking them to the bunker. I can't manage the boys too. They're in a state."

"We'll get them." Michael nodded and ran past, with Ashleigh on his heels.

Stephen stood crying from his crib and Charles framed the wall, back pressed tight against it as if frozen in place. Both boys were petrified. Roving lights filtered in through the window and danced across the floor, alerting them to the Zep's nearness. *Oh dear God, please keep us safe.*

Another explosion almost shook the ground. The wail resounded again.

Michael grabbed Stephen from the crib and Charles rushed to cling to his side. Ashleigh scanned the room and the empty beds. A certain five-year-old was nowhere to be seen. Her gaze flew to Michael's where fresh awareness dawned.

"Where is Lance?"

An explosion to their left shook the building and sent Stephen's cries into a new volume.

"He might have come looking for me. He does that when he's afraid."

Ashleigh threw a blanket at him from the bed and started from the room. "Get the boys to the bunker. I'll check your room."

"No, Ash."

But she was already out the door, running down the hall to Michael's room. She slammed open the door and looked around the room, no sign of the boy. "Lance?"

Her mind spun through possibilities. She snatched a blanket from Michael's bed and started down the hallway, pushing open doors and peering inside. "Lance, darling, please come out."

Suddenly a thought came to her. The pantry. The sister who brought Lance to them said he'd almost starved before they found him, and had a tendency to hoard food. In fact, Kara mentioned finding him there on several occasions, food stuffed in his pockets. It was worth a chance. She ran into the small room they used for dry storage. Huddled in the corner sat the dark-haired runaway.

"Oh, Lance, come here."

Ashleigh opened her arms and the boy ran into them, a loaf of bread in one hand and crackers in the other. "We must get to a safe place."

They stumbled down the hallway, passing rooms where some of the furniture had turned over from the explosions. She grabbed Michael up in her arms as they descended the stairs, but another explosion sliced through the corridor separating the hospital from the East Wing.

A massive dust cloud blasted toward them, blocking her vision. She placed Lance on the ground and tossed her apron over his head in an attempt to keep his airway free of the particles. She tried to stifle her breathing, but the dust cloaked her throat, suffocating her and burning her eyes.

She coughed and stumbled forward, trying to make her way to a safe haven, but how far was she from the back door? *Dear God, help me.* Corrupted oxygen squeezed into her raw airway, resulting in more coughs.

Another high pitched whistle pierced the intermediate silence, a preemptive warning to another explosion.

"Ashleigh."

Someone grabbed her arm and drew her out of the cloud. A door slammed behind her and engulfed her in immediate darkness, but she emerged into clean air...and safety?

Where was she? A closet? She collapsed to the floor, coughing to clear her lungs but keeping a hand to Lance. He shuddered against her with a whimper.

She bent forward, tears wetting her face, each smoke-stained breath a battle. The debris slid deeper than her cough could reach, into her lungs.

A massive explosion shook the room, followed by a crash outside. Lance screamed and she pulled him close, shielding his head with her body. A thud rattled the door. Ashleigh tried to make out the other adult in the dark room, but her blurred vision combined with the darkness didn't help. She rocked from side to side, trying to force deep breaths into her saturated lungs. Dizziness hinted at the edge of her consciousness, seeking control. She couldn't give in.

Lance whimpered into her chest.

She closed her eyes and held the crying child closer. "It's all right, sweetheart." Her hoarse words sounded eerie in the dark closet. "We're going to be fine."

"You could use something to drink from the sound of it." A woman's voice came from the darkness, familiar...and surprising. Were Ashleigh's ears as clogged with dust as her throat?

"Catherine?" She tried to clear away the dust scratching her throat. "You're still here?"

"Dr. Ross needed extra help in surgery, so I stayed." A shudder accompanied her words. "Amputation."

Another round of coughs shook through Ashleigh body, followed by a sting of pain in her lungs. She swallowed hard. "I could have taken that one. You didn't have to—"

"You'd worked hard enough for one day, Ashleigh." Her words held an edge of reprimand tinged with...concern? Catherine was concerned for her? Maybe her ears *were* clogged. "But instead of rest, we all received the benefits of a gentle German goodnight."

Her ears weren't too clogged. She caught every ounce of Catherine's sarcasm.

Lance's body slowly relaxed. "Why didn't you go to the bunker? I heard Michael mention it to you last week."

Ashleigh's eyes began to adjust to the darkness. Small hints of light strained through a window anchored above them, perhaps large enough to crawl through, if necessary. She made out Catherine's silhouette and the faint glimmer of light against her face.

"I was on my way there, but I heard you calling for Lance, so I..." She shifted and leaned back against the wall. "You should have been in the bunker too."

Quiet swelled into the darkness. Catherine had worked long hours the past two weeks, proving her capabilities. They'd shared short, simple conversations since their talk in the garden, but nothing of much consequence. Their relationship had shifted since their garden-discussion – in both of them. Catherine's edge softened, Ashleigh's apathy disappeared. They were trying.

"You've worked a lot this week too."

Catherine stood, her shadow moving toward the door. She gave it a shove, but it wouldn't open. Something must have fallen against it in the explosion. She beat it a few times and then turned with a sigh. "It's safe to say I have no excuse for not writing letters now."

309

The full impact of Catherine's declaration hit a few seconds later and Ashleigh laughed, encouraging another round of coughs. "I should think you've gotten plenty of practice?"

"Everything from sweetheart letters to children to grandmothers." She slammed her hand against the door again.

"You've become a fairly impressive amateur nurse too."

Catherine shook her head. "I'd rather leave the messy parts to the professionals, but..."

"It's sobering, isn't it?"

She nodded and hugged her stomach. "Seeing all the suffering and loss, it...it changes things. You're a good nurse."

The unexpected compliment took Ashleigh's response. She couldn't remember the last time she'd had a kind word from her sister. The little girl in her almost wept – longing to find a connection they'd never experienced.

Catherine turned her head back to the door, her body going straight. "I hear someone. Do you?"

A muffle of noise rumbled outside the door. Male voices. Catherine slammed her fist against the door again and called out. Ashleigh stood and pulled Lance with her. She stepped close enough to Catherine to see her face.

"Ashleigh."

"Yes."

Catherine's shoulders fell forward and she braced her palm against the door. "I can't talk about it yet."

Ashleigh squelched another cough, igniting a sharp pain in her chest. "There's plenty of time, Catherine. We'll talk when you're ready."

She nodded. The voices were louder and something scraped against the closet door. Her gaze met Ashleigh's.

"Soon, but I…I'm not as brave as you."

Ashleigh hadn't seen her mother hold her head with such confidence in years. Roth Hall teemed with soldiers in the previously closed up East Wing, nurses roamed the back stairs to the kitchen, and solitude was a commodity for a few private rooms at the far edges of the house. Despite David's request to use Lady Cavanaugh's grand house as a temporary hospital due to the Zep's damage to their current building, the grand lady refused to allow anyone except officers for convalescence, which left David pulled between two facilities. Ashleigh took over some leadership in the makeshift surgical theatre, while one of the newer nurses, Margarite, managed control at other times, when David visited the officers at Dothan.

The relationship with Lady Cavanaugh was tedious at best. Her bitterness against the Dougall's provided a solid threat of continued financial support as long as the wounded stayed in Roth Hall, but since she wasn't willing to open up Dothan for all the soldiers, there was little else to do. New wounded arrived every week and needed attention, with or without a new facility. The sheer acknowledgement of her mother's service to the wounded had her mother strutting about town sharing her magnanimity to anyone she met. Interesting how tragedy brought a sort of restoration to her family. The memory of a few shared smiles with Catherine from across the dinner table deepened the understanding.

God truly worked all things to her good.

Ashleigh pushed her tears away. Would He break the long silence from across the Atlantic too? Each week unraveled another thread of hope, and a deeper sting of rejection. Would she always long for him like a part of her was missing?

Michael's gaze asked questions, her heart wouldn't answer. He could give her a family, the children she longed to mother -- and there would be contentment...mostly. Her body sagged against the surgery door, exhaustion weighing her shoulders. Weariness left her on the edge of tears, and a pulsing headache kept her seeking snippets of solitude to quell the ache.

Stifling her coughs during the day became more difficult, especially with the jabbing pains in her chest. The wheezing had grown more pronounced, like the cancerous breaths of a dying patient. She was sick, possibly pneumonia, but there was little time to focus on it. Kara needed help adjusting the children to their new home on the north side of Roth, wounded needed medical care, and David wasn't as readily available as he'd been at the hospital.

A flush of heat moved from her neck to her face, confirming her earlier hints of a fever. Her eyes watered in response. Helping in surgery wasn't an option with her mind making foggy choices, but she could still assist with basic care, couldn't she? Perhaps if she rested a few moments. She stepped toward the stairs and the shift sent her vision spiraling.

"Ashleigh?"

David's voice came from the surgery. She turned to him, but went off balance. Her body moved forward; a cloud of darkness framed David's advance toward her. The haze in her periphery darkened out the sight of everything except the sound of her cough and a voice calling her name.

Chapter Twenty-eight

Guilt was not a healthy bedfellow. Sam rubbed his aching head, another restless night forcing fingers of pain over his skull. He couldn't get Ashleigh out of his thoughts, and he hated waiting for letters. He'd spoken a few times with his father, sharing bits and pieces of what had happened in England, and his father's response was to pray about it.

Pray about it. His solution to everything. Having Mother back had probably driven Father to his knees more than usual, so practice must be worthwhile because his father seemed the very picture of contentment.

Unlike Sam. And sleepless nights. And the gnawing ache guilt left behind. Finally writing to Ashleigh gave him a sense of peace, even if the letters felt awkward and impersonal. He was trying. Desperately trying to sort out what his next step needed to be. He couldn't throw away their friendship, if nothing else, but he didn't want to settle for friendship either. He loved her, with each day the strands of guilt, love, and longing tightened the cluster of pain in his chest.

He'd resorted to sending a telegram yesterday in hopes of some sort of resolution. Some word.

Would she write him back? Would he be too late?

He crossed the footbridge over the creek on the path to Faith Church. Its rock frame, built from the field stones of the mountains, stood as a beacon of confidence Sam had trusted since childhood. Life wore a hole in his faith, which probably accounted for his current sleepless nights. Just one look at the small chapel nestled among dogwoods wrung his heart. *Too long.* When he'd first come home, he didn't attend because he was angry. Angry that God would bring his mother back, apparently unscathed, and even help his father forgive her!

His assumption about his mother's life shot down his argument.

He stayed away longer because of guilt. Guilt in his behavior toward Ashleigh, his frustration with his father, and his bitterness against his mother – even his anger toward God. But as he rounded the path and stared at the afternoon sunlight casting a halo through the trees around the church, a deep longing drew him forward. A haven for lost people.

He pulled to a stop as the chapel's dark blue door opened and his mother stepped out. Her straw bonnet shadowed her downturned face, but it seemed she'd been crying. *For him?* The possibility nudged a jab of guilt. She looked up then, wide eyes registering her surprise. A few tears streaked her cheeks.

He should walk past her, give a polite nod and nothing more, but his rebel feet stopped right where she stood waiting. Did God invest in glue for the bottoms of Sam's shoes?

"Rosellyn," he said, unable to form the word 'mother'.

Her gaze met his, the softest smile upturning her lips. Lines carved wrinkles at the edges of her amber eyes and a few around her mouth, but her eyes glowed with an inner light. Her smile welcomed him, honest and gentle – two things he never used to describe her in his head. Caution reared its protective casing, but with a weaker grip.

"Sam." She inclined her head and her smile bloomed. "Fiona will talk of no one else but you."

Sam's ducked his head with his smile. "She's a spunky sort."

"Yes, I believe God piled all of the energy from my

lost children into her. She brings an immense amount of joy."

Lost children? Pain anchored a line of grief behind her eyes, sobering his thoughts and dulling the bitterness. "I can imagine she does."

He shifted his weight, unsure what to say. Why did he suddenly feel like a child who needed to be found? "Has Scott enjoyed having her about? He's used to being the youngest."

"He's been charming." She squeezed the parasol. "As has Emily Dougall. I wish so much I'd gleaned from her wisdom years ago before—" She paused, golden brows drawn. "Before I left."

Sam's jaw tightened. He rubbed it with his palm, a question broke free. "Do you plan to leave again?"

Her gaze rose to his, direct and intense. "If God allows me the opportunity to be a part of your life..." She drew a deep breath, but her stare never wavered. "I'll only leave if you ask me to leave."

Sam tried to make the demand, but couldn't. The joy in his father's expression curbed his need. Fiona's sweetness stole some of Sam's bitterness and the unexpected gentleness in this woman broke something in his chest he couldn't identify.

"Sam, I didn't come for reconciliation. I sought forgiveness from your father...but mostly from you." She took a small step forward, searching his face, eyes glistening. "Your father has shone grace to me by seeking more than I ever asked, by offering me a chance I don't deserve." Her voice grew raspy and she paused. "I would be a better wife now. I would love him in the right way – because now I know what the right way is."

Sam studied her, breath as uncertain as his emotions. His father had told him over and over his mother had changed. She'd given her heart to Christ, he said. All the evidence pointed to it. His soul lured him to believe.

She pressed a handkerchief against her eyes and cleared her throat. "But I won't stay if it will cause a break between you and your father. If you want me to leave--" Her chin tilted as if ready to take whatever verdict he handed down. "--I will leave."

With her admission, the doubt clenching a fist around his faith loosened. His eyes burned. His heart ached and his mind resembled a wood-scrap pile on the shop floor – jagged and mismatched. He was messed up from the inside out, a heap of broken pieces. *Much like his mother used to be.*

Broken.

God shows mercy to the broken. Ashleigh's word resurrected and posed the question. *Have you ever been broken, Sam?*

His throat closed for a moment so he paused his response. Slow. Honest. "I don't know what to think or feel when it comes to you, Rosellyn."

Her lips shifted up on one side and a single tear made a path down her cheek. His lungs tightened at the love on her face. An ache started deep and worked its way up through his chest, increasing the burn in his eyes. He had little practice with a mother's love, but the sudden craving nearly sent him crying like a baby. A lost love, found?

"That response was more gracious than I expected." She lowered her head and turned toward the path home. "Good day, Sam."

He watched her go, the longing in him growing. The yearning swelled into blurry vision. A few more steps and he pushed open the familiar door of the church; the strong scent of cedar its familiar welcome.

The solitude of calm quiet ushered him inside. The

chapel's stained glass windows, lining each of the side walls, filtered red and blue light over the pews. He stepped further in, the sanctuary empty except for long shadows making a pattern of rainbows against the floor.

Tears covered the burn in his eyes, but he stopped their spill. What did God want him to do?

"Sam, glad to see you." Pastor Markson stepped from a room near the back, his words on a whisper. His dark eyes showed no surprise. Had he expected Sam to come? "Are your ears burning, son? People have been praying for you all day. First your father." He nodded toward the closed door behind them. "And your mother just left." His gaze locked with Sam's. "Waiting for forgiveness is a hard burden to carry, and one she's borne for a long time."

Sam looked down at the rock floor. "So I understand."

"She cares about you, you know." Pastor lifted one shoulder. "And your father comes nigh every day to pray for you, seeking God's guidance for your heart and your future."

Sam had hundreds of memories of his father praying by the bed, seeking God's peace and direction on behalf of his son. Even praying for his mother's forgiveness? Why hadn't he trusted his father? Why had he fought so hard against what he knew was right? His pulse beat in his throat an answering rhythm.

Why haven't you trusted me, Sam? The question sliced to his spirit.

"I don't know what to do."

"'Tis the business of the Almighty to change people. You and me." His dark eyes leveled Sam. "And your mother. Circumstances broke your mother and tempered her hard heart to clay for God's work. He does that to us, Sam, my boy. He loves us enough to break our hardness." Pastor Marksman placed a hand to Sam's shoulder, a Bible clutched in his other hand. "Perhaps it's time to realize how much you've been loved – and how much you've been forgiven, so then you can give back."

"How can I take her back as if nothing ever happened?" Sam's palms opened in defeat. "I can't do that."

"She doesn't want you to love her as if nothing's happened. She wants you to grow to love her *through* what's happened." He looked back to the front of the church. "You belong to God, but you haven't given Him everything. You're holding on to your pride with both fists tight, but it won't help you. What is it your heart craves?"

Peace.

He breathed in the word. Pastor Marksman's palm squeezed Sam's shoulder then released it. He pushed his own Bible into Sam's hands. "You're sick for His peace, Sam. Dying for his reassurance and truth."

"Sick?"

Pastor Marksman folded his hands in front of him and met Sam's gaze with a steady challenge. "God only has use for broken people. 'Tis for the sick he came." He turned and took a few more steps before stopping. "I think you'd do wise to open that Book to Luke seven verse thirty-five in particular. You might find yourself and your mother there."

Sam stared at the pastor's retreating back and slid into a pew in front of him. What did he know? He wasn't the little boy betrayed. And Sam had grown up as one of the good kids, obeyed, even worked in the furniture shop and placed photography in the background to keep his father from hurting even more.

Ashleigh came to mind and he groaned from the fresh ache. And he'd always been honest to her, a true friend. Faithful.

He winced. *Faithful?* The vision of Ashleigh in tears as he left her in Edensbury singed his pride. If he'd been a faithful friend, he would have tried to learn the full truth – sought to understand.

He looked at the threadbare book and sat down, running a palm over the worn cover. Curiosity and a little rebelliousness against Pastor's challenge encouraged him to draw the book into his lap. He flipped to Luke. It had been so long since he'd read a Bible – so busy with life, the words caught his attention, pricking at his heart. The story dug the pricking deeper. A woman. A sinner, the Bible said, anointed Jesus' feet. She was called 'a woman of the city'.

A fallen woman.

She washed Jesus feet with her tears. Yes, he could see his mother in this. A sinning woman. A woman who needed much forgiveness. But hadn't Pastor Marksman said Sam would find himself in the story too?

Sam read back through it and paused on a verse. It reached from the page and wrung his heart with sudden awareness. *He who is forgiven little – loves little.* The words tinkered to a crawl in his mind.

Do you love Me, Sam – as I have loved and forgiven you?

The revelation broke into the silence of his soul. How much had he been forgiven? His sins? His pride? His lifelong anger? Had he loved so little because he'd never really recognized his brokenness? Sam's hand clenched against the pew in front of him and he came to a solid resolution. He was going back to Ashleigh – even if it meant traveling third class and suffering through another sea voyage. He had to know the truth. Make things right. She was worth a second chance and so much more. God knew, he didn't deserve someone like Ashleigh Dougall, but maybe…maybe she believed in forgiveness a whole lot more than he had.

The hairs on the back of Sam's neck rose with a sudden awareness. Someone watched him so intently he felt their stare burning the side of his head. Was God so close as that? The discomfort heightened. He scanned the sanctuary and lost his gaze in the fiery stare of Jessica Ross'.

With a wave of peppermint and a creak of the pew, she sat beside him. "I've spent the last ten minutes praying God would keep me from killing you, Samuel Miller. And I couldn't find it in my heart to attempt a murder while you were praying." Her words hissed close to his ear. "It was a tough battle between God's grace and my anger. Thankfully for you, God's grace won out."

"What are you doing here?" Sam barely kept his voice to a whisper in the silence of the chapel. A sudden fear gripped him. "Is Ashleigh all right?"

Jessica Ross slapped his shoulder. "What do you think? She's grieving for you." She placed her hand against the pew in front of her, which was a good thing since he was pretty certain she wanted to hit him again…harder. From the fire in her eyes, it might actually sting. She released a stream of air from her nose, an obvious sign of her battle for his life. "You broke her heart, Sam Miller. I came to tell you that you are an idiot." Her gaze blazed with accusation. "And if you do anything less than rush across the Atlantic to admit your stupidity to Ashleigh's face, God's grace for your life might not win out next time– no matter how hard you…or I pray."

"I…sent a letter, and a telegram." The admittance sounded weak. Clearly, he was an idiot. He sighed back into the pew. "Jess, I'm a lost man here. I shouldn't have left the way I did."

Jessica narrowed her piercing gaze, studying him for a moment. "I'm tempted to believe you are a good man – but your response to the news I'm going to share with you will prove it or not." Her expression turned sorrowful. "You were wrong about Michael."

He drew in an audible breath at her announcement, but she lifted her hand to stop his reply.

"The truth is much worse than you could imagine." She shook her head. "Making your rejection more devastating."

"What do you —"

Jess placed an envelope into his hand. "Here's the truth, Sam. Ashleigh asked me to deliver this in person because Heaven knows when her mailed letter might arrive." Jess rolled her eyes to the ceiling. "She needs you *now* and I know you are a man who can handle the truth." Her gaze drilled a hole in his. "Don't prove me wrong."

"I can't make any promises, Jess. My track record right now isn't so good."

Her pursed lips twisted into a slight smile. "Well, your awareness is a good place to start." A braid of anger and sadness reflected in her eyes. "Brace yourself, Sam. You're not prepared for this."

Jessica left him sitting in the pew. The creak of the church door closed at her exit and left him alone, with the letter, his heart, and God. He slid a finger under the lip of the envelope and drew the white sheets from their casing, his pulse throbbing in his ears.

Jessica's warning proved accurate. Ashleigh's story ripped apart every raw emotion he possessed. It divulged a secret wound too hideous and dark to believe, and yet, every piece made sense of all the questions he'd had regarding her behavior for years.

Nausea jarred to pain in his stomach. How could any father…any man hurt a child? Especially in such a cruel and demoralizing way? He squeezed his eyes closed. *Oh God, heal her. Give her strength.*

He flinched from the memory of his final words, his blame, as she begged him to listen, but he'd ignored her and embraced his fury. Blindly blaming her. He rubbed an ache at the center of his chest. She loved him, and he didn't deserve it. She'd been wounded in the deepest, most intimate way by someone who should have protected her heart. As he should have done.

Tears branded his cheeks with their warmth. He'd rejected her. He'd betrayed her trust. He'd…*abandoned* her. The pain in his chest pulsed deeper, harder, riveting him to the spot with his own sin.

Do you love Me, Sam?

Like the slow filter of morning light over a horizon, recognition dawned. He loved little, because he never realized the depth of his own sin. Pride. Self-righteousness. Ashleigh had trusted him with her heart. She had faith he would trust her – believe in her through pain, and when she'd needed him the most…he left her. *Like his mother.*

I've come not for the righteous, but for sinners.

Like his mother--a broken woman.

Like Ashleigh – a wounded child.

And like himself – a recovering Pharisee?

As sharp as lightning's flash slashes into darkness, God's truth penetrated him to the core. He shuddered, a reflection of his sin mirrored back to him. Haughty, arrogant, unforgiving? He leaned forward and moaned under the scrutiny.

"Save me. Save me from myself."

A tide of relief swept over him, crushing through his spirit and breaking his assumptions and pride apart. He sobbed at the clear image of his sin, the dark consequences of his pride, and the wounds both left behind in the lives of others. As the hurricane in his soul washed to calm, a profound peace remained in its wake. Peace and clarity.

Ashleigh, his mother, and he all stood on level ground – covered by the grace of God.

He buried his face into his hands, the wash of his hurt pouring from him and into the love of Christ. *I love You with an everlasting love.*

"Forgive me, Father. Help me love like you love, and forgive..." His breath stuttered. "As you have forgiven me." His thoughts turned toward Ashleigh, the weight of her possible unforgiveness almost unbearable. Was this what his mother felt? Grief and disquiet uprooting her soul?

Who knew how long he sat there, tears dripping to the floor, but when he looked up, the late morning light had shifted to afternoon and his father sat beside him.

"I have to go to Ashleigh."

His father smiled as if he'd known the answer all along, which he probably had. "Yes, son, you do."

"And I'm sorry for...for being so hard on you about Mother."

Sam's heart pulsed a need for forgiveness, but his father wouldn't hold to pride as his son had. Without hesitation, he took Sam into his arms. "I love you, son. I forgive you."

"Even though you know I don't really deserve it. I've been a boar." Sam shuddered.

His father shook his head. "If we waited to give forgiveness to the deserving, there would be a lot of bitter people in the world. Thank God, He didn't wait until we deserved forgiveness – and *He's* our example."

The peace of his words tightened Sam's hold on his

father. How had he made it all these years without realizing the true love of God – the true forgiveness? Had bitterness and hurt distorted his vision to such a point he compared himself to the actions of his mother and thought he deserved God's grace? What a fool! God expected perfection. He breathed out a long, shaky breath. He was far from perfect, but amazingly, God still loved him. How could he ever make up for the hurt he caused Ashleigh? His soul ached to see her – to beg her forgiveness, and no matter the cost he'd find a way to earn her trust again.

They walked out the church doors and started back down the footpath toward Emily Dougall's fine Victorian.

"Sam."

Fiona came running toward them, her face almost as red as her hair. She puffed out a long breath and stopped in front of them, kneeling over bent knees to catch her breath – very unladylike. "Grandmama told me to find you at once."

"What is it, bug?" Sam rested his palm on her shoulder and her grin spread at the endearment.

She handed him a small envelope. "It's a telegram. I don't know if it's good or bad news, but Grandmama got all excited about it and rushed me right out the door to find you."

Sam took the card and shot his father a glance before opening it. Had Ashleigh responded to his telegram? Was this a note to let him know she'd forgiven his stupidity? He slipped the card from its envelope and his breath froze in his lungs, a whoosh of dread rushing his skin cold.

Ashleigh near death. Pneumonia. Please pray. C.E.D.

Chapter Twenty-nine

Dr. Ross pulled the stethoscope from Ashleigh's chest and turned his jade eyes to Catherine. His expression spoke of the seriousness in her sister's pale, nonresponsive face.

"You say she started coughing after the bombing?"

Catherine nodded, unable to pull her gaze from her sister's death-like pallor. Three weeks of working near her, watching her, and replaying memories forged a clearer picture of Ashleigh's status as spine of the Dougall family. How had she managed to love them all? To survive amidst the massive grief plaguing her past? *No wonder everyone loved her.*

It was good Catherine had sent the telegram to Grandmama, feeling pride in at least one thing she'd done, but the grim realization of her sister's condition evoked emptiness in the center of her stomach. Uncommon humiliation and regret had haunted her solitude since Ashleigh's declaration of her past. She'd ruined her relationship with her sister with blind envy and selfishness. Was it too late to seek any sort of reconciliation? To beg for freedom from the shame trilling her nerves into a timbre of sleepless nights and guilt-filled days?

I'm so sorry, Ashleigh.

She'd pleaded with her nonresponsive sister last night as she knelt by her bedside. Cried for mercy and forgiveness of all the ways she'd abused her, adding painful wounds atop the scars she already carried. How could she ever make up for the damage she'd caused? How could she live with the weight of her shame? Pride and jealousy bore hefty penalties in her soul.

"As I told you and your mother earlier, pneumonia is

an unpredictable condition. We've provided what care we can, the rest is up to the Almighty and your sister."

Catherine crossed her arms against the chill his words inspired. "You mentioned the benefits of her age earlier? Do you think she might...survive?"

Dr. Ross slid a hand around Ashleigh's limp wrist, stilled a moment as he felt her pulse. "She's strong." He released her hand and Catherine replaced him at Ashleigh's side. "Tonight will be our test." His gaze met hers as he stepped toward the door. "If she survives the night, then there will be more hope tomorrow. Her coughs have been productive today, but she's exhausted from them. Her fever is persistent, despite the cool bath. I'm not certain how much fight her body has left."

Catherine managed to keep her expression controlled, though a tremor nearly shook her to her knees. All those years of wishing Ashleigh dead whispered accusations from the shadows. "What can I do?"

"You can pray."

Her breath whooshed out in a silent laugh. "Pray? Me?" She shook her head and stepped away from him. "God doesn't listen to the prayers of someone like me."

Dr. Ross turned from his exit plan, a sudden light in his eyes. Warnings skittered across her skin. He was going to speak about his faith. A fascinating magnetism lit his expression, like one of the lecturers at the World Exposition in Paris she'd seen when she was ten. With any other man in her current acquaintance, she'd have taken the glow as the flare of attraction, but not David Ross. For weeks his words and the dangerous glint of his faith terrified and tempted her – and now, in the room of her dying sister, she was trapped with him...with *it*.

Part of her wanted to run away – the part writhing from her dark secrets and stains.

But another part feared if he left, the glow of hope he carried might leave her alone with her shame and the death waiting in the shadows.

"Someone like you, Miss Dougall? You don't strike me as the vagabond-type."

She raised her chin in defiance. "You don't really know me, Dr. Ross, not really. I'm as scathed and outcast as any vagabond."

His green gaze softened, inviting her to listen. The room closed in around her, bringing her vision and thoughts into focus on him.

"I know a woman who has devoted her time and energy to helping at the hospital. A woman who possesses a quick mind and a willingness to serve others. A woman whose tender attentions have given many a wounded man hope for healing...or peace in dying."

She scoffed. A few weeks work in a hospital couldn't redeem her horrible actions -- actions which reverberated to her future with the clarity of an unborn child.

Her hand rested on her stomach and challenged Dr. Ross' rose-colored assumptions head-on. "I've made terrible mistakes and hurt a lot of people. In fact, I'm a remarkable liar." She stuffed another wave of tears hard into her soul. "God doesn't want someone as ruined as me tainting His Heaven."

Dr. Ross' intense gaze flickered into compassion, a strong-forceful compassion which held her attention in a vice. "On the contrary, you're just the sort He wants in His Heaven. God has no use for people who can save themselves, but for those who know they can't make it on their own." He drew a step closer. "Those are the ones He can do something about."

The tears edged from her grip and warmed the rim of her eyes. "You don't know all the things I've done, Dr.

Ross. The compromises I've made." She stifled the sorrow, keeping a stubborn hold against the growing warmth in her eyes. "I know my Bible stories. I'm not worth His love or His life."

Dr. Ross too another step forward, without releasing his hold on her gaze. "I beg your pardon, Ms. Dougall, but it appears you may have heard the stories but didn't listen to the message. Christ even says he came for sinners."

Her eyes narrowed. "If you and my sister are characterized as sinners, then there's no hope for me. Do you realize how broken I am?" Her voice cracked. Cool tears on her cheeks surprised her. She pulled to her full height. This man clearly needed a lesson on his faith. God didn't take lying, thieving fornicators. "I stole money my grandmother sent to Ashleigh. Money intended for *your* hospital."

Dr. Ross stopped his forward motion, but kept a solid hold on her stare.

"And I've spent the last ten years, at least, trying to ruin my sister's life in any way I could. I can't understand why she still loves me." She couldn't stop the confessions yet. Not until she'd opened the pure Dr. Ross's eyes to what broken really looked like. He seemed to brace himself, as if he sensed the grand finale. She swallowed away the scratchy tears, but they invaded into her words even more. "And I'm almost certain I'm pregnant with a rogue's baby."

That declaration finally rattled him. His chest deflated, and she knew, God wouldn't take her now. She was utterly lost. No one wanted her. Even the unflappable Dr. Ross? No, her sheer presence would stain his pristine reputation. He'd walk out of the room any minute, without a glance back.

She steadied her chin as he straightened, but he didn't

turn away. He focused the full impact of those green eyes on her, unswerving. She shuddered--her stains open to his perusal, her soul naked against the honesty of his gaze. New tears broke free, spilling down her cool cheeks.

"Miss Dougall, Christ loves you more than your poor choices and sin." His hand came back out, a welcome gesture. "When it comes to our hearts, we're both in need of grace and forgiveness. You." His lips tipped into a gentle smile, the alluring light returning. "And I."

Catherine's breath lodged tight. She gripped a fist to her chest and shook her head. "You can't mean that. Not after what I've told you. How can God ever want someone like me?"

He closed with another step, his grin flickered a dimple she'd never noticed. "He's loved much worse than the likes of you, no matter how much you wish to win the competition."

Catherine couldn't move. His reaction contradicted every social expectation, every human probability, every notions she had of God. He should shun her, as God should do, but Dr. Ross added another handful of shock.

"I'll pray with you, Miss Dougall."

She forced air through her tight throat. "Here?"

"God is everywhere, even here." His brow sent a question only she could answer. "Especially here."

If the intensity in his gaze, the hope in his smile, hadn't boasted such confidence, she would have rolled her eyes at the simplicity of his claim. Every social corner of her world would label her a whore, or at the very least refuse to allow her entrance into their homes.

But here? Now? Dr. Ross offered the promise of something new, something drawing her forward as if a string tugged at the cords of her soul.

What did she have to lose? She shrugged one shoulder

and placed a palm to her hip, hiding in the ruse of the familiar. "Fine. What do I do?"

"We pray to our Father in Heaven."

She cringed and drew back. "Father? I don't have the best opinion of any father's love at present."

Dr. Ross tilted his head, examining her again with those piercing eyes. "Very well, what if you saw him as a…" A hint of red splotched his cheeks. "Lover?"

Catherine laughed. Behind Dr. Ross's pristine demeanor, he was crazy. Well, at least it made him more approachable. "God as my lover?"

"He pursues you as His bride, even though you continually give yourself to others." Dr. Ross recovered from his embarrassment with a step forward. "He knows your wounds. He sees your hunger for gentleness and complete acceptance, your longing to be seen as beautiful and treasured, and He can give you what your soul aches to possess."

Catherine could hardly catch her breath, every word resonating to her core. She tempered her shaky voice with a defiant edge. "And what is that?"

"Love." He whispered the word, but it blasted through her disbelief. "Love beyond every mistake or longing. Love to comfort your darkest bruises and deepest scars. He knows about them all, has seen every choice you've made, and He gave His life to love you forever and passionately."

His chest shook with the same shallow breaths as hers. Did he feel the warmth of the room? The presence of something…or *Someone* pressing on all sides, even inside of her?

He extended his hand, expecting her to take it. Holding her hand could brand him as flawed as she was. Her fingers flexed.

He sighed and lowered himself to his knees in front of

her. "Shall we pray?"

She stared at the senseless doctor who spoke of God as a lover and knelt before her in her dying sister's bedchamber. No doubt, he was crazy – but certainly crazy had never been in finer company. After a moment's hesitation, Catherine followed suit, dropping to her knees. Dr. Ross lowered his head and closed his eyes. Catherine glanced up at her sister's sleeping, pale face, and then followed his lead. Ashleigh's labored breathing filled the silence and stung deeper, another knife to Catherine's pride. If Ashleigh died, without knowing the depths of her regret...

"Dear God, we come to You as broken children in need of Your love."

Broken? Yes, but she was much more than broken. She was deceptive, angry, ruined.

"Our choices have separated us from You. Our pride shunned You, holding to our own strength to help us succeed, but we have failed. We come to You powerless and in utter need of Your grace. I pray for Catherine." His voice gentled her name, like a caress. "Be the lover of her soul."

Lover of her soul? *Her* soul, as wretched and marred as it was? She didn't even like herself, how could God?

A sob broke free, unexpected and soft warmth encircled her hand. *David Ross.* He squeezed her fingers and another sob shook her body. The sweet idiot kept breaking social convention. She tried to pull her hand free of his, but he pinched tighter. Poor man was going to ruin his reputation.

"Capture her with Your love. Break through her misconceptions and rescue her from her lostness."

She stopped struggling and listened. Lostness? Her heart quivered. Yes, she was lost. She'd been lost a long time, struggling in a world which taunted liquid happiness and paper dreams. She'd thrown away her future to a man who cared more for immediate pleasure than her heart, wrecked her past on a lie she'd been determined to justify, destroyed her present...

Her breath hitched and shuddered out. No, not her present. Could God really find her in this quiet moment by her sister's deathbed? Did He truly want her? Would He sincerely love her?

She pinched her eyes tight, and forced words on a shaky breath of hope. "Rescue me?"

Her whisper broke into the silence like a brushstroke of pale light, but crashed through her soul with the force of a cymbal. She had nothing to lose. Why not offer it all and see if David and Ashleigh were right? "Forgive me if You can. What little I have is Yours, if...if You want it."

A wave of warmth flowed from her head down the length of her body and finally pooled in her chest. The weight in her heart loosed and her breathing came easier, lighter. Something...no, Someone embraced her soul.

You are Mine.

The words kissed over her spirit, healing and restoring.

I love you anyway.

Tears coursed a heated path down her cheeks. Anyway? Despite it all? Could her body contain the warmth of this love?

I love you always.

"I believe."

Time mixed with tears. She was loved completely? Whole? Found? She released a breath she felt she'd been holding her whole life. When she finally opened her eyes, David cradled her in his arms. Catherine had been in plenty of men's arms, but not men like him – and never with a sense of belonging like this. A new heat coursed up her neck and planted firmly on her cheeks. She pushed away, gesturing to his damp, wrinkled shirt.

"I'm afraid I may have ruined your fine shirt."

He followed her gaze and stood, bringing her with him. "I think your soul might be worth the cost of my shirt."

It took her a few seconds to recognize he'd broken with his usual seriousness and she smiled. "I don't know if I would gamble on that notion, Dr. Ross. You might very well lose." She stepped away from him and swept her fingers over her wet cheeks.

His gaze sobered, the clinical-side of this quiet complex man taking control of his expression again. "I only bet on a certainty, and what has happened here, Catherine Dougall, is certain. A miracle."

Miracle? Did miracles burn up your soul and replace it with a lighter one as a rule? No wonder they were fairly infrequent. If they didn't heal people, they probably killed them from the inside out. Catherine glanced back at her sister. "Well, I hope I haven't used up my only one, because if anyone deserves a miracle, it's my sister."

"Then I suggest you take your newfound faith and put it to good use." His gaze pulled from hers and fastened on Ashleigh. "She'll need every prayer we can give her."

Chapter Thirty

"Welcome back."

Ashleigh unglued her eyelids and tried to bring the shadowy world into focus. Her limbs hung heavy against her sides, as heavy as her weighed-down eyelids.

"Is she waking?"

The woman sounded like Catherine.

"It's a good sign that her fever has broken." The male voice reminded her of Dr. Ross.

"Oh thank you, God."

No, that couldn't be Catherine. Thanking God? Certainly not in her sister's vocabulary.

She tried to talk, but her throat burned out the words before she started. Dry and sore.

"Try this." The deeper voice soothed close. Yes, Dr. Ross.

Something cool touched her lips. She received the liquid and almost smiled at the smooth balm it left as it coated her raw throat. Green eyes came into focus.

"Dr. Ross?"

"Happy to see those eyes, Nurse Dougall." Everything processed slowly – sights, sounds. "You had us worried for a while."

Ashleigh tried to clear her throat. "Worrying is a sin," she whispered.

Dr. Ross chuckled. "I think you are going to be just fine."

An audible sigh drew Ashleigh's attention to the shadow at David's right. Catherine emerged at his shoulder, cloth in hand, the faintest hint of a smile on her face. A nice smile. Ashleigh blinked her into clearer view and the smile grew a few degrees.

"And you accuse me of using extravagant means to gain attention?"

The gentle humor in her sister's gaze softened the edges of her face, in fact, there seemed to be a general softening of her entire countenance.

"Next time you can take the stage." Ashleigh forced her words above a whisper, a scratchy whisper. "Or in this case, the sick bed."

Catherine wiped the cloth across Ashleigh's forehead and cocked a brow. "I think I'm due time out of the spotlight for a while. Too much attention isn't healthy for what matters most."

Yes, there was a distinct difference in her sister.

"How long have I been unconscious?"

David wrapped his hand around her wrist, and Ashleigh mentally counted her pulse along with him. The rhythm of her heart beat in her throbbing temple.

"Two days," he said and released her hand.

"Three, if you include the day you kept trying to save me and Michael from drowning on the *Lusitania.*" Catherine's grin hitched wider. "And if you'd had the strength to get out of bed, you would have chased poor Mother out of the room in search of a lifeboat."

David even quirked a smile. "You were somewhat delusional from your fever."

"Somewhat?" Catherine pinched her lips together to hold in her grin.

A fresh wave of heat coursed up into Ashleigh's cheeks but ended with a rasped laugh. "Well at least my near-death experience provided some humor."

Catherine's gaze sobered and she placed a hand to Ashleigh's arm. "I'll find humor elsewhere in the future, Ashleigh." Her words softened to a whisper as she slid her hand away. "I never want to see you like that again."

Their gazes locked and a long-denied emotional connection hovered into existence. A lifetime of change happened in a span of three days? It had to be God's work.

"I'm going to let the others know you are awake." David bowed his head and backed toward the door. "Unless you don't feel up to somewhat exuberant visitors?"

Ashleigh pressed herself to a sitting position and her vision spun a few times. She pressed a hand to her head. "Of course."

"Good heavens, Ashleigh, saying 'no' is not a sin." Catherine shook her head and shot David a warning look. "I think you should take the long way to the drawing room, Dr. Ross. Perhaps by way of the garden." She returned her pointed stare to Ashleigh. "To give my sister time to prepare for all of Mother's hysterics."

Ashleigh relaxed back into the pillows as David exited the room. "You sound like an overly concerned sister."

Catherine's brows drew tight, but her eyes sparkled. "Perhaps you are still a bit delusional?"

They shared a smile and then Catherine's expression grew serious. "I'm sorry for so many things I haven't the time to mention them all, even if Dr. Ross takes three turns around the garden."

Ashleigh placed her hand over Catherine's and breathed a long sigh. For so long the pain of the past separated them, and for the first time the possibility of a healthy relationship edged into view. Those old wounds didn't seem as important as they once did.

God gave her yet another opportunity to practice forgiveness. First Michael, now Catherine. It came a little easier this time, perhaps from practice. "I forgive you, Catherine."

Tears glistened in her sister's indigo eyes. "I'll try to

make it up to you, but I'm certain I'll manage it poorly."

Ashleigh laughed. The same saucy temper simmered beneath the calmer surface. She would make a good nurse. "What if we start new from today?"

Catherine nodded, lips pinched. "Can we make it a fresh start from tomorrow?" She shrugged and sat down on the edge of the bed. "Because after I tell you the trouble I've brought on myself, you might want to reconsider."

Ashleigh smiled. "Catherine, after all I've had happen to me over the course of my life, I doubt there are too many things you could have done to change my mind."

Catherine reached into her apron and pulled out a bulging envelope which she placed on Ashleigh's lap. "Here is all that's left. I took it."

"What are you talking about?"

"The money meant for your orphanage. Each and every note Grandmama sent, Marsh brought to me and I took half to keep for my own plans. I thought it was another example of how someone else in our family loved you more, so I...I stole it."

Ashleigh touched the envelope and flipped through the paper. Tens of pounds waited to be counted.

"I'm sorry, Ashleigh. I'm thankful for God's forgiveness, but I...I need yours too." Ashleigh lifted her eyes to Catherine's, her regret as clear as the tears on her cheeks. "There is at least a hundred and fifty pounds there. I had already spent some, but will pay it back to you."

A tickle started in Ashleigh's stomach, rose up to her chest, and finally came out in raspy laughter. Catherine's wide-eyed expression responded she thought Ashleigh might still be a bit delusional.

"It's perfect timing, Catherine. Perfect."

"What do you mean?"

"Do you realize how desperately we need the money

now more than ever? If we'd had this before the Zeppelin attack, it would have already been spent on something else, but now it's vital to us keeping our patients at Roth Hall."

"What?"

"We lost most of our surgical equipment in the attack, but Lady Cavanaugh won't provide funds for new equipment for the soldiers housed *here*." Ashleigh's laugh came again. "Now we can purchase our own." She looked up to the ceiling and welcomed the joyful tears. "God took another broken thing and brought something beautiful from it."

Catherine's ebony brows almost met her hairline. "Are you certain you're not still delusional?"

Ashleigh closed her eyes and smiled, a sweet, sleepy peace stilling over her. "It's been a long journey for the both of us, Catherine, but I believe I'm beginning to understand."

"Please, enlighten me."

Ashleigh squinted through her lashes at her sister's smirk. "Stealing and lying are wrong, of course, but don't you see? God can take all of the wrongs and somehow make them right. Even those wrongs we do to ourselves." She sighed and squeezed Catherine's hand. "And somehow God's taken all of the wrongfulness between the two of us and worked it into something right."

Catherine's hand went to her stomach, a slight hint to Ashleigh of a secret unspoken. "Turning our wrong to something right," she whispered. "There have been a lot of wounds along the way, Ashleigh. Me to you. Michael. Father."

"We'll still suffer the natural consequences of our own choices, and the wrong choices of others, but we're not lost. God gives us opportunity to see His healing and grace."

Catherine's expression turned thoughtful. "I think you

just described the meaning of second chances."

Ashleigh's smile matched her sister's. "And hope."

Tears glimmered in the lantern-light's reflection of Catherine's eyes. "I'll embrace a love like that any day, any moment."

Ashleigh sighed and left her tired eyes drift closed. "I think we already have, Catherine."

Michael kept a friendly hold on Ashleigh's arm as she climbed the stairs back to her room after dinner. His glances and attention confirmed his hopes of renewing their relationship as soon as Ashleigh gave him the regard, but her heart wouldn't turn.

"It's been four weeks, Ashleigh, and no news. Do you think...maybe? We could talk about...possibilities?"

Ashleigh came to the landing at the top of the stairs and turned to him. "I'm sorry, Michael, but it doesn't work so easily. I can't make my heart fall in love with you any more than I can make my tongue enjoy the taste of turnips."

"So you're comparing me to turnips?" His grin did little to cover the hurt in his eyes.

"Michael."

His palm lifted to stop her. "I don't want to take Sam's place, Ash. I want you to be open to the possibility he might not accept the truth with grace." He slid his hand down her arm. "You want a family? I can give you that. Your past wasn't your fault – and Sam will realize it too, eventually, but it's a difficult image from which to recover."

A cringe pulled her back from his hold.

He sighed. "I'm sorry." He ran a hand through his hair, immediate regret deepening the lines in his forehead. "I really don't want to hurt you any more than I already have." His hands cradled her shoulders. "I'm trying to make things right, here. Make up for my stupidity. I can give you what you've always wanted."

"By marrying me?" She rested in his hold, his intentions hazing clear. "Dear Michael, you're forgiven. You don't have to try and prove anything to me."

He searched her face, eyes wide. "I can help you. You don't have to be—"

"No, I won't be alone." She cupped his cheek. "I care about you and adore Stephen, but you'd be marrying me for the wrong reasons – as wrong as they were a year ago."

His brow wrinkled into a tighter bunch and he opened his mouth.

She lifted a finger to stop him. "And so would I." She dropped her hand to his shoulder. "Marriage built on friendship is one thing. Marriage built on regret is another."

His gaze softened into acceptance. "I want you to be free of the hurt in your past. I thought maybe marriage and a family would help do that."

The thought settled into her heart like the fit of a glove. Free from her past? For years it controlled her, waited in the folds of her sleep. It curbed her choices and inflated her self-doubt. It fogged her vision of love and marred her choices with the poison of bitterness. She held on to her anger with a life-grip, when it only produced the fumes of death.

God abides with me.

She knew what she needed to do. Christ's love, His strength, would be enough – with or without Sam.

Her smile spread to pierce her cheeks. "Michael, I think I know what I must do." She leaned close to whisper. "But I may need a nice distraction to sneak past a certain doctor and a currently overprotective sister."

Michael's familiar glint sparkled bright. "A distraction? I have a boat-sized mischievous streak and five children at my disposal. If you need a distraction, just tell me when and where."

Sam waited in line at the train station for his turn with the ticket agent. The last time he'd arrived at the Edensbury Train station, he and Ashleigh had hired a car. He shifted his weight, hoping his pointed stare into the back of the head of the man in front of him might spur him along. He didn't have time to wait. He was already six days and a choppy sea trip behind. He shook his head. No, he was over a month behind, with enough regret pumping through his veins to fuel the hired car.

He glanced at his pocket watch and recalculated the time from America to England. It was nearly four in the afternoon. He could be to Roth Hall within an hour if he left soon. *Please let Ashleigh be alive.* He prayed it for the thousandth time, all the way across the Atlantic. The importance of grace nailed into him. Grace for one more moment with her – one more instance to let her know he'd been wrong. That he loved her and would spend the rest of his life showing her how much.

Oh Father, please help her forgive me.

He'd make it right.

The man in front of him finally moved and Sam stepped to the counter.

The ticket agent adjusted his wire rim glasses and fit a smile between a gray moustache and beard. "May I help you, lad?"

"I need to hire a car for Roth Hall."

The agent clicked his tongue and shuffled through some papers. "American, are you? Hire a car?" He adjusted his glasses again and opened his own pocket watch. "Well now, we only sent out our car not ten minutes ago, but if you'll have a seat our driver should return within the hour or so."

Within the hour? Or *so?* Not an option. Sam placed a palm on the counter and tried to keep the edge out of his voice. "Sir, I don't mean to be rude, but I've traveled all the way from the States to find out if the woman I love is still alive. And if she *is* alive, if she still loves me. And if she still *loves* me, if she'll marry me." The agent's brows elevated with each sentence. "So, I'd be much obliged to you if there is *any* way I can get to Roth Hall as soon as possible."

"Well now," the man said, rubbing his beard. "I've heard of the Dougall daughter's illness. They've had a hard time, make no mistake. After the hospital was hit, we wondered what would happen to everyone."

Sam gripped the counter. "The hospital was…hit?"

"Zep attack. Destroyed one side and took about six souls with it. Pure miracle it didn't take more than six." The man filtered through another set of papers. "But for the Dougalls taking in the wounded, there's no knowing what might have happened to the lads. Some say the poor nurse worked herself into pneumonia."

Sam squeezed his eyes closed. It sounded like something Ashleigh would do. Risk her own welfare for the good of others. His heart pumped faster, warmth stemming through his chest. *Oh, how he loved her.* "Have you heard if she is recovering?"

The agent shook his head, the downward tilt of his moustache, foreboding. "Last we heard she wasn't expected to make it through the night, but that's been a few days ago. Heard nothin' since."

Sam leaned in closer, determination morphing into desperation. "Please, is there anything you can do to get me there? I'll pay for whatever it takes."

The agent perked a brow and glanced to the right, out a large window. "There is *one* other option, sir."

Sam followed the man's gaze. Staring at him through the window was the treacherous face of a cream colored horse, which looked too much like Sugar for his own comfort. His jaw tightened along with his stomach. A horse? Really? He shot a look toward Heaven, the irony almost humorous. Almost. *Lord, was my pride truly as bad as that?*

For Ashleigh?

"I'll take it." Sam placed his money on the counter. "Just tell me its name isn't Sugar."

The agent grinned and shook his head. "No, sir."

Sam's shoulders relaxed. He didn't trust anything with a name as sweet as Sugar. It never rang true, and his existence hung in the balance.

"That mare's name is Honey."

Of course it was. Sam's gaze fastened on the agent, whose moustache twitched from a hidden smile. With a deep breath, and a prayer of complete dependency, he faced Honey and possibly the end of his life.

Chapter Thirty-one

Kara emerged in Ashleigh's doorway as a squeal echoed from downstairs. A crash followed along with a child's laughter. Kara's auburn brow jotted north. "I believe you ordered a distraction, Nurse Dougall?"

Ashleigh reached for her cape, a smile at the ready. "Exactly what sort did Michael conjure up?"

Kara folded her hands in front of her and closed her eyes in surrender. "He told the children they could play hide-and-seek from the salon to the state drawing room, of course being mindful of the wounded."

Ashleigh felt her eyes widen from cheekbone to hairline.

"Michael Craven!" Her mother's voice carried through the corridors.

Kara didn't so much as flinch. "Needless to say, your mother is having fits."

"No doubt." Ashleigh pulled her cape around her shoulders and snatched her cane, unsure how well her legs would manage the walk.

"If you're going out, Miss, would you tell me which direction so someone will know to keep a watch out?"

Another crash sounded from below and Ashleigh peered passed Kara to the hallway.

"Whoa, whoa there, little fella, that silver platter is much too heavy for—" Michael made a sound like a groan and Kara shifted her attention toward the stairs, more concern lining her face.

"I'd better go and help him before someone truly gets a beating."

Ashleigh's grin pulled against her cheeks. "I believe

his plan might have spread broader than he expected." She placed her hand on Kara's arm and gave it a gentle squeeze. "I'm walking east toward the family cemetery."

Kara's chin tucked in assent. "Then you best be on your way." Another round of children's laughter rippled toward them. "I don't think your distraction has a long life if Mrs. Dougall's nerves have much to say about it."

Ashleigh slid from the room and down the back stairway. No doubt the near-destruction of the main floor had pulled all extra hands to secure control again. Michael's plan worked perfectly. She'd have to give him a hug of thanks later.

A cool breeze and the rolling hills greeted her like a friend, welcoming her into the open spaces. Nursing at Roth had kept her indoors recently, and compounded with her illness, it had been a long time since she'd taken in the freedom of a country walk...or ride. Though her steps weren't as quick as if she'd been at full health, she made good progress, breathing in the fresh scent of magnolia blossoms. Today, their aroma hinted of lemons.

Tears blurred her vision and faltered her steps. *Lemons.* The pulse of Sam's love beat warm waves of sweet longing through her veins. But God would be enough.

Refusing Michael's proposal strengthened her certainty.

Dear God, please help me let him go, if I must.

The footpath curved away from the house and followed a hill to a walled garden. Dark red and pale pink rose vines climbed the entry to the family cemetery. Their fragrance ushered her to stop and take in the sweet scent. She glanced through the entry. Centuries of gravestones lined from one wall to the next under the canopy of a great white magnolia. She caressed a soft rose blossom between her fingers and then picked two crimson blooms, stepping over the threshold into the solemn place.

Substantial roots weeded across the ground, twining through the pale gravestones to finger across various areas of the cemetery. White Magnolia blossoms fluttered down to the earth, a gentle rain of tender touches to the graves of her family members who had passed on, bringing a white-washed beauty to the solemn place. Years had worn its hands across the stones, fading names and dates, cracking stone against stone, but memory served as a faithful guide.

She weaved a path between the markers, her gown leaving a hush of noise at her feet as she stepped over the patches of tall grass and faded earth. Nothing breathed as quietly as a cemetery. Even the wind faded to silence between the rock walls, barely nudging more blossoms from the bow overhead. Determination moved her forward, pushing her to take her future into her own hands and find some resolution. She couldn't be ruled by her past any more.

Sunlight filtered a flickering thread between the green-swathed branches of the magnolia, shadowing a patchwork against the ground and broken stone. Sparse grass reminded her of the relative newness of her father's grave among the others. Her mother, brother, and sister had brought his body here for burial. She knew which plot he would take, but she'd never seen it.

Though his gravestone boasted a chiseled appearance from the well-carved and well-paid hands of the stone cutter, its cold surface mirrored the lifeless lot of the rest of his ancestors. Ashleigh smoothed the roses' petals between her fingers, mentally rehearsing her words to the ghost of her past. He'd asked to be buried here, brought all the way from America.

A cross marked the top of the stone with the sharp

edges of his name underneath, followed by the dates of his birth and death. Her father. Anger flared its familiar flame, stirring up the ready hatred. She fought it and dropped to her knees. Rehearsing her prayer had given some confidence, but in the wake of seeing his name carved in stone, her courage dwindled a little. She'd clung to her anger for so long, could she let it go?

"I cannot do this on my own, God. You promise to be my good and loving father. Give me strength to do what I cannot do."

She unfisted her hands and placed the twin roses on her father's grave, their dark blush a stark contrast to the gray stone. She closed her eyes, breathing in the fresh strength of hope and releasing her anger in a long steady breath. The shadow of his sin lurked near her, tempting the fury to rise. Her father's whispers breathed of distorted love and twisted promises. She battled them with Christ's words and her trembling faith. *My peace I give to you; not as the world gives do I give to you. Let not your heart be troubled, neither let it be afraid.*

"I forgive you."

Her breath stilled. A sudden swell of peace whispered through her spirit. No trumpets. No fanfare, but an understanding of what true freedom involved. Sacrifice. Of her hatred and bitterness…and herself.

The breeze brushed cool against her tear-dampened cheeks.

Her eyes flickered open to a sight which encouraged…laughter? It bubbled up and joined the chorus of wind and birdsong from over the wall. The white magnolia blossoms fell to her father's grave and covered over the crimson roses like snowfall. *Though your sins are like scarlet, they shall be as white as snow.*

White. Pure. For her? She looked up into the sky, new

tears streaming unguarded down her face. God's grace makes her pure. "Thank you, dear God." Her whisper hushed with the gentle rustle of leaves, as life swirled into the quiet. New life. New...hope.

She wiped a hand over her cheeks and stood, leaning against the cane for support, as she followed the path out of the cemetery. With one last glance over her shoulder she left the bitterness of her past where it belonged--with the dead. There would always be scars, but with God's grace, the shame wouldn't haunt her any more.

The countryside stretched green and alive from her perch on the hill outside the cemetery. Edensbury's smokestacks and a few roofs lined the horizon. She breathed in the air of a free woman and marveled at how her clarity of spirit even seemed to affect her vision. Brighter colors. Fresher air. God would be with her, even if the rest of her days were spent alone.

A sudden movement in the distance flickered into view among the sprawling hillsides. She took a few steps from the shadow of the cemetery wall, examining the steady movement of a horse and his rider. They rode with purpose, at a gallop, but the rider's posture marked him as ill-equipped for the endeavor. A novice, no doubt.

Stiff and tight, his jacket flew behind him like a wave of panic. She touched a gloved finger to her smile as the memory of her ride with Sam ushered another sense of longing. The poor rider even reminded her of Sam, golden head bright with afternoon sun and a tense posture which was sure to have him sore in the morning.

The horse turned in her direction, its graceful run and the rider's rigid style a distracting mismatch. Perhaps they brought a missive for a soldier in treatment at Roth, or a message from Grandmama. A current of concern pushed her a few steps toward home, but then she stopped. Instead of taking the road toward Roth Hall, the pair started for the hill. The cemetery hill. The one in which she stood.

Who on earth...?

Her heart quivered to a faster rhythm. Breathing shuddered shallow. A sudden weakening of her knees had her shifting her weight to her cane. Every gallop which narrowed the distance between her and the rider cast more clarity on her tentative suspicions.

Sam?

As the horse scaled the hill, his face came into view. *Sam.* His gaze locked with hers and time suspended. Sam was here? On horseback? She pressed a fist to the pounding pulse at the base of her throat, old insecurities swooping in to threaten her newfound peace. Had he received her letter? Did he know the truth?

Heat fled her face, her cane bearing more weight than it had only moments ago.

The horse slowed to a stop a carriage-distance from her. Sam followed with a clumsy dismount. She would have grinned, if she hadn't been so concerned about her weakened knees keeping her upright. His skill resembled the status of her stomach at the moment – off-balance. With a stumble and a toss of the reins over the saddle, he turned the full, lovely attention of those cerulean eyes on her, lips set in a frown.

Breathing congealed in her lungs. He marched toward her with purpose, his red-rimmed gaze holding her in place. Tears even glistened on his cheeks. What would she say to him? How would she explain?

He didn't give her a chance to sort it. Without a moment's hesitation, his palm slid across her cheek, cupped the back of her neck, and pull her to him. She barely had time for a gulp of air before he drew her into a kiss to bring all her doubts to a full and utter stop.

It took every ounce of strength he had to control the impulse to run to her. Alive. The shadows under her eyes and the pallor in her cheeks hinted at her recent illness, but she stood as a vision in royal blue, mouth as wide as her eyes. His chest tightened with each purposeful step he took. Her eyes widened as he closed in, those beautiful eyes he loved. Tears burned. She was beautiful and breathing. *Thank God.*

He was like a starving man, craving one touch. He'd almost lost her, and in his pride, he'd almost given her up. Never again. A gasp escaped her as he pulled her to him and covered her soft lips with his. She tasted of sugar and home. Sweetness and safety. Everything he ever wanted, God wrapped in this dear friend. A sob rattled him. Was it hers or his? *Oh, how he loved her.*

His hand roamed to her damp cheek – damp from her tears! He lurched to a halt. With the hurt he'd given her, not to mention the pain from her father, how could he nearly attack her like this? He cringed and tried to pull back, but couldn't.

Her hands held him against her, knotted into his hair. And she was kissing him back, with the same fury as he'd started. She wanted *him.* Another sob shook him into action. He kissed her everywhere his mouth touched – her violet scented hair, the soft curls at her temples, her cheeks, salty with the taste of tears. No one else could satisfy his heart. Her skin beneath his lips, her body melting into his, soothed the ache he'd built at the thought of losing her, and ignited a swelling fire. Ashleigh. *His Ashleigh.*

He couldn't get enough. One hand dug through her hair, while the other tugged her deeper into his embrace. His palm smoothed down the line of her back, pressing her closer. He left a trail of kisses across her jawline to her ear. When her voice broke through the silence with a gentle moan, it drew his mouth back to hers. Her fingers moved, cool and trembling against his cheeks and her lips opened for him, warm and inviting. This was home. Right here with her. Why had God been so good to him?

He kissed her until her sobs melted into raspy breaths that matched his, until her fingers tangled in his curls, until he couldn't get any closer and still be respectable. She was alive and…from the way she kissed him, she still cared about him. Still loved him? Her smile spread against his lips in answer as she drew back.

His gaze roamed her face, and his fingers followed. He caressed her swollen lips which held a ruby glow from his assault. Her palm slid down his neck to rest on his chest just over his heart.

"Sam."

The sweet whisper of his name urged him forward for another quick kiss. He pushed tear-dampened tendrils back from her face and palmed each of her cheeks. "I was a fool, Ashleigh. Please, forgive me for hurting you. For not listening to you when you had so many wounds." His chest shook with a stifled sob. "For not being the friend you needed me to be."

"You…" She gazed at him in wonder. "You received my letter?"

He trailed his thumb across her cheek and outlined the corner of her lips until she smiled. "More like a personal message from a terrifying American nurse."

Ashleigh's smile spread wide, eyes aglow. "Jessica?"

"Mmhmm."

"And…and you still want to kiss me like—"

He stopped her words with a kiss to dispel her doubt. His hand slid down her arms and back up to cradle her face. He touched his forehead to hers, surveying every part of her face. From the walnut-colored eyes to the tip of her puffy lips. He'd almost lost her. "I love you my dear, beautiful friend."

She released a shaky breath. "I didn't think you could."

He pulled back and hoped he forced every bit of love into his gaze. "If I could change the hurts from your past, I would do it, but I would never change the person you are right now. You're the most beautiful woman I've ever known." He flicked a tear from her cheek with his thumb. "Please forgive me. I've been so blind."

She traced her thumb across his lips. "I forgive you. I...I love you."

He wrapped his arms around her and rested his cheek against her hair. Her body relaxed into his, so closely he felt her heartbeat against his chest. Right where she should be. *Oh, thank you, God.*

"And I have something for you." He reached down into his jacket and drew out a small package wrapped in brown paper. "Actually, it's for your bracelet."

Ashleigh looked down at her wrist, her charm bracelet boasting the three charms it had before he left. "More?"

He nodded and took one charm from the paper, placing it in her palm. A gold heart with a small diamond in the center. Her smile softened, knowingly.

"My heart. For you." He lifted a brow. "If you'll have it."

A single tear trailed down her cheek and she held out her wrist for him to fasten the tiny charm. "I'll treasure it always."

He thumbed away her tear and took a deep breath before bringing the final charm from the papers. At the time he bought it, he thought it exhibited Ashleigh at her core, but he had no idea how much until he read the letter.

She examined it and looked up at him, a question in

her eyes. "A rose?"

He cleared his throat of emotion, touching the silver stem of the charm. "Yes, with thorns. I thought of you when I saw this. No matter what pain came into your life, what thorns pricked and scarred, you bloomed into someone beautiful."

She stared at the charm, and then she reached to touch his cheek. "Thank you, my dear friend."

He turned to kiss the inside of her palm and then proceeded to add the charm to her bracelet.

The soft whinny of the horse broke into their privacy. Ashleigh tilted a brow up to him, eyes glistening with a sheen of tears. "You rode a horse to find me?"

He brushed the back of his fingers down her cheek. "Impressed?"

Her grin followed the angle of her brow. "It does add a great deal of credence to your statements of love, I must say. Horseback riding across country?"

"On a horse named Honey."

Her laugh darted straight to his heart. He rewarded her with a kiss right on her smile. He happened to reap the benefits of that reward too, especially when she nuzzled in close to make it last longer.

"You're so important, in fact, that I don't think I can manage another lengthy separation." He shook his head and steadied his palms on her shoulders. "Definitely not any time soon, so I have a...um...proposal."

"Do you?"

"Would you care to be kissing friends for, let's say..." He looked up to the sky in thoughtful silence. "The rest of our lives?"

Her gaze widened and then her lips took a playful slant. "The rest of our lives might be a very long time, you know."

"I was hoping it might be."

She gripped his jacket and pulled him close. "With lots of opportunities for kissing, I should think."

"I was kind of hoping for that too," he whispered, their noses almost touching.

Her smile faded and she tightened her hold on his jacket, her gaze locked to his. "I love you, Samuel Miller. And I would gladly be your kissing friend for as long as you'd have me."

"How about till death parts us?"

She laughed and he swooped her off her feet and into his arms. "Let's go tell your family."

She nodded toward Honey. "Riding would get us there faster."

He answered her with a long, slow kiss that left Ashleigh sighing into him. She rested her head against his shoulder, her warm breath fanning his neck. "Now that I think about it, I'm not in a hurry. We ought to take our time, in fact."

"We should?"

She lifted her head and looked over at him with an apologetic shrug. "Once we reach Roth Hall, we'll have to share our time with twenty-four soldiers, an emotional elder sister, a somewhat irrational mother, and five children under the age of ten."

He lowered her to the ground. "Maybe I'm not in such a hurry either." He squeezed her hand and renewed their walk at a much slower pace. As they stepped in time with each other, Ashleigh leaning against him for support, he reached into his pocket and pulled out a pack of LifeSavers.

"Care for a LifeSaver?"

Her gaze met his, sweet love warming him all the way through. Oh yes, he was grateful God didn't give him what he deserved. She was much too good for the likes of him, but as his father said, no one ever complained of getting something too good for them.

"Yes, thank you."

He popped a yellow from his pack and offered it to her with a challenge in his voice. "Want a yellow?"

She snatched it from him and placed it in her mouth with a smile. "For the rest of my life."

Acknowledgements

A special thanks goes out to the lovely ladies of Seekerville, who started me on the road to publication with their encouragement.

Laura Frantz, for writing stories to inspire my imagination beyond the world I know.

My lifelong buddy, Jessica, whose namesake in the book carries the same spunky and encouraging personality.

The amazing Alleycats, without you this journey would be a lonely road. So thankful for you! And Ang and Amy, couldn't have finished this book without your solid support.

My awesome agent and friend, Julie Gwinn, who loves my stories as much as I do.

To my beautiful, fun, and crazy family! I cannot thank God enough for the joy you bring to my life.

To my parents, who have been dreaming this dream with me ever since I was a little girl creating tall tales.

And to the ultimate Storyteller. I am eternally thankful He wrote His story in me.

About the Author

Pepper D. Basham is an award-winning author who writes romance peppered with grace and humor. She's a native of the Blue Ridge Mountains, a mom of five, a speech-language pathologist, and a lover of chocolate. She writes a variety of genres, but enjoys sprinkling her native culture of Appalachia in them all.

She currently resides in the lovely mountains of Asheville, NC where she works with kids who have special needs, searches for unique hats to wear, and plots new ways to annoy her wonderful friends at her writing blog, The Writer's Alley. She is represented by Julie Gwinn of Seymour Literary Agency. *The Thorn Bearer* is Pepper's debut novel and the first book in the *Penned in Time* series. You can learn more about her at www.pepperdbasham.com.

Dear Reader,

If you enjoyed reading The Thornbearer, I would appreciate it if you would help others enjoy this book, too. Here are some of the ways you can help spread the word:

Lend it. This book is lending enabled so please share it with a friend.

Recommend it. Help other readers find this book by recommending it to friends, readers' groups, book clubs, and discussion forums.

Share it. Let other readers know you've read the book by positing a note to your social media account and/or your Goodreads account.

Review it. Please tell others why you liked this book by reviewing it on your favorite ebook site like Amazon or Barnes and Noble and/or Goodreads.

Everything you do to help others learn about my book is greatly appreciated!

Pepper Basham

Plan Your Next Escape!

What's Your Reading Pleasure?

Whether it's captivating historical romance, intriguing mysteries, young adult romance, illustrated children's books, or uplifting love stories, Vinspire Publishing has the adventure for you!

For a complete listing of books available, visit our website at www.vinspirepublishing.com.

Like us on Facebook at
www.facebook.com/VinspirePublishing

Follow us on Twitter at

www.twitter.com/vinspire2004

and join our newsletter for details of our upcoming releases, giveaways, and more! http://t.co/46UoTbVaWr

We are your travel guide to your next adventure!

CPSIA information can be obtained
at www.ICGtesting.com
Printed in the USA
FFOW03n1322110515
13300FF